DEDICATION

To Susan, my Isabel

MAP SHOWING
KEY LOCATIONS FOR
SWORDS OF HEAVEN

Swords of Heaven

A Story of Magna Carta.

by

C. D. Baker

PrestonSpeed Publications

PENNSYLVANIA

A note about the name PrestonSpeed Publications:
The name PrestonSpeed Publications was chosen in loving memory of our fathers,
Preston Louis Schmitt and Lester Herbert Maynard (nicknamed "Speed"
for his prowess in baseball).

Swords of Heaven
by C. D. Baker
© 2006 by C.D. Baker
Published by PrestonSpeed Publications,
51 Ridge Road, Mill Hall, Pennsylvania 17751.

This book is printed on acid-free paper, and its binding materials have been chosen for strength and durability.

ISBN 1-931587-45-0

PRINTED IN THE UNITED STATES OF AMERICA

WWW.CDBAKER.COM

PrestonSpeed Publications
51 Ridge Road
Mill Hall, Pennsylvania 17751
(570) 726-7844
www.prestonspeed.com

JUNE 2006

ACKNOWLEDGMENTS

As usual, I am indebted to a wide circle of friends and strangers who helped me in the research and writing of this story. My wife, Susan, is my first critic and an excellent one. Editors Nancy Drazga, Beverly Schmitt, and Rachel Schmitt contributed much. I also need to thank those helpful guides and passers-by in England, Wales, and Ireland for their kind help and hospitality. My son, David, was an encouraging traveling companion. Most of all, I wish to thank PrestonSpeed Publications for their generous and enthusiastic support. They continue to inspire me with their deep passion for history.

INTRODUCTION

There is a river of time that carries us each towards the end of a journey. Its currents flow from the deep springs rising in the mouth of the Almighty. The river runs a varied course, sometimes slow and sometimes not, oft' driven hard against a yielding bank to carve a mighty bend that forever alters the currents for those to come.

Like her own Thames River, old England was shaped into many bends by the forces of her past. And those things that etched her green valleys were in due time borne away to other lands where they shaped yet other times and places. These tides and eddies, torrents, and still pools of England's ages have flowed towards us and moulded us in ways we should consider. For this cause we do well to pause and see those things which time has used to make us what we are.

England was home to tribes of Celts who had dwelt within her forests long before anyone measured the years. Roman legions then claimed her and called her "Britannia." For generations her gentle hills and hardwood forests were under the Caesars' watchful eyes until Rome grew old and weary. By 425A.D. the legions had sailed away and Britannia was abandoned to hordes of immigrating pagan Teutonic (German) tribes known as Angles, Saxons, and Jutes. These wild peoples drove the Britons into the rugged lands of Wales and Scotland, where they joined their Celtic cousins.

In the next few centuries the Teutons slowly converted to Christianity under the courageous influence of the Celtic Church and were baptised by missionaries following the example of such notables from Ireland as Brendan, Brigid, Columcille, and the famous Briton, Patrick. The land's name gradually changed to "Angleland" after the Angles, though it remained dominated by

Saxons—such as the remarkable King Alfred, who so effectively integrated Christian ideals of liberty and justice into a decentralised political framework.

In 793, Danish Vikings landed on the English coast and over the next hundred years established themselves throughout much of northern England. Mostly free farmers, the Danes infused the realm with a spirit of political independence and a defiant sense of individualism. Eventually, they converted to Christianity, and their amazing King Canute sanctified their Nordic notion of limited government by declaring himself a ruler submitted "under God."

The Vikings had invaded other parts of the world as well. Early in the tenth century Norwegians seized the coast of France from the Franks—a Germanic tribe that ruled most of central Europe. The area was soon called "Normandy"—the "land of the Northmen." Called "Normans," these Christian converts quickly developed a formidable presence by effectively implementing their cultural disposition towards independence within a clearly defined order. As a result, they established powerful layers of military relationships that advanced Europe's drift into a feudal system under which protection was granted in exchange for military service.

Ambition was another characteristic of these Normans, as it had always been with their forebears. By the middle of the eleventh century they had turned their eyes towards the narrow Channel that separated them from England's green charm. William I, more commonly known as William the Conqueror, believed he had a rightful claim to the English throne, and his army sailed across the English Channel to defeat the Saxon King Harold in the famous battle of Hastings. The event ushered such change into Britain as cannot be properly considered here. However, a few basic points are of interest. First, the Normans had adopted the Franks' language into their own, creating Norman (Norse)-French. Soon after they arrived in England, their Norman-French quickly changed the sound, the rhythm, the vocabulary, and the structure of the language of the Saxons. Over time, English became the rich, hybrid tongue that would eventually supplant Latin as the language of the world.

It should also be noted that, as England's ruling minority, the Normans ultimately established a class system that is evident yet today. More importantly, the Normans were shrewd enough to embrace, and not destroy, those features of the conquered Saxons that were of great value. The Norman ideas of a free man's liberties were consistent with ancient Saxon traditions and the Norman high regard for order was easily superimposed upon the efficient, decentralised framework of Saxon counties and shires. As a result, the Norman rulers were inclined to embrace both the traditions and the political organization of England's past.

The blending of these streams would prove to be a wondrous gift to the peoples of Britain in the centuries that followed. Though the ebb and flow of competing interests exacted terrible costs in blood and property, eventually a grand principle would emerge as the treasured hallmark of this incredible juncture: that the rule of just law, and not the rule of man, should be supreme. Indeed, it was on June 15 in the Year of Grace 1215 when a new dawn broke on a meadow by the Thames. It was the day when the currents of time had, indeed, converged. The wisdom of ages past had been brought to bear against a tyrant, and a simple document, Magna Carta, was forged. This Great Charter memorialised what had gone before by becoming the set-stone for the life of liberty that followed.

Over the centuries to come, it was the spirit of Magna Carta that provided the builders of the English Constitution with a firm foundation. And it must be stated that the Great Charter itself stood upon a premise that liberty and justice are ultimately grounded upon the absolute truths of the Creator. This English Constitution—an evolving collection of statutes, custom, and common laws—provided the legal balance between personal freedom and order. Its evolution eventually shaped the roles of both the Crown and Parliament and even laid the foundations of the English Reformation. Time would eventually carry this Constitution across the sea to the New World, where another people would embrace the great principles established in the meadow by the Thames. There, men in whose veins flowed the blood of both Saxon and

Norman would welcome those from other lands to share in the joys the virtues of liberty offered. And there, in a place called Philadelphia, the spirit of Magna Carta would fire freedom's champions once again.

The tale to follow is the untold story of Magna Carta. Indeed, while every school child may have heard of the Great Charter, and perhaps may even know something of the players, few have been escorted through the mists of history to see the faces of our nearly forgotten heroes. Few know of the family who once lived in the damp castles of old England and served us well with courage and with wisdom. Their names are unfamiliar, yet they are deserving of our high honour. It is their true story that must now be told, the story of a beautiful Countess and her knightly husband—the story of the remarkable family that saved England for England and Magna Carta for us all.

It is our good fortune that the lives of our story's heroes are not completely blotted from history's account. A record of the knight's life was penned by a poet hired by a loving son with the unrealised hopes that it might be sung as a tribute throughout the ages. The song was written as a poem entitled, *Histoire de Guillaume le Mareschal*. (The History of William the Marshal). Its author is thought to be one Jean d'Trouvier (John the Troubadour), though others contend it was another John. It is one thousand, nine hundred and seventy-four lines long and has provided us a rare biography of this man of those times and his family. This poem and the excellent research surrounding it have provided many of the facts upon which this book is based.

Our story is an historical fiction. By fiction, of course, it is meant that the author has enjoyed those literary liberties necessary to provide the reader with a pleasurable encounter. By historical, the author means that the story is rooted firmly in the factual particulars of life in the period as well as in chronicled events. Great care has been taken to research fine details from a wide variety of sources, and every effort has been made to present a credible accounting of the times. Most of the principal events and their dates are as factual as could be determined, and the great majority of the book's characters were living persons. The standard applied is that our story be based on either what is known to be true, or what could have been true.

For any interested in sorting out fact from fiction, William Crouch's *William Marshal*, (Harlow, England: Pearson Education Ltd., 1990) is recommended. It is a comprehensive, non-fiction work based on the medieval poem referenced above and, though some may dispute fine details or contentions, all should find this work an informative read. Other recommended books are Winston Churchill's, *Birth of Britain*, (New York: Dodd, Mead & Company, 1956) and Robert Bartlett's *England under the Norman and Angevin Kings*, (Oxford: Clarendon Press, 2000.).

Having said all of this, we are now ready to begin our journey upstream in the river of time. We must sail back, far beyond America's War for Independence, past Cromwell and his Roundheads, past the masts of Drake's Golden Hind, the smoke of the Lollards, and the Black Plague. We must go farther back, until we finally take our rest on the pleasant shores of the quiet Thames. A meadow awaits us—and a lovely Countess. It is almost June and the birds are singing, the war-horses are grazing, and all Christendom is watching. The sun shines overhead, the reeds bend lightly, and the world has fallen still at the place called Runnymede.

CONTENTS

This England

This royal throne of kings, this sceptered isle,
This earth of majesty, this seat of Mars,
This other Eden, demi-paradise,
This fortress built by Nature for herself
Against infection and the hand of war,
This happy breed of men, this little world,
This precious stone set in the silver sea, . . .
This blessed plot, this earth, this realm, this England.

William Shakespeare
Richard II, Act 2, Scene 1

SWORDS OF HEAVEN

CHAPTER I

THE MEADOW OF THINGS PAST

ARROWS suddenly sang over Sir John's shoulders. "Turn men, turn!" the knight cried. His company of royal scouts reined in their mounts and wheeled them desperately away from the surprised sentries of the rebel army. "Hard, men! To the wood!" Sir John d'Erley and six mounted men were returning from a distant reconnoitre. They had stumbled upon the rebels' flank and several companies of Welsh archers.

"Raimond is hit!" cried a rider, as a comrade tumbled hard to the ground.

"Forward!" ordered Sir John. He looked over his shoulder and groaned. A column of mounted knights was now bursting from the enemy's camp and charging towards him. He turned, and set his jaw towards a dark forest lying directly ahead. The deadly hiss of a crossbow bolt grazed his horse's head. "Hurry on, men!"

The scouts roared into the wood at a full gallop. They dashed below the gnarled limbs of ancient oak and between the thick, trunks of English hardwoods flush with the tender green of springtime. The earth trembled with the hooves of the heavy horse thundering from behind and Sir John's mind whirled. His mount, a sleek hunter, was frothed with sweat and sucking air wildly through wide-stretched nostrils. John leaned forward and drove his spurs hard into his horse's flanks guiding him across a narrow clearing and into another tangled wood. Here the forest had been twice timbered and was thick with brush and saplings slowing the frantic scouts. "Sir John!" cried a sergeant. "We've lost the advantage…we must find open ground."

The man was right. Their hunters were quicker than the heavy war-horses bearing hard upon them, and though the thick brush shielded them from bolts and shafts, it had also slowed their

1

pace. John reined his horse and stood in his stirrups. The rumble and tremble of the approaching cavalry grew louder. "There," he shouted as he pointed. "Follow me."

The scouts lunged forward through a stinging thicket as shouts filled the air behind them. A hundred yards ahead, a clearing now loomed bright and washed in sunlight behind a thinning wall of trees. Hopeful, the men pressed all the more, desperate for open ground. A volley of bolts suddenly snapped twigs and branches overhead as mounted cross-bowmen shot from behind. A scout's horse was pierced through its rear leg, dumping both beast and bellowing rider to the ground. "On, men!" roared Sir John.

The six that remained raced forward, leaning hard upon the sweat-soaked manes of their straining mounts and praying for God's mercy. They finally broke from the shadowed wood and dashed into a wending field of winter rye.

"On, men! On!" John's horse was heaving hard for air, his men wide-eyed and panicked. For the first furlong the fresher mounts of the armoured column kept pace. By the second, however, Sir John's men began to pull away, and by the third it was clear that the rebel knights' heavy chargers could not catch them.

John threw his chin over his shoulder to see the cavalry falling behind. His heart lifted and he ordered his men to slow. Suddenly, however, four horsemen sprinted from the centre of the knights' column and dashed furiously towards the scouts. "Sir John," cried a comrade. "Light horse."

"Aye, lad." The man's eyes flew this way and that. He stretched in his stirrups and peered down a long slope to his right. "There, to the bottom," he pointed. "We needs lay an ambush."

The scouts turned and galloped straightaway towards a dry wash at the distant end of the field. The wash was rutted and strewn with rocks. Crossing carefully, the men hurried to find cover in a thick wood at the other side, where they waited with drawn swords.

As Sir John expected, the approaching foursome had been sent to engage the scouts and delay them until the main column could catch up. They were riding light horses and, like his own men, were wearing only leather vests and padded shirts. He watched them slow their pace and pick their way warily over the dry wash. He could see their eyes nervously sweeping the landscape as they moved ever closer.

The four sensed danger and entered the wood slowly as Sir John readied his men. A battle-seasoned knight, he knew the armoured cavalry was only minutes behind and he could not hesitate. With a shout and a wild cry, he sprang his ambush, pouncing on his foes from two sides.

A savage clash of swords rang loudly through the forest as the horsemen fought furiously. The first to fall was a royal scout, dropping to the ground with his belly opened by a slashing blade. A rebel fell next, then two more. Sir John turned against the last and the two fought savagely from atop horses now pressed flank to flank. The earth began to tremble again as the armoured column neared. "We've no time!" cried Sir John to his men. "Ride. Warn the King."

John's anxious scouts reluctantly obeyed. They kicked their mounts hard and dashed away, leaving their captain to fight for his life alone. The stout-hearted knight was courageous and resolute, but not more so than his foe. The two warriors were of nearly equal skill and of nearly equal age. Both were brave men of middling years and they fought for causes of nearly equal virtue—one for proper order, the other for ancient liberties. Regrettably, only one of the men would survive and Sir John d'Erley watched without joy as his worthy enemy fell dead to the ground.

Gasping for breath, the chivalrous, grey-haired knight had no time for courtesy. The rebel cavalry was now driving towards him down the slope and would soon rumble over the wash. He saluted his fallen foe and dashed away.

Within the hour, Sir John found his men resting by a quiet brook. He dismounted and received their happy embraces, releasing his horse to the sparkling water. He took a moment to feel the agreeable warmth of the mid-May sun, then plunged his face into the cool stream. Drinking deeply, he thanked God for sparing his life.

Refreshed, John wiped his brow and stared towards the western horizon. "Men," he began. "We needs warn Lord William at once. He believes the rebel army to be much farther to the north. With them here, near St. Albans, London will soon fall, and I fear all may be lost. Pray the King sues for peace before mid-Summer's day."

✳

"Do not be anxious, m'lady."

A fair, slender woman with long braids of faded, cherry-red hair stood quietly under the morning sun. She nodded, then returned a kindly smile. "Ah, good Aethel, my oldest and dearest friend, 'tis a word that is so very familiar."

The two paused and took each other by the hand as they gazed hopefully across the English meadow called Runnymede. Before them, at the farthest edge of the lush field, lay the tree-lined bank of the River Thames, and as far as they could see in any direction was the wondrous, well-watered green of good England.

It was Sunday, the fourteenth day of June in the Year of Grace 1215, and the sun had barely chased the Sabbath dew from the golden buttercups, the yellow sow-thistle, and the white-petalled feverfew that were sprinkled hither and yon. Patches of purple willow herb, pink bindweed, and white clover also dotted the grass now pressed flat upon itself by the hooves of the mighty war-horses that had trotted nervously between the camps of two opposing armies.

The Countess Isabel, aged forty-three, was the gracious wife of Lord William Marshal, Earl of Pembroke and King John's most valiant knight. She stood calmly by her maidservant of nearly forty years. "I love two men in this meadow and I pray each serves God according to honour."

"Aye, m'lady," answered Aethel. The stout, buxom, heavy-legged servant took her beloved Isabel's hand and squeezed it gently with a kindly grip weakening with age. Now fifty-seven, the devoted attendant surveyed the dappled colours of springtime sprinkled throughout the meadow. She drew the pleasant scent of

4

grass and wildflowers through her nose and cocked her ears to the happy chirp of a dashing swallow. Turning to speak to her mistress, she noticed the Countess gazing solemnly at the tents of the King and his dwindling army that was pitched in the direction of Windsor Castle.

A light breeze rustled the green, silk gown draped atop Isabel's noble form, then flew to dance with the willows by the river's edge. A rabbit, a species no more native to England than the Saxons, the Danes, or their Norman rulers, scampered silently into a nearby hedge. "Our family herald is there," said Isabel, as she pointed to her left at a small collection of brightly coloured flags. "I pray my lord husband and Archbishop Langton are close to finding the proper bit and bridle for King John." Her restrained tone belied her frustration and fatigue. "My husband's honour is wasted on this tyrant."

Isabel turned her blue eyes away from King John's camp and swept them across the flat meadow before her, pausing briefly to rest them on the vacant, red tent covering an empty throne in the centre of her view. "Years of suffering and now civil war. Aethel, my heart tells me that on the morrow this business shall end. Pray it is so; pray for Monday."

She removed her hand from Aethel's and adjusted the yellow wimple banded to her head by a red linen cord. She ran a finger between her chin and the silk *barbette* that circled her face. With Aethel's help, she loosed and retied the two silk belts that wrapped her waist, and brushed bits of bramble and flying dandelion from her silk *bliaut*—her ankle-length over-gown. She ran her hands down each of the long braids that fell below her waist to be sure their plaits were in order. Her clothing and hair adjusted, she surveyed the scene once more. "See there," she said, as she turned her head to her right. "The rebel barons are still hoping."

Aethel's eyes found the canvas tents and brightly coloured banners of the twenty-five barons who had been appointed to be the representatives of the rebellion against King John. The other barons, along with their heavy cavalry and archers, had wisely kept out of view. They saw no advantage in goading the prideful King who was infamous for foolish fits of fury.

"I see so many familiar colours flying there." Isabel surveyed the barons' flags carefully. Among them were the burgundy and gold of Richard de Montfitchet, the red and silver of Robert de Ros, the blue and gold of Richard de Percy, the silver cross of Eustace de Vesci, and the tri-colour shield of Gilbert de Clare. The Countess gave no heed to these, however, believing most to be little more than symbols of the greedy tyrants of petty realms. What she sought, instead, was the twin-panelled banner of green and yellow that bore in its centre a red rampant lion. It was the flag of the Marshals that, in this trying time, was flying both with her husband in the King's camp, and with her eldest son, William the Younger, warring on the side of the rebellion.

"Ah, yes. There it is, Aethel. I see it furling a hand higher than the others." Isabel stared proudly for a moment. Like her Irish mother, she was one to reflect and ponder. "It gives me peace to see it flapping there, for it is the same breeze that brushes both my son's banner and my husband's." She closed her eyes and lifted her face to the sky. "Yes, I feel quite certain that the winds shall move things in the councils of the King today. There blows a change that shall unite the whole of the realm for generations to come." Isabel brightened. "Ah, I think this day may earn a poem or ballad—a good Irish one, perhaps?"

Aethel grumbled. She had little time for the Irish, or, for that matter, the Welsh, the Scots, the Cornish, or even the Bretons of France. She lumped them together as uncouth and barbaric, savage and untrustworthy—all Celts, who "should be corked into the holes they mine so well." A Saxon by heritage with a bit of Dane mixed in, Aethel was proud to call herself "English"—a name derived from the early German tribe of Angles who, with their cousins from Saxony and Jutland, had conquered these lands nearly eight centuries prior.

Isabel, very much aware of Aethel's views, laughed. Herself a mixture of two cultures, she often teased Aethel with her "Irish ways." Her mother, the daughter of a wild Irish king, had taught

Isabel Irish myths and legends. The Countess had learned to speak Gaelic as a small child and remembered much of it. Her father was a Norman—the descendants of the Norsemen who had settled the western coast of France and who had conquered the English some one hundred and fifty years before. Hence, Isabel also spoke Norman-French—a dialect resulting from a blend of Norse and French. Having spent most of her youth as King Henry's ward, she had also learned Latin from her royal tutors and English from the Saxons who worked in the Tower.

The Countess and her servant re-joined the entourage of attendants waiting patiently nearby. Isabel received a goblet of morning mead and sat atop a square blanket in the shade of a widespread beech tree between her husband's favourite old dogs, Alfred and Canute. "Ah, good fellows," Isabel said with a smile. "Always sleeping in the shade." She scratched the ears of one and the belly of the other. Alfred was a huge, grey, wire-haired Irish hound—courageous, devout, and with a disposition that had inclined towards gentleness with age. Canute was a boarhound of equal size, though more the colour of harvest wheat, and smooth-haired. His stalwart, bold, and loyal ways reminded all of his master, the earl. Like his Viking forebears, Lord William loved liberty and sought to see it guarded faithfully, so he had named each dog after two great kings of England: the Saxon, Alfred the Great, and the mighty Dane, King Canute.

Isabel handed her servant the clay cup and closed her eyes. She began to hum softly and, as she did, she lifted a delicate golden cross suspended on a fine chain from within her white chianse, or under-gown. The necklace had been a gift from her husband at their wedding. It was a relic that she believed had served them well.

"A rider, m'lady," cried Aethel suddenly. The Countess's small entourage turned to see who was thundering towards them. Isabel stood warily, but as the rider drew close, she recognised him immediately as her husband's most faithful knight and her personal favourite, John d'Erley.

Sir John, recovered from the adventure of the previous month, dismounted and hurried to the Countess. "My good lady," he said with proper courtesy, "I bring you news from Lord William. We may be near the end of this matter. God be praised. It seems the wisdom of thy lord husband and the Archbishop may have prevailed upon the King's mood for the good of all."

"Ha, I knew it!" cried Isabel, clapping happily. She was relieved beyond words and closed her eyes. She understood all too well that the alternative would have been a protracted civil war with her husband and her son soon facing each other on the field of battle. "I had a feeling at this morning's Mass, dear John." She smiled and handed the knight a goblet of mead.

"Aye, m'lady," smiled John. "I've learned to trust thy feelings." The knight was one like few others. Although of common size and skill, he was, nevertheless, steeled unlike any other with a devotion to his lord and his family. He was a man of grace and unshakeable courage. Close to the same age as Isabel, d'Erley loved her and had spent most of his adult life in the service of her household.

Isabel took John's strong, war-hardened hand in hers. "I've had a feeling since the day this business began that something is about to be born. You may say it is my odd ways, but women know of new life. A mystery is upon us that shall be nurtured into something that we shall never fully know, dear John. 'Tis so, and I believe it just, just as—" her voice began to fade and her face tightened—"as I believe in the curse of that awful Scottish priest."

"Nay, m'lady. You have not been right on all of your feelings. That curse, that blasted hex has no more life to it than—than—" He glanced about frantically until he spotted a leafless limb on a nearby tree—"than the branch on that willow." It was an unfortunate choice.

Lady Isabel, now pale and quite ghostly, stood erect and rigid; her attendants quiet and motionless. "Are you quite certain, *Messire* John? Do you so swear on all that is good in this sad world that the curse has no more life to it than that very branch?"

John struck a characteristic pose. He set his clean-shaven chin upward and planted both fists on his hips. "I so swear," he barked.

The Countess brushed past the knight, snatching a short-sword from his belt. She walked towards the willow branch with a resolution that seemed to always mark her stride and took the leafless limb in one hand as she sliced its bark with the other. With no emotion, she marched back to Lord d'Erley and handed him his short-sword and a strip of green, wet bark. "Perhaps the worms have eaten the leaves, kind sir, but the branch is very much alive."

❉

Lord William the Marshal was named, like his father, for his title as the marshal of the King's stable. As such he was the master of the King's personal knights and commander of the royal military forces. In his mid-seventies, the man was the marvel of all Christendom. He had lived a life of steadfast integrity and unmatched courage. Lean and still handsome, the gallant knight towered over nearly every other man in the King's camp.

William sent for his wife and her entourage in the forenoon and when Isabel arrived, the earl embraced her with a tenderness that was the envy of womenfolk throughout Britain. The great lord stood dressed in a fine, bright green embroidered robe. It was sleeveless and belted atop a tight fitting *chianse*, or under-tunic, exposing its white sleeves. A silver-handled dagger was placed securely in his wide leather belt.

Isabel thought he looked drawn and weary, no doubt preoccupied with the weighty business of the past several days. Nevertheless, his short-cropped grey hair was impeccably groomed, his moustache properly trimmed, and his face clean-shaven. He stood tall and erect, his wide shoulders upright and his chiselled features still exuding the strength of character that had steadied the bone and sinew of his being all these many years. Though more than three decades her senior, Isabel thought him to be the pride of English manhood.

It was about half-past ten in the morning, the customary time for dinner, when William bade his wife enter the large dining tent set in the King's camp. His usher led her to her place on the long table to the right of her husband and beside that most inspiring servant of God, Archbishop Stephen Langton.

Dressed in a finely loomed red chasuble—or robe—draped by a yellow stole that hung behind his neck and over his shoulders, the great Archbishop stood quietly, his golden cross-staff gripped securely in his right hand. When some degree of order had finally been attained beneath the canvas, he raised his arms upward in order to pray for those gathered under both this tent and "under the larger tent of the King of Kings." He bowed his tonsured head—one shaved in the middle, leaving a ring of hair symbolising Jesus' crown of thorns. "Good and gracious Father in Heaven, forgive us, Thy most wicked and perverse servants. Grant us Thy favour by Thy blessed Grace. Bless us all, Father in Glory, that in Thy liberty we shall find the liberty Thou hast most graciously imparted to us, Thy unworthy vessels. Bless King John, bless his holy army, bless the Church and all who serve therein. Bless those we call our enemy according to Thy commandment. Forgive all who have violated thy holy ways. Lead the people of this good realm called England into a union of thought and deed that shall bear the fruit of Thy justice and wield the arm of Thy power in the generations to follow. *In nomine Patris, et Filii, et Spiritus Sancti.* Amen."

Lady Isabel smiled with approval at the Archbishop's fine prayer. Like Lord William, he was a man of uncommon gifts and of uncommon spirit. He had stood by her husband's side against both princes and popes and she called him "Heaven's hound of liberty."

A scholar, Stephen Langton had been the one to organise the books of the Bible into chapters, and all of the books into a standardised order. It was like a Norman to do such a thing, for they, like their Nordic ancestors, craved orderliness. It was why they had organised their world so ingeniously, with its many layers of feudal titles and relationships.

With the sulking King John eating alone in Windsor Castle, Lord William and his wife were the first to be presented trenchers covered with a thick slab of bread and laden with roasted venison. With the exception of the archbishop, the other guests would have to share these thick, wooden planks by twos, threes, or fours, depending on their rank.

Within a few moments the ushers had served all and with their knives the diners eagerly lifted great chunks of dripping meat into their gaping mouths. Drooling and happy, they washed each mouthful away with tall beakers of English ale. Dogs prowled below the table, lunging at strips of fat tossed to the ground. Their backs proved to be suitable hand-wipes. A few hooded falcons screeched from their perches and a bishop's monkey drew loud objections as he scampered directly across a silver tray of cheese!

The late-morning meal progressed with additional servings of fowl and pork, a pot of boiled beans, and garden salads, until the stuffed *courtiers* leaned away from the table to settle into a babble of rumour and speculation. Knowing that William Marshal and Archbishop Langton had always been sympathetic to the barons' cause, it was believed that the present negotiations had been shaped, in large part, by their counsel. *The Articles of the Barons* that would be presented to the King on the morrow was thought to be the product of Langton's genius and William's resolve. Yet no one had the slightest interest in raising doubts of either man's loyalty to the King. Creating controversy at this time would prove unwise, for the civil war that had ravaged England had been terribly costly for all. And, since France—that eternal thorn, that pesky briar 'neath the saddle of all Britain—was poised to join the rebels, it would be prudent for all Englishmen to serve the cause of peace.

Isabel smiled contentedly at the knights belching loudly and rubbing bellies filled with venison, roasted ox, and boiled hare. "Ah, good usher, more comfits please. I'd be most grateful for some sweets on such a warm day—and some honey with my fish?" Isabel loved to eat, and all marvelled that she had remained slim for all of her life. She also liked to cook—a skill that had given much consternation to her kitchen staff.

A pleasant breeze wafted beneath the brown canvas tent just as the bells of sext rang in Windsor's nearby church. Called to his religious duties, the Archbishop rose to excuse himself and soon disappeared with a column of dark-robed clerks and an armed escort.

The churchmen gone, William's knights took their ease with the ale and the red wine set in pitchers along the trestle table. Their language quickly became coarse, their manners nearly forgotten, and, as Isabel could have expected, a brawl ensued between the large, brash, and always-unkempt Sir Henry Hose and William's foppish Jordan de Sauqueville. To the eye, one would have thought Jordan to be a delicate fellow. He was an actor who loved to wear flowers in his hair and dance on the tips of his toes. In a brawl, however, he was tenacious and quick-fisted—in combat, vicious and unmerciful.

The contest proved to be a short-lived affair, born of some off-handed remark that had stung Sir Henry's Saxon pride. The two rolled across the table, clearing it of both patron and partridge. They kicked and bit, punched and scratched each other until Lord William would have no more. "Enough," he bellowed. A sporting brawl at dinner was not uncommon, but under these tense circumstances it was not welcome. The old earl took several long strides and separated the pair with a scowl. He stood between them with crossed arms and clenched his jaw while he thought.

Lord William's face suddenly relaxed and the corners of his lips turned up, ever so slightly. It was a look of satisfaction that cast a pall of dread over the combatants. He winked at his wife, then said, "Henry, receive the kiss of peace from thy worthy comrade."

Sir Henry Hose groaned; it was as he had feared. The kiss of peace was oft' given between faithful vassals and their lord. Placed squarely on the lips, it was a sign of affection, loyalty, and camaraderie. He looked at Sir Jordan like a droop-eared pup submitting to his master's rebuke.

Jordan drew a long draught of cider, licked his lips slowly and cackled a wicked laugh. "Ha—*mon ami. Mon amor.*" He strode towards poor Henry with opened arms and puckered lips. Then, as his fellow knights roared their approval, Henry Hose closed his eyes and submitted.

❋

With a call for the dogs and a kiss for her husband, Lady Isabel beckoned her entourage to follow her to the banks of the nearby Thames. The sun was past noon and felt warm on the skin, yet the air was cool and refreshing. It was a glorious day, a gift of time in which the very best of memories are oft' born. "Come, come, Aethel! We've a wondrous day to walk by my most favoured river in all the kingdom."

"Aye, m'lady, but we've needs wait for d'Erley. I think the lord has sent him as escort."

"Fine, fine, though I am sure Twigadarn is security enough." She turned and smiled at her ever-present bodyguard, whom she had often described as a shadow—silent, looming, and forever close. "*Air fhaicill*," she proclaimed. "Always on his guard."

Twigadarn nodded. "*Seadh*," he said, "It is so." It was typical for the man to say little more than necessary, if anything at all. His first language, of course, was Gaelic, and he could understand only a little English, and even less Norman-French. The son of Poch ab-Rhys of the valley of the Wye, the Welshman was a giant of a man, a head taller than Isabel's husband. In his middle thirties, he was thick-built, broad-shouldered, and wore his black hair shaggy and long like his beard. His skin was very white, like the peaks of Snowdonia, and his eyes were such a ghostly, light blue that they turned many away in fear. "A spirit of sorts—devil, perhaps, warlock or soul-slave, most likely," is what the priests oft' mumbled. After all, no one had ever seen the man sleep, nor even recline, for that matter. He was vigilant and menacing, appearing from nowhere and vanishing in the mists, guarding his precious Isabel with the transcending perceptiveness and nether-world ferocity attributed to Celtic warriors throughout all time. Though he owned no land and had never been knighted, Isabel often referred to him as "*Messire*"—abbreviated as "Sir"—Twigadarn, out of respect for his valour and courtesy.

"Come, come, all. Sir John shall come forthwith." The Countess impatiently bade her entourage begin their walk along the sluggish Thames. Followed by some dozen attendants and her hounds, the lady stepped lightly under the silver willows rustling lightly in the soft breeze. A frog leapt from beneath a clod of river grass, a turtle slipped beneath the dark water, and a shrill bird dashed above. "Marvellous," exclaimed Isabel. "I do love the water so."

A group of late-born ducklings scurried by, frantically peddling the water to keep stride with the sure strokes of their mother. Isabel paused. "See, Aethel. I count ten." She smiled.

"Aye, m'lady. Ten little ones—just like what followed you all over the King's realm."

Isabel bent midst ankle-blooms to pick and toss a flower aimlessly at the mother duck. "She seems like a good mother, do you think?"

By her tone, wise Aethel sensed a need for affirmation. "Aye, m'lady, but no better mother in all God's Creation was ever than you—other than the Virgin Mary, of course."

Isabel's eyes moistened. She wasn't so sure.

"Lady Isabel," sounded a panting voice. It was Sir John d'Erley.

"You've come to walk with us. Good; I had hoped you would."

John bowed and smiled broadly. He was dressed in a black-belted, bright blue over-tunic, or *cote*, that fell to mid-calf, exposing white hose beneath. The sleeves of the tunic reached to his forearms, widening at the ends into a great bell-shape that would have hung to his knees, except that on this occasion they were knotted up at his wrists.

Isabel placed her hands together and bent slightly as she welcomed her favourite, all the while staring at the man's stuffed sleeves. "Did you pack a snack from the table?" she teased.

John blushed. "Ah, no. I've a gift for you and thy lovely handmatron, however." He proceeded to untie his sleeves, releasing a huge bundle of wildflowers that he and Lord William had picked while talking after dinner. Henry Hose had added a few (without much enthusiasm), along with the dandy de

Sauqueville, who had been delighted to contribute some from his hair.

Isabel clapped. "Ah, good John—and good lord husband." Her eyes moistened; it was good to feel loved. Isabel gathered the many colours into her hands and lifted them to her nose. She breathed deeply and raised her eyes to Heaven.

"My lady, thy husband bids you not wander far from the King's camp. You'd be a good hostage for a baron who doubts the morrow."

Isabel shrugged. "My son is with the barons; there's no need to fear. But, I shall yield to my husband's wishes, for he's enough on his mind and does not need a wife's distraction. Aethel, gather the servants and let us move to yon bank. 'Tis clear of brush, and wide—perhaps a little steep, but a good place to recline—and perhaps to swim." Her eyes twinkled mischievously; it was a trait that Lord William had loved from the moment he had met her.

Aethel groaned, then obeyed, and, in a few moments the lady's entourage had spread a cover of colourful woollen blankets atop the grassy riverbank and beneath the wide-spread limbs of a large sycamore. Isabel had John's flowers sprinkled atop the blankets and bade all to rest within their fragrance while she and Aethel prepared to swim. "Is the bathman with us?"

Aethel peered about, half-heartedly. Her nose wrinkled. "Aye, m'lady. So he is."

Isabel smiled. "'Tis a good day for a bath. We ought wash away the troubles of the past three days and prepare ourselves for the hope of tomorrow."

The bathman travelled with Lord William's staff wherever it went. Unlike King John, who took few baths—some saying not more than three a year—Lord William and his household followed the more common Norman preference of bathing whenever possible. He and his knights washed their hands faithfully before each meal, and when a drawn bath was impractical, all were expected to sponge bathe as often as they could, with their bathing bags of oatmeal and dried flowers.

"Thy servant, good lady," bowed the bathman. He handed Aethel a large block of soap and a boar-bristle brush.

Though most bathed in mixed company, Isabel preferred her privacy—perhaps at the prodding of her jealous husband—and summoned the screens.

"Aye, m'lady," answered the servant. The man ordered a large, square sheet be lifted as Isabel and Aethel undressed. In moments, the Countess tip-toed lightly down the grassy bank and slipped gracefully under the dark waters of the Thames, delighting in its refreshment.

Poor Aethel was not designed to make an entrance nearly as elegant. With a grumble and a grouse, she removed her final under-garment, folded it, and laid it atop her other clothes. Then, dressed in only that which the Creator had granted at her birth, the full-bodied woman turned towards the waiting water and secured the braids that were rolled by her ears like the horns of a great ram.

Facing her duty squarely, she then set one ample leg before the other, lumbering and toddling on spreading feet down the steep bank, only to slip as the hound, Alfred, dashed by. The trumpet-ing servant landed hard atop her full buttocks just in time for Canute to clamber over her bare belly on his way to a swim! The furious matron lay howling in river mud until, with a few choice oaths and a gentle hand from Isabel, she stood to her feet. Finally, with a grunt, a deep breath, and a heave, ample Aethel launched into the Thames, all four limbs pedalling wildly like a great white cow struggling in a deep ford.

"Oh, dear Aethel!" giggled Isabel. "My dear Aethel. Thank you for joining me."

"Aye." scowled the handmatron. "The water's a bit cold, m'lady," she quipped.

"Perhaps," tittered Isabel. "Have you the soap?"

"Indeed. Somehow I kept it fast whilst I tumbled in! And, by the Virgin's help, I saved the brush as well." The woman's frown began to give way to a grin and soon a big smile spread across Aethel's broad face as she began to laugh uproariously.

The two old friends splashed and dunked one another, then

scrubbed each other with tallow soap scented with herbs. The scrubbing tingled their skin and the cool water enlivened their bodies. For a brief time they did not feel like ageing women, but rather like young misses, romping and giggling under a smiling sun. At last the dripping pair climbed up the bank to dry and re-dress.

"Are you refreshed, m'lady?" asked Sir John, as the two emerged from behind their screen.

"We are, indeed," Isabel answered.

"I suppose *courtesie* denies me the knowledge of what troubles Aethel suffered?" The knight smiled and winked

"You, Sir John, are so very correct," Isabel tittered. "Some things are best left unsaid. Now, it is my wish to gather you, Aethel, and Twigadarn by my side—over there—away from the others."

The curious three followed their lady some ten yards or so along the bank, where they spread a fresh blanket atop the grass. Aethel brought a basket of treats—some cherry preserves and honey cakes, a flagon of red French wine, and a clay jar of cider, cooled in the river.

Lady Isabel blotted her braids dry with a hand towel as she bade the others to recline. Twigadarn hesitated; it was never his custom to lie down. He remained standing. "*Le cead; le ur cead?*" he asked, with a bow.

The Countess stood and took him gently by the arm. "Of course, dear friend. You have my leave."

The group relaxed and looked about the pleasant meadow happily. Their lives had been pressed in these past months and they were glad to rest. The green was healing, the bright colours of the countless wildflowers invigorating, and the high sun as comforting as a friendly hearth.

After a brief time, Isabel turned her eyes from the pleasures of nature and laid them on each earnest face before her. *Good and faithful d'Erley*, she thought. *He's suffered much and stood the test. A keen mind and clean heart, strong arms and a steady eye. Quiet, caring, dependable as the dawn. William is right to love him so.*

She turned to Aethel and smiled. *Only she would follow me into rivers and seas, lakes and fishponds! Oh, what life would I have had without her?* She sighed, sadly, realising that her friend was age-ing. Would that her children had lived. She greets her late years with such strength and devotion.

Twigadarn—always Twigadarn, she thought. *I thought him an odd gift from William—but now I know. Her mind then drifted to one not present. Oh, I pray the good dwarf is safe. I do miss him.*

As the others chattered lightly, Isabel lay back and stared at the puffed, white clouds far above. She saw in them the images of a lifetime: knights on horseback, towering cathedrals, stubby chapels, and the battlements of castle keeps. *There*, she thought. *'Tis my father's ghost?* Isabel closed her eyes and pictured her father, not quite knowing if it was her own memory or the words of those who had so oft' described him to her.

Isabel's father had been Lord Richard de Clare, called Strong-bow, a Norman knight who had climbed from little means to become one of the greatest landholders in King Henry's kingdom. In alliance with the Irish king, Dermot MacMurchada, the red-headed, freckled, warrior had won land with both his sword and his clever mind. Perhaps the respect Isabel felt for her father was what caused her to so honour her husband, for William, too, had been little more than a knight-errant before winning his wealth through boldness, honour, and a strategic marriage.

Her thoughts quickly flew to her mother, the quiet, golden-haired Eve. Few had known her well and she, least of all. It was a denied affection that still left a void in her heart. "I hope I pleased her some. I fear her life was a sorrow."

"My lady?" asked John.

Isabel sat up with a start. "*Oui?*"

"You were—whimpering some. Is everything all right?"

The Countess nodded and reached for the cider. "Would you all gather close—might we spend a special time on this uncommon afternoon?"

John and Aethel looked at each other, curiously.

"Twigadarn—*labhair san dol seachad*. Yes, Twigadarn?"

The giant nodded.

Isabel smiled and took the knight and her servant by the

hand. "I am getting older and looking at you two, I should say we are all getting on a bit."

The three laughed.

"As my time passes, I have learned to treasure it all the more. It is a sad irony to me that time's very value is in its passing. It is ever more clear to me that the memories of a lifetime ought to be recalled when one can, for in such recollection is discovered the gifts we may have left the world we shall soon leave."

"Gifts, m'lady?" asked Aethel.

Isabel nodded. "Yes, we would so hope. Gifts like—like a kindness shown or a mercy offered, a loss for another's gain, a word of comfort or of wisdom. Perhaps, Aethel, a gift of example—honour, courage, devotion. Perhaps a gift of instruction such as what might better another's life. Maybe new ideas or old ones made better, of things clever or beautiful. Perhaps during our time we have rooted out corruptions and wicked ways, exposed evil or chased the demons from the common path. Most of all, however, I would hope we might have left behind the greatest gift of all: love to others, so that they, like us, might love as well, and in so doing, fill the future with the love of the Giver of all things lovely."

Aethel remained silent. She had never considered her life more than one expended in the service of the great Countess and her family. She smiled, suddenly wondering if her life had been one of lasting value after all.

John d'Erley's face was ribboned with tears. "Good lady, you make us weep and tremble with hope. Oh, would that we leave behind such gifts. But it is you—"

"Ah, nay, Sir John," scolded Isabel. "Nay. It is *you*, and *you*, my dear Aethel, and *you*, Sir Twigadarn. It is you that have so bravely served the cause of good. It is also my beloved husband, our ten children, the rugged circle of our knights, the good men who have come and gone in my time—so many, dear John, so very many of you have left good gifts all about the seasons of my life."

The four fell quiet, listening to the occasional lap of the river Thames, the pleasant chirps of unseen birds, and the rustle of leaves. A pair of swans drifted within view, and Isabel smiled. She swallowed another draught of cider and reached for a sweetmeat. "Would you indulge my present melancholy?"

"Whatever you desire, m'lady," answered John.

"Good; then hear me. I should like to spend this afternoon in times past. We have shared much of life together. Our lives are entwined like—like the vines on that distant tree. What one forgets, another remembers. Would you treat me with a roundtable? Might we fly from here and soar among the many years now gone?" Isabel's voice was excited and hopeful.

John and Aethel nodded. How could they refuse such a pleasant invitation? They, too, had taken little time to swim in the great ocean of their lives' stories. "Aye, m'lady," they chimed. Twigadarn smiled and agreed. "*Gu dearba*—certainly," he added.

Lady Isabel clapped her hands with joy and passed the basket of treats. "So then, Sir John, my Aethel, *Messire* Twigadarn—let us begin—let us remember."

CHAPTER II

THE KING, A PRINCE, AND A GENTLEMAN

LITTLE four-year-old Isabel de Clare was taken by royal escort from Dublin's Holy Trinity Church immediately following the burial of her father, Richard (Strongbow) de Clare, in April, 1176. Strongbow had pursued a chequered career of intrigue and violence, having warred and plotted within the complicated web of feudal alliances that characterised Norman rule. At one point, King Henry II had seized most of his lands. In response, the combative, though soft-spoken Strongbow had made a powerful alliance with the Irish king, Dermot MacMurchada, eventually winning Dermot's daughter and his many lands in Leinster, a province of eastern Ireland. Later, needing Strongbow's support, King Henry had restored most of the lord's lands in Wales and in England which, added to his Irish holdings, had made him-- and now his little daughter-- amongst the most wealthy landholders in the kingdom.

The child was taken aboard a royal ship on which she sailed to Wales under grey, foreboding skies. She was then promptly delivered to a waiting column of mounted soldiers who were to provide protection for her overland ride to the Tower of London.

"And there you will do as you are told."

Bouncing within a royal carriage, little Isabel de Clare lifted her chin and turned away from her attendant. Sheltered beneath a heavy canopy, she stared thoughtfully through the budded branches of the trees lining the rutted roadway. The April day was heavy and grey. "Then, *Madame*, when shall I see my mummy?"

The answer was swift and harsh. "Do not ask me that again, else you shall feel my hand. Forget your mother; you are now a ward of King Henry."

Refusing to look at the ill-tempered woman beside her, Isabel folded her hands on her lap and struggled to fight the tears now forming beneath her eyes. In five years of life, the young heiress had never ventured beyond her father's Irish lands. In these past weeks, however, strangers had taken her from all she had ever known. The child wanted desperately to be brave; it was a quality her father had spoken of endlessly. But now she did not feel brave, or safe, or happy. She lowered her face and stared at her shoes until a voice from outside the carriage startled her.

"M'lady?"

The girl looked up at one of her mounted escorts. "Aye, Sir Knight?"

The young soldier was saddle-sore and coughing. He had ridden alongside Isabel's heavy-wheeled carriage all the way from the faraway docks in Wales. "All's well, m'lady?"

Isabel nodded.

"Good." He looked casually about the damp landscape, then at his tiny charge. "Won't be long now," he said as he nudged his horse closer to Isabel. "I thank the Holy Mother for our good fortune. You are the King's fine prize, you know. An army of saints could not have protected us had we lost you to highwaymen or to raiders."

Isabel said nothing. She understood enough to realize that her inheritance exposed her to grave danger and she had been assured by many that the King's protection was a good thing. Nevertheless, she didn't like the sound of being called the 'King's fine prize.'

"Well, we're well past Windsor and we ought be at the Tower soon enough. You've a stew and a soft bed waiting."

At the sound of the word, 'tower' a chill shivered through the girl's body. She had been told that the hand of man had cast no longer shadow in all of Britain than that cast by the cloud-capped heights of London's Tower Castle. Imagining herself as a helpless captive within those massive walls gave her cause to fear. Her heart began to race and a clammy feeling crept over her skin. *Soon*? She bit her lip and stared forward, still resisting the temptation to look at her attendant. She suddenly wanted to leap from the carriage and sprint across the flower-tipped meadows now lining the Thames. Instead, she dried her eyes with a silk kerchief and chose to face the woman, boldly. "*Madame*, when shall I be taken home?"

The cruel woman abruptly slapped the determined child hard across one cheek, then the other. "Now stop it, else I find the rod." She cast a hard look at the young soldier who grumbled and faded away.

Smarting, Isabel shrunk into her red woollen cloak with a whimper and, daring to say no more, sat silently for a long while as the groaning carriage jostled closer to its destination. Lonely and frightened, Isabel sank ever deeper into herself, one hand holding the cloak close to her nose where she hoped to capture one last, fleeting scent of her mother's lavender. *Oh Mummy*, she thought as a wisp of fragrance graced her nose. *Oh Mummy, I can see you.*

She drew upon the wool deeply once again and shut her eyes. A wondrous memory came to her mind and she smiled. It was as if she had been suddenly returned to the special morning in the summer before when the sun was shining brightly over Ireland. Her father and her mother were walking with her through green grass. *Your hair was like gold, Mummy.* Isabel felt suddenly warm. *You picked me up, Papa, higher than ever.* Isabel's hair had not been braided that morning and it had blown freely in a brisk morning breeze. She remembered that, too, for it was then—with her berry-blond hair streaming behind-- that her mother, Eve, had pronounced her blessing. Isabel now whispered the words to herself: "May none ever bind thy spirit, child; bold currents are thy kin. For you are special born, my dear; a daughter of the wind."

Isabel sighed. "Oh, Mummy, where are you?"

"Stop muttering," said the attendant.

Shrinking from an expected blow, Isabel looked up at the woman's hand. The attendant looked away and Isabel fixed a suddenly defiant stare on her, gathering her cloak to her throat. *Leave me be*, she thought.

After a short while, Isabel escaped behind closed eyes once more, but now her mind flew to the anxious moment when her mother's trembling hands had wrapped the very same cloak tightly beneath her chin. It had been just weeks before in the damp graveyard of the church--mere moments after her father had been lowered into his grave.

The child released her grip and turned to stare blankly at the unfamiliar countryside around her. She wanted to be home—in Ireland. She thought of her father again, before he had gotten sick, moving about his castles with his long-sword at his hip. She remembered him telling stories of her grandfather— her mother's father, King MacMurchada—the wild, free Irish King.

Though deeply grieved, Isabel could at least understand death; it was the companion of her times. She had already witnessed death and dying in most of their forms. So though her father's death had been excruciating, being torn from her mother's arms at her Papa's graveside had been something else, altogether.

The sounds of heavy horse startled her. She quickly leaned forward and saw a mounted company of royal guards approaching. Her carriage was reined to a halt as the guards arrived. A few shouts were exchanged, and when all was in order the captain of the royals nudged his horse alongside the carriage.

"Is the girl well?" he asked the attendant.

"A bit strident, but red-cheeked and robust."

The captain dismounted with a grunt. He opened the carriage door. "Let's have a look." With two strong hands fixed on Isabel's waist, he lifted the child from her velvet seat and set her softly on the ground.

Isabel looked away as he opened her cloak to study her for a long moment. She knew her woollen cloak had been soiled from the journey and her black leather shoes were stained with dried mud. She stole a brief look down her grey linen over-gown and was relieved to find it only soiled at her ankles. She hoped she was 'presentable' as her mother had so oft expected.

Satisfied, the soldier bent over and stuck a short finger in her belly with a smile. "Aye. She looks rosy and well-fed, and those blue eyes of hers are bright and keen. The King will like her hair. 'Tis not unlike his own. You'll need to have it braided or at least combed a bit better."

"Of course, sire," answered the attendant.

"And a bath?"

"Certainly."

The captain squatted on cracking knees. "I am sorry for your father, young Lady de Clare." Isabel liked the tone of his voice. "I served with him against some wild Welsh pagans. He was a brave man indeed—a fair Christian, too." The man became melancholy. "Hard to imagine the mighty Lord Richard Strongbow de Clare dead from a mortification of the foot. He should have fallen in battle. Still, m'lady, he will be remembered."

The captain stood, slowly, and lifted Isabel back into the carriage. He turned to the attendant. "So, where's her mother?"

Isabel's eyes widened.

"Strongbow left her a small holding in Wales where she is being held."

Isabel looked back and forth between them. *Held?*

The guard nodded. He looked at the young heiress. "Do you know your duty now?"

She did not answer his question. "Sir Knight, what does 'Mummy being held' mean?"

"Ah. Well, your mother is safe and well-kept in a good castle in Wales where she shall live. Your duty, now, m'lady, is to be a proper ward of the King."

The captain waited as the little girl tried to sort things through.

"Do you know what a royal ward is?" he asked, patiently.

"I think so."

"I see. Well, King Henry shall keep you safe and he shall see that you are fed and clothed properly. Priests will teach you of heaven and earth. Then, when the King is ready, he shall marry you to a man deserving of your father's great wealth. Have no care, all will be well for you."

"Must I marry the man he chooses?"

"Aye."

Isabel thought for a moment. "You are certain?"

"Yes, m'lady."

"Until then, might I leave when I wish? Can I go to Wales?"

"No, m'lady."

"Am I a prisoner, then?"

"No, m'lady."

"But I am not free."

The captain paused. "And who is?"

The child and the old veteran looked at one another for a long moment until Isabel nodded.

"So, my dear," he said. "To the Tower, then."

✽

Isabel had been fortunate to be of high birth, a member of the Norman ruling class that had divided the wealth and power of Britain amongst itself since the day its armies conquered the Saxons more than a century and a half before. Thankfully, the privilege she enjoyed had not begun to taint her character as it had so many of her peers. Those who knew her well believed she might never be so stained, for she, like her mother, was sincere in her faith--a faith not encumbered by the weighty apparatus of the Roman Church.

Hers was a station spared the random cruelty that terrorized the common folk. Yet the aristocracy to which she belonged was exposed to its own particular perils to be sure. Her elders were entangled within a complex web of financial relationships, legal procedures, and military obligations that resulted in shifting alliances, assassinations, boundary wars, and the like. Lacking adequate restraint, the tyranny of advantage ruled them all. It was this unbridled power that had sprung from the very centre of the web and had stolen Isabel from her mother's arms.

"And what shall I say to him, Father?"

An old Welsh priest named Adderig bent low. "Perhaps you'd best leave him speak." The cleric paused. "Are you frightened?"

She nodded.

26

Adderig laid a hand lightly on her head and said a prayer. "God goes with you, my child. And I shall be at thy side."

Isabel had been delivered to her new chambers late in the prior afternoon where she had met a small staff assigned to attend her. Now, with the old priest on one side and an indifferent soldier on the other, she waited nervously at the entrance to the royal hall. It was eleven o'clock in the morning and the huge room was crowded with a stifling collection of hungry courtiers busily consuming the main meal of the day. A large fire roared in the gaping hearth situated at one end of the rectangular chamber and the royal hounds were prowling for scraps. The scene was not unfamiliar to Isabel; she had seen lords gathered in her father's castles before. But this particular hall felt different to her. There was an unfriendly sound to it, a grating buzz that made her want to run away.

The faceless soldier started through the archway. "Follow me."

A million questions swirled through her mind. *Will he be cruel to me? Will he think me ugly? Am I presentable? Will he let me go home?* She slipped her hand into Father Adderig's and stepped forward.

Isabel was led towards the King ceremoniously down a long aisle, and on either side diners fell silent in her wake. They studied the heiress carefully as she passed, each wondering how they might exploit her value. These lords and ladies were no strangers to the clever machinations of a world that had become the whispering realm of conspirators. In efforts to plunder the expansive Le Clare fortune of the child's father, many had already sent their lawyers to the King's ear with petitions and clever offers. The King, however, had made it very clear that he would preserve the rich estate through the wardship of Isabel. In so doing, the child would remain the King's possession until he bartered her and her inheritance to serve his own interests.

Isabel walked closer and closer to the huddle of courtiers gathering close to King Henry's huge chair. She was dressed in a green silk over-gown that was wrapped at the waist in a bright red sash. The perfectly tailored gown fell to her ankles, and then trailed behind her in a short train. Her hair had been plaited into two long braids and atop her head she wore a gauzy, yellow wimple tied loosely beneath her chin. She was a miniature of those elegant ladies of the court now craning from afar.

As Isabel approached, she closed her eyes and prayed. Then, as the great King rose, she felt her mouth go dry. She was immediately encircled by royal knights. Clutching the priest's hand, she raised her chin proudly. Little lady Isabel--the tiny, vulnerable daughter of the mighty Strongbow--now stood boldly in the shadow of giants. Her father would have been proud.

Father Adderig bowed. "Sire, allow me to present thy ward, Lady Isabel de Clare, daughter of Lord Richard Strongbow de Clare of Ireland and Wales."

The hall was silent as the priest whispered into Isabel's ear. She quickly curtsied. "My King."

Henry smiled. "Welcome, Lady Isabel." His voice was strong and clear.

"Are you my new *père?*"

Father Adderig winced and a gasp rustled through the hall as the forty-three-year-old monarch crouched down to face his ginger-haired ward, eye to eye. The King thought for a moment, and then answered. "*Non, mon enfant*, I am not your new father."

Isabel kept her chin up. "Then I should be very pleased to see my mummy, sire."

The court sniggered, but fell silent as King Henry rose with a hard-set jaw and folded arms. He glared at the wretched ring of over-indulged, petty, self-important nobles suddenly feigning deference. The King could barely stomach any of these courtiers: his mumbling advisors and idiot lawyers, his grasping lords, his effeminate accountants, and his pompous priests. The only members of the court he enjoyed were his knights who also did what they could to avoid these hissing serpents of the Great Tower. Henry turned from one pallid face to the next—emissaries and courtesans, barons and their brides—or more likely, their paramours—men no more sincere than a Judas kiss;

women worthy of Scripture's reproach-- resplendent vessels filled with corruption. "If only Marshal were here," he muttered.

The King cast a final frown to the farthest reaches of the stone-walled hall, then knelt once more and took Isabel's pink cheeks tenderly in his coarse, rough hands. "Child, you are now my precious jewel. Look at your fine gown. You are so pretty in green. *Messier* de Glanville shall see to your happiness and he assures me he has already selected hand-servants to see to your cares." He leaned close to whisper, "And I vow you this, you'll need not suffer the devils lurking here."

Isabel now smiled, albeit cautiously. She suddenly liked King Henry. His red hair and freckles reminded her of Papa. So did his barrelled chest.

"Now, child, listen well. Your mother is safe in a keep and you need not fear for her. You are now part of my household. Have no care, little Isabel de Clare, all shall be well for you."

Isabel looked into her King's face with clear eyes. "Shall I be free, sire, free like the wind?"

Henry raised a brow. "Like the wind? Well, I confess I have no answer for such a question."

A long pause followed.

"Who shall you marry me to?"

"Ah, little flower," chuckled the King. "There are already suitors by the score, but I shall wait and when you are ready you shall have the bravest, strongest, most honourable knight of all."

❅

"Ha, you missed," laughed Isabel.

A lad of about twelve, stormed towards the girl, tossing his bow aside. "What say you?" he screamed.

Isabel braced herself. "I said you missed the target, and badly at that."

The soon-to-be-squire angrily bent over and set his nose against the maid's. "Look at me—do you not see who I am?"

The little girl flinched, but just a little. She had been in residence at the Tower for well over a year now and she certainly knew the darting eyes and rage-flushed face pressed close to hers. "*Oui*, m'lord," she answered with feigned humility. "You are Prince John." She curtsied.

"Indeed. And you—you are nothing." He closed his mouth, rolled his tongue, and then spat into Isabel's face before striking her and pushing her to the ground.

At that moment, a small boy who had been retrieving the prince's arrows shouted angrily. "Leave her be."

The prince whirled about. "D'Erley, guest or not, you're a little fool. She's a ward of my father and nothing more."

"She's a lady." The boy, no more than five years old, stuck his chest forward and planted his fists on his hips. "Chivalry demands her protection."

Isabel smiled at the plucky little fellow and climbed to her feet. She was about to speak when a voice boomed from behind.

"Hold fast, there." It was Isabel's favourite handmaiden, Aethel, a fifteen-year-old English girl with a broad, ruddy face and stout body. She came running from the apple shed. "Prince or no, you'll leave m'lady be." Panting, she placed herself between John and Isabel.

"Is that so?" The prince glared at Aethel, then turned a cold eye on Isabel. He curled his upper lip like a snarling wolf and kicked dust atop both their shoes. "Do not ever dare insult me again." Then, with a string of ear-singeing oaths, he turned on his heels and stormed away.

The handsome young prince was a miserable lad—cunning, crafty, shrewd, and vindictive. He was cold-hearted and given to sudden fits of fury. The youngest of Henry's four sons, it was a relief for all that his ascendancy to the throne was unlikely. Some thought his rage was rooted in bitterness over the King's imprisonment of his mother, Queen Eleanor, some four years prior. Yet, it seemed to most that John already understood, or perhaps even enjoyed, matters of royal politics, leaving it generally agreed that the lad was simply wicked seed.

"You misjudged the prince," scolded Aethel.

Isabel nodded. "Aye, it would seem so." She had remembered following the boy one day in the summer past, soon after his father had beaten him with a willow wand. He had run to the chamber housing a small menagerie of exotic animals kept there for the King's pleasure. Isabel, too, loved animals and thought anyone who sought them out for comfort must surely have a heart of some tenderness.

Isabel sighed, and then turned towards the stranger. "I thank you, young master. Might I ask your name?"

The little lord blushed, and then bowed deeply. "I am Master John d'Erley of the west country."

Isabel curtsied. "And I am Isabel de Clare, ward of the King."

John d'Erley smiled. "We shall meet again, m'lady." He then bowed once more and hurried away.

Aethel took her charge into the cold shadow of the castle's newly built outer wall. She knelt, wiped the spittle from Isabel's face with her hand and tucked the girl's hair under her wool cap. She snuggled Isabel's cloak more tightly beneath her chin and fixed it with its silver clasp. "By the saints, young lady," she grumbled as she wagged a stubby finger. "He could have ordered you beaten for that outrage."

Isabel giggled. "And you as well."

Aethel looked about nervously. "Aye, m'lady. And me as well. I think we found him on a good day—and he really did miss his mark."

"*Oui*, and badly." Isabel thought quietly for a moment, and then rubbed the small bruise rising on her face. "I pray, Aethel, that he never becomes our King."

※

Later that same day, Isabel and Aethel were walking through the wet leaves of the courtyard. Isabel had become quiet, almost inward. Her mood was darkening like the day around them. The day was April the tenth, one day after Easter and two days after Lent. The season of Lent had lasted its normal forty days and had denied the devout the pleasures of sweetmeats, comfits, and the other forbidden delights. Easter, of course, had released everyone from their moderation so Aethel led the way towards the King's kitchen where she begged a spoonful of plum preserves in the vain hope of raising her lady's spirits.

The castle was relaxed and its workers at ease. The King was travelling about his kingdom; none were quite sure if he was in England or busy about royal business in his Norman cities of Rouen, Cain, and Bayeux. He might also have been touring his other French holdings, such as the duchies of Aquitaine, Poitou, Maine, or Anjou. The courtiers who remained at the Tower were now free to speak openly of the King's nagging melancholy which had troubled Isabel greatly. Messengers had reported that Henry was lethargic, his spirit yet wounded by the death of his mistress, the fair Rosamond, some fifteen months prior. For Henry, young Rosamond had been an angel sent to comfort him, a gentle dove who had rested lightly upon his arm and cooed kindly in his ear. She was the essence of feminine beauty—fair of skin, blond-haired, blue-eyed, and shapely.

Isabel and Aethel agreed with most that the King's wife, the contentious, hard-edged and ageing Queen Eleanor of Aquitaine, had most likely ordered the poisoning of Rosamond. Of course, Eleanor had no cause to cast stones. She had been the wife of the religious and soft-spoken King Louis VII of France when the dashing nineteen-year-old Henry appeared at the French court. He had swaggered his way into the royal hall like a champion stallion, heated with ambition and lusting for adventure. Eleanor's affections were immediately fired and she divorced King Louis in order to fly to Henry's strong arms where she buttressed his claim to the English throne and lands in France. It was the stuff of troubadours and balladeers and gave birth to an age of poetry and music devoted to courtly love.

Eleanor's dubious virtue notwithstanding, Henry's indiscretion had been but a harbinger of things to come. In addition to any number of lesser sins, the King went on to defy the pope on issues of supremacy and was believed by some to have ordered the murder of the Archbishop of Canterbury, Thomas à Becket. King Henry, however, was now obsessed with "that toddling toady" King Louis and his perpetual, vengeful plots against the English.

Kicking rotting acorns that had fallen from a pair of tall oaks, the two passed the stables and the smith's shed, an armorer's booth, and a wagon laden with rushes destined for the floors of the damp castle. Isabel's favourite priest, Father Adderig, came out from behind a shed. The ruddy-faced Welshman spent much of his time teaching her Latin and the ways of Holy Scripture in the lively spirit of St. Patrick. "Isabel, *a h-uile là a chì 's nach fhaic,*" he said with a twinkle in his eye.

Isabel smiled, politely. "And the best to you, Father."

"So, my dear child, what is troubling you?"

The maiden shrugged, and then deflected his question. She pointed to one of the four tall towers that rose at each corner of the castle's central keep, itself nearly ninety feet tall. "I've been up there." Her strawberry-blond braids fell back as she tilted her head.

"Aye?"

"*Oui, Père.* The King takes me up sometimes. Its—its—"

"The observatory," added Aethel.

"*Oui.* King Henry shows me the stars and the moon. He says he goes there to dream—and so do I."

Father Adderig bent forward and set his finger under the girl's chin. "Aye, little flower. Ye ought to dream always. Why, methinks even the angels do dream some."

Isabel nodded. "I see angels in my sleep. I see them flying over there, too." She pointed to the ramparts fringing the top of the castle's walls like so many gapped teeth.

"And what are you dreaming of now, little sister?"

"I am not dreaming at all, Father." She turned her face away.

"I see. Well then, should I ask if you were at Mass this morning?"

"*Oui,* Father." She, like the entire King's household, attended Mass every morning. Six-year-old Isabel, however, unlike most of her elders, found true purpose in her religious duties.

"Good. And didst thou say thy *Pater Noster* before thy breakfast?"

Isabel's mouth dropped. She turned a scolding eye to Aethel, who had forgotten as well. "*Non, Père.*"

Father Adderig grinned. "Nor I." He laughed. "So, come by me, Isabel, and thee as well, fair Aethel, and we shall say it twice, once for what was due, and once—"

"For penance," blurted Aethel.

The priest smiled and shook his head. "Nay, sister. I thought a second one in case we forget on the morrow!"

Aethel and the old fellow roared.

"Aye, aye, enough. Now, shall we recite in Latin, Norman-French, English, or—Gaelic?"

Isabel knew Norman-French, of course; it was her primary tongue, but she had not wanted to bother with the French of King Louis' France-- the *Langue d'Oïl*. She knew her King had little good to say about the French, so she had no interest in their dialect. On the other hand, she happily studied Latin, Gaelic, and even the guttural English of the common folk.

The priest waited patiently, though he had much to do. As a cleric, he, like all the other 'clerks,' had a number of tasks. It fell to him to provide assistance to the castle's chaplains in matters of prayer, conduct the Divine Offices of the Day, masses, baptisms, and burials, but also to serve the King's household as a tutor, an accountant, and occasionally as a scribe. "So, Lady Isabel, what is thy choice today?"

Isabel thought carefully. She really was in no mood for this. "I suppose English."

"Good, then both of you on your knees."

> *Ure fadyr in heaven rich*
> *Thy name be hallyed ever lich*
> *Thou bring us thy michell blisse:.*
> *Als hit in heaven y doe,*
> *Evar in yearth beene it also.*
> *That holy bread that lasteth ay,*
> *Thou send it ous this ilke day,*
> *Forgive ous all that we have don,*
> *As we forgivet uch other mon"*
> *Ne let ous fall into no founding,*

Ac shield ous fro the fowle thing.
Amen.

Duty done, the little girl rose to her feet. The figure of a lad carrying a bow dashed near and at the sight of him Isabel could no longer contain her troubles. "Father, I…I…"

"Yes, child, please, what is it?"

Aethel took her hand and the pair sat down on a sawed log. Isabel began to tear. "Father, I fear the King might marry me to Prince John."

Startled, Aethel and Adderig looked at each other. "And why do you think this?" asked the priest.

"He looks at me oddly."

"Who?"

"The prince."

Adderig thought for a long moment. Finally he shook his head. "I dare not imagine why the prince stares at you, but this is my thought on the matter: I see no advantage for King Henry in marrying you to his son. The Crown already controls your wealth and any gain to be had would need to come from outside his reach. Do you understand?"

Isabel shrugged.

"I do," blurted Aethel. "He would be wiser marrying you to a lord he needs in alliance, else a foreign born prince, but his own son adds no purpose."

"Foreign? A Frenchman?" Isabel was not comforted.

Adderig feigned a chuckle. "No, no, child. King Henry is no fool. He'll be sure to marry you to one who strengthens his position. He will certainly not marry you to Prince John, or even to his others sons. Do not give it another thought."

Isabel began to brighten. "Are you sure of it, Father?"

Adderig nodded, feigning confidence. He would surely pray that he was right.

CHAPTER III

CHRISTMAS AND THE DREAM

THE winding Thames reflected the passing seasons of grey and green, orange and white. The city on its shores was crowded with heavy-laden ox-carts driven from England's nearby plains and wooden crates from ships tethered to London's many wharves. According to the season, the markets were heaped with ells of cloth and barrels of fish, with spice baskets, sheaves of grain, bales of wool, with tinker's wares, silver craft, and gold. And amidst the turning of time and the rhythm of a city's life, storms and troubles had come and gone, drifting across life's landscape like the shadows of great clouds. All the while the Tower stood tall and mighty atop the river's bank, the massive symbol of a kingdom's power and, by the Year of Grace 1184, still the home of Lady Isabel.

"Aethel, have you found my wimple?"

"Uh, no, m'lady. Ah—yes, m'lady. Here it is, a bright red for Advent, with a winter vine headdress. I shall lay it by this chest until the last. Now, off with yer day clothes and make ready for the feast."

It was sometime past sext, the sixth hour of light. The days' hours were calculated by dividing twelve into the available daylight of the season. Hence, a winter's daylight hour was considerably shorter than a summer's. Terce, at nine o'clock, was the third hour of the day and marked the time the ladies of the castle should be well on their way to dressing for first dinner of the Christmas feast. Isabel opened a shutter of the narrow window that overlooked the bailey below and laughed as she watched the clerks bustling towards their prayers. "Look, there is Father Bigod. I think he has the perfect name."

"Please, m'lady, we needs hurry." Aethel was feeling anxious, for it was her duty to have her mistress properly prepared and punctual. With the help of two other attendants, Aethel removed Isabel's outer garments, reducing her to the white, linen chemise she wore as her undergarment. It was a comfortable, shin-length shift, cut simply and sleeved in winter. Aethel led her lady to a wash basin and washed her face, hands, and feet in rose water. She stepped back and smiled at the young mistress standing in the castle's dim light. "You've the curving hips of a lovely maiden," she said with admiration.

Isabel blushed. She had changed from mere slip of a girl into a shapely, young woman of twelve. Not yet married, she was beginning to wonder. "Do you think the rumours are true?"

Aethel smiled. "One can ne'er know about the court, you know that." She led the maiden to a stool by the fireplace and ordered more logs. It was a chilly December day and the castle chambers were damp. A light snow had fallen and the sky was grey and foreboding. Aethel began the slow process of unwinding the plaits in Isabel's strawberry-blond hair in order to brush and braid them once again, though with the added accessory of a thin, yellow ribbon.

Isabel nodded, excited about what might be, and then took Aethel's hands in hers. "Forgive me for thinking only of myself when you must suffer another Christmas alone."

The woman nodded and fought the tears now welling in her eyes. Five years ago she had married a free man, an Englishman named Stephan Yourk. A saddler by trade, he had come to London to serve the groomsman of the royal stables. Since Aethel, as the daughter of an English sheriff, was free, all that had been needed was the permission of the King's *seneschal*--the overseer of the household. For a fee he had agreed, and the two were married on a Thursday in March. Unfortunately, their union proved to be troubled. Aethel's first child was stillborn and her second died of an infection. Later, her beloved Stephan was called to duty as a royal archer and killed in Normandy in the recent wars between King Henry and his rival son, known as Henry the Young King, now also deceased.

Aethel stared blankly for a few moments, and then muttered,

"I hear over and over again how young Henry repented before he died, and how his father forgave him." She shook her head. "I find it hard to forgive."

Isabel thought for a moment. She had spent so very many hours at the knee of Father Adderig that, though she knew a veritable armoury of verses with which to answer, she had also learned what not to say. She took her lonely friend's hands in hers and squeezed them, saying nothing.

Aethel took a deep breath. "I suppose I am in need of forgiveness m'self. I was so very glad-hearted when I learned how the Young King suffered and died, lying on a bed of ash in his hair shirt, his head on a stone pillow and a noose wrapped round his neck! Seemed right and fitting for a rebel." She shook her head, perhaps for her own unresolved bitterness, perhaps in contempt for the man who had taken away her life's love.

Isabel answered softly. "I'm told young Henry died clasping his father's ring of peace to his heart, and that his favourite knight, Lord William Marshal, has taken his cloak and heart to Palestine for burial near the Holy Sepulchre." The wounded look in Aethel's eyes made Isabel regret not binding her tongue a little longer.

"My Stephan's buried in a dark hole in France. No one took *his* heart anywhere. And as for William Marshal, I—I hope it was not for his honour that my Stephan lost his life. For years the court has whispered his name. 'A warrior like no other,' they say. 'Ne'er once lost a joust,' they say. Now he's taken arms with the Templars and sheds the blood of infidels. Even the clerks speak his name in reverence and I'm told King Henry trusts him like no other. Imagine, him, the very man who supported young Henry."

Isabel looked away. She knew that Lord Marshal never slew a man in hatred, that duty was his code, and that honour was his life's blood. She had heard that he had long been sworn to the Young King—even with King Henry's blessing—and that he had had little choice but to honour his vow when the younger man rebelled. But she would not speak of it now. Her thoughts were of Aethel only, for the last year had been difficult for the English-woman. She longed for Aethel to be cheery again, to put back the pounds that had fallen off her bones, and to find the happy glint that had so often danced in her eyes. But Isabel also knew the pain of grief. Her brother, Gilbert, had died a few years ago, after suffering an agonising bout of pleurisy complicated with whitlow—a miserable eruption of boils.

"So, no matter," said Aethel bravely. "I swore to Stephan 'afore he left for war that I'd not quick marry again. He did not demand the oath, though he said the thought of me with another drove him near to madness. I gave it as a free pledge, for I did love him so. And I miss him." Her chin quivered, but she quickly regained her composure. "But enough of this. I made another pledge to him; that I'd strive to enjoy m'life, that his memories would be my faithful companions." She nodded her head and set her jaw. "I have failed in this, m'lady. Methinks this Christmas to be a good time to start afresh."

Isabel smiled, approvingly. She wondered if she would ever love a man so. "God bless you, Aethel of Salisbury."

"Now, m'lady, you needs dress. You, Ida, hand me the hose." The other servant, recently sent from nearby Windsor Castle, handed her superior two purple woollen socks from a wardrobe chest set against the plastered wall of the bed-chamber. Aethel proceeded to replace Isabel's day hose with these, pulling them up to her knees and fastening them with garters. She then called for a pair of freshly oiled leather shoes. She had Isabel step lightly into each one and then secured them by wrapping the leather cords round her ankles.

"Now, Ida, fetch me the chianse from the perch—Nay, y'dunce, not that one—the one on the long peg—the red one, aye." With a scowl Ida handed Aethel the under-gown. Two days ago, the long, linen shirt—cut like the chemise—had been twisted while wet, or "broom-sticked," and set to dry before the fireplace, to achieve a crinkled look. Aethel and Ida lifted the ankle-length under-gown over Isabel's head and upraised arms, and then pulled it down over her body. It was tight-sleeved but loose at the neck, where it was tied by a criss-cross of leather cord.

Content that the first two layers were in order, Aethel pro-

ceeded to the next. "You there, Carly, hand me the *cote*." A timid
Saxon girl reached for a finely spun, grey-dyed woollen over-gown.
Again, the handmaidens helped pull it over Isabel's head and arms
before smoothing it. Its wide sleeves, short enough above to reveal
the sleeves of her red under-gown, lengthened to a point below
her wrist, almost touching the ground when her arms were at her
side.

Aethel circled her mistress with folded arms and a furrowed
brow. It was important that the damsel be the jewel of the Christmas feast. With a few nods and satisfied taps of her finger on her
chin, the matron-servant ordered the barbette and wimple. The
barbette—a comfortable, white chin-band, was wrapped length-
wise from beneath Isabel's chin to the top of her narrow head. The
affect was to frame the beauty of the wearer's face. Aethel then covered the girl's head with the red silk wimple that fell from her head
like a soft veil, open at the face. It was secured by a circlet of woven
ivy pressed lightly atop the lady's head.

"You, Carly—the bear mantle."

Isabel smiled. She loved bears the best, and had spent many
hours in the King's menagerie feeding them fish from the castle
pond. The King of Norway had given Henry a polar bear many
years before and when it had suddenly died, the disappointed
English King had had his furrier fashion both Isabel's mantle and a
boastful winter cloak for himself. The girl smiled as she remembered herself and the King going to Mass as a matched pair.

Aethel wrapped the stole around her lady and fastened it at
her throat with a lovely golden clasp purchased from a returning
crusader. Heavy and finely crafted, it was tooled in the shape of a
Norman ship and bore the sign of the cross at both bow and stern.
Isabel loved it, for it reminded her of a wonderful journey across the
Irish Sea so very long ago. She closed her eyes and imagined the
smell of salt air and the sounds of sea birds.

The three attendants stood back and studied their mistress
one last time. Aethel eyed the maid's waist-length braids to be sure
they fell properly along her youthful bosom, and then gasped.
"We've forgotten her belts."

Carly scampered to another chest and withdrew a handful of sashes and buckled belts. "Which, *Madame?*"

Aethel thought for a moment. "That—and that." She pointed first to a black, colourfully embroidered sash that she quickly wrapped tightly round Isabel's waist. Then she added a thin, sable belt with a silver clasp. "Ah, wonderful."

Isabel was asked to turn from front to back and to front 'midst the approving mutterings of Aethel.

"I should have thought green ribbons in the plaits to be better," blurted Ida.

Aethel disagreed, with a frown.

Ida reached forward and adjusted the sash, complaining that the cote was a bit too short, that too much of the under-gown was exposed at the ankles. "Too much red at the feet," she offered.

Aethel disagreed.

Ida offered one last suggestion. "Methinks a pellice, rather than the mantle, would have been a good choice. At Windsor they are quite the fashion. With a long waist-coat she'd have no need of a cloak and—"

This time, Aethel disagreed loudly. With a red face and clenched fists, she reached for the long green woollen cloak she had selected and laid it over Lady Isabel's shoulders. "There, my lady, you are as I wish you to be."

❋

Young Isabel followed an escort through the busy, torch-lit chambers that separated her apartment from the Great Hall of the Tower. The corridors were lit by pine torches, and the flames from these cast shadows that danced in the wake of hurried passers-by. Isabel's heart was pounding as she joined the stream of courtiers. She was so very eager to take her place at King Henry's Christmas feast. *Oh, if only he were here!* she thought. She had learned to love the King, despite his shortcomings. She also feared for his present safety. The court was filled with rumours that the adventurous Prince Richard was conspiring to seize the throne. She hadn't met

Richard save for one time, a brief and enjoyable episode at the castle's fishpond, where the young man had slipped a perch inside a squire's shirt!

Her mind turned to Richard's brother, Prince John, that 'cunning, grasping, treacherous man' for whom she had abandoned all hope. She shuddered, and thought, *I feel evil all about him*. King Henry had recently made John the Lord of Ireland—an investiture many thought the Irish deserved.

"My lady," bowed a well-dressed usher. "Please, to the hall."

Isabel took the man's arm and was escorted with ceremony into the Great Hall of the Tower Castle, and as she entered beneath its pointed archway, her breath was taken away. The green-bedecked hall was aglow in the soft light of unnumbered candles and countless rushlights, each a tiny beacon of joy bending and wending in the castle draughts. Huge iron candelabras hung from the ceiling on long chains and slanted torches hung from their brackets along the tapestry- covered walls. At the far end, near the platform reserved for the royal family, roared an open hearth. It was the height of a tall man, perhaps even higher, and lined with tiles that reflected its heat far into the chilly room. Two hearth-attendants hurried to and from the wood-bay with armloads of heavy logs. Meanwhile, the chandler and his servants kept a sharp eye on bending candles and smoky torches.

The room was long and wide, buttressed by stone arches. High above hung royal banners suspended along ropes strung the width of the hall. The centre of the huge chamber was filled with a long series of table tops laid end to end, resting on oak trestles and covered by heavy white cloths. The floor was heaped with fresh rushes and sprinkled generously with dried flowers from the summer past. Isabel closed her eyes and smelled the fragrance of lavender and camomile, marjoram, mint, and pennyroyal.

"Please, young mistress, follow me."

The enchanted damsel took the usher by the arm and was led past the envious glares and jealous whispers of women well past their prime. She smiled politely, but not seductively, at the lords and prelates who paused to enjoy the alluring youth, and was delivered, at last, to a young, brown-eyed lad, near to Isabel's age. He was standing nervously by their places, midway down the table's length.

"My most fair and gentle lady," said the youth as he bowed deeply. "I have been waiting without breath for thy coming."

Isabel smiled and dipped a shallow curtsy.

"You bring the sunshine and the warmth of a summer's day to my table. Thy smile, ah, thy smile is like the happy parting of a flower's petals at a dewy dawn."

Isabel blushed.

"And the pink of thy cheeks. Oh, the blush of rose, the–the–the red of–of a September apple—"

Isabel lowered her chin and restrained a laugh.

It was now the young lord's turn to blush. He fumbled for another word, and then began to wring his hands. Mercifully, Isabel spoke. "I, gallant sir, am Isabel de Clare, daughter of the late Richard Strongbow de Clare."

Relieved, the lad bowed again. "Your pardon, m'lady. I am John d'Erley, son of William of Erley, late chamberlain of the King, and I am pledged as a page to England's greatest knight, Sir William Marshal."

Isabel thought for a moment, not terribly impressed, but interested. "I remember your father, but not you, master John."

The lad winced a little. "I live in Windsor Castle as the King's ward. Before that, I was at the keep of Erley, but had spent some time here, with my father." John looked down. "I–I do remember you."

Isabel raised her brows. "Me, you remember me?"

"Aye, m'lady. I was with Prince John one day when you mocked him. He spat in your face and pushed you down."

Isabel smiled. "Indeed, I remember. You were gallant."

John d'Erley brightened. "Lady Isabel, hear this pledge:" He lifted his jaw and set his fists on his hips. "I swear on the relics of this great hall that I shall defend you always, no matter the foe, no matter the cause."

Isabel blushed.

✳

It was nearly three years later when John d'Erley and Isabel met again. Unfortunately, circumstances were not nearly as pleasing as they had been at the Christmas feast, for all Christendom was reeling from shocking news.

"It can not be so," gasped Isabel.

John nodded, sadly. "It is true. It stings my ears to hear it. I am told that the whole of Windsor Castle is draped in black and that Westminster is filled with mourners." The young man sat on a barrel in the bailey by the castle wall and hung his head. "Just past Lammas my master returned to Normandy from Palestine. I met him in Rouen where he told of his years in those lands. He said he had prayed earnestly at the Holy Sepulchre with unnumbered Christian knights. He had taken Mass each day with the Templars, bathed in the Jordan, and given alms without reserve. He raised his sword against the hordes of the infidel but would say nothing more about it. It is rumoured that he drew blood enough to fill the River Thames. I thought him to be weary, and troubled that the worst might happen, and it has."

Isabel was still reeling from the news. She leaned against the cold stone of the castle walls and stared aimlessly at the bare branches of the trees. All was grey; all was heavy. The air felt damp and the sky was foreboding. It was truly November, the blood month. Throughout the Christian world, the seasonal slaughter of sheep, hogs, and oxen was well underway. "I–I thought the rumours to be an evil gossip, an impossible scandal. How is it, Squire John, that Jerusalem could have fallen?" A tear rolled down her cheek.

John looked away. "Oh, Jerusalem!" he cried. "The Holy Cross lost to the infidels, the streets of our Lord defiled by unworthy feet." He stood and railed against the wind. "I shall rally with Prince Richard. He and King Philip are gathering an army even as we speak." The young man's eyes were fired and he began to pace. "It is for me to take up the sword—I shall be knighted on the battlefield of our Lord."

Isabel was thoughtful. "Perhaps the armies of Christ should be prudent; perhaps they ought pause to gather their wits."

D'Erley was not listening. "He looked weary, like one who had seen more than a man ought."

"Who?"

"Sir William—William Marshal. Did you know he is near to fifty years old? Ha, yet I'd not like to joust with him."

Isabel was still thinking about Jerusalem. "But tell me, how could it be that the city fell?"

The fourteen-year-old squire sighed and sat on his stool once more. "It seems that some months ago our Christian knights fell out from one another. They became rivals for the kingship of Jerusalem and began to war amongst themselves. The vice-regent, a Templar named Raymond of Tripolis, actually allied with Saladin and led a band of Turkish horsemen against his Templar brethren! It was a breach of honour that Sir William wept over. Then, early in the July just past, Saladin and his Muslim hordes fell upon our Christian armies in the very place where Christ preached his Sermon on the Mount. Our comrades were driven to the desert, where they nearly went mad for thirst. The day next a savage battle destroyed our armies. Were that not enough, every captured Templar was butchered. It was the beginning of the end."

Truly, it was. Saladin's Islamic army had overspread Palestine, seizing city after city from their Christian defenders. At last, with only Tyre, Tripolis, and Antioch yet resisting, Saladin's vast army had destroyed the Templars at Hittin before camping at the ancient walls of Jerusalem. Of the city's one hundred thousand Christian citizens, most were women, feeble old men, or children. Its Christian knights had been lost to other battles and only a relative handful remained to defend the Cross. Not willing to desecrate Allah's sacred city with Christian blood, Saladin offered a reasonable, though suspicious peace: safe passage to land in Syria in exchange for the opening of the city's gates.

Jerusalem's devout flatly denied the infidel's offer and mounted a brave, but hopeless defence under the leadership of Balean of Ibelin. After fourteen days of courageous resistance, the defenders realised that the walls by St. Stephen's gate had been undermined. The cause was lost.

The army of Saladin charged through the city crying, "*Allah akbar*" along the same streets where "Christ victorious!" had been heard almost one hundred years before. Crowding in terror deep within their churches, the Christians waited and prayed. Determined to not have his city defiled by Christian blood, Saladin again offered a conditional mercy. This time, the beleaguered Christians had little choice and they stepped from their hiding places with hands folded in prayer. In the end Saladin remained true to his word and released the great majority of his captives, even sending some away with gifts.

The city theirs, the army of Allah dragged the Holy Cross through the mire and excrement of Jerusalem's streets. Gleeful soldiers melted church bells and purified the floors and walls of the mosque of Omar with rose water. It was a story that shook the foundations of Christendom.

Isabel folded her hands and closed her eyes. Her lips moved quickly but silently, praying for those yet suffering on the sands of Palestine. Having heard enough, she begged John's leave. "Now, Squire, I wish to find Father Adderig and pray further on these matters."

John bowed, respectfully, and watched her drift lightly across the bailey. His eyes followed her until she disappeared in the shadows of a dark archway. "Good-bye, Isabel—"

❋

King Henry Plantagenet was in failing health, and his two surviving sons, Richard and John, were adding to his miseries. He was often seen staring at the family emblem embroidered on his hat. The emblem was that of a yellow-flowered, wild plant known as a broom, or *Planta Genesta,* its Latin name, from which his surname—Plantagenet—was derived. He had never quite recovered from the death of his beloved, though ambitious, eldest son Henry—who had died of dysentery—and he had grieved the death of his third son, Geoffrey, who had been trampled to death in a recent tournament. His youngest son, Prince John, had been given responsibilities in Ireland, while the adventurous Crusader, Richard the Lionhearted, was busy defending the royal lands in France from rebellious barons and the designs of King Philip, son of the now deceased Louis VII.

But, despite his troubles and his poor health, when the King was in residence at the Great Tower, he still delighted in a number of things, including his menagerie of exotic animals. The collection now boasted a leopard, an old elephant, two lions, several bears, some odd birds, and a few snakes. No doubt he believed these friends to be more trustworthy than the pretenders within his court.

The man also wandered through the castle's many chambers to admire their decorations: wainscoting of Norwegian fir, wall hangings of painted fabric, murals of "men and women rare for their exquisite beauty." He spent dark nights staring at the night's sky from his tower-top observatory before rummaging through the castle's buttery for wine, its pantry for fresh wheat bread, or its kitchen cupboards for black manger and mustard.

It was on such a night that the King stumbled upon his favourite ward standing forlornly in the gap of the rampart atop of the castle's eastern wall. "Ah, greetings, my young mistress," bowed Henry.

The startled Isabel cried out, nearly falling over the wall.

"Ho!" cried the King as he grabbed her arm. "*S'il vous plaît, Mademoiselle*, my heart is far too weak for such a fright."

Shaken, Isabel climbed from the stone perch and dropped awkwardly to the wall-walk. Embarrassed and terribly surprised, she dipped politely and lowered her face.

"Now, my Isabel, what on earth are you doing hanging over my wall in the middle of the night?"

The young woman took a deep breath. *Let him not be in a foul humour.* "Lord King, I–I was praying for Jerusalem. It seems all hope for the world is fast fading."

King Henry stood quietly, impressed as always by the maiden's piety as well as by her unconventionality. He had only ever prayed by altars. He looked south-eastward, towards Palestine, then removed his wool hat to rub a hand all over his large, round head. "Jerusalem's fall is not to be laid at my feet. Nay, nay. Blame it on that idiot German Emperor, Barbarossa, or better yet, the French. I sent crates full of English silver to support the Templars— a king's treasure, to be sure. Add to that the alms, the investitures to abbots. Humph. I've established priories, nunneries, given grants to bishops and archbishops; I tell you, sweet Isabel, I have done all I know to prompt God's mercies. I've filled reliquaries with the bones and hair of saints, our Saviour's thorns, and the bloodstains of the martyrs. I've punished evil doers as the Holy Scriptures command, and I've repented of my many sins with tears."

Relieved to hear him call her 'sweet Isabel,' she listened, sympathetically. She knew Henry's reign had been one of greys. Like the November landscape, his rule had been neither white in its purity nor wickedly black. His tenure had proven offensive to some, glorious to others. "My lord, God works His ways as He wills. Jerusalem is His city; His Will be done." She spoke softly, respectfully.

The King shrugged and took the damsel by the elbow. He escorted her from the cold walls of the stone fortress to a pair of stools set before a warm fire in a small, candlelit apartment adjacent to his own quarters. A guard followed at a distance and a servant immediately brought the pair a flask of red wine and a pitcher of warm cider. "Please, Lady Isabel, sit with me. I need to clear my mind."

Clear his mind? With me, she thought. The very idea of it had both confused and delighted Isabel. Yet she could not imagine what would now be expected of her. Shall I simply listen, like some mute statue? Shall I offer something—dare I instruct a King? The young woman looked about the tiny anteroom timidly. Her heart began to beat. She took her seat and wrapped her cloak around her, tightly.

King Henry turned to the suddenly flushed fifteen-year-old and poured her a tankard of warm cider. "My dear, have no fear, you are the most precious flower in my garden. Your virtue is secure."

"*Oui*, my King."

Henry removed his boots and hose and held his bare feet towards the fire. In the shadows of the flames Isabel thought him to look weary. The man had reached his fifty-fourth year, yet his shoulders were still bulky and his arms were muscled like that of a younger man. It was his haggard face and bagged eyes that troubled Isabel. Though still bull-necked and upright, his visage had lost its fire. When he rose to add some logs to the fire, however, Isabel nearly laughed out loud, for his legs were more bandied than ever, bowed all the more from years on horseback.

The King spoke slowly. "In these past few years, my slumber has been given to dreams. I lay my head upon my pillow, and as my eyes close, it is if I am carried away to far places. I saw the Holy City a fortnight past. Its walls were shimmering gold and its towers mounted with huge sapphires. Atop its battlements stood the knights of Christendom in blazing glory, staring down at a siege of devils, black as soot and spread as far as my eye could see." The man shuddered.

The King stared into the hearth. "On Candlemas Eve I saw a mighty lion prowling an orange sky. My chancellor said it portends the coming Judgment. I heard the lion roar like a thunder never heard before and lightning burst from his nostrils."

Isabel listened respectfully.

"Ah, but I had another dream not long ago. 'Twas of you."

"Me, sire?"

The King looked squarely at her. "*Oui, Mademoiselle.* I was strolling alone on the bailey of your father's castle in Pembroke on a summer's morn, and there I found you standing alone. You were smiling as if in perfect peace; your gown was white, your head crowned by a ringlet of wildflowers. You were standing on bare feet atop an open Bible with your arms stretched forward and your palms opened upward. As I watched, a shadow spread around you but did not darken you, for it was as if you were illumined by an unseen light. Then, floating from a dazzling blue sky came the *Book of Kells* which settled gently on your right hand. The earth opened and a score of scrolls flew from its bowels and swirled about you like leaves caught in a whirlwind. They circled you until, one by one, they settled atop each other on your left hand.

"You stood still, smiling, still illumined in the centre of the shadow. Then you began to whisper, your voice riding a quiet breeze to an unseen ear. With each word the shadow grew, and as it grew, you began to sing.

"As I watched, my heart beat lightly and my soul rejoiced, until a blinding flash burned your eyes. You dropped the books and covered your face with a loud cry. Then, with a soulful wail, you lowered your hands and the shadow slid away. As it faded from your view, the light left you and you were gone, vanished as if you never were.

"I sat up in my bed and staggered to my window where I threw open my shutters to stare at the heavens. And as I did, it was as if I saw your star fly away to be lost amongst all the others. I turned away, but as I climbed back into my bed I heard a chorus of voices sing from a time not yet come. It was a happy, grateful choir—perhaps of souls unborn? I do not know, but they soothed me and I fell into a deep sleep."

Isabel's spine tingled and she felt chills run through her limbs. She stared into the King's fire and wondered what the dream could mean.

CHAPTER IV

THE ROYAL SURPRISE

HENRY took a deep breath and sighed, heavily. "I beg your pardon, good lady, forgive an ageing man his visions. Perhaps it was a bit too much saffron in the fowl." He smiled and reached for a flask. He filled a goblet with red wine and changed the subject to other matters pressing hard on his heart. "Prince Richard has taken the Cross, impetuous lad. He's taken the Crusader's vows and is begging money from my barons in Normandy. Yet he wants more. He knows he shall be king but he already plots against me—why? I am certain his mother is behind his ambition. I've commissioned a painting at Westminster, you know. It is of four eaglets preying on their parent. These are my 'beloved' sons. Humph. Oddly, I fear it is the fourth eaglet, John, who will be the one to pry out my heart."

The weary King sighed again, then muttered, "I hear rumours of that scoundrel Philip winning the ear of Richard. I know they are in conspiracy to take the throne before I'm cold.

"But, to other matters. My heart is burdened to fund a third crusade. What say you to a heavy tax on my subjects. A new tithe—perhaps I should call it a 'Saladin Tithe?' A good name, do you think?"

Isabel was speechless. *He's asking my opinion on a tax?* She thought. "Would your barons accept such a thing?"

The King's face darkened. "Eh? What does that matter?"

Isabel paled. "I–I—forgive me, my lord."

"They need pay what I tell them to pay. It is the royal will that matters."

"Of course, my lord."

Henry stood and paced, only to stop and howl and hop on one foot to a wooden chair. "Cursed dogs." A broken chicken bone had been hiding deep within the straw. He picked a shard from his

51

bared foot. Cursing, he glared at a rivulet of blood dripping from his heel.

Isabel shivered. Her father had died from a simple infection of the foot.

The King's mood quieted and he became reflective. "Isabel, did you know my veins run with both Norman and Saxon blood?"

"*Oui*, my lord."

"Hmm. How so, then?"

Isabel blushed, shyly. "Your grandfather, sire, the first King Henry, chose to marry a woman named Matilda of the Saxon royal line."

"*Oui*, good."

"The tutors you have given me are excellent."

The King nodded. "And why, Isabel, does this matter?"

The young lady thought for a long moment. "The Normans are but a few compared to the English folk. I should think the common people to be more loyal to a King of mixed lineage."

"Aye. I have spent a lifetime honouring the folk—they are cousins to me, and I long for the day when we *all* share the name of 'English.'"

He sat quietly, dabbing at his bleeding foot with a scrap of cloth. He took a deep breath. "Young lady, do you think I have ruled well?"

Isabel nearly swooned. Her mind began to spin.

Henry nodded. "*Oui, oui*. Have no care, you have my leave to speak freely, but you must swear to be truthful."

The young girl swallowed a sip of cider. She straightened her shoulders and stiffened her back. Be careful. "My King, I am thy faithful ward, as is required of me. I have not been witness to much more than rumour and hearsay."

King Henry leaned forward.

Isabel thought for a long moment. "What I do know is that you have been a strong hand on men who need firm reins. You have been faithful to thy prayers and no more harsh with your servants than what is due. Perhaps you have erred from time to time, but in what cause I could not say. I am quite certain you have sinned, for so have we all." She hesitated.

"Go on, girl."

"There is one thing, my lord, that conscience requires me to add."

Henry leaned yet more forward.

"I–I believe you were wrong to let the monks whip your bare back. You are the king, anointed by God."

Henry's eyes squinted with interest.

Isabel hesitated, looking at her feet nervously. "I know little of–of–of the murder of Archbishop Becket—but whatever the truth, it is God who is supreme, not the pope nor any king."

"Yes, yes—go on."

Isabel knew she was considerably out of her depth. "My King, perhaps I speak of things I do not understand." She turned her eyes quickly to the floor, now wishing for all the world that she had not ventured to the castle wall this night.

Henry pressed. "Unlike my courtiers, your thoughts are unsullied. I can see you've a keen mind, one that has absorbed wisdom like sand soaks the rain."

"Yes, my lord, as you will." Isabel took a deep, confident breath; she had spoken truthfully and had survived. "My unlearned thoughts are these: that temporal things are holy things, for they are fashioned by the Hands of God. And spiritual things are holy things, for God is Spirit. Together they ought to serve one another, for at the final Resurrection both body and spirit shall be rejoined.

"Therefore, I confess doubts as to whether the pope was truly called to rule over the kings of the earth. Could it not be that good kings are ordained to rule their realms under God, like the pope rules the Church—under God? The kings carry the sword in defence of the Church so that the Church is free to serve as Christ served? Perhaps there are to be two Kingdoms under the sun until the Day of Judgment, both sacred, but separately serving each other."

King Henry considered her words carefully. The minutes passed until he finally spoke. "Lady Isabel, you are speaking the notions of the old Celtic Church. The Roman pope uses his power quite differently. He may place a king under anathema or lay a whole kingdom under interdict. All the knights of Christendom together cannot save a single soul from banishment to Hell. I fear the pope is, indeed, supreme."

"With respect, my lord, I am told that the pope's reach was once not as grasping as it is now. Perhaps in times to come, things will change again, for I cannot help but believe it better that the Law of God be supreme, not that of any one man, whether pope or king. Both ought to serve the Law of God together, as two oxen plough the field for their common master."

Henry stood, shaking his head and punching his fist into his palm. "No. Law cannot rule. 'Tis nothing more than a fanciful notion, a fool's vision. Law has neither knights nor archers—not even a name. Should one say, "King Law?" Preposterous. Rule must come from a ruler who can be seen, one with the power to gouge eyes, to crush bones, to shatter teeth-- or even to send a soul to Hell." Henry was now agitated and he gulped more wine. "So, I suppose you think me to be a poor king, then, eh?"

Isabel felt anxious again. She may have gone too far.

"Consider what I have done. I have built a royal administration that uses the councils of the folk in their counties and their shires to keep all of England under the King's Peace. But more, my courts now rule by English custom. I have taken the ancient ways and melded them, slowly, like a clever cook who softens vegetables in a stew. My England is now one; laws exist that are common throughout the whole realm. From Cumberland to Kent, from Norfolk to the Welsh Marches, one law serves under my sword. Now, what say you to that?"

Isabel had listened carefully. "My lord, might I ask a question?"

Henry nodded with folded arms.

"How did you persuade the barons to accept these things?"

The King laughed heartily. "Ah, indeed. My vision did come at a price; most do. I offered the barons something they had heard of from the English Danes: trial by jury. The barons liked the idea that any free man might stand before a judge who simply oversees the decision of the accused's peers."

"*Oui*, my lord." Isabel liked what she had heard and her keen mind quickly carried King Henry's ideas far beyond the man's self-serving purposes. *Rules of the King's Peace, rules of custom, rules of trial and evidence—all taking root as rules of law and not of rulers.*

Now feeling tired, King Henry rose and summoned his guard. With a bow, he kissed Isabel's hand lightly. "My dear, you have been enlightening. I have enjoyed this time very much. Sleep well and may your dreams be pleasant."

Isabel curtsied. She felt suddenly light and warm and as she took an escort's arm, she smiled. After all, she had just counselled a King.

※

A sudden rap on Isabel's door gave Aethel a start. She had barely recovered from her night with the King the week prior. She stumbled to the door and opened it warily. A solemn-faced page, dressed in a fine surcoat bowed. "Aethel? Aethel of Salisbury?"

The woman narrowed her gaze. "Aye? Who is asking?"

"I am Hubert of Bayeux, valet of the King, instructed by his *seneschal* to escort thy Lady Isabel to the carriage waiting. Her hand-servants are permitted as well."

Aethel was flustered. "I—she—we are barely awake. We've not tended to Mass, washed—"

"Shall I tell this to the steward, *Madame Domestique?*"

Aethel's eyes were baggy and her hair unkempt. She let the command settle into her brain, then abruptly slammed the door and dashed to Isabel's bed. "My lady!" she shrieked. "Hurry, hurry—be quick about it. Ida—Carly, come, come—bring me—bring me the heavy chemise and hose—quickly—and the green wool chainse—and—and—"

"And what on earth are you doing?" mumbled Isabel, as Aethel dragged her by one arm from her bed.

"A valet says a carriage is waiting."

"Now?"

"Aye, m'lady."

"But for what?"

"I—I am not sure, m'lady—now hold your breath—" Aethel flung cold water atop the naked girl's body.

"Aaaah. Aethel! What are you doing?"

The servant didn't answer, but bound the girl in a thick blanket and began raking through her hair with a coarse brush.

"Ouch! Aethel. Enough. I think not. Where is the valet?"

Aethel paused only long enough to point.

Isabel pulled away from her servant, donned her undergarment, wrapped herself in a heavy cloak and opened the door. "We beg your pardon, young master. Please tell us again why you are calling."

"*Oui*," the youth answered with a bite and a hard eye at Aethel. "The King requests Lady Isabel's presence at Windsor Castle. A carriage awaits."

Her eyes widened. "I see. And when is my audience to be?"

"On the morrow, *Mademoiselle*."

"Ah, *merci*." Relieved, she cast a sideways glance at Aethel. "Then we beg thy indulgence for us to attend Mass and enjoy a light breakfast. We shall be delivered to the carriage no later than the bells of terce."

"Yes, m'lady, as you wish. I shall tell thy escort to be at the ready. God's peace on the journey."

Isabel leaned forward, shyly. "Kind page, would you happen to know the purpose of this summons?"

The lad glanced about nervously. He hesitated, but the warm blue of Isabel's imploring eyes melted all reluctance. "Yes, m'lady, but tell no one, else I've a hard price to pay." He laid his lips by Isabel's ear and whispered, "The King plans to inform you of your betrothal."

The young woman stared at the boy blankly. Her heart began to race and she spun round the door frame to lean limply against the wall of her chamber. She clasped her hands to her chest and breathed quickly.

"What is it?" asked Aethel.

Isabel was flushed with excitement and she could not speak. With a nod and a nervous smile, she quickly bade her servants to prepare her for the day.

❈

Windsor Castle sat above the Thames on the edges of ancient Saxon hunting grounds one good day's march west of London. It was for this reason that the royal *seneschal*, or steward, had wanted the lady removed soon after dawn, especially given the early nightfall of early December.

To Isabel it was as if her journey to Windsor was atop the back of the wind. She had little recollection of her morning, but Aethel had taken curious note that the secretive damsel had not taken a single bite of breakfast bread or even a nibble of cheese. Isabel had seemed distant at Mass and now seemed dreamy and frightfully distracted midst the hurried pace of her anxious escort.

Arriving at the castle, the young woman lighted from her carriage with a flushed face and racing heart. For so many years she had wondered who would be the man that King Henry would marry her to. Would he be handsome—or not—wise, clever, of good humour, and devout? Would he be courageous and strong, literate and courteous—a man of chivalry? Would he hail from England or Normandy, Aquitaine—perhaps Norway, Spain, or the Holy Empire of the Germans? Would his skin be clear—or scabby? Would he have his teeth? Would he smell good? Would he learn to love her?

"My lady?"

"Eh?"

"With thy leave, Countess Isabel de Clare, I should escort you to thy chamber."

Lady Isabel looked surprised. She had not been addressed as

a Countess in the past. Since she had been the King's ward and all her properties held in his trust, she had not really considered herself a landed woman. She suddenly realised she was almost of age and would soon inherit her father's vast estates. She dipped, shyly.

"*Complaire*—my arm."

Isabel laid her hand lightly atop the man's forearm and followed him past the score of knights and sergeants that had shepherded her journey. The soldiers stood erect and proud, dressed in chain-mail coats covered by sleeveless, colourful robes. As the Countess passed, each nodded and offered his name—"Guy de Ros," "William fitz Robert," "William de Vere," "Roger FitzWilliam,"—one after the other, each typically Norman: strong-featured, rugged, fair, clean-shaven, and lean. At the end of the line was a dusty squire holding a lance. "My lady, John d'Erley." He bowed.

Isabel paused and smiled.

It was an hour or so past vespers, deeper in the night than any would have preferred, but the young Countess and her servants were directed to an anteroom set up as a makeshift dining hall. Tabletops had been removed from their storage against the walls and set atop trestles. An ample, though long overdue supper of stewed meats and squash was served, after which the King's guests were escorted to their sleeping quarters.

Isabel had spent little time outside the walls of the Tower Castle, save a few hunts she had joined with the chamberlain's greyhounds. From time to time she had picnicked by the Thames in summer—moments she cherished. But for most of her life she had faced either the stone of the Tower, its courtyards, or the sky its walls had framed. Yet the fifteen-year-old maiden gave little heed to her new surroundings. She now lay on a feather mattress, snuggled deeply beneath heavy woollen blankets. Her eyes were wide open, wondering who it would be that would soon join her in a bed like this in some castle yet unknown.

Morning came and Isabel informed Aethel of the day's purpose. Trembling and as anxious as her lady, Aethel saw that Isabel was quickly dressed, fed, prayed over, and delivered by royal ushers to the King's chamberlain and the chancellor. The chamberlain was a weary old fellow with an inviting smile but eyes as penetrating as his position required. He was the senior staff member of the royal household, answering only to the *seneschal* and the King. The chancellor, one Bishop de Fontineu, was a clerk of middling years who now served the King as his personal chaplain and who ruled all the clerics serving the King's household.

"Hmm." The chamberlain studied the trembling Countess as if she were a prize heifer. "A bit thin, I should think, Bishop. But a good, upright chin and clear skin. Hmm. Hips—good for birthing. I understand, *Mademoiselle*, that you are the daughter of Richard de Clare, the Strongbow."

Too nervous to speak, Isabel nodded. The man continued to circle her. "Tall, long armed, lanky. Hmm. Hair like berry-stained wheat! I like that. Eyes like the sky—and bright. You've a bit of spirit! Good. You shall need it."

Isabel trembled. *What did he mean by that?* she thought.

Sensing her discomfort, the chancellor interrupted. "My child, it is fitting that thou should'st be prepared to accept God's Holy Will. His lot for thee is intended to serve the interests of thy King and countrymen." The bishop's tone was strained, his words urged on by a quality of unease that did not go unnoticed.

Isabel covered her face with a thin veil and bowed her head as the churchman prayed over her. She could hardly keep her mind on the man's earnest entreaties, for she felt something was not right; a dread had begun to creep along her skin. At that moment, a draught tilted the torches of the chamberlain's room and the young lady gasped. She closed her eyes and began to pray as she heard the door open.

"Now, Countess, please, follow us." The chamberlain and the chancellor, as well as a company of well-armed footmen led Isabel through numerous dank rooms, a narrow corridor, and a smoke-choked stairwell. The castle was damp, very cold, and draughty. The lady gathered her cloak tight to her throat and glided within the ring of her escort, flush-faced and near to tears. The column soon exited the keep and hurried along the bailey until, to Isabel's utter confusion, they arrived at the mews, the building housing the royal falcons.

King Henry, an insatiable hunter and engaging sportsman, welcomed Isabel into the stone shed. "We meet again, Countess."

Isabel curtsied and kept her eyes to the ground.

The King sighed. He was sick and near to exhaustion. The differences between him and his sons had continued to gnaw at him. Prince Richard was insistent that Henry's intentions regarding succession be formally announced and blessed by the pope. The ambitious firebrand had delayed his crusade while he waited, but now many feared he might just take the crusading money his father had given him and raise an army to seize the throne. King Henry was clearly distracted; he loved his son and the thought of Richard's likely betrayal had deeply wounded him. He turned to Isabel. "I loved to hunt with these hawks at your father's Pembroke Castle. Ah, the south of cursed Wales, 'tis where the very best birds nest! A wild one once dropped my own best Norwegian hawk at my feet.

"See, here, I've nestlings. These are long-winged ones, peregrines. Those over there are sakers, and those are lanners. See there, the short-winged ones? Aye, they are goshawks. Look about you, young mistress. 'Tis a kingdom of feathers."

Isabel was pleased. She loved the sounds of the birds and the flutter of their wings. She walked slowly atop the gravel floor and marvelled.

"Do you know that the females are larger and more powerful than the males?"

Isabel smiled.

"You like that notion. Indeed. We call the females 'falcons.' The males we call 'tiercels.' Each is quite an investment of my time and, of course, that of my huntsmen. We train them with lures and bait, teach them to ride on our forearms, wear the hood, and strike fast and hard. Ha! Sounds like the work of a young wife."

Isabel's heart began to pound.

"So, enough of this." Henry set a gerfalcon from his arm to its roost. He patted it lightly on its back and turned to Isabel.

"Since you were a small child I've had suitors at my door. I've pushed them all away until now. My decision is made; I have betrothed you."

Isabel looked at her feet. Her slender frame trembled faintly. *"Oui, mon Roi."*

King Henry looked sad. He took the damsel by both her hands and looked into her face. "You have been my ward for these many years—I think more than ten. I remember you as a spindly little thing, laughing and racing about the bailey. I've spent many years in France and other times throughout my England, but I dare to say, I've not seen a more lovely, more precious jewel in all my Empire." He lowered his hands and set them on the lapels of his thick coat. "But you are a child no longer. It is time for you to serve."

Isabel hands were clammy and she felt hot all over. She held her breath.

Henry's demeanour changed, though Isabel thought it did so against the man's inward will. No longer the doting visage of a grandfather, he became suddenly the King Henry the world had known. "Your father left you many lands, the estates at Pembroke by the inlet, those of Chepstow, those along the Wye, as well as something of a kingdom in Ireland. You are a Countess of great wealth. You are valuable to me and so is the alliance thy marriage shall secure." He hesitated, then looked away. "You are to be wed to Lord Raimond fitz Mallet."

Isabel shifted on her feet. She had never heard the name. Her mouth went dry, but she dared not speak. *Oh, dear God above, have him tell me more.*

King Henry turned his back on his beloved ward and called for his guard. The dumfounded maiden sadly yielded to a soldier's touch and followed the King's officers onto the windy bailey towards the arched door of the keep. She walked away erect and proud, but weeping softly. She turned her head back to the mews, back to the King she loved, hoping to see his face one last time. It was not to be.

The bishop came up and stood by her side and sympathetically took her hand. "Raimond is young," he offered. "Not handsome, but strong. He is a knight who has slain the infidel on Holy Crusade. His father has large holdings in Northumberland, Cumberland, and Durham—lands the Scots covet endlessly. I pray God's mercy on thee."

Isabel could not speak. It was as if she were caught in a whirlwind. Her legs were wobbly and her hands shook. Her belly felt nauseous and cramped. Her heart cried to Heaven, *Oh, dear God, Mother Mary, spare me this thing! Something is amiss; I feel it.*

Once in sight, Aethel raced towards her, arms spread wide. And when Isabel saw the familiar face of her dear friend, she collapsed into her embrace.

✺

Isabel cried all that afternoon. She lay atop the bed in which she had dreamt of love the night before. Now terrified and feeling abandoned to the arms of a stranger about whom she knew nothing, she could not be soothed. "Oh, Aethel. I can feel it; I can feel something wrong in this thing." she sobbed. "Why could not he have picked someone the court knows, someone I might know something about? I feel that I am in peril."

Angry, Aethel held her lady tightly, stroking her hair and wanting so very badly to offer words of hope. But she had once been through Northumberland on a brief journey to Scotland as a youth. "The Gate of Waste," she had called it. Little more than a landscape of barren, stony hillsides, sharp winds, dull villages, and meagre towns, it was not the green garden that Isabel cherished.

Soon after nones—midway between noon and dusk—a light rap sounded on the oak door of the Countess' bedchamber. Aethel hid her mistress by closing the heavy curtains that surrounded the four-poster bed. The lady's modesty protected, the servant opened the door. She dipped, politely, but warily. "Good evening, master John."

John d'Erley bowed, looking past the servant into the cold room. "Is your lady about?"

"She is unable to receive you."

John was in an agitated, anxious mood. "Might I please come in—I've—I've news."

Aethel balked, but the urgency in the young man's face begged that she yield. She opened the door wide and hurried to Isabel whom she wrapped in a cloak and removed from her bed. Isabel was pale and drained and the meagre light of late dusk made her look all the worse. Respectfully, the squire looked down.

"Squire John, lift thy head. How might I serve thee?"

John faced the Countess squarely. "My lady, please, I beg thee, hear me out." He lowered his voice. "Countess de Clare, my master sent three of us here from Colchester to spy on the court. My lord believes the King to be in grave danger, no doubt from untrustworthy counsellors. Our spies report that King Malcolm of Scotland has new designs on the northern counties and is in league with disloyal English barons to seize them."

Isabel felt a flutter in her belly, for she knew that her husband-to-be was a large landholder in those counties. Her interest was piqued. "*Oui*, Master John, go on."

"My lord believes that King Henry is being deceived about Raimond fitz Mallet, to whom you are now betrothed. Sir William is confident that the man is in plot with Malcolm and also with King Philip of France. A monk told us that Raimond had secretly pledged fealty to King Malcolm and is promised rewards with fiefs in the lowlands. Any fealty to King Henry is a ruse. Sir William says the man is a knave; he is neither chivalrous nor true. It is said that Raimond killed two knights near Toulouse by striking each from behind.

"My duty, *Mademoiselle*, is to confirm my master's fears and expose the villains quickly."

Isabel stood erect, chin out. "*Oui*! I felt it all along; I knew this was amiss!"

"*Oui*, Countess. We've loyal knights here at Windsor. For now, take hope, m'lady, and take heart."

As the squire disappeared into the darkness of an outer chamber, the two women stared at each other. Isabel walked to the shuttered window of her room and stared through its cracked louvers into the failing light of that cold, December evening. Her mind raced and she closed her eyes. Suddenly, she whirled about. "Would it not be reasonable that Raimond would have emissaries here, now, to keep watch over Henry's pledge to me, to see that it is honoured?"

"Of course, m'lady."

Isabel began to pace. "Of course, indeed. If I am a pawn in his game, he'd need to be certain of the King's move. Aethel, take the others and go; learn from the King's house who and where Raimond's ambassadors are—and go quickly."

CHAPTER V

SQUINTS, CURSES AND THE GIFT

OBEDIENTLY, Aethel rumbled through the door with her staff in tow and disappeared into the bowels of Windsor Castle.

The next hours were difficult for Isabel. She stepped about the herb-laced rushes of her apartment, wringing her hands. She fell to her knees and begged God's mercy, imploring help from the Virgin Mother and the departed saints of Ireland, especially St. Brigid, whom she felt might help her best of all. About two hours past vespers, Aethel stormed into the chamber.

"Oh, m'lady, we've done well."

Isabel held her breath.

"We've learned that one party of Lord Raimond's men left soon after the King pronounced your betrothal. But others stayed to keep watch: three knights, a Scottish clerk, and a big squire. They share an apartment near the kitchen of the Great Hall." Aethel's eyes were wide with delight, like a child at a May Day feast.

"Yes, yes, go on."

"Ah, m'lady, the cook tells us of 'squints' in the kitchen wall where the staff can peek into the guest chamber. What devils they are. He says Raimond's men drink late into the night and speak loudly. For four pence I've rented the squints from him."

Isabel clapped. "God be praised. Now, let's have a look."

Aethel hesitated. "But, m'lady. I thought we ought send for Squire John."

Isabel was a wise young woman, but on this night, more young than wise. The temptation of adventure was too much to resist. She hurriedly dressed herself. "Yes, yes, of course. Send Carly and Ida to find John. While they are searching, let's have a look ourselves."

The Countess and her servant stole through the darkness of

Windsor Castle. The fortress was filled with a muffled silence, broken only by an occasional laugh from drunken men cavorting deep within its walls. The corridors smelled dank and the air was heavy with torch smoke. The pair arrived at the kitchen, careful to enter the doorway quietly so as to not disturb those in the adjacent chamber.

Aethel pushed open the kitchen's squeaking timber door and touched her candle to others about the room. The kitchen staff had slipped away, leaving the room an eerie chamber of suspended knives and cleavers, hammers and saws. Shelves and hanging hooks were cluttered with an assortment of tinker's wares, paddles, dough-breaks, and spice bins. Fat shadows from large iron pots climbed the stone walls by a small charcoal fire glowing sleepily in a baker's hearth. At the opposite end of the room were a dim-lit cupboard and a panelled wall.

Aethel led her lady forward to the panelling and tittered. "Here. Here is the common wall to the apartment and see, this opens." She pulled on a small knob and opened a narrow section of panelling that was deftly hinged by hidden leather straps. Behind was the stone of the castle. Aethel's fingers ran along the mortar until they touched upon several cork plugs which she removed. "There," she whispered. "Look."

Isabel laid a wide eye against one of the squints and peered into the amply lit chamber next door. She could see the black shoulder of a robed priest and the legs of two men partially covered by their *braies*—their under-leggings. Another man walked by laughing. He was young but huge, and playing with a menacing dagger. The men were loud and clearly celebrating some good news in grand fashion. As Isabel watched, she shuddered in a cold draught; it was as if evil had found its way through the squints. She withdrew her eye and laid her back against the wall, holding her nauseous belly.

John d'Erley rushed into the kitchen, accompanied by Ida and, to everyone's surprise, the royal chancellor. "My lady," rasped John. "I think it unwise for you to be here."

Isabel nodded, shyly. "Yes, master squire. But I think you need to see, and to listen. Where are your knights?"

"Two are rummaging about, looking for what you've already found. The rest are following Raimond's other men, somewhere on the road north. The chancellor is witness enough should we learn something." John and the bishop strode to the squints. They looked through the peep-holes, shifting from eye to ear and muttering to each other. Unfortunately, they witnessed little more than fitz Mallet's men belching and singing debauched ballads.

John and the chancellor listened for one hour, than two, before becoming concerned about the yawns and heavy lids now quieting the room. "John," grumbled the weary bishop, "I see gluttony and hear blasphemy, but I find no treachery. If thy thoughts are to accuse Lord fitz Mallet thou hast better bring me evidence—and quickly." The chancellor had not believed William Marshal's suspicions from the outset and had counselled the King to proceed with the betrothal in all haste. If Raimond fitz Mallet's loyalty was tentative—and he doubted that—he thought of no better way of securing it than the gift of Isabel de Clare.

"Please, lord Bishop. These men hold the key."

Isabel was listening carefully. "John," she offered. "I have a plan."

The squire drew close.

"It seems most men brag amongst themselves with little reserve, but when they brag to a woman, they have none. I shall feign I am lost in the castle, that I am a ward of the King and my name is, is, um—Edith, and I am from Durham—in the north. I shall ask them who they are and why they are here and so on. With so much ale I think they might just babble the truth."

Aethel shook her finger at her lady. "Indeed not. 'Tis a foolhardy scheme. They've surely heard of your beauty and would know you straight away. No, m'lady, I would block the door myself."

John turned his eyes on the broad-shouldered matron. *Hmm* he thought. *If anyone could handle herself in there, Aethel surely can.* He nodded and turned to Isabel. "*Oui*, m'lady. Your handmatron speaks well. 'Tis not safe in the least." He turned back to Aethel. "*Madame*, I'm told you love thy lady?"

"With all my life," boasted the woman.

"Would you take risk for her?"

"Aye! I'd stick my head in the mouth of a lion, I'd lay under an elephant, I'd stand in the ramparts, I'd—"

"*Oui, Madame.* I understand. Then listen well." Young John's voice hardened. "Enter the room with a jug of fresh ale. Sit with them as an ale-wench might, and get them to talking once again. You know what needs to be said."

Aethel turned white. "But–but—"

"Go!" ordered the bishop. "This business must end, and soon."

Isabel reluctantly handed her friend a stout jug of ale and squeezed her arm. "God be with you."

In moments the squints were filled with nervous eyes watching Aethel enter the villains' chamber. She seemed stiff at first, but after closing the door behind her, she claimed her role well.

"Ach, what do you want?" barked a young Scottish squire.

Aethel dipped. It was a typical Aethel curtsy, squat and a bit awkward. The room burst into laughter. The woman did a second, exaggerating her lack of grace while grinning from ear to ear. "Ale, good sirs?"

"Come 'ere, ya buxom wench!" slurred one of the knights.

Aethel feigned shyness and looked to the floor. Her cheeks were red as roses. She put both hands on the braids rolled at her ears and adjusted them, flirtatiously. "But, my lord—you're wearing only your unders." She forced a giggle.

The room roared as Aethel climbed into a pawing man's lap. The knight had carried many a heavy thing, but he quickly realised he had misjudged this woman badly. "Saints above, wench, m'legs are cracking."

Aethel cast a fetching smile to the others and laid her large arm around the man's neck. "Are y'not man enough for as much a woman as me?"

The men howled. An old priest poked a long, bony finger into Aethel's ample side. "Lots there to love, my son."

The knight offered a muffled answer. His face was pressed sideways and he was pinned hard to his chair.

Aethel leaned into him all the harder and asked his comrades, "If love is not his game, what of sport?"

"Nay," roared one. "He's ne'er won a joust—ne'er won at chess—he's ne'er won at anything."

To the guffaws and bellows of his fellows, the man reddened with anger. More jeering jabs were thrown until the nearly suffocated knight rallied. "Get off me you, you—you great sow." He dumped Aethel on to the floor and climbed to his feet. Standing straddle-legged over her, he thumped his chest and proclaimed, "I have bested the King of England. 'Tis me who has stolen my lord a bride and—"

Another knight climbed to his feet. "Ya fool. You've done nothin' more 'an ride yer horse. 'Tis me what's tricked old Henry."

"Nay!" roared another.

"Aye, 'tis so." The room quickly filled with curses and flying fists. Now drained of all courage and desperate to get out, Aethel crawled slowly across the floor, through the legs of brawling men, past a hard-punching squire, and out the door.

In the kitchen, the bishop and Squire John watched and listened with opened mouths as they witnessed brags and counter-brags of the grand deception of King Henry by Raimond fitz Mallet. Lady Isabel kept her eye fixed on good Aethel and did not look away until the woman's feet were out the door.

Within the room the brawl continued until at last the priest brought quiet with a shout. He held a rolled parchment high in his hand. "Enough. No more. This, good sirs, is what we've *all* won today. I hold the document sealed by Henry and witnessed by his fool chancellor. This is what grants all the lands of the damsel to our Lord Raimond.

"With this we win much. With this our lord is to be the Earl of Pembroke, Lord of Chepstow, and more. With this power he will easily tip the scales against Henry so that Malcolm can seize the north with ease and Philip can have his way in France. We've cause to sleep proudly, men, for black-hearted Henry is about to pay for his sins."

The shocked chancellor had had enough. The "Auld Alliance," that bedevilling alliance between Scotland and France, had been invoked with cleverness and craft. The bishop loved his King and was furious at his own blindness. He cursed, then made an angry, loud exit from the kitchen as he stormed away to call the royal guard.

Unfortunately, the slamming door piqued the suspicion of Raimond's squire, a young Scot who had been ordered to remain sober and attentive. The sixteen-year-old cocked his ears, then slipped away from his chattering fellows to take ten long strides to the kitchen. He kicked the door open and burst in with a growl. "What is this?" he barked, as he spotted Aethel.

"Uh, uh," stammered the exhausted woman. "I've come for more ale."

John stepped towards the Scot, one hand on the hilt of the dagger tucked under his belt. "You've no business here; begone."

The Scot sneered. He was a big youth, overdue his knighthood. Shaggy-haired and unkempt, he swore a string of oaths at John. "*A' cur fo smachd mo mhiannan as làidire.* I'll not begone—what's yer business in here? Are ye serving ale as well?"

John thought quickly as Isabel closed the panel. The Scot, however, heard the creak of wood and his eyes flew to the lady's hand. "Eh?" He took a determined step towards the squints as John blocked his path.

"You've no business in the King's kitchen. Now I say again, begone from this place."

Aethel drew Isabel away and the two faded into the shadows. The Scot peered down into John's defiant face and snarled. "Ye'll be giving me leave to pass, else I'll be taking yer heart to Edinburg."

John lifted his jaw. "Shut your mouth, *y'imbécile.*"

"Frenchman, eh?"

"Nay, English."

With that, the intruder grabbed a cleaver hanging from a hook and swung a ferocious swipe at d'Erley's head. As John ducked, the Scot yanked a dagger from his belt with his right hand and thrust it at the dodging Englishman.

John plucked his own dagger and crouched like a lion ready

to pounce. The two young men eyed each other warily, until the impetuous Scot charged with a yell. John planted his feet and sprang forward, low to the ground, blocking the Scot's dagger thrust with his left arm and driving forward with his blade. He caught the man just beneath the ribs and plunged the dagger deep.

The Scot bellowed like a wounded bear, but had enough fight left to swing the cleaver one more time, nearly taking off the top of John's head. D'Erley countered with a kick that knocked the man to his back and then fell upon him to finish the bloody thing.

Isabel and Aethel stood holding one another and trembling. As John rose to his feet, the two ran towards him and embraced him. Another voice at the door turned all heads.

"What is this? What hast thou done?" The Scottish priest from Raimond's entourage came running into the kitchen, torch in hand and comrades in tow. He was an old, hawk-faced clerk, thin-lipped and evil-eyed. He stared at his dead countryman, then turned a hard face at the three. "Murderers. What is this wicked deed?"

The others, unarmed and tottering, stared blankly.

John planted his fists on his hips. "He attacked me, *Père*, and paid the price. And you, Father, had best be on your knees."

"Eh?"

"Aye, there." John stormed to the panelled wall and flung open the secret door. "We are witness to your conspiracy—yours and your lord's."

The priest darkened and hissed, sinking deep within his black hood. He whirled about when the corridor suddenly filled with torches and soldiers well armed and angry. They burst into the kitchen and fell upon the knaves. For a few moments the room was filled with shouts and cries, until the conspirators were bound and gagged and dragged into the corridor.

The officer of the King's guard turned to John d'Erley and the corpse at his feet. "All is well?"

"Aye, sire."

The man nodded. "Lady Isabel?"

"*Oui*, m'lord," she answered.

"Please, my guards shall escort you to thy bedchamber. The King sends his regrets and begs thy pardon."

Isabel bristled. *Begs my pardon?* she thought. *'Tis all he says? He begs my pardon?* She took Aethel by the hand and took two steps towards the guard, when the wrist-bound priest suddenly shrieked from the company of his fellows.

"I curse thee, Countess Isabel de Clare. A curse I put upon thy life. Listen well."

"Take him," boomed the officer of the guard. But as the soldiers began to drag him away, the priest shouted his horrid curse:

> A sword from heaven's gates shall fly
> with wings that none can stay. Its
> edge shall split thee from thy love and
> tear thy heart away. Thy tears shall
> never dry nor cease, thy grief shall
> never fade, Lest angels err and brace
> thee so that thou can'st join the blade!

Countess Isabel felt a shiver race through her body. She stared numbly as the priest's couplets etched their poison deep within the most tender recesses of her young mind. The words turned over and over in her head and she clutched at her ears with her fists. She could not hear Aethel rail against the man, nor the pleadings of good John to "let the words just fly away." Instead, she paled, then silently followed King Henry's guards through the cold darkness of Windsor Castle.

❋

Between the curse of December 1187 and the troubled July of 1189, the French side of King Henry's empire became a whirlwind of battles, truces, sieges, and intrigue. Always the firebrand, Prince Richard had engaged his sometime friend, King Philip, over territorial squabbles and the personal affronts of some barons. For two years the soldiers of both realms had ravaged the land, robbing it of its crops, murdering helpless peasants, and disturbing the peace and safety of villages, towns, and castles with torch and sharpened steel.

Yet neither side truly wanted to be at war against the other. Both Prince Richard and King Philip wanted desperately to be on crusade together, and King Henry was exasperated with the mounting expense of keeping his army in the field. In the summer of 1188, King Henry had sailed across the Channel from England through a dangerous storm to end the unnecessary conflict. But upon learning that a truce had failed and that an angry King Philip had chopped down the ancient elm of Gisors, his heart sank. The elm had been the traditional site of treaties between the kings of France and the dukes of Normandy for more years than any knew. Its destruction portended a future far different than the past.

The war went on, its tide first turning against the French, then against the English. King Philip was a cunning king, however—clever and ruthless. He wanted the conflict to end, but for numerous reasons, he also wanted Prince Richard on the throne of England. To prompt his ends, he began circulating rumours that Henry had already decided succession in favour of John, and against Richard. It was a ruse he was certain would evoke an angry response by the bull-headed, blind, impetuous Richard. Philip's calculations were correct. The seeds of deception he planted sprouted quickly.

Not quite ready to swallow the bait in whole, Prince Richard continued the war against the French, alongside his father, until it had finally settled into a wearisome and costly siege between the two camps. The two kings finally agreed to confer at the castle at Bonmoulins, where Philip offered a proposal for peace in the "hopes that we may join our swords against our common foe, the infidels." Among other things, Philip demanded Richard's succession to the English throne.

Henry was furious. Sick or not, weakened by age and malady or not, the man roared his refusal and stormed away from the conference. "I'll not be blackmailed by some puffed-up Frenchman. My throne is yet mine and I shall dispose of it as I will."

Henry's outburst served to convince Prince Richard all the more that his father would deny him the throne, and he promptly summoned another conference with the French king. He was bewitched by Philip's deceptions and was out of patience with his father. At the conference, instead of renegotiating with the King of France, as everyone had expected, the Prince turned to his father in front of all present. "My lord King. Do I have thy word before the witnesses here gathered, that I am to succeed to the throne of England?"

Henry did not answer. He lifted his square chest and set his jaw. The King would not be cornered by anyone, including a son he patiently loved.

Believing his father's silence to be confirmation of the rumours, the red-faced Richard turned towards the wry King Philip standing near. The castle's hollow chamber fell as silent as the stone surrounding the court. Then, to the utter astonishment of all, Richard then flung his sword and belt upon the ground at Philip's feet and knelt before the French king. True to the ceremony of homage, he then bowed his bared head and pressed his hands together, placing them upright within those of the King of France. With a loud and angry voice he swore his fealty to Philip for all lands in Normandy, Poitou, and Aquitaine, and for "all service due in France save that which conflicts to homage owed my King Henry." He then stood and kissed Philip upon the lips, thereby becoming a vassal to Philip with "both sword and mouth."

Father and son stared at one another for a long moment, the former broken-hearted, the latter bitter; then each walked their separate ways without a word.

The web of feudal obligation was extraordinarily complicated and Richard's actions busied the lawyers of two realms. The system rested on a simple but sacred ritual called homage, in which either a grant of land or a promise of alliance was given in exchange for a man's commitment of military service and his fealty, or loyalty. The man granting the land or protection was the lord, the man swearing loyalty was the vassal.

In most cases, vassals were given land, called fiefs, and they usually sub-granted that land to their own vassals, who did in kind. This created a pyramid of sorts, a layered structure of lords and overlords ruling those below.

The system was fluid, however, for positions often changed when vassals were released from their oath by the defeat or death of their lord, a change in a lord's own fealty, or realignments of relationships due to marriages. Shifting relationships then required shifting military alliances. A knight might storm the ramparts of a castle one year, only to become the same castle's defender the next. As a result, warfare was considered more as a business activity than a matter of principle, and was waged by the rules of courteous conduct that were included among the virtues of chivalry.

Richard had sworn fealty to Philip, but as the system had become so complex, such pledges could be assigned to very specific situations. Richard had technically only offered Philip his fealty for lands Richard held on the continent, and only to the point that it did not violate his competing fealty to his father. For this reason, King Henry did not anticipate that Richard would take arms against him. But in the months that followed, Richard's disaffection drifted quickly towards outright treason. He quickly compromised the remaining fealty still due his father by openly joining his troops to those of the French king. Together, the two decimated Henry's army, finally chasing the English to Le Mans, the city where King Henry had been born.

"My King," begged Sir William Marshal. "We will soon be trapped inside this castle. The city is in flames—we need to retreat to safety." The great knight was Henry's most trusted soldier and the commander of his troops.

King Henry stared over the ramparts at the smoke rising from Le Mans. With a sad sigh and a nod, he assented. "Good William, protect the rear with what troops you need. God be with you."

Sir William immediately provided cover for the King and the bulk of the English army as it slipped out of the castle. Sir William and his remaining soldiers would delay the enemy's forward assault as best as they could. Presuming the King to be a safe distance away, William abandoned the castle and fought his way out of the burning city.

In the midst of the furious combat, William ran past a woman trapped in her burning home. Ever valiant, the knight removed his helmet and charged directly into the billowing smoke and snatched the shrieking woman from the fires of death. William's face was singed, he had nearly choked on the heavy smoke, but he retained enough presence of mind to secure the woman within the shelter of a chapel before returning to the battle. It was the kind of deed that had so characterised his career as a soldier.

Finally, Marshal and his men escaped beyond the blood-stained walls of Le Mans into the safety of the countryside. But Richard was not finished. Ruthless and brash and wishing to ride like the wind, he stripped himself of heavy armour and threw his weapons to the ground. He cried for an entourage of light horse and began a hot pursuit of his routed father. The petulant thirty-three year old Prince charged forward, flying out of the smoke of Le Mans, past the burning suburbs, beyond the terrified villages, and on towards his prize—the throne of England.

The wild warrior had failed to consider his move carefully, however, for one player yet remained on the King's board. Waiting in ambush was Sir William. Calculating the prince's impulsiveness, Marshal had set a brilliant snare into which the prince and his unsuspecting horsemen flew. William's men sprang the trap, falling upon their surprised prey with the righteous wrath of all Heaven. His seasoned veterans were the royal mesnie, the King's own household of knights—the very best of knighthood. With William at the fore, they swept in from all sides and exacted a slaughter without mercy—no mercy, that is, save for the King's wayward son.

William Marshal, England's knight of knights, ran the prince down with his well-lathered war-horse. The steely man-at-arms raised his lance and charged forward, fully prepared to dispatch the rebellious prince until Richard cried out. "By the mercies of God, Marshal, spare me! I am unarmed—and at thy mercy."

William paused and glared at the terrified prince until he finally shouted, "A price. A price for treason must be paid." With that, he spurred his mount forward and threw his lance hard, crying, "I shall take the horse; let the Devil take you!"

Prince Richard collapsed atop his slaughtered steed and tumbled into the dust unharmed. William circled the man from atop his white charger and said nothing as the two locked eyes. With disdain, the King's man then reared his horse and ordered his column forward to join the English camp.

Dust-covered and smudged with soot, William found poor Henry suffering in the heat of the royal tent and nearly stricken to death with exhaustion. Saying nothing about his incident with Richard, the knight informed the King of the army's present predicament and pleaded, once more, for the King to sue for peace.

Vexed with an ambitious, foolhardy son and pressed by his enemies, Henry had only one friend on whom he leaned heavily. He dismissed all talk of the crisis, for he had lost all interest, at least for the moment. Instead, he smiled weakly and bade William sit before him. He intended to bless William with a gift born of deep gratitude, one for which no selfish advantage had been calculated. "*Mon cher* William, my friend and faithful knight," Henry began. "Save for my son, John, it is you and you alone who has kept faith with me. I fear my end is coming—my son may soon have the crown."

Henry stared into William's large grey eyes. Taller than any in the English army at six foot two inches, his disciplined bearing had always provided the King the confidence he often needed. Nearly fifty, William's face was still strong. Symmetrical and sharp-featured, it was as if chiselled by a master sculptor. His chin was square and cleft, his neck thick, like his broad, muscled shoulders. "Remove your coif, Sir William."

William obeyed and dropped his open-faced mail hood backward to his shoulders.

Henry pointed to the man's dark brown hair. "A mere sprinkle of silver for an ageing hound." The two laughed lightly. "Silver in the hair is a treasure, like silver in a strongbox. It comes with wisdom and seasoning; it is a sign for others to honour. Given your life, sir, I should think you'd have more."

"Aye, m'lord." William bowed, modestly.

The King pulled himself off his cot and stood on tentative legs. He laid a hand on William Marshal's shoulder and smiled as if he were simply a familiar friend and not the King. He called two clerks to his side and bade them bring a quill, ink, paper, wax, and the King's seal. The priests hurried to comply and waited for the King's command.

Finally, the succession, thought William. *But who might be the better King? Richard is more of a man than John—more courageous, more devout, more sincere, but disloyal and impulsive. John is a fool, a wicked and sly rogue.* William watched the clerks' anxious faces, each waiting—as was all of France—for this business to be brought to a finish. *But where is the chancellor?* wondered William. *The deed needs a bishop's blessing.*

With his eyes fixed on the Marshal's, King Henry dictated his pronouncement:

"I, King Henry Plantagenet of England and Wales, Duke of Normandy, Lord of Aquitaine, Brittany, Maine, Poitou, Gascony, King of lands in Ireland, do this day, betroth Lord William Marshal of my royal household to Countess Isabel de Clare, daughter of Richard Strongbow de Clare, deceased Earl of Pembroke, of Chepstow, Lord of fiefs throughout Normandy, and of the Kingdom of Leinster in Ireland."

William Marshal, the middle son of a modest lord, the once knight-errant who made his living winning tournaments all over France, stood speechless and dumfounded. He had seen Lady Isabel on his various errands to the Tower. She was often the object of the fanciful thoughts of the young knights in his charge, but to imagine her as his wife was more than a dream come true. The veteran knelt and took the King's hands in his own. "With every gratitude of my heart, dear King, I vow to rule her lands with thoughts ever fixed upon thy kindness."

Henry darkened. "Good knight, pledge this also. Pledge thy faithful affection to my precious flower. I near erred in a way that shall vex my heart until its final beat. I do love the damsel. I've more a need to know that you shall treat her well, that your affections shall be set upon her and not her lands. Swear it, sir."

William nodded. "*Oui*, sire, I do so swear. I confess I saw her once as a tender shoot, bowing over her image in the fishpond. My heart was smitten then, sire, as it is now." His heart was racing more at that moment than it had done while in wait for any battle of his life. He nearly wept for joy. A bachelor of almost fifty, he found the solitude of his bed something to grieve. Devout and pious, he had remained true to his honour in a world fraught with men of far less virtue and rampant with temptation. But more, he longed to see the faces of children gathered at a table in a place he might call his own. *Children*, he thought. *God be praised. It is a fresh beginning in my fading years.*

Tears of joy overcame the sturdy knight. His chain-mail coat felt suddenly heavy, his sword a clumsy appendage at his hip. At that moment he wanted nothing more than to rid himself of the weight and coldness of steel, and embrace, instead, the silk-wrapped curves of his young bride.

CHAPTER VI

FAREWELL TO A KING

THE day following, the fifty-six-year-old King fell desperately ill and was escorted by William Marshal to the city of Tours, where he met with King Philip to negotiate a peace. Feeble Henry was tied atop his horse so that none might know of his failing condition. He listened to Philip's terms: he was to pay homage to Philip for all of his French possessions, he was to pay a huge indemnity, marry Richard to Philip's sister, Alice, and yield three castles as a pledge of good faith. To this, the ailing King quietly assented. He then rode slowly out of Philip's sight before collapsing into the strong arms of Sir William, who eased him upon a litter and returned him to the keep of Chinon.

King Henry had asked only one thing from King Philip. He had asked that a list of the knights who had abandoned him in favour of Richard be given to him. Knowing he was about to die, he wanted to perform an act of mercy. His intention was noble and rooted in a heart that had softened over time. He wanted to offer forgiveness to those who did not deserve it. He wanted to formally relieve from their vows of homage those who had betrayed him, thereby restoring them to honour.

King Philip had been all too happy to comply. He thought that waving such a list of friends and former allies under Henry's nose was just the sort of humiliation the man deserved. He pictured Henry's wounded eyes dropping from one treasonous name to the next, names of men he had feasted with and revelled with for all these many years—men who had pretended loyalty while they had truly only ever served themselves. He laughed to himself as the messenger galloped away. "Bitter medicine for a dying King."

Lord William was not pleased to present the list to his lord. He begged the King to withhold grace from men so vile and self-interested as these. Unable to sway the quiet King, he unrolled the parchment and had a clerk read him the names. He would take careful note of the unrepentants; he would remember them. But his ears fixed themselves at once on only one name, the first name—and he groaned. "Enough, clerk," he moaned.

William entered the King's chamber with the scroll in hand. "My King, this list is a fabrication, an insult, to be sure. I shall return it to that devil Frenchman with some words of my own!" William squeezed the parchment hard and hid it behind his back.

Henry looked carefully into the Marshal's eyes and he knew the man was protecting him from further injury. "Sir William, it matters little. This old anvil fears no blows. I know most that have betrayed me. I simply wish to present their names to my bishop. Now, good friend, I insist you hand this to me."

So, with compassionate reluctance, William obeyed. He drew a deep breath and waited.

Henry opened the scroll slowly. His eyes fell immediately upon the first name. It was his own son John's, and at the sight of it, the shocked King lurched forward with a gasp. It was too much to bear. With all hope in life suddenly gone, Henry turned slowly to his sad-faced knight. "Remove me to the altar in the chapel," he stated weakly. "I am beaten."

William nodded. He and a small band of faithful barons slowly carried their liege lord to the chapel, where the King received Holy Communion and the prayers of the priests. The heart-broken King was soon semi-conscious and delirious. He uttered a rambling confession and lifted his eyes towards Heaven, no doubt longing for life in a better Kingdom in a place far, far away.

The King was taken to his bed and left to rest. A short time later, on Thursday, the sixth of July 1189, Henry Plantagenet released his soul. He died alone, except for a few menial servants who had abruptly stripped his body and robbed his chamber before running away. It was the royal *mesnie* who found the cold and stiffening corpse. Aghast, a knight covered his King's body with a robe and summoned Sir William.

Henry's remains were washed and escorted by a column of

barons and a grieving William Marshal to the abbey of Fontevrault in the valley of the Loire. Here the King's favourite nuns prepared the corpse to lie in state and here the royal household waited nervously for the arrival of Prince Richard.

For William Marshal, the wait was nerve-rending. He had served Henry as faithfully as any vassal in the realm, perhaps more faithfully than any knight had ever served a king. He was respected by the barons as a man of honour, the very "flower of chivalry." Yet he was virtually landless, and though his position as the royal marshal paid handsomely, it existed only at the pleasure of the King. Now he would be at the mercy of Richard, the very man he had nearly slain. But his heart feared far more than a loss of position. What made Sir William tremble was a question that had haunted him since he had found the King's cold, naked corpse: *Is Countess Isabel still mine?*

※

Prince Richard stood tall and well-muscled, clean-shaven, and handsome alongside his father's corpse as it lay in state in the abbey church of Fontevrault in Anjou, France. Feeling sudden remorse for his past betrayals, he now stared disdainfully at the throng of courtiers and knights feigning their sorrow. He took some pleasure in knowing he would soon be belted as the Duke of Normandy and crowned King of England. He was satisfied in the knowledge that the duchies of France still claimed by the English throne would be his as well, despite Philip's technical overlordship. Yet he never sought these titles and privileges for vainglory; he intended them as no more than means to a more sacred end. He had longed to rule *so that* he might have the power to reorganise and re-finance his plans for the third Holy Crusade.

The soon-to-be-crowned King had one troublesome concern. He did not trust the ambitions of his younger brother, John. He intended to placate and distract the man by protecting John's interests in Ireland, yet with the scheming prince in Britain and himself far away in Palestine, to whom might he dare entrust the knights of his kingdom? Surely not his barons; they had proven their lack of virtue by joining him in his betrayal of King Henry. "Who among these serpents is a man of honour?" He looked about the circle of the Angevin Empire's most wealthy barons and hardened knights. His eyes moved from one to the other, some of good repute—men of chivalry and piety—but most of selfish ambition. Many had served his prior purposes well, but he dared not let them near his throne. He leaned towards his senior counsellor, Lord Longchamps, and grumbled, "Whom can I trust? Must I choose among those who have betrayed their virtue the least?"

Longchamps answered bluntly, "No. He who'd steal an egg would surely steal an ox." He was one to know. The man was a baggy-eyed, bald, and pompous politician who scowled both day and night, even cursing the Virgin when his stew was cold. Richard trusted him, however, for the man was vulnerable. It seemed that Richard's spies had informed him of Longchamp's darkest secrets, shaming ones that could leave him a legacy of mockery and disdain. For Richard, secrets as these were worth more than a company of Norman knights. The counsellor leaned forward and whispered something in Richard's ear.

"Ah, of course." Richard stood to his feet with feigned bluster and pointed his long arm at a group of soldiers. "William Marshal, sit with me," he commanded.

The knight removed his coif and sat on a stool by the acting King. "*Oui*, Sir Richard," he said, coolly. His choice of salutation did not go unnoticed.

"You would have killed me that day had I not deflected thy lance with my arm." blustered Richard.

William bristled. Neither the charge nor the facts were true. He stood to his feet. "No, sir. It was not my will to kill thee, for had I wished to do so, you would now be stiff and mouldy in thy grave. I have nothing to repent."

Pleased with the man's pluck, Richard's eyebrows arched upwards and he cast a sideways glance at the nodding Longchamps. William Marshal was every bit the soldier of character the court had claimed him to be. Well-seasoned, respected, too naïve to be treacherous and too pious to abandon faith, he would surely do. Richard rose, approached his father's former marshal and spoke in a measured tone. "I pardon thee, Sir William, and I bear thee no rancour for thy act."

William chafed at the misplaced pardon but bowed respectfully. He was suddenly aware that his betrothal to the damsel, Isabel, might be in jeopardy.

Richard then bade the man stand before him and receive the kiss of peace. William balked, but the code of *courtoisie* to which he was bound required that he honour Richard's request. He walked forward, stiffly, and allowed the future King to touch his lips to his own.

The deed done, an unhappy general of Richard's cried out, "Sire, he slaughtered our soldiers by the score. Make your peace if y'must, but know that your father gave him Countess de Clare. Pardoned or not, he ought not steal a gift from thy father's grave."

Richard whirled about. He grabbed the hilt of his sword and stepped towards his general with a menacing stride. "Nay, I tell you this—hear me, all of you. This man has received *nothing* from my father. The pledge is buried with the worms. I am King; I grant or deny as I so will."

William's heart sank.

Richard sat with Longchamps for a few long moments, then rose to take several long strides towards the hard-faced knight. "Upon thy pledge of fealty, you, Sir William, are appointed the Marshal of England. I set the knights of my household and all my armies under thy care. And hear me well. It is I sir, and not my father, who does give you the maiden de Clare. I shall receive thy homage and you shall serve me as you did King Henry."

Relieved, William bowed. "My thanks to you, sire. I shall serve with honour."

"*Oui*, with honour—I would expect so." Richard was pleased. He had just secured his kingdom with the services of England's greatest knight. "Then sir, let not time fail us. Grant me thy oath."

William Marshal did not hesitate. He fell to both knees and

placed his hands within Richard's. A priest laid a relic of St. Vedast at the King's feet while William proclaimed, "My lord, with gratitude I do pledge thee my fealty for all lands I receive by marriage. My sword and my honour are thine against all enemies and as long as you shall live. I so swear in the name of the Father, the Son, and the Holy Ghost, Amen."

"Then rise, Sir William," Richard commanded with a smile. Knowing his kingdom would be safe, he was overjoyed to begin his plans to storm the walls of Jerusalem. He laid both hands upon the Marshal's broad shoulders. "Faithful knight, serve to the glory of the Christ. Ride, now. Take thy charger and gallop away. Sail on, Sir William, seize thy bride and claim what lands are thine by right-of-wife."

On the sixteenth of July Sir William Marshal rushed into London, Richard's writ in hand. He and his entourage had travelled from France at breakneck speed, crossing Anjou, Maine, and Normandy in only two days. He had arrived at the dock in Dieppe, only to leap upon a waiting boat with his horse and crash through the half-rotted planks of its deck. His horse survived with no more injury than a few ugly cuts, and the undaunted knight limped away with one very bruised leg. Visions of Isabel had consumed him, and if he could have filled the sail with his own breath he would have blown the boat across the English Channel with a single blast.

Immediately upon his arrival in London, he sent messengers to the royal justiciar—one reluctant and rather obstinate Ranulf de Glanville. Ranulf would be the one William needed to advise the Holy Church of the marriage and to arrange the legal affairs in matters of land holdings, rents, etc. The justiciar resisted, perhaps envious of the ageing knight's good fortune, but upon feeling the cold steel of the impatient marshal's sword on his neck, the man yielded on all points. In the meantime, another messenger had been sent to the Countess.

✳

"News, m'lady." Aethel's cheeks were flushed as she handed a copy of the betrothal to Isabel. John d'Erley stood in the doorway.

Isabel held the parchment in trembling hands. "Squire, I am to marry your lord? William Marshal?"

"*Oui*, m'lady."

"And in just five days?"

"*Oui*, m'lady."

Isabel staggered to a chair. In a matter of five days she would marry a man she had never met. Feeling overwhelmed and suddenly anxious, she cast a terrified eye at Aethel. "Squire, I am—I am breathless! You say it is Sir William Marshal, the knight oft' spoke of at court, King Henry's favourite?"

"*Oui*. The old King had pledged him to you himself before he died. King Richard has honoured the pledge."

Isabel stared at Aethel again. Both had known the reputation of William Marshal as a man of impeccable character and a champion among knights. For all her life Isabel had heard of his heroics, his courtesy, his virtue. Some had said he was cold as winter steel, however, and illiterate. The seventeen-year-old Isabel had a more troubling concern. "Squire. Tell me of your master's age."

"I am not certain, *Mademoiselle*. I believe he is fifty, but even he is unsure."

Isabel turned away. "Fifty!"

"With pardon, m'Lady," urged John, "he is strong and full of life. I have seen him dance and seen him joust. He laughs heartily and knows of courtly love."

"How so?"

"Queen Eleanor loved him as a brother and she taught him words of love. It is said that in the court at Rouen he made the ladies swoon."

Isabel nodded. "A bachelor all these years?"

"Aye, m'lady."

"How many illegitimates?"

"None, m'lady. He is devout and pious, a man of uncommon virtue."

Isabel took a deep breath. "I see. I would have thought illegitimate sons an advantage for a man of means like he. They prove to be loyal soldiers."

"Indeed, Countess. He is no man of means, however. He was given a small grant in Cartmel two years prior. 'Tis all he holds."

"I should assume he is to inherit lands from family, then?"

"Perhaps, m'lady, but it is not certain. His brother received what little the family possessed."

Isabel was astonished and she scowled at d'Erley. "I should have thought him to be of better station. No large holdings from the King he served so well?" She wrung her hands and let her anger loose. "I thought I might marry a young earl—now I am to marry an old pauper. And an illiterate one at that. What do I care if he wins at tournament, if he makes old hags swoon?!" Isabel's face was flushed. It was a side of the maiden rarely seen.

D'Erley stiffened. "M'lady, he is a man of character, something rarely found in men of means. I would have thought you to give that sort of treasure greater heed than mere silver." John's tone was sharp, his insight deep.

"Master d'Erley," boomed Aethel in defence of her charge. "How dare you!"

Isabel felt suddenly ashamed. She fell quiet and walked to her window. She looked out into the bailey and the stone walls that had surrounded her all these many years. She took a shallow breath. "Thank you Aethel, but *I* am in need of rebuke." She faced the squire. "Master John. Well said. Forgive me. I do thank thee for your message and pray God's blessing on what comes of it. Now I beg you give me leave."

John d'Erley bowed deeply and left the chamber. Isabel stared blankly at Aethel for a long moment, then burst into tears and ran into her arms. Neither knew whether she wept for shame, for fear, for disappointment, or anger. No matter, the maiden simply sobbed; it was the privilege of her gender.

❋

Nearly a week later, on Friday, the twenty-first of July of 1189, the Lady Isabel, Countess of Chepstow, placed herself in the capable hands of her exhausted handmatron and a company of attendants. She had finally surrendered to her destiny and now waited for her moment almost serenely, like a butterfly carried by a gentle breeze over which it had no control.

Aethel bustled about the young woman to be certain that her beauty would be displayed in its full radiance for the wedding of that afternoon. She had purchased new clothing from a London seamstress, bypassing the royal staff with which she had grown so very weary. She had ordered the damsel a bath, being sure the bath-maiden scrubbed her clean with pumice and refreshed her with scented water. Her staff then covered the young bride's supple skin with a white linen chemise before drawing new white hose over her feet and calves. Atop the undergarment was then hung a yellow under-gown, its colour chosen from the Marshal's herald.

Isabel smiled approvingly as her outer-gown was presented. It was made of expensive green samite, green being another of the Marshal's colours. In front, the gown fell to the ground by the bride's feet but at the back formed a, flowing train—some twelve feet in length—that was to be carried by attendants. On top, its bell-like sleeves reached to her wrist; below, they were so wide that their ends nearly reached the floor. The Countess curtsied play-fully and her staff clapped.

Isabel's strawberry-coloured hair had been braided into two long plaits through which were wound thin, red ribbons. Red was the Marshal's final colour. Her face, covered by an application of sheep fat mixed with vermilion and white powder, was then framed by a scarlet barbette snugged beneath her chin with some care. Aethel laid a white linen wimple atop the bride's head and secured it with a crown of wildflowers picked that very morning from the Tower gardens.

Aethel wept. "Oh, God forgive me, but I doubt the Virgin Mother could have been more wondrous. Here; see yourself." She handed her lady a small mirror. It was a costly accessory, but one that Isabel had always enjoyed.

The young Countess held the looking glass at arm's length and stared at her likeness. She peered deeply into her own blue eyes and wondered what course she was about to be set upon. Content, she lowered the mirror and smiled at Aethel. "You have done well. I could have never had a more skilled attendant than you." She then turned to Carly and Ida, two seamstresses, the florist, the bathmaid, and some helpers. "All of you have done so very well. I am proud to bring you to my new life."

The servants were relieved. None knew if their lady's intentions would be to keep them or dismiss them to King Richard's steward for reassignment.

"Are you ready, m'lady?" asked Aethel proudly.

Isabel nodded, nervously. She took Aethel's hands in hers. "I wish you could stand with me."

"Aye, m'lady. And me as well. Can you just see that? A servant by her Countess. I think not. I am content to watch from a distance, and from there I shall pray for your joy and for a full nursery."

The Countess blushed and smiled at Aethel with eyes melted in admiration. A large lump filled her throat. The servant loved children like nothing else on God's earth, save Isabel herself. With her own children in cold graves, the poor woman could do little more than dream of the motherhood she had been denied. Yet good Aethel did not despise the same dream for Isabel, nor cast envy on the slender young virgin standing before her. Indeed not, for it was with a full and sincere heart that she wished her lady every joy that life might offer. Isabel vowed to herself at that moment that she would never be tended by ladies-in-waiting, those false friends hired to be companions. No, she would surround herself with genuine friends, like Aethel, regardless of their station.

Isabel gave her handmatron a tender hug and a gentle kiss, then stepped towards the door of her bedchamber at the head of her company of attendants. Unable to pass through the door without a final look, she turned. This room in the Tower Castle had been her home for so many years. Her mind filled with memories of her happy days as a lanky little girl tumbling atop the straw covered floor with laughing Aethel. She closed her eyes and felt the cold nights of winters past, but also the torchlit feasts of Christmas and the Epiphany.

Her mind then flew to summer ringdances where her hair had been loose and flowing and the world filled with song. She remembered what fun she had had splashing in the fishpond, climbing the trees of the small orchard, and picking flowers with Father Adderig. *Ah, I miss him so,* she thought. Her mind turned to King Henry entering through the castle portcullis on his huge grey charger, bedecked in his blue royal robes and followed by columns of mail-clad knights. Pennants and banners, tournaments amidst the gardens, minstrels and passion plays, walks by the Thames; this had been her childhood. With a final sigh and a turn, it was all behind her.

❉

William Marshal had arrived in London with no thoughts other than of his bride-to-be. He had little money, no fine clothes; no preparations had been made whatsoever. But he was resolved to claim his wife quickly, lest any twist of fortune might deny him his dream. He sent his knights on a wild chase to make ready.

Given the wealth that William was about to enjoy, he certainly had no problem with credit. The city of London was filled with moneylenders, mostly Jews whom the Normans had imported after the Conquest just over a hundred years ago. William was reluctant to go to them, however, for fear of their high rates of interest. Usury, of course, was a sin between Christians and a sin between Jews, but no one considered interfaith loans sinful! William did not blame the Jews for their rates: after all, it was their Christian clients that had often failed to honour their debts, which forced the powerless moneylenders to sell their loans at a discount to an abbot or bishop who could excommunicate the delinquent debtor! Rather than become entangled in all that, William chose to borrow money from a willing Christian merchant, one Richard fitz Reiner who would not charge him interest. It was a relationship that would serve the Marshal well in the years ahead.

The nervous groom rummaged about the shops of London with his entourage and bought the necessaries for both his wedding and his honeymoon. All items in hand, he and his fellows then found a bathhouse where they paid the proprietor six *deniers*—pennies—for a refreshing bath, complete with a generous supply of eye-burning lye soap and a pleasing rinse of rose water.

When finished, John d'Erley helped his lord climb into a fresh pair of *braies*, his knee-length undershorts. He then pushed on a pair of good wool hose and tied them fast around William's calves with bright red garters. Sir Ralph Bloet, newly joined to the entourage, and Eustace de Bertremont, a knight-errant from France, helped the lord with his undertunic—a dark green, ankle-length robe with tight sleeves. It was bound tightly to his waist with a thin leather cord, its throat laced loosely, exposing the man's sun browned skin beneath.

An over-tunic was then pulled atop this. It was a glorious yellow robe falling to just above his ankles with long, full sleeves and belted by a bright red sash. On his feet he wore black leather shoes tied snugly at his ankles. His face was clean-shaven except for a moustache; his brown, grey-streaked hair was shorn typically close on the sides and back and parted down the centre. Atop his head he donned a red, linen coif, cut loose at the jaw and fastened beneath his chin by thin ribbons.

Eustace laughed. "Y'look like my father's peacock. Spread yer wings!"

The others roared. "Aye, dandy man. You look like a lady's garden on legs. All y'needs is flowers in yer hair and you'd be quite the fop."

Eustace belched. "I'd feel like a fool, would I look like that. Eh, John?"

The squire dared not answer but he did laugh.

"Too timid y'are, boy? So, Sir William, too bad you've no lookin' glass."

William Marshal was beet red and flushed. He gave Eustace a playful shove and threw John d'Erley across the room. "A fop? Who says I've the look of a fop?" He pulled a dagger from within his clothing and romped about the bathhouse, chasing his comrades like an embarrassed schoolboy.

The play ended, William gathered his fellows in a circle and begged their patience in the life that must now change. "I've a bride now to tend, lads. You, Ralph, you know what that means."

Ralph Bloet rolled his eyes and grimaced. "Aye, sire, that I do."

With a roar, the laughing men burst from the bathhouse and into the streets of London. It was time for a wedding.

⁂

Since William had little time to make preparations, Isabel's ceremony would not be attended with the pomp of which she had so often dreamed. She had once been told of a lord's wedding near her family's Welsh estate in Chepstow. The bride was of rare beauty and the groom as "good a man as ever walked the earth." All the barons and the prelates from the surrounding lands had formed a large parade in which they danced their way by the salty Severn to a fortnight of feasting. It was said the seabirds cried for joy as they flew above the splendid scene, and that fish so filled the bay that fisherman were blessed with extra-heavy nets for one year to the day.

Countess Isabel now knew her day would not be like that. Father Adderig had once told her that some dreams had a way of giving pleasure for a season, only to exact a price in the end. "But ah, my little flower, dream on and on, long past the ones that fail thee, for what would life be without them but a journey of despair." She placed her fingers upon a delicate golden brooch her mother had sent her as a wedding gift. It was the cross of an Irish saint they both loved, St. Bridget of the Eternal Flame. She closed her eyes and tried so very hard to picture mother Eve. She had some image of fair hair and skin, of a light touch and the sounds of songs and stories, but little more.

The guard that was waiting just beyond her door led the

Countess and her company through the Tower and to the men waiting on the bailey. The King's justiciar had ordered a large armed escort for the Countess, unwilling that she become the hostage of some pirate or the victim of a jealous baron. She was led with every courtesy through the Tower Castle's gate and to a royal coach standing in the centre of a long column of armoured knights. Isabel smiled at the score of mounted men looking so very handsome and strong in their flowing robes of green, blue, crimson, and white. Their presence helped the moment seem suddenly more special to the damsel. It was then that Isabel set aside all thoughts of disappointment and chose to face her future with hope.

The carriage rolled at a comfortable speed along the roadway just beyond the city. As they approached Bishopsgate, the column halted in order to allow a troubadour to light upon a small cart now following the Countess' carriage. Isabel's eyes lit with surprise and delight as the singer presented himself with a deep and spectacular bow. "Thy groom, fair maiden, hast sent me to lighten thy heart and kindle thy spirit with a song of his enduring love."

The musician sang wonderfully well. He played his lute and lifted his eyes to the skies as he sang of beauty and gardens, of seascapes, and joy. "Thy husband's love is like the vintner's finest fruit, sweet, strong, bursting with nectar, and longing to please thee."

Isabel was enthralled. She held Aethel's hand and the two were swept away as their retinue passed by Cripplegate, St. Bartholomew's priory, and finally Newgate, before arriving at the Temple Church, the life centre of England's Order of the Knights Templar. The Temple grounds provided for the needs of the military monastery, including dormitories, gardens, an infirmary, herbarium, workshops, and the like. A newly built round church formed the centre of their premises and within its simple archways and plain pillars, Lord William and the Countess would soon be joined in marriage.

Lord William, once having served with the Templars, had been smitten with an affection for the order bordering on obsession. It was fitting, thought his comrades, that he should wed in their church, though none knew how such an unusual event had been arranged.

Isabel bade her bowing troubadour farewell and hugged Aethel. She was helped to the ground and escorted to the Temple Church on trembling legs. Two short parallel rows of Templar knights formed a corridor of white robes distinguished by their renowned red Templar crosses. She was quite taken by these warrior-monks and felt secure in their presence. She passed slowly between them, straining her eyes to see her husband-to-be for the first time.

William Marshal stared from the church and watched his bride's carriage arrive. His hands were wet and clammy; his clothing felt heavy and uncomfortable. A playful jab in the ribs by Eustace put him at some ease. But when Isabel stepped upon the ground he nearly wept. She seemed to him to be an angel sent from heaven. Her silk moved so lightly, so softly, he thought Heaven must have clothed her in gossamer. His breath left his body and his chest tingled with joy. "Oh, my Isabel—*my* Isabel."

Three musicians ran to greet the lady. One strummed his lute, a second blew lightly on his panpipes, and a third rapped his fingers on his *tabour*, a small drum hanging from his neck. Isabel s eyes widened with wonder as three pink-faced children then ran towards her sprinkling flower petals before her every step. The damsel began to weep.

Aethel had been crying all along. She wiped her swollen eyes with a kerchief and blew her nose from time to time, trumpeting loudly and earning looks of contempt from her fellows. She craned her neck to watch—with the other servants—from her distant vantage and prayed God would bless her beloved lady on this most wondrous day.

CHAPTER VII

TO GOD, LORD WILLIAM AND HIS BRIDE

THE young Countess was approached by two of Sir William's personal knights and one very happy, though somewhat jealous, John d'Erley. The knights stood to each side of the bride and the young squire took a position at some distance behind, holding the train of the lady's gown. The foursome walked slowly towards Sir William, who was waiting with the Master of the Temple and two green-robed priests in the doorway of the church. With each step, both bride and groom's eyes became ever more fixed upon one another until, at long last, Lady Isabel de Clare stood face to face with her betrothed, Sir William Marshal.

The moment was quiet and respectful. Isabel curtsied, albeit a bit stiffly. William bowed, though a bit awkwardly. The Countess then lowered her eyes shyly and waited. With a nudge from Sir Ralph, William then extended his hand to receive hers. Without raising her eyes, Isabel lifted her small hand upwards and in a moment, it was tenderly lost within the mighty hold of her groom.

At the touch, Isabel closed her eyes and trembled. A shiver rode her spine and she felt as if her hair was rising. Her heart began to race and she wanted to cry out for joy. It was right, she knew it was to be a good thing, a life as God willed—and now as she willed.

"Sir William Marshal, Lord of Cartmel, " began the master. "Dost thou come willingly to take this woman, Countess Isabel de Clare, as thy wife?"

"*Oui, Père*. I do come willingly."

"Countess Isabel de Clare, daughter of the late Richard de Clare, Earl of Pembroke, Lord of Chepstow and of Leinster, dost thou come willingly to pledge thy tryst to this man, William Marshal, Lord of Cartmel, as thy husband?"

Isabel lifted her eyes with certainty and answered in a strong voice befitting the daughter of a nobleman and the granddaughter of a king. "*Oui, Père*. I do come willingly."

The master nodded and adjusted his white robe. He turned to William. "*Messire* William, dost thou now take this woman to love and defend as Christ does love and defend His Holy Church?"

"*Volo!*" William assented with such enthusiasm that even the priests had to restrain a smile.

"Countess de Clare, dost thou now take this man to honour and obey as the Holy Church does honour and obey Christ?"

Isabel answered, "*Volo*."

The Templar turned again to William. "Hast thou a token of thy tryst?"

William nodded and fumbled through a small purse tied to his belt. He retrieved a golden ring, once wrested from a goldsmith in Normandy during his wild ride to this moment. His shaking fingers placed the ring on the fourth finger of his bride's right hand, the finger that returned blood to the heart. "With this ring I pledge thee my love; with my body I wed thee."

Isabel received the ring from England's greatest knight and smiled. She already loved this man.

"Sir William. Hast thou a symbol of the dower?" asked the master.

This was the moment that had troubled the mighty warrior from the very beginning. The dower was a gift from the groom to the bride that would assure the bride's financial well-being in the event of her husband's death. Typically, a husband would grant up to one-third of his wealth. But William Marshal had virtually no wealth. What he received from his marriage was already destined to be returned to his wife at his death. He felt terribly embarrassed, but dutifully reached into his purse. "Good wife. I offer this symbol in dower. I have little of this earth to pledge, but this golden cross was touched by my hand to the Holy Sepulchre in Jerusalem. It has protected me from my enemies, it has assisted my prayers, and has healed my wounds. It is now for thee to keep as a token of my undying love. It shall serve thee when I am gone."

Isabel was overwhelmed. *A relic? A holy relic?* She squeezed the cross and its chain within her palm and her heart swelled with wonder at this man. She received her dowry with grace and poise, and with reverent appreciation. She was indeed the woman that her groom had hoped for.

The master nodded, equally impressed with the dower. Few would be selfless enough to surrender a token of such spiritual consequence. Who but William Marshal would have given it to his bride?

Content that the marriage was conducted in all ways proper, the Templar laid one hand over each of their heads and raised his face upwards. "Under Heaven and by witness of Christ's Holy Church, the Virgin Mother, and the saints above, I declare thee husband and wife, *in nomine Patris, et Filii, et Spiritus Sancti*, Amen."

❋

Countess Isabel, wife of Lord William Marshal, had few memories of the wedding Mass that followed. She had a vague recollection of lying prostrate on the cold stone floor alongside her husband and before the altar; of squeezing bread between her teeth and feeling warm red wine roll over her tongue. She thought she had heard the low chant of priests and smelled a pungent incense. The one memory that did fix itself in her mind, however, was that of squealing Aethel and her staff charging towards her as she came out of the church door!

Isabel was now riding in a canopied carriage next to her proud husband. The carriage was a solid-wheeled high cart drawn by two spirited horses. Before the carriage and behind it rode a rugged column of William's own *mesnie*. Each was in full armour and heavily armed. To a man they wore the robes of the Marshal—yellow and green panels with a red rampant lion at the centre. Their lord's wife was now their lady, the precious, fragile treasure they were sworn to defend to the very death. Following behind were carts carrying Aethel, her handservants, and a group of minstrels. At the very end of the column, covered in dust, rode Squire John.

William and Isabel held hands and smiled as the lutes and drums, the dudelsacks and panpipes joined a chorus of glad-hearts in happy song.

"Wife, I shall try to love you well," offered William tenderly. "I hope you will love me as I do you."

Isabel blushed. At seventeen she had not known love, but the weakness in her body and the inexplicable joy filling her heart was a clue that perhaps it was her time.

William had one nagging fear. He was well aware of the difference in their ages and needed to be reassured that it would not be a matter of secret resentment for his bride. The man mustered his courage and said, "I am many more years thy elder; I think my age to be near to fifty. I–I should think you'd prefer a younger man." His face was tight and his lips were pursed in dread of the answer he expected.

Isabel thought for a moment, aware of her husband's concern. It was true, she had hoped for a younger man. She would have rather awakened in the morning to the bright eyes and boyish frame of an eager young groom. Yet there was a depth in this seasoned man, a well of wisdom rooted deeply in life's experience that she had never known in the young knights who had dashed about the Tower in her childhood. She felt safe with William, as if this giant of a man was now her very own living, loving, castle keep that would be her haven in a perilous world. But there was more. He brought to her a delightful smile, an endearing shyness, and a tender touch that lifted her heart. Indeed, Isabel was well-pleased and answered boldly, "Lord husband, I am content with God's will."

William nodded bravely. It was hardly the answer he had hoped for. He replied with a steady tone, "It is good that you are content."

Isabel's mind raced. She immediately realised her words had been poorly chosen. "But I am most *pleased* with God's will," she blurted.

"Truly?"

"*Oui*, my lord."

William felt better. He took a deep breath and let it out slowly. "I am happy to hear that."

Isabel nodded and fell silent. In fact, both said little more for the next two hours. It was an awkward and uncomfortable silence between a timid bride and a terrified groom. It was not the kind of silence caused by regret and filled with misery, but rather one of simple unfamiliarity cloaked in a fear of spoiling the day that Heaven had made so very perfect.

The Marshal's column wound its way south of London, through the well-watered green hills of Surrey, and finally to the house of one of William's many new friends, Lord Enguerrand d'Abenon. Lord William offered his bride his outstretched hands and lowered her lightly to the ground. Her young body felt soft to him and light as feathers. To Isabel, the man's huge hands wrapped round each side of her waist felt strong and sure. She stood on the ground and looked up at her husband's handsome face, and smiled. It was a smile that assured the man that all was well.

Lord Abenon sent his ushers hurriedly to the carriage and carts. Groomsmen led the horses to the stable while the knights were escorted to their quarters. The lord's steward appeared with a gracious bow, then bent to one knee, as had become the fashion, and presented the bride an armful of flowers cut that afternoon from the rose garden.

Isabel received the roses gracefully as her husband offered his thanks on her behalf. William then took his new wife by the arm and followed the steward through the tall oak doors of the manor house, past the great hall, and into a scented bridal chamber decorated with drapes of French silk and flowers of the season. Here a new life began for England's greatest knight and his enchanting Countess, Isabel Marshal.

❋

The Marshals' honeymoon lasted several weeks. It was a dreamy season for both bride and groom, one filled with summer breezes, singing birds, and vivid colour. William dismissed all thoughts and concerns about the conditions in the wider world instead, he thought of nothing other than the love he held in his arms, the most wondrous creature in all Christendom.

In gratitude to God for his kindness, William sent a messenger to his new steward residing at his wife's castle of Chepstow. The steward was the overseer of all the lord's new lands and was ordered to transfer William's personal estate at Cartmel to the Augustinians for the purpose of founding a new monastery. It was a gesture that further pleased his bride. The man's charity was genuine; he had always done what he could to be generous to the brothers and the nuns. He was renowned for his alms and was thrilled to know that his new found wealth would afford him the means to maintain the services of an almoner to oversee more regular gifts to the poor.

Indeed, William's resources were impressive. With the marriage, King Richard had released all of Isabel's estates except for holdings in Pembroke and in Ireland, both of which King Henry had seized some years prior. Richard held Pembroke for himself and the Irish fiefs for his brother John, in hopes of distracting him from other ambitions. Nevertheless, William Marshal was now Lord of Chepstow and its cliff-top castle that dominated the forest of Wentwood and the lowlands along the Severn estuary in western Wales. But Chepstow Castle, like most others, was merely the administrative centre of an estate of properties scattered widely throughout Wales and England. The Chepstow estates were comprised of many thousands of acres, yielding enormous fees and taxes.

But his marriage brought him other lands as well. He received the estates of the castle at Usk, became overlord of several lesser castles, and landlord over estates in Normandy. Richard also allowed William to buy the office of sheriff in Gloucester, thereby getting service fees from its castle and its Forest of Dean. It was fair to say that Lord William Marshal had become a magnate, and in the years to follow his wealth would expand all the more.

※

While the happy couple spent days walking through their

host's gardens, and evenings staring at the stars, Aethel's staff and the lord's *mesnie* enjoyed one anothers' company over ale and hard cider in a large, torch-lit hall near the stables. One raucous night followed another, each more cheery than the next. It was the joining of two households that would serve and defend each other for decades to come.

"Aethel, I do love thee," pined Sir Ralph one Tuesday, long past vespers.

Aethel reddened and shoved her would-be lover hard away. "Try to kiss me again, and you'll be kissing my fist."

The revellers rollicked. Ralph took a long, dramatic guzzle of ale and wiped his mouth on his sleeve. "So, a hen with pluck, eh?" The knight widened his eyes and spread a grin across his face. He opened his arms and lunged for the feisty matron, only to step square into the iron fist of Sir Alan de St. Georges.

Alan was a lanky thirty-three year old whose long blonde curls fell to his shoulders like a great mane. It was an outlandish signature more in keeping with his Viking forbears than the well-groomed convention of his Norman comrades. He was clean-shaven, however, and handsome, with bright, green eyes and a strong nose. His wife, Sybil, was the *bonne d'enfant*—the nurse—for William's future children.

The room grimaced with the sound of Alan's knuckles greeting Ralph's nose. "Aaah!" bellowed the knight. "*Sacre bleu*, you've broken it." The bloodied knight tilted his head back and placed a rag over his face.

"Leave the woman be," growled Alan as he guarded Aethel.

Ralph spat and faced de St.Georges with a snarl. Blood ran from his nostrils and his eyes blazed. Alan was a newcomer to William's *mesnie* and Ralph was not about to cower. Two of his fellows moved to his side, leaving Alan badly outnumbered. "If I want a go at that sow I'll 'ave it."

Alan smiled. "Aye? It'll take more than three of you."

Exhilarated by her defender's bravado, Aethel folded her arms and planted her feet. She raised her chin defiantly until her goading eyes prompted a lunge from Sir Ralph.

Alan caught Ralph by the arm and threw him violently on to the floor. With that, Ralph's comrades pounced, knocking de St. Georges backwards atop a table, then kicked him and punched him until a shrill battle-cry rose above the din. It was Squire John.

To the roars of a ring of cheering knights young John leapt upon the back of one of Ralph's fellows, burrowing his fingers in the man's eyes and biting his scalp. The man howled and spun, finally crashing John into a post, whereupon he pounded the lad without mercy.

Having a moment's reprieve, Alan managed to better both Ralph and the other knight, kicking and punching them about until the bellow of the *mesnie's* senior brought order. It was Sir Baldwin de Bethure, William's close companion and unofficial master of the *mesnie*. The man was rugged, quiet, withdrawn, and rarely seen except in moments of necessity. "Enough!"

The revellers fell silent and the combatants dragged themselves to the centre of the room where they wiped blood off their faces and knuckles. Baldwin circled about with a menacing eye and stopped at Squire John. He looked at the badly bloodied youth and said nothing for a moment. Then, to the surprise of all, he smiled and laid a large hand upon John's shoulder. "Well done, brave lad," he said.

With that note of honour the whole room cheered and the squire was glad-handed by all. Peace restored, the combatants kissed and a toast was offered to the future happiness of their common lord and lady. Sir Ralph then wrapped one arm around Sir Alan and raised a tankard of ale high in the air. He looked for Aethel, who had retreated with the other servants to the dark edges of the room. "First, to Aethel the Saxon. May she defend the Countess as she does her virtue."

"To Aethel, to Aethel!" hurrahed Lord William's knights. The woman blushed and curtsied.

Ralph turned to his fellows. "And now this: to comrades old and comrades new, may our hearts be one, and our steel be true."

A deafening roar saluted Ralph's toast. The men pounded their tankards atop the table and cheered until Sir Baldwin raised his hands. He looked about his knights and nodded as the room became silent. "God go with us all, each and every one. May His arm fall hard upon our enemies, may He shatter their bones before us and make them tremble at the very name of William Marshal's men."

Each knight stood to his feet and raised their tankards one more time. "To God, Lord William, and his bride."

✳

Over the next four years, Isabel's world changed. Immediately after her honeymoon she followed William to Normandy on the King's business, and while there she gave birth to their first child, a son named William Marshal the Younger. A year later, Isabel delivered a second son, Richard, named after her father, Richard Strongbow. A happy Lord William was now content, for the birth of a second son practically assured him that his family name would survive. In the year following, Isabel delivered a third child while in London, a girl named Matilda.

The fortunes of William had further improved as well, for the de Clare lands in Ireland, they being the whole of the island's south-east kingdom known as Leinster, had been returned to Isabel. Prince John, the former holder, had mounted a predictable revolt against his brother and was besieged at Windsor Castle. As part of his punishment, King Richard relieved him of his lordship, though he did not strip John of his title of King of Ireland. By restoring Leinster to the Countess, Lord William became the holder of these lands by right-of-wife and entitled to the great wealth they produced. Prince John, by virtue of his position, became William's overlord and as such, received William's oath of fealty *in absentia*.

In this present year of 1194, Isabel and William finally returned to their primary home of Chepstow Castle in the south of Wales. It sat squat and threatening, perched atop a limestone cliff and overlooking the river Wye near its mouth at the Severn. Despite the cold of January, the sight of Chepstow's stone was a great joy to Isabel. She hurried her three children and their nurse-maid, Sybil, through the yawning gate between the castle's massive twin towers. A roaring fire in the great hall was there to greet them all, and a resounding hurrah from Chepstow's residents was raised with sincere enthusiasm.

The castle was typically Norman, begun one year after William the Conqueror had defeated Harold the Saxon at Hastings. Lord Marshal had already ordered improvements to its eastern wall, introducing the latest in French castle architecture. Chepstow's walls were high and thick, made of local stone and remnants of red brick from the ruins of a nearby Roman fort. Unlike many other fortresses, it had not begun as a motte-and-bailey castle—the early Norman strongholds built by constructing a keep atop a mound and surrounding it with a timber stockade. While these had served as excellent temporary protection for the Norman invaders, it was the high stone walls, the ramparts, and the round towers of castles like Chepstow that ultimately secured the lands of men such as William Marshal.

William owned several castles by right-of-wife, though none as fine as Chepstow. From them he administered his vast estates through two separate households. One of these was his *mesnie*, his military household. William's knights now numbered some twenty-two—half travelling with him, others left to supervise the defence of his properties throughout Wales, England, and France. In addition to these, the lord was served by a scattered garrison of sergeants—unknighted cavalrymen—squires, pages, footmen-at-arms, watchmen, porters, armourers, and archers, as well as their wives and children, who often worked as servants in the domestic staff. In total, the Marshal's military household numbered about two hundred and fifty souls, not counting mercenaries who might be hired for special military campaigns.

Supervising his warriors from time to time was William's old friend, Sir Baldwin de Bethune. Baldwin was a great lord in his own right, but loved William and found it both enjoyable and profitable to serve in the capacity of acting marshal when called upon. So, when needed, he came to supervise weapons-training, the lord's stable, and the groomsmen, carters, messengers, deliverymen, blacksmiths, wheelwrights, harnessmakers, and saddlers.

The other household was that of the domestic staff, supervised by the chief *seneschal*, or steward. William had hired Roger of Nottingham, a thorough, fair-minded man of middling years. It was Roger's responsibility to manage the business of Lord William's many estates, including the collection and distribution of money, the hiring and disposing of staff, and the organisation of wardrobe, foodstuffs, furnishings, and sundry chattels. Furthermore, he needed to be sure of the household's spiritual health, travel across three kingdoms to adjudicate disputes, head the councils of knights, and serve as the lord's ambassador at court. Roger was newly arrived to this position, having happily been released from similar duties in Nottingham Castle, which had been so recently granted to Prince John by his brother, the King.

The steward delegated his responsibilities to two lower offices. The first was that of the chancellor—the household chaplain. Most argued that the chancellor, as a priest of the pope, was ultimately outside of the jurisdiction of a mere steward. It was an argument not unlike the pope's spat with King Henry in which the pope declared temporal supremacy. Henry's defeat notwithstanding, William Marshal made it clear that his chancellor would serve *under* his steward—a scheme of things no doubt prompted by the Celtic notions of his wife. She had whispered to him that the Church ought serve souls *under* the lord's protection.

It was the chancellor's duty to both shepherd the souls of the lord's household and provide secretarial duties. The chancellor was to personally administer Mass to the lord and his family, and was the keeper of the lord's seal. His priests and novices were to entreat God, the saints, and the Holy Mother on behalf of the general household, as well as care for vestments, assist in liturgy, and protect the relics. Since these clerks were literate—that is, they could read and write Latin—they were responsible for all record-keeping, correspondence, and auditing. The Countess had urged William to recruit a priest from Pembroke in the west of Wales to fill this post. She had learned of the man's reputation from a trusted pilgrim but had further calculated the advantages the choice might provide her husband in his legal haggling over claims to Pembroke Castle.

The second office was that of the chamberlain. Also usually a priest, the chamberlain's duties included oversight of the lord's possessions and his domestic staff at each castle, as well as the details of the lord's entourage. Due to the distances between the various castles and manor houses, the diversity of William Marshall's possessions, and the size of the staff, it was a difficult position. William's domestic household had grown to over sixty, and included ushers, valets, chambermaids, butlers, pantlers, cooks, cupbearers, laundresses, tailors, bakers, poulterers, barbers, and doctors.

Isabel had recommended that her husband select an Englishman, one Father Edward Shoulderlock of Canterbury, for this position. She had known of him by reputation while at the court of King Henry and, in a brief meeting some years prior, she had noted that he was a keen judge of character and a man obsessed with order. She had learned that he was a respectful, thorough, and meticulous man, neither uncharitable nor unkind. She admitted two disadvantages, however, the least being a physical oddity that was a bit distracting and no doubt affected by the second.

The second disadvantage was one that some argued was actually salutary—a paradox not uncommon to many human qualities. It seemed the man was an extraordinary precisionist, a stickler for exactness to a degree that kept him in a nearly perpetual state of frustration. His lofty expectations of others were regularly denied by the realities of the fallen world, and the man found in each new day cause for hand-wringing and heavy sighs.

✳

It was a chilly day in late March 1194, when Sybil brought good news to her lady. She held the bundled, one-year-old Matilda tightly in her arms. "Countess, she is much better. The doctor said 'twas neither winter fever nor *la grippe*, but only a touch of coryza that ought to pass within the week. He's given me a tincture of camomile and Spanish fennel. Look, she smiles."

As if on cue, the child cooed and her mother brightened as she took her in her arms. "Ah, God be praised. I've prayed to St. Brigid all the night and read my Psalms all this morning." She kissed the golden cross—her wedding relic—hanging from her neck. "Thank you, as well, Sybil. You are a worthy nurse."

Sybil sank her slender body into a deep, respectful curtsy, nearly touching her long black braids to the floor. She turned her grey eyes downward and her porcelain skin pinked. A young widow of an errant-knight of Stokesay, she was now happily wed to the dashing Sir Alan de St. Georges. She loved children, and, like Aethel, had lost hers in their early years. One was taken by the pox, another to mortification from an injury at play. Unfortunately, she would have no more children. The Welsh raiders that had slain her first husband had pierced her body with an arrow and her injury had left her barren.

Isabel took Sybil by a hand and lifted her upright to embrace her. "My dear Sybil, thank you for thy good care. I am glad to call you my friend."

Aethel smiled from a close distance. She loved her lady dearly, but not with a possessive, jealous love. Her heart was large enough to be filled with affections that were neither conditional, nor self-serving, and she was pleased to share her friend with others.

Father Edward Shoulderlock suddenly appeared at Isabel's door. "Countess?"

Isabel turned and bade him enter. "*Oui*, Chamberlain."

"I am just arrived from Usk and am pleased to inform thee that all is in order, save a quarrel between the baker and a grooms-man."

Isabel smiled. "I assume the matter is now settled?"

"Yes, Madame. The groom remains in thy employ; the baker is dismissed. It was a rather tedious charge regarding missing oats and some loaves of coarse bread." He self-consciously snugged his mantle under his chin and shivered within his black robe. "I am not here to talk of these things, however, for I come with news. King

107

Richard has sent a messenger to thy husband. The King is to arrive at the port of Sandwich from France near mid-month and requests Lord William's attendance at court in Huntington. And, I should add, the house needs to be prepared for a long absence."

Aethel cried, "The King returns?"

"*Oui*, a blessed day, sister," Shoulderlock said. "But there is more, and I fear few among us will be pleased. The King has commanded the end of the siege at Windsor. Prince John is to be released on account of the King's pardon."

"Pardon?" Isabel was shocked. She handed Matilda to Sybil and cast a distracted eye to her two boys playing by the fire.

"*Oui*, m'lady. As one who has been forgiven much, King Richard is aware he is hardly able to deny others. As distasteful as it oft' is, *Madame*, it is Christian grace, nonetheless."

Aethel bristled. "Christian grace? 'Tis as foolhardy an error as I've e'er heard. John would have gladly mounted his brother's head on a spike by the Thames. Now he is given pardon?"

Isabel could only imagine her husband's outrage at the injustice. His royal troops had successfully contained John by besieging the traitor and his soldiers at Windsor all this cold winter past, only to be ordered to release the black heart without consequence. Even though William was a sworn vassal to John for lands in Ireland, he had nothing other than contempt for him. She shook her head, then remembered some words of old Father Adderig. With a low, almost reluctant voice she answered her friend. "Aethel, 'tis God's mercy that pardons us all." She sighed, heavily. "We ought not despise the forgiveness that Richard shows his brother."

The handmatron scowled. "I say m'rosaries and my pater nosters; I do all what's required—as do you. John does naught but evil."

Isabel smiled and took her friend by the hands. "Dear Aethel, what good we have done is good indeed, but hardly enough to commend us to a perfect God. We need to be thankful for the grace that pardons us, and we ought not to begrudge the grace that pardons Prince John."

All in the room were quiet and reflective for a long moment until Shoulderlock cleared his throat. With characteristic objectivity, he said, "I believe the crusade must have touched the King's heart, for if ever a man deserved the hangman, it is Prince John. While our Richard the Lionheart warred against the infidel, the treasonous scoundrel fell into league with the French and lied to all England that Richard was dead. God bless the barons; they held for the King."

Isabel nodded. "Like my husband, they do honour the King for his valour. They happily assent to his rule, for they know he serves the Cross well. I do confess, however, my astonishment that his crusade failed. I fear God did not go with them after all."

Shoulderlock folded his hands at his chest and sighed sadly. "I can not speak for God, but it would seem so. The German emperor was drowned. Richard and Philip quarrelled like schoolboys brawling for a comfit, while our Christian warriors poured their blood across all Palestine."

The Countess nodded. "Yes, *Père*, and for naught but a 'thin truce,' as my husband calls it. Then to have our King shipwrecked and imprisoned by the barbaric Germans."

"*Oui*, my lady, to think their Emperor Heinrich defied the pope and the tearful entreaties of all Christendom to satisfy a grudge and keep poor Richard in his dank cell. The barons paid a ransom of 150,000 marks to free the King—twice the crown's income for a year! I truly disdain this sort of disorder."

The Countess was well apprised of such matters, for William regularly shared the news of the world from his pillow. She nodded. "Prince John offered the German 80,000 marks to *keep* Richard under lock until Michaelmas, his own brother."

The chamberlain's face tightened and he spoke with a tone of harsh judgement. "John is as wicked a man as I have e'er known. I fear the Serpent darkened his soul long ago; he has become a man of trickery and deceit, faithlessness and betrayal. God be praised he is not King."

Shoulderlock became quiet and stared through the window of Isabel's room into the heavy, Welsh sky. "So, to other matters. Countess, I need to prepare for the journey. Aethel, thou need'st inform thy handservants we are to leave on the morrow next, at prime."

CHAPTER VIII

A JOURNEY AND A FRIGHT

FOR the next several hours Isabel's staff was a bustle of activity. They knew that once they left Chepstow, it would be certainly months, if not years, before they returned. Furniture would need to be readied for transport, while bedding, wardrobes, jewelry, and other personal effects would need to be packed securely into iron-strapped chests. It was a task requiring many hands.

The staff busied itself for several hours until, late in the afternoon, Lord William burst into his chamber. The man's eyes were red, his face tight and hard. He motioned stiffly for all to leave the chamber, save his wife. The man stood quietly, even patiently, as a flurry of silent handmaidens scurried past him and out the door. Sybil carried Matilda; Aethel dragged William the Younger and Richard in tow.

The great lord then faced Isabel for a long moment, saying nothing. He rarely revealed his heart, save for anger, but when it was filled with sadness, or with fear, with confusion, or with jealousy, such that he could barely contain it, he would finally empty himself within the privacy of his bedchamber. Isabel, saying nothing, waited wisely for her husband to speak first, and when he did, his heart gave way. "Oh, it cannot be so." He leaned into the soft embrace of his young wife.

Isabel stroked his greying hair and wrapped her small arms around his wide frame. "Tell me, dear husband," she whispered. "Tell me."

William slumped forward on the side of the bed and Isabel wiped his eyes and nose with a kerchief and kissed his cheek. "My brother John—is dead." At the sound of his own words his eyes swelled again.

Isabel groaned. Though the two men had little contact, John

was William's only living family and he loved him dearly. She remembered them laughing and romping like little boys just two years prior when William was passing through Lancashire.

"He died in Marlborough and is to be buried in Cirencester. I have sent knights to escort his body and his widow, and we must hurry to follow. I am summoned by the King as well."

Isabel was confused. "But, sire, surely the King can wait a few days. Surely he would understand a brief delay to bury thy brother."

William stood. His wife's words offended him and he suddenly composed himself. "My duty is to my King first; it is to him I have pledged my sword." His words were delivered with an unnecessary bite, as if to chastise his wife for tempting his honour. But the look on her face gave him pause. His tone softened and his eyes drifted off of hers as they cooled. "He needs to attack a remnant of John's rebels at Nottingham; I must be at his side." He turned to the window and opened the shutter. The cold, damp air of a Welsh March blasted into the room, scattering ashes from the hearth. The man stared blankly at the grey sky before turning to his wife. "I love you, Isabel, but 'tis only you I love more than my King."

The woman's eyes moistened and she embraced the man. The two held each other for a quiet moment; for Isabel it was as if the world had vanished. She lost herself in the beating of her husband's heart and the rising of his body as he breathed. She did not understand the man's passion for duty, but she felt his love of her and she thanked Heaven for it.

With a kiss on her head, William turned and vanished into the bowels of the castle. Isabel sat on her bed and clutched her heart, happily. To be loved by such a man as William filled her with warmth and so softened her that she wanted to sing to all the world. She closed her eyes and fell backwards upon the soft blankets of her yet unpacked mattress and her mind whirled joyfully— until the words of the curse crept into her thoughts. She sat upright with a start. Aethel and Sybil entered the room to find their terrified lady staring wide-eyed into empty space.

"Oh, dear Countess, what is wrong?" exclaimed Aethel.

Isabel said nothing.

Sybil laid her hand tenderly on Isabel's. "M'lady, can we help?"

Isabel turned her eyes into Sybil's. She took a light hold of one of Sybil's black braids. "I see his black robe and his black eyes."

The servants looked at each other anxiously. "Whose?" asked Aethel.

"The priest, the Scottish priest." Isabel stood and wrung her hands. She suddenly looked frantically about the room. "Where are my children?" she cried.

Sybil pointed to young William and Richard playing in a dark corner, to Matilda lying in her cradle.

"Forgive me," said Isabel in a low tone. "It–it is that devil's curse. I think of it often—it follows me wherever I am."

"That blasted Scot. If only I could, I'd pull his little head off." Aethel shook her fist in the air. "Forget his nonsense; it means nothing."

Isabel's chin quivered. "I fear it does; I saw his eyes. 'A sword from heaven's gate shall fly with wings that none can stay; its edge shall split thee from thy love and tear thy heart away.' Oh Aethel, dear Sybil, 'tis William whom I love—William and these children. Should any of these perish by sword, my heart would be surely torn."

Aethel and Sybil had nothing to say. The servants all knew the curse, the whole of it—and it had been a matter of argument for some time. None could decipher its meaning, but all had the wisdom to never discuss it in their lady's presence. Matilda began to cry and Sybil hurried to lift her. Young William and Richard began to quarrel and Aethel ran to them. The room slowly filled with others returning to their chores. At last, the sombre Countess walked away to stare over the ramparts of Chepstow Castle.

❄

The journey to Cirencester was hurried, though uneventful.

Lord William's entourage crossed the Severn on several ferries, then proceeded due west into the wooded humps, the rushing streams, and rolling pastures of the Cotswolds. Time did not permit Isabel to satisfy her curiosity over the strange stone circles that rose in the open fields. Though the names of places like The Devil's Quoits, Goose Stone, and The Rollright Stones enlivened her imagination, she dared not ask her husband to tarry. In fairness, Lord William denied himself his desire to detour to the Templar preceptory in Bisham. Instead, he pressed his entourage forward until they finally arrived at the Cirencester abbey.

Here the lord sought out his brother's widow and paid his proper respects. He then made his way to his brother's corpse where he grieved quietly for a short time. Yet, his honour demanded he follow a higher duty, that to the King to whom he had given homage. Messengers from Richard had been awaiting his arrival, and now pleaded with him to hurry to the King's side. "Lord William," said one, bowing. "The King begs thy presence with him at once. He's waiting at Huntington; he is in need of Thy sword."

William Marshal's grey eyes turned to fired steel. *Needs my sword?* These were the words more dear than any others. He let them ring in his head.

Isabel knew the look. "Take my leave, lord husband, and go with God." She removed the relic from around her neck and hung it over William's. "Your children and I shall follow quickly."

William refused the golden cross politely and kissed his wife tenderly with one eye on his waiting mount. He donned his mail coat and heavy helmet, snatched a lance from the armourer and secured his belt and sword. "Until Nottingham then," he stated. His voice was sharp and excited. William turned to Baldwin and pointed to a newly acquired knight, his nephew, Sir John Marshal, the son of his deceased brother. "Baldwin, send him and two others with my brother's body to the priory at Bradenstoke. Let them bury the man, let young John give his mother comfort, then have them join us in Nottingham. Call de St. Georges and Sir Ralph. They will ride with me to Huntington. You and the others escort the household to Nottingham where we shall meet."

With his military house in order, he paced about impatiently, searching for the chamberlain. "Isabel, where is Shoulderlock?"

"Here, sir; here he comes."

At the sight of Father Edward parading towards him, Lord William grumbled. He had trusted Isabel's advice on the selection—he nearly always trusted her advice—but watching the man never failed to draw a rolled eye, a flush of embarrassment, or an occasional chuckle from whomever was near. Poor Shoulderlock had been born with an odd and rather distracting gait. While walking, or worse yet, while running, the long-limbed man's arms failed to swing. It was as if they were locked at his shoulders and had earned him his surname. Added to that was an unfortunate high lift to each step! Isabel had kindly advised the man to walk with his hands folded at his belly, as if in prayer. "You would look thoughtful and collected," she had said charitably.

"Chamberlain," barked William.

"*Oui*, m'lord?"

"Prepare my household. You must hurry to Nottingham."

"*Oui*, m'lord. Shall we have accommodations at Nottingham Castle?"

"Ha! Indeed we shall."

"Very good, sire. I shall send a messenger to Steward Roger now at Kilkenny. He shall be pleased that Nottingham is finally to be freed from John."

"Indeed, chamberlain. Also tell him I need a full accounting of the villages throughout my Irish lands. I need to know what sort of rebellion there I ought to expect."

William's entourage was large and growing larger as the man acquired more holdings and the courtiers who came with them. The lord was travelling with about thirty knights as well as their squires, valets, and groomsmen. Lord Baldwin quickly put good order to his men, but Shoulderlock had a more difficult task.

The chamberlain needed to quickly assemble the domestic travelling household, which numbered around eighty persons, not counting the children of the lord, his knights, and the servants. Supplies and transport for over one hundred souls required a great deal of organisation. Pack horses were used to carry the lord's household goods. These included Lord William's dismantled bed, his sheets, mattress, and heavy blankets.

The forlorn beasts were also laden with the lesser chattels of the greater household: the wardrobes of both the lord and his entourage, the contents of the buttery—the household beverages, kitchen utensils, the portable altar, and vestments. Squat, lumbering carts of either two or four solid wheels were stacked with foodstuffs, furniture, weapons, and armour. None rode within the wagons save the carters who drove them, for it was uncomfortable and considered a disgrace. Only young children, the very old, the infirmed, or prisoners rode in these springless, groaning boxes, the rest riding atop comfortable saddles or in padded, canvas-covered carriages.

Isabel was dressed in a warm outer-gown and a heavy wool cloak. Her head was covered in an otter hat and her hands kept warm within rabbit mittens. The day was sunny, so she refused her carriage in favour of her horse, upon which she sat side-saddle. Her mount was a young, bay-coloured hunter, standing nearly sixteen hands and sleek, bright-eyed, and dependable. Lord William had won the mare in a joust a year after his wedding.

The other women and the male servants rode atop palfreys or hunters of lesser breeding, while the knights pranced along on their magnificent war-horses—their chargers. Lord William's favourite was a huge white stallion with blazing eyes and high-stepping black feet. He was another of the lord's conquests at tournament.

Considering the value of horseflesh, the knights and their grooms had quite a responsibility as well. The common palfreys cost their lord about one mark each—a month's wages for a skilled tradesman. The knights' chargers cost nearly five times that amount. Added to that was the cost of harnesses and saddles, iron shoes, armoured hoods, and stirrups.

So, just hours after Lord William and two of his knights had dashed away to meet King Richard, Sir Baldwin took his place at the head of the assembled column and led it forward. The Marshal household wound its way along the ridgeways of the Cotswolds, north past Gloucester, into the orchard-filled Vale of Evesham, and along the Avon River. The weather was remarkably dry, though a bit cold, and the roads were hard and easy to pass. Sir Baldwin kept a hasty pace in order to take every advantage of the weather, and succeeded in covering between fifteen and twenty miles a day—an astonishing rate, considering most such columns did little more than twelve.

It was the chamberlain's responsibility to send procurement agents ahead of the retinue. These *herberjurs* were responsible to billet the company from night to night and when they failed, they were the ones to bear the news that the night would be spent under canvas! As monasteries were the preferred accommodation for travelling lords, Shoulderlock's agents did what they could to open the doors at the cloister of Pershore.

Roger, Lord William's almoner, assured the resident monks that his master would be more than generous and the company spent a comfortable night eating good wheat bread and drinking stout English ale in the refectory. The following night they were less fortunate, for the castellan of Warwick refused hospitality. The third provided the knights a comfortable stay in Coventry, though the servants found themselves scrambling for cover amid the squalor of the town's hovels.

The fourth night brought an altercation between William's knights and a larger band of knights belonging to a baron named Lord Hugh fitz Gerald of East Anglia. Both travelling retinues stumbled upon the hapless monastery of Leicester at nearly the same time. To the dismay of Lady Isabel, swords were drawn and blood was spilled upon the cloister's gate. A company of armed monks emerged, their prior at the fore. They drove a determined black wedge between the combatants and enforced the peace at the price of one obstinate squire's life.

The fifth night found the Countess's entourage camped under canvas in the pouring rain within the safe bounds of King Richard's army and the weakening walls of Nottingham Castle. Lord William was happy to greet his wife and to salute his knights. "Good fellows, we can use more arms. And my lady, you look a bit white."

Isabel nodded. She had been feeling sick over much of the

journey, vomiting each morning. "I think I am with child, lord husband."

William smiled and pulled his helmet from his head. He shook his hair and wiped the rain from his face. "*Oui*? Wonderful! Another lad, perhaps?"

Aethel ducked under the tent and curtsied reluctantly to her lord. "Sire, the lady is weary." The servant was cold and wet, sore from a week's travelling, and out-of-sorts. William scowled. It was the look of one whom few should cross, and Aethel shuddered. "Oh, begging pardon, my lord, I–I—"

Isabel cast an imploring look at William and the man softened. He reached into a satchel and tossed Aethel a sweet cake. "Stolen from the King's pantry," he quipped.

Aethel smiled. Relieved and repentant, she thanked her master and removed herself. Sybil then entered with Matilda in her arms, and young William and Richard following.

William brightened. "Ah, let me see them." He knelt to face William the Younger, and as he did, his wet, leather leggings squeaked and his mail coat jingled. The four-year-old smiled. "Hello, daddy."

The knight embraced the blond-haired lad. "Ah, hello, good fellow. Let me see your eyes." William peered deeply into his son's blue eyes. "They've my fire, but thy mother's wisdom." He felt the boy's arms and shoulders. "Strong and lean; warriors arms for sure." He turned to Richard. "Look at you." He patted Richard's white-haired head, then reached for Matilda. He lifted her to the sky. "Someday, you shall be wed to the finest knight in all Christendom."

A messenger entered the tent and summoned William to the King's council. "Tomorrow, sire, tomorrow we storm the ramparts."

Isabel chilled.

❋

Dawn delivered a damp fog through King Richard's camp,

but the clouds above had begun to retreat and a clear day was breaking. The wet, April grass had been laid flat by horse hooves and wagons, and a heavy dew lay atop the canvas tents. Morning campfires drifted a lingering, eye-stinging smoke through the encampment as yawning, belching, stretching soldiers ambled to the latrines before preparing for battle.

Lord William hastily donned his leather leggings, padded under-tunic, and knee-length mail coat. Atop this he placed his sleeveless robe, then tightened his thick sword-belt around his waist and reached for his helmet and his shield. Ready to lead his knights on behalf of the King, William first kissed his wife and children.

Lady Isabel dreaded these moments like no others. She feigned calm as she straightened her husband's belt and un-kinked his armour. She picked over him like a young mare grooming her colt, then took his face in her hands and said a prayer. As he left the tent, she fell to her knees, clutching her relic and praying hard against the curse.

The grooms held the war-horses as William's knights climbed into their large saddles. Baldwin presented the mounted line and William rode before them proudly. Each of his knights was clothed in his lord's robes—the well-respected yellow and green panels with their red lion. Above their heads fluttered William Marshal's matching herald flag. The great knight paused to seek out young John d'Erley, the squire, standing behind the horses. "You there, lad."

"Aye, sire."

"Mount; you ride with us today."

To the cheers of his comrades, John's eyes went wide and his mouth fell open. He ran to the armorer and quickly pulled a mail shirt and coif over his head and torso. He added a new helmet—a flat-topped pot helmet with a visor and thin eye slits. He grabbed a sword and a lance. "Ready. I am ready, my lord."

As the sun drove the mist away, Lord William thundered forward to join his King and the army assembling before the castle's walls. There, an excited Richard welcomed his troops for battle.

The man lived for combat; it was war that pumped through his veins, not the affairs of court, and certainly not the intrigue of courtiers. The King enjoyed the company of women and took delight in fine wine, but it was the comradeship of men in steel, galloping hard through flying arrows and singing bolts that gave the man life.

Richard ordered his knights into a tight cluster a little more than a bowshot from Nottingham's ramparts. To each side he aligned rows of footmen and archers. Three catapults had finally arrived from service in nearby Lincoln and were loaded with heavy boulders capable of breaking great holes in the castle walls or smashing down the gates and interior portcullis.

Chivalry required he offer quarter one more time to the rebel barons within. They had been abandoned by Prince John, who had been pardoned and was now pouting in France. But they were a stubborn lot, and had imagined they might soon see the flags of King Philip marching over England's green to their rescue. Instead, they peered through the gaps of their battlements forlornly, facing, instead, the siege cannons of King Richard and a whole company riding under the banner of the dreaded William Marshal.

The royal army rustled impatiently. Like a heaving stallion pawing near a trembling mare its restless flanks tensed and strained, ready to bolt towards its prize. "The fools had better not yield," growled Richard. "My blade grows dull in boredom."

William surveyed his men and gave a steadying smile to John d'Erley. "A good day for you, lad," he chortled.

John looked awkward in his armour. He raised his visor and smiled nervously at his lord. "Aye, sire. Any day is good when a man follows you to battle."

His fellows roared their approval. But suddenly King Richard shouted blasphemies to Heaven. "By the saints, no. May the cowards ne'er forget their shame." A white flag had been run up the castle tower.

To loud oaths and jeers the castle's gates opened slowly and from within its walls drifted the dejected defenders. The disappointed King's men pounced upon them and immediately stripped them of their weapons, horses, servants, and valuable armour. They would soon be disenfranchised from their lands as well, and would become the vassals of others.

Flying to Sir William's side, the King roared, "I'd rather have cut them to pieces."

"Aye, sire, but the day is won, nonetheless."

Richard spat. "True enough. But I'd have rather won it with steel."

With a wave, Lord Marshal reined his horse and ordered his men to return to camp where they would celebrate King Richard's final victory. With Prince John defeated and the French King still at bay, Lionheart was now the unchallenged ruler of England, the Duke of Normandy, and the sovereign of much of France.

✷

Night fell quickly and, while a much relieved Isabel went to her guest chamber within the occupied wall of Nottingham Castle, King Richard bade Lord William and his knights to the feast in the Great Hall. For hours the wine poured freely and laughter reigned. Poultry and venison steamed in mounds atop silver trays, and pots of rolling stews drew wild applause. Loaves of hearty bread and jars of honey were pilfered from the pantry, as a handful of minstrels played their lutes and beat their kettles. A half-dozen tumblers, fools, and jesters romped throughout, stealing hats, spilling wine, and doing tricks. *Jongleurs*, recently imported from the courts of France, sang songs and recited poems of love and war. Atop wooden roosts and a few forearms perched hooded falcons, and high above fluttered several popinjays and two bright parrots. A half-dozen or so hounds roamed about the rush-strewn floor and the King played endlessly with two monkeys sent as gifts from Philip.

William was eager for the night to proceed. He had a surprise in store for one his most beloved fellows. Finally, sometime around midnight he bade the King stand with him and as the two raised their hands, the hall hushed. The very sight of the King, the *Coeur de Lion*, inspired his barons with admiration. He was the glorious veteran of Holy Crusade, a dashing, moustached warrior of unquestioned courage, the grand adventurer—Richard the Lionhearted.

Beside him stood Lord William, the royal marshal, tall and proud like grey granite. He was the unhesitating soldier, the honourable Christian knight, the very flower of chivalry.

"Brothers," cried King Richard. "Hear us. We call before you the squire, John d'Erley."

At the far end of the long table, the twenty-year-old's eyes widened with a start. His heart began to beat. *Could it be? And by the King's own sword?* he wondered. The young man stood and began a nervous walk forward.

With a wave from Richard's hand, a row of trumpeters blasted three notes, each for a member of the Holy Trinity. John's mouth felt dry, his legs went weak but he walked slowly past the welcoming eyes of men otherwise hardened by war. John arrived before his master and his King, humbly and without a word.

Williams's eyes were searching the hall. He turned to Baldwin and whispered, "Where is my new chancellor? Isabel assured me he would be here for this."

"He's arrived just hours ago. He was clearly instructed to be here after matins."

"Matins? The bells are long since rung. I wanted this to go well."

"Aye, sire." Baldwin's voice quieted to a low whisper. "I should warn you, however, your new chancellor is a bit—"

A titter rolled through the hall and William strained to hear. "What? He is what?"

Two hooded figures dressed in black robes entered the far archway. From William's vantage the first was easy to identify as Shoulderlock. The other was a dwarf, not much taller than a grown man's thigh. William turned a hard eye to Baldwin. "Tell me I am seeing a jester in priests' robes."

Baldwin shook his head. "Nay, sire, 'tis thy new chancellor."

121

William gawked at the pair hurrying towards him. "*Sacre Bleu*," he mumbled. "My house will ne'er be the same."

King Richard leaned towards him with a smile. "Lord William. A jest?"

"Nay, m'lord. It would be my new chancellor."

Richard's eyebrows lifted and his moustache raised at the corners. "I dare say, good fellow, but they seem a rather odd pair." He snickered. The hall's titters turned to chuckles and a few loud guffaws.

For his part, the flush-faced Lord William wished he might blame this embarrassment on his wife. *She told me she had found the very best of both offices. Indeed. A gangly, strutting goose and a runt of runts. Oh, Shoulderlock, you fool, swing your blasted arms—and—and don't step on the little fellow.*

His frustration restrained, the man stood stiff as hard timber until the pair of priests arrived to face both King and lord. Each bowed respectfully and lowered their hoods. The King returned the bow, albeit a bit embellished and with a whimsical grin.

Shoulderlock leaned forward and grumbled, "Lord William, thy pardon for our tardy arrival. *He* was late. *He* claims he was distracted by some book."

The King and Lord William turned four eyes on the dwarf.

"My King," the new chancellor bowed. "I do beg thy leave." His voice was surprisingly resonant and rather strong; his words were offered with respect but with a quality of pluck that caught William's attention.

The King and William waited but that was all the little priest would say. Lord William cleared his throat and bent low to face his new officer. He rallied his courtesy. "I, *Père*, am thy Lord William Marshal."

"Indeed, sire. So I supposed by thy great height and advanced age."

William gawked.

The chancellor bowed and extended his small hand until it was swallowed by the giant grasp of the great knight. "I, Sir William, am blessed to be thy chancellor, *Père* Hubert fitz

William. However, it gives me pleasure to be called quite simply, *Le Court*."

Le Court? Lord William nodded and stood upright. He filled his chest with a deep breath. *Oh, Isabel,* he groaned inwardly. As chancellor, this fellow would have a highly visible position—an equal rank with the chamberlain, each serving just beneath the Marshal's steward. It would be this priest's responsibility to shepherd the souls of the lord's household, manage all things related to liturgy, relics, and vestments, and provide secretarial duties. William had only ever seen dwarves leaping about as jesters in the court. He shook his head, unaware of the amazing difference the fellow might someday make.

CHAPTER IX

SIR JOHN, THE DWARF, AND THE JOURNEY

LE COURT now stood alongside his lord, barely taller than William's belt. His arms were misshapen, his legs a bit squat, and his rump tilted upwards, but his face was made pleasing by intelligent brown eyes and his manner was winsome. Quite aware of his lord's shock and the surprise of the gathered guests, Le Court climbed awkwardly atop the table and bowed to the King once more. "With permission, sire." He then faced the assembly and raised his hands. "I greet thee, every one, in the name of our Lord Christ. I am *Père* Hubert fitz William, known better as simply, Le Court—the Small One."

The hall filled with a low rumble of muffled mumbles. Humility of character expressed so publicly exposed deep confidence and no little reserve of courage. The knights in the hall recognized these virtues at once.

The tiny chancellor continued. "I am quite aware of my limitations, but equally certain of what good gifts God's grace has granted. It is my great joy to serve King Richard the Lionhearted." He grabbed a goblet and filled it with wine. "So, first, to our good King."

The knights stood and toasted Richard.

"And next, to my new lord, Sir William Marshal."

The hall resounded with a great hurrah.

Le Court lifted his goblet once more. "And now to the purpose of my presence, all hail Squire John."

❉

William was now moved to admiration. *Such courage one does not oft' see*, he thought. *The fellow stands to face a hall of war-*

riors without shame and without fear. William bade the chancellor take a place to one side, and turned to John d'Erley who had been standing patiently to one side. The great knight had been looking forward to this moment for almost as long as the young man now waiting breathlessly before him. "Squire John, come here, before us," William boomed. "Sir Baldwin, the cloth and the sword." The hall fell quiet and all faces stared eagerly towards the ceremony now beginning.

Following William's lead, King Richard moved to a position directly in front of the squire. He drew his war-battered sword dramatically and laid it atop a wooden chest filled with miracle-granting relics—bits of bone from ancient martyrs, the chasuble and alb of St. Edmund the Confessor, the dried blood of St. George, and a bit of hair from St. Peter. He bade Le Court say a prayer and a mighty one was offered. The King then grasped the sword's long handle in both hands and pointed the blade upward to touch it to his lips. In a booming voice he then suspended the flat of the sword over Squire John's head. "In the name of Christ and to the glory of God, I, King Richard of England, do dub thee Sir John d'Erley, knight of the realm." The King touched the sword to John's shoulders and head. "Arise, Sir John."

The proud new knight was beaming. He bowed to the King and received a kiss, then turned to his lord and embraced him.

Lord William took another sword from Baldwin. "Now, *Sir* John d'Erley, bend to thy knees once more."

The hall fell quiet and the young man knelt before his liege lord and prepared to become his vassal. William held the long sword horizontally by each end and stretched his arms towards John. He then lowered it into John's opened palms with a loud voice, crying, "Receive this, my sword, to be sworn in defence of all lands to which thou shalt pledge thy fealty."

Still kneeling, John accepted the marshal's sword. He held it out as Le Court moved to William's side. The chancellor laid a hand upon the blade, and prayed in a strong, clear voice: "Almighty Father in Heaven, cast Thine eyes kindly upon this, Thy servant. Dispose his heart towards righteousness, lift his arm in defence of the good, be his Shield against all evil. Let this, Thy sword of Heaven, be borne for only that which is right and good. *In nomine Patris, et Filii, et Spiritus Sancti,* Amen."

William then took a razor and shaved the crown of the lad's head like the tonsure of the clerics, symbolizing the man's devotion to God. He then wrapped John in a white robe for purity, a red robe for his willingness to die for righteousness, and a black robe to signify his willingness to accept death.

Le Court prayed again.

William returned to his position directly in front of the kneeling knight. He removed the sword from John's palms and handed it to Baldwin. John then placed his hands together and held them upright between the hands of William. "Sir John d'Erley," began William, "under God I do swear with all my heart to defend thee, thy household, and the property I shall grant thee. Dost thou swear thy troth under God; dost thou so swear thyself in defence of my household, my person, and my property against all enemies, save those shielded by thy honour?"

John assented boldly. "I do so swear, my lord."

"Dost thou, Sir John, then pledge thy fealty to me?"

"I do sire, and to no other in favour, save the King."

Pleased, William lifted his new vassal to his feet and kissed him. With weeping eyes the new knight then turned to face the thunderous approval of his comrades.

In the days to come, William would enfeof John with lands of his own, but for now he presented him with the "ward robe" of his *mesnie*. He first removed the three ceremonial garments and donned his vassal with the herald robe of the Marshal's men. He then gave him a golden spur, a golden ring, and his sword, now sheathed and suspended from a wide leather belt. It was a good day for Lord William and a good day for John d'Erley—a very good day, indeed.

※

"But must we, lord husband?"

"*Oui*, it is as the King bids."

"But I am newly with child and the crossing shall be difficult."

William looked at his wife sympathetically. "Yes, 'tis true enough. You might go to our manor house in Crendon, but if you must remain behind, I'd prefer you to be closer to the port. I shall demand hospitality from Lord Raimond de Cluny near Pevensey, or from the monks at Battle Abbey near Hastings."

Isabel was quiet. In the five years of her marriage she had been rarely apart from her husband. She reasoned that it was mid-summer and the Channel crossing should be quiet, after all. The sea did frighten her a little, though, and this pregnancy had already proven to be uncomfortable. She thought for a moment, then looked into her husband's imploring grey eyes. *He loves me so*, she thought. Isabel smiled. "Sir William, I would like very much to sail with you."

William brightened. "Good. It is settled then. I shall inform Shoulderlock that we must prepare to sail within a fortnight."

Father Edward was soon scurrying about the accommodations at Nottingham Castle preparing to vacate the chambers that the household had occupied for the last four months. He had secretly hoped to be returned to Chepstow so that he might confer with the Steward Roger, recently returned from a miserable time in Ireland. Shoulderlock wanted to review the provisions being consumed at a seemingly alarming rate by the travelling *mesnie*, as well as a request by William to procure more art for his various manor houses. In addition, he wanted to discreetly discuss his objections to the disorderly behaviours of one Chancellor Le Court.

The diminutive chancellor had made a powerful impression on the Marshal household. While the lord's retinue had been in Nottingham, he had not only served the family well, but he had also managed to tour William's castles and manors in Cartmel, Lancashire, the Netherwent of Wales, Weston in Hertfordshire, Parndon, and Chesterford, as well as the abbey in Tintern, of which William had become the patron. He wisely postponed a trip to the Irish estates, though he was excited to sail to the mysterious lands of Patrick and Columba. At each stop, Le Court endeared himself to the local stewards and the household priests through his quick wit and charity.

It was his unusual ways that had attracted the Countess to him. Though born in Normandy and educated in Rome, he was not like most priests. He had told Isabel that the pope's personal chapel, the Holy of Holies in the Lateran Palace, had held no special charm for him. "My own favourite chapel is a good oak on a hill by Pembroke!" he had told her once. "The pope bends the knee midst relics of every imaginable type—even the very crown of Christ—yet he can not feel God's breath in the wind, nor feel His kindness under the sun." The words had made her smile, for they reminded her of something Father Adderig might have said. "And more—I'd sooner climb the cliffs at Chepstow than mount those blasted twenty-eight Holy Stairs upon my bony knees!" Isabel had laughed all that night as she pictured the tiny man attempting to stretch one knee above the other on those cold, marble steps.

Le Court had returned a fortnight past and was sleeping under the summer sun when the Countess approached. "Good day, Chancellor."

The priest was sprawled on his back atop good English grass and snoring. "Eh?"

"I say, good day, Chancellor."

Le Court hopped to his feet and bowed. He was sprightly for a man in his mid-thirties. "My lady, so good to see you."

"I've heard wonderful reports of your travels to our houses. Thank you."

Le Court blushed, and bowed again. "I fear Shoulderlock is annoyed with me again. I lost a barrel of red wine and three quills, two geese and a swan. I really have no memory of how I lost them."

Isabel smiled. The chancellor was more than eccentric, he was sometimes absent-minded and easily distracted. "My husband has requested Steward Roger to acquire more art for our homes—French tapestries, goldware from Italy, and silver from England. I fear Roger lacks skill, and is in need of some direction.

Perhaps you might send a messenger to Chepstow before our departure?"

Le Court smiled. He loved art, music, and fine food. The only things he did not enjoy were warfare and order. "The ancients of Rome and Greece knew of beauty, as do the Celts. My grandfather was a Breton, so I suppose that is what accounts for my own passion for things beautiful. I do cherish their eye for God's artistry. Have you e'er seen the Irish *Book of Kells?*"

Lady Isabel shivered. She suddenly remembered King Henry's dream. "*Non, Père.*"

The chancellor put his fists on his hips. "Then either I shall borrow it, take thee to Kildare to see it, or I shall so describe it as you might think it is held by thy hand. 'Tis a glorious masterpiece of Celtic art—knots and swirls, the psalms and prayers—all in magnificent colours. Some think it is art by no human hand at all, but rather of the angels."

Isabel answered quietly. "It sounds wonderful." Beautiful things in the midst of a troubled world always gave her hope.

"*Oui.* It is wonderful. I've seen it three times. But, to answer your question: indeed, I shall instruct Steward Roger on the essence of beauty in such a way that even his fool's eye might spot a glimmer of it! I fear, however, that it is you who ought to acquire these things and allow the steward to busy himself collecting taxes and counting money."

"And why so, sir?"

Le Court led the lady through Nottingham Castle to a small office in which he kept his travelling desk, an ample store of parchment, quills, and ink, and a chest filled with a treasured collection he had gathered over his lifetime. Along the way, he explained. "Beauty consists of four primary constants. These are, first, allegory. Allegory is the expression of eternal truths in outer forms. Art should always contain some element of truth.

"Second is symbolism, and that, dear Countess is thine own heart's expression. We each *feel* the Creation around us in our own way. The art of thy household needs to reflect what you feel.

"The third constant is proportion, that being a balance to

the eye. As in music, art of all forms needs to bear a mathematical relationship that is pleasing. I do confess this is of the least pleasure to me, as I prefer the disorder of a whirlwind.

"The fourth and final constant, dear sister, is brilliance of colour! I *do* love this one so. God is light, so what light that shines through bold colours is nothing less than bits of God, as it were. He reigns in Heaven and shall on earth again. We must proclaim His glory in the *radiance* of our art.

"So, if you must send the dull Roger, at least send him forth with a firm command to seek bright colour, in good form, that reveals his lady's heart, and God's ways."

The Countess clapped. "Ah, good Father, you are wonderful."

The chancellor smiled, pleased with himself. In an effort to salvage his humility he pointed to a large open chest by his desk. "Countess, in there lay things truly wonderful—the thoughts of men far wiser and with minds more keen to splendid things than mine."

Isabel walked slowly to the chest and stared at a pile of scrolls, most made of parchment, but a few of expensive vellum—a sheet of calf skin. With a timid look that prompted a nod from grinning Le Court, she reached a hand to grasp the first scroll.

"Please, my lady. Open it."

The Countess unrolled a sand-coloured parchment and scanned the fine Latin script. "*The Song of Roland?*" she exclaimed.

"*Oui*, at least a few lines of it. What you see are my copies of many wondrous books that I've found in monasteries and cathedrals all over Christendom. Some have come from returning Crusaders; others are from the ancient times of Christendom.

"My early days were those of a copyist in the cloister at Cluny, so I learned to move my quill quickly. When I have visited Paris, or Rouen, Canterbury, Oxford, Milan, or even Rome, I have always taken time to locate a great book and copy a portion for this little *scriptorium* in a box."

Isabel's eyes sparkled. "I never knew. 'Tis wonderful, just wonderful."

Le Court plunged his hands deeply into his chest of scrolls, sinking his arms to the elbow like a happy miser playing with his gold. He lifted a bundle of parchments to his chest and stood grinning from ear to ear like a schoolboy showing off an armload of fresh-caught fish. "All of these I share with you," he said. "Please, come whenever it pleases you and read; read what I have discovered—'tis magic."

The Countess opened one, then another. The chancellor had copied pages of works dating from antiquity to modern times. "Here," said Isabel. "It must be from Plato's *Republic*—and here, *The Argonautica*. I've only heard of these in King Henry's court; I never imagined I might read from them."

Le Court beamed. "And see, here, m'lady. Here is Lucan's *Pharsalia*, and—and here is one of my favourites, *The Life of King Alfred*, by Bishop Asser of Sherborne."

"You enjoy King Alfred?"

"*Oui*, I love him—and England's past. We've much to learn from him and his times."

"When I tell Aethel she may kiss you on the lips for saying such a thing," Isabel laughed. She was excited. Her days in the Tower had been well spent with tutors who had taught her the wonder of literature, the value of history, and the delights of poetry. She had learned to read well and only wished her husband could share in that joy. Isabel opened one after the other and began to see a pattern of interest. "So, you enjoy history?" she asked.

"Indeed, Countess. It gives us eyes for where we've been so we better know our future course. I am particularly taken with the history of politics and the state."

Isabel was suddenly disappointed. It was a subject of some interest, but the schemes, the trickery, the artifice, and the subterfuge of life at court had soured her to the subject. "I see," she answered politely.

Her tone did not go unnoticed. Le Court smiled. "So, you've little interest in such things. Well, in time I think you shall warm to them."

"I do like history and King Henry oft' talked of the monarchs past and their ways. I listened and I learned, but it seemed to matter little, for I had no matter of power or influence of my own to wield."

Le Court listened and nodded. He looked at Isabel with a penetrating eye. "My lady, dear sister, I believe King Henry may have planted seeds for a later harvest. Thy lord husband may play a role in England's future. A wise and informed wife would be a great advantage to him! So, please, come to my chamber at whate'er time pleases thee and read whatever you wish. Make the effort to read that which does not at first delight you. You may find thine eyes taken by that which you did not expect."

Isabel smiled.

The chancellor then bent over his library and dug through his parchments until his hand settled on one that he held high overhead. "'The Countess is worth as many queens as the cost of a gem in pearls and sards.'"

Isabel blushed lightly and chuckled. "You are quoting from a verse?"

"*Oui*, m'lady. A new work from the court of France. I copied the first part a year prior. It is titled *Le Chevalier de la Charrette*, and it was written by Chrétien de Troyes. What a wonderful story—with only a pinch of politics." Le Court winked. "I think you should take it with you."

The Countess took the unopened scroll with a curtsy. "Many thanks, good *Père*. I shall enjoy it on our voyage to Normandy."

※

A messenger had been sent from Wales with sad news, but he was having great difficulty finding the Marshal family, now hurrying on their way to Dover. Lord William's retinue had paused only at two sites, the first being the Canterbury Cathedral. The lord thought it to be an important stop since Canterbury had been the seat of the Church in England for centuries. Christianity, of course, had come to Britain by way of the Romans, but upon the collapse of the Roman Empire its preservation was left to the Celtic Church. Centuries later, Pope Gregory had seen Angle slaves for sale in the Holy City. He had been so struck by their fair beauty that he had cried that they were 'angels, not Angles' and sent Augustine with a band of monks to England. Canterbury soon became the foundation stone for the Roman Church's ultimate domination of all Britain.

In addition, the cathedral in Canterbury housed the holy remains of Saint Thomas Becket which had been quickly claimed as a source of miracles. Pilgrims from all over Christendom were now flocking to the cathedral in search of hope.

Lady Isabel entered the crypt with scores of pilgrims and fell to her knees, flanked by Aethel and Sybil. Nearby knelt Lord William, John d'Erley, Le Court, Shoulderlock, and a row of lessers. The Countess prayed earnestly at the wall of the sarcophagus, peering through its two small openings at the bones of the murdered saint. Isabel could not help but grieve at the sight, for here were the remains of the man her beloved King Henry had suffered over. It was his angry remarks that had inspired four wicked knights to slaughter the archbishop near this very place.

After the brief delay, the entourage then travelled some seventeen miles over flat roadways dotted with fish carts and peddlers until they arrived, without incident, for their second pause at the preceptory of Temple Ewell some three miles north-west of Dover. The preceptory was a two-storey keep made of flint and mortar, and finished with stone from Caen. This and the buildings surrounding it provided the monks with strongholds for their own defence as well as the mounting treasuries of silver they guarded for others.

Isabel watched as her husband dismounted to confirm their arrangements for the night's stay. She was sometimes jealous of her husband's affection for the Templars whom he loved like no other body of men on earth. Some said his love for them surpassed all other loves. The Order of the Knight's Templar had filled all Palestine with courageous warrior-monks who were devout for the faith, steadfast in battle, and charitable in peace. Isabel knew her rival for the man's heart would never be another woman, but rather the honour, the valour, the piety, and camaraderie represented by the Templar sword and robe.

Yet unaware of the pursuing messenger, Lord William's entourage resumed their journey the day following and soon entered the port town of Dover where they were quartered in the nearby priory of St. Martin's-le-Grand. Here they waited for the heavy rains and unfavourable winds to abate before they could board their ships bound for St. Valery on the coast of Normandy. It was here where Isabel began hearing whispers at night, whispers that filled her with dread.

❈

Three days later, morning finally broke bright and blue over Dover and a dusty rider dismounted in front of Sir William. It was the determined messenger.

"Sir William Marshal?"

"Eh? I'm busy, man."

"Sir, a letter from Wales."

"Wales? From Chepstow?"

The weary messenger shook his head. "Nay, sire. From Lord Geoffrey Montfichet."

"Who the devil is that?" William was annoyed.

"The husband of thy wife's mother, sir."

William took the note and summoned Shoulderlock. "Read it to me."

The priest held the small parchment at arms' length. "To Sir William Marshal, husband of the Countess Isabel de Clare Marshal. With condolences we commend the wife of Lord Geoffrey Monfichet to the mercies of God. Please inform thy wife of her mother's passing. We entreat thy prayers on her behalf. Signed, Father Robert Fitzhugh, Chamberlain."

William drew a deep breath. "She'll be heartbroken. She had wanted to visit with her on several occasions but her husband had forbidden it. Fool. I should have marched against his manor house with steel." The man took the letter from Shoulderlock. "See this man is fed, Father Edward, and then be about your business. I'll meet you at the dock soon enough."

William stared blankly at the letter in his hand, then began walking slowly towards his wife's chambers. *I'll not know how to comfort her; I'll not know what to say.*

❋

Isabel had not eaten her breakfast that morning, nor had she attended Mass. She had awakened with a heavy heart, mysteriously aware of her mother's death. Just before dawn, she had heard the whispers again, only this time they had been unmistakable. Knowing, she had risen from her bed and wrapped herself in a robe. Then, with her hair shaken loose in the morning air, she had walked quietly through a courtyard from where she now spotted her husband through tear-blurred eyes.

"Isabel?"

She nodded. "It is well, William. Mother is gone but she is at peace."

William took her hands in his. "How did you know?"

"I was told in my dreams."

"I am sorry, dear wife."

Isabel leaned into William's breast. "And I as well."

The pair held each other for a long time, hearing nothing but the other's breathing. The rising sun was warm, the air cool. Isabel sobbed lightly, and then kissed her husband tenderly. "I love you, dear William. I'm sure she would have loved you, too."

"I should have knocked down the devil's gate and took you to your mother's side."

Isabel stroked his cheek. "I would have never asked that of you. She was held in the will of her husband," she said softly. "But his hand could not stay the power of her love for me. She spoke to me, William. She wanted me to know that she is at peace; she knew I needed to know that." Isabel wiped her eyes. "And if she is at peace, husband, I am, as well."

※

With Isabel left to be consoled by Aethel, William reluctantly returned to the dock to supervise the loading of the holds and decks of three large merchant vessels called 'busses'. Each was a cog, built high at both bow and stern, as was typical for the Norman ships. A huge square sail was rigged on a tall central mast and a steerboard was mounted on the right side of the ship, henceforward known as the 'starboard' side.

Once loaded, the quiet Countess and her staff were positioned in the fresh air of the lead vessel's deck where they watched with interest as the twenty-one man crew pattered about the boards on bare feet. The fat ropes tethering the ship to its moorings were released and a fresh gust immediately filled the belly of the sail and the ship groaned forward midst the cries of gulls and snaps of canvas.

Lord William's vessels heaved and splashed their way eastward. Isabel faced the wind and drew a long breath of salt air through her nose. With her strawberry hair flying behind her in the breeze, she smiled. '*May none ever bind thy spirit, child; bold currents are thy kin. For you are special born, my dear; a daughter of the wind.*' She turned her face westward and gazed at the white cliffs. "Sybil, could you fetch my children?"

"Aye, m'lady."

Sybil returned, quickly, leading two-year-old Richard and three-year-old William to Isabel's side, and placed Matilda in her arms. William had become a handsome young lad with agreeable features. His will was strong, and Isabel loved how he would stubbornly set his jaw. He was deep-thinking and sometimes melancholy. Richard was fair, like the de Clare family, a feisty lad, and one quick to quarrel.

Isabel kissed her daughter's cheeks made rosy red from the sea breeze and bade her sons sit with her as she watched the waters of the Channel roll past the crashing bow of the cresting ship. The sun was warm and the air clean and fresh. The Countess was suddenly happy with her world.

Lord William's vessels heaved and splashed their way eastward in a good wind that kept the ship's masters in reasonable humour. It hadn't taken long for Aethel to find the seamen to be of particular interest. They were a hardy race of men, made swarthy by years of salt and sun. "Hallo yon maiden," cried one from a barrel atop the mast. He waved vigorously until Aethel returned the gesture with a giggle.

"Oh Aethel, you've found your man at last," tittered Sybil.

Red-faced, the handmatron smiled like a young damsel just pinched by a lad she favoured. "Nay, goodness nay. Those are devils—pirates of sorts. And very un-Christian."

"Ah, but look at them! Strong backs and knotty arms," answered Sybil with a wink.

Isabel turned her face to the wind and drew a long breath of salt air through her nose. She smiled as the sun lit her strawberry hair. Now twenty-two, she was still a beautiful young woman. She cast a final look at the white cliffs of Dover already beginning to shrink behind her. Aethel shuffled close. "A crewman tells me that with this wind, we've only a day and maybe half the next on the sea."

Isabel was relieved.

CHAPTER X

NORMANDY

WITHIN a few months of the Marshals' arrival in Normandy, the lord was finished with royal business and had settled his family in a small castle he held in Muellers. William had precious few lands in Normandy and he was frustrated by that fact. The gentle landscape of Normandy was the home of his youth and he knew it well. He had been sent there at age twelve to serve the Lord of Tancarville as a squire.

The Lord of Tancarville had been known as the father of knights and had trained the youth carefully in the arts of war, including the art of *tilting*. Tilting was a training technique in which a mounted squire pointed a lance at a two-armed, pivoting post called a *quintain*. On one arm hung a bag of sand, and on the other a spiked ball. The object was for the squire to strike the sandbag and ride through at enough speed to avoid being struck in the back by the whirling ball! William had learned tilting well, then swordsmanship, and all manner of combat. Soon he had been tested in battle; afterwards, he was knighted, and remained undefeated in joust, whether in Normandy or in the neighbouring kingdom of France—the *Ille-de-France*.

At Tancarville, William had also learned of life at court, including table manners, rules of courtesy, dances, the hunt, and games such as chess and backgammon. Yet, as appealing as any of these diversions had been, the man's greatest love had always been serving his liege lord under arms.

It was a cold night in December 1194 when Sybil answered Aethel's cry. "Coming, my lady," she answered. The nursemaid was also the midwife, and she charged through the castle at Muellers with a bundle of cloth, a sharp knife, and a look of steady resolve. She entered Isabel's chamber to find Aethel and Carly hovering over their lady with words of encouragement. Sybil shouldered her narrow body between theirs and wiped Isabel's brow with a wet kerchief. She examined her mistress and smiled. "All shall be well with you."

Aethel breathed a sigh of relief. Giving birth was under Eve's curse and it was no odd thing to bury mother and child alike after hours of desperate agony. "Then, we need not call the barber?"

Sybil shook her head. The barber was a Frenchman that few liked. He did not travel with the family, but was a servant in residence at Mueller. His duties, like those of all barbers, included shaving beards, trimming hair—and performing surgeries! "No, I prefer our chances without him."

Isabel cried out. "Oh, Sybil! Do not leave me!"

"Nay, m'lady."

"And is good Aethel here?"

"Aye, by your side, always."

Isabel smiled and waited for her next moment. She looked at Sybil's fair skin and black braids, then turned to Aethel's ruddy face and sturdy frame. She was thankful for friends as these. In the interim she smiled at Aethel. "So, the sailor never sought you out?"

"Ha!" bellowed Aethel. "Give me a man of the soil, one whose feet are planted on good sod and one who doesn't walk with a roll in his step."

The three laughed. Isabel grimaced, then cried out again, this time much louder. With every contraction, her hands squeezed those of her servants until the pain faded. "Oh, dear God above," panted the Countess. She lay quietly, then whispered to Sybil. "And your husband? Sir Alan is well?"

"Aye, m'lady. He follows Lord William gladly and is ready to lift the sword for him—so he says nearly every night."

"These men and their swords," sighed Isabel.

Sybil was anxious to keep the Countess' mind off her pain, and she had become more and more concerned about her weakening condition. She whispered to Aethel, "Go, pray twelve *Ave Marias*—one for each apostle. Then three *Pater Nosters* for the Holy Trinity. Find a relic from Le Court and hold it fast while you do so. And hurry." She turned to Isabel with a loud, resonate voice. "I've sent Aethel to tend the children. Now, you and I needs be about our business."

Isabel groaned, then clutched her belly with a shriek, and so it went far into the night until, at long last, sometime after matins, Isabel granted the world another soul. Before midday meal, her newborn child would be baptised Gilbert Marshal.

✳

The next years were wonderful times for the Countess and her family. The gentle green hills and wide forests of Normandy gave her much pleasure. Her growing children were happy as well. Isabel was pleased to play with her three sons and daughter and was now nearly ready to give birth to another. She enjoyed teaching them according to their abilities and had spent hours feeding birds with them, hawking, hunting for squirrels with a sling, shooting little longbows, and even kicking the bladder ball. She read them stories from Le Court's grand library of scrolls—*The Song of Roland*, and stories of King Alfred. Young William especially loved *The Song of Roland* and often recited his favourite verses, to the delight of his father:

> Ten snow-white mules then ordered Marsilie,
> Gifts of a King, the King of Suatilie.
> Bridled with gold, saddled in silver clear;
> Mounted them those that should the message speak,
> In their right hands were olive-branches green.
> Came they to Charlemagne, that holds all France in fee,
> Yet cannot guard himself from treachery.

Lord William, too, loved time with his children. Himself being rather unlearned, he was, nevertheless, capable in matters of courtly behaviour and enjoyed playing at mock table scenes where he taught his boys the arts of carving meat, pouring wine, and the courtesies of conversation. He also taught his sons to play at 'knights' with him. When he was busy at court, Isabel, Aethel, and Sybil were worthy substitutes in the game, all playing together in a tournament-style grand *mêlée*. The game was played with stalks of plantain, each yet bearing its head. The combatants would duel as if with swords and the first to strike off his opponent's "head" would be proclaimed as *le champion de tournoi*.

As much as the Countess enjoyed her play, she was also mindful of her children's need for a formal education. Herself well-taught, she was one to appreciate the value of learning. She had every intention of seeing that her children were properly educated—the boys in their various schools, and her daughter, or daughters, with the most excellent tutors she might find. And she was determined that her daughters, unlike those of most others, would learn more than the singing of songs, the arts of poetry, and the skill of embroidery.

William the Younger was now six years old and had been tutored under the gentle eye of Le Court and his clerks for the past year. He was about to begin his studies at a nearby monastery in which an elementary song-school was held. Here William, along with others aged six to eight, would begin his education under the hard eye of strict masters.

Le Court took his young pupil by the shoulders and looked directly into his round blue eyes. "As all the Christian world knows, young William, 'manners maketh the man.' Therefore, you shall begin the journey of thy formal education by studying basic courtesy. It will be followed by an earnest study of Latin, beginning as we have begun—with the singing of hymns and songs."

The boy looked stone-faced but courageous. He had little choice but to yield to his elders, but he was wishing for all the world to remain with his younger siblings and spend his days by the fish-ponds or at play in the forests, in the stables, or in the shadows of battlements. "*Oui, Père.*"

"Good lad. We've worked hard at thy Latin, for it is the common language of the civilised world. Labour at it with all your might, for it is necessary for thy Bible reading and for all correspondence."

141

William shrugged. He knew the song-school was just the beginning of many years of sitting atop hard benches in cold rooms. Though he doubted he'd ever be sent to the university at Oxford—his father thought too much learning was an unhealthy excess—he did understand that he would eventually move from his song-school to the grammar school. There he'd spend years surrounded by black-robed clerks hovering over him with birch rods and palmers—flat discs used to slap a delinquent's palm.

In the grammar school he would learn the *Trivium*—a three-fold curriculum that taught grammar, logic (the art of argument), and rhetoric (the art of presentation, both by pen and by mouth). He hoped his father would be content with his mastery of the *Trivium,* so that he might be released to train as a squire in his early teens. Otherwise, he would have to spend more years studying the dreaded *Quadrivium*—a four-part curriculum including arithmetic, geometry, music, and astronomy. It should be noted that the arithmetic young William feared was not yet simplified by the system of Arabic numerals with their logical columns of tens, hundreds, thousands, etc., and their most helpful 'zero'. Instead, the lad would need to suffer the interminable agonies of arithmetic processes in Roman numerals, including the calculation of fractions.

While his eldest son began his formal education and the rest of his family happily enjoyed their surroundings in Normandy, Lord William spent the next year shuttling to and from King Richard's court at Rouen, according to the King's pleasure. Throughout his married life he had insisted his family accompany him wherever he went, but, given his rapid movements, he had agreed to place his family in more permanent quarters at his castle in Muellers. During this time Isabel gave birth to a second daughter, named Eva.

William missed Eva's baptism, for he had been charged with keeping a wary eye on the menacing ploys of France's King Philip. To the chagrin of Philip, King Richard's Angevin Empire had maintained a threatening presence on the Continent. With Normandy under the direct control of the English monarch, as well as the duchies of Brittany, Aquitaine, Poitou, Anjou, Gascony, and

Touraine, Philip's kingdom—the "*Ile-de-France*"—was, in reality, less than half of what was commonly considered "France." As a result, King Philip was obsessed with stretching his shrunken kingdom into territories lost over time through marriages and by war. Normandy was of particular interest. Though the English king was theoretically the vassal of the French king in Normandy, in reality it was the English king who reaped the profits from its generous soil and hard-working peasants. Philip longed for the time when the grip of the Anglo-Normans would be broken, and he pursued a policy of war intended to do just that.

Warfare consisted primarily of destroying the wealth of one's opponent. So King Philip sent his soldiers into the villages of Normandy where, with unspeakable cruelty, they slaughtered pitiful peasants, destroying their homes, their livestock, and their harvest. Since it was ultimately the folk who wrested the wealth from the land, the losses they suffered immediately impacted the coffers of their lords.

Richard's lords of Normandy naturally rose up in defence of their lands and battled with Philip's raiders as best they could. In addition, Richard's barons sought revenge by conducting sorties into the *Ile-de-France*, and Philip's province of Champagne to exact an equally brutal cost. This bloody exchange continued for years, interrupted only by truces worth less than the parchment they were scribbled upon.

The adventurous King Richard, however, loved warfare and found the contest to be stimulating. He amused himself with taunting the French king from time to time, and constructed a castle atop a high crag by a bend in the river Seine near the important Norman city of Rouen. He called the light-coloured castle Château Gaillard, meaning the "Saucy Castle." It was an amazing three-walled stone fortress with an intricate design of outworks, battlements, water defences, and bridges.

The Saucy Castle invoked the wrath of Philip and also that of the Church, for it was built in violation of a sworn truce. The bishop excommunicated Richard while Philip roared to his court, "Even if its walls were built of iron, I would take it." But the Lionheart dismissed the interdict and enjoyed the outcry. When he heard of Philip's bravado, he smiled and sent an answer with a dare: "Ah," he bellowed with a laugh, "and if its walls were made of butter, I would hold it!"

❋

On a comfortable morning in the spring of 1197, the Countess gave birth to her sixth child, a son they named Walter. As with all infants, the baby was immediately wrapped tightly in linen swaddling cloths. The binding was thought necessary in order to prevent the child's limbs from bowing in his early months. Sybil held the little fellow in her arms as Aethel tended Isabel, who lay perspired and exhausted in her bed. A rap on the door turned all eyes.

Aethel hurried to answer. "Ah! Sir John d'Erley. We've not seen you for some time."

John bowed. He had been serving Lord William in Richard's army and had been in combat all over France. "'Tis so good to find thee in health, Aethel." He smiled politely and requested entrance.

Aethel blocked the door. "I think not, sire. The lady has given birth within the hour, and I was about to send Ida with word to Lord William."

John brightened. "Good news? Boy?"

Sybil called from within the chamber, "Girl."

"I see." John's eyes betrayed his disappointment.

"Really, Sir John! Sybil is toying with you, but you ought be ashamed. 'Tis a boy, another warrior in waiting—does that please you more?" Aethel's eyes were scolding and her fists were planted hard on her hips.

"I did not mean—I think I—well, indeed, God be praised! The Virgin Mother was once a daughter to someone and—"

"Enough, Sir John. You are digging a very deep pit for yourself. Now, what brings you here?"

The knight cleared his throat uncomfortably. "Lord William has been summoned to battle at the castle of Milly-sur-Thérain near Beauvais, on the northern borders."

Isabel whimpered and Sybil came to her side.

Aethel nodded. "A castle on the frontier. Shall it be heavy combat with King Philip's army?"

"*Oui.*"

"You shall take word to him of his son?"

"Of course."

The Countess called from her bed. "Sir John, come to me, please."

D'Erley strode across the room and knelt on one knee at Isabel's bedside. "Yes, my lady?"

With Sybil's help Isabel sat upright, supported by pillows propped against her back. "Sir John, please tell my lord husband that his son is fit and well, and as we agreed, is to be named Walter. He shall be baptised this very day."

"Yes, m'lady."

She reached behind her neck to unclasp her necklace. "Take this, Sir John, and give it to my William."

John stared at the relic. "But, m'lady, I am certain he would not wish it so."

Isabel's eyes rarely flashed in anger but at that moment she levelled a look like the points of two lances. "It is as I command, sir knight."

The young man closed his hand around the relic, and bowed his head. "As you wish."

Isabel softened. "Now tell me, John, how long a campaign do you expect?"

· John took the Countess' hand respectfully. "Methinks one hard fight ought to break Philip in the east. If we take the castle at Milly-sur-Thérain, Lord William says the barons of the borders will shift fealty to Richard. That will insure Philip's hasty withdrawal to Paris."

"And is this castle well-fortified?"

"I do not know, m'lady."

Isabel squeezed John's hand lightly. "I shall pray for my husband, John, but I shall also pray for you. Lord William loves you as he loves his sons." Her voice was soft and kindly.

The knight smiled. "I do love him, as well, m'lady. And you. I shall serve you both with all the might God grants my arm." With that John d'Erley stood and hastened away.

The Countess took her baby in her arms and sobbed lightly. She was ever mindful of the curse and at every birth or every battle it brought a chill to her.

"I fear Lord William will object loudly to the relic," said Aethel, as she poured Isabel a tankard of cider.

"Indeed. Let him," sighed Isabel. "But if I must crawl on my belly to lay that blessed cross around my husband's neck, I would do it, and gladly."

Another rap on the door turned all heads. It was Le Court. "I beg entrance, my lady?"

"*Oui, Père*, please, you are welcome."

The chancellor entered. "I just learned of this little one. May God grant him long life and joy. Thy wish for the baptism?"

"Today, father."

"Indeed. You are able to join us?"

"*Oui*. Lord Marshall has appointed the godparents in advance; you should have their names."

"*Oui*, m'lady. I do. Among them is to be Lord Baldwin—in absentia—and wife, Lord John Marshal—*in absentia*—and wife, and Sir John d'Erley."

Isabel smiled, pleased with her husband's choices.

"And two others." Le Court paused and then, with great drama, turned to the Countess' servants. "Lord William respectfully requests Sir Alan de St.Georges—*in absentia*, and his wife, Sybil, as well as the Saxon, Aethel, widow of Stephan the Archer."

The two servants stared dumbstruck and speechless. For them to act as the godparents of a lord's child was an astonishing break from custom. The Countess smiled and gathered them to her side. "Dear, dear friends. 'Tis you whom I do so love. Good William loves you as well."

Aethel started to bawl, loudly. She embraced Isabel roughly as her broad back heaved with her sobs.

"Ouch!" laughed Isabel. "Please, Aethel, not so hard." The

Countess took the servants' hands. "I am so glad my lord husband has not burdened me with ladies-in-waiting. I need no pretend friends as long as I have either of you. One Candlemas I saw the Duchess of Aquitaine strut past with a squawking flock of her ladies. Silly fops. I doubt that a single one of them care one whit for her."

Aethel and Sybil smiled and squeezed Isabel's hands lightly. It was true, they were mere servants and Lord William often wondered why Isabel refused to add ladies-in-waiting to her staff—women of high birth that could accompany her at court and represent her dignity in matters of dress and style. Isabel would have none of it. She had spent her childhood nearly alone in the Tower Castle and was content to spend her time with friends deserving of the word.

Little Le Court smiled, then cleared his throat. "Good then. Come to the chapel after the bells of terce. The tub shall be ready with warmed water. In the meantime, Lady Isabel, we need to offer a prayer of thanksgiving for thy son and prayers of safe-keeping for thy husband, his brave knights, and the whole of King Richard's army."

✹

The castle of Milly-sur-Thérain was situated along the Thérain River in a wide landscape near the town of Beauvais on the northern frontier between Normandy and the kingdom of France. King Richard had assembled a determined army of subjects, including some four hundred knights-in-service from both the continent and the isle of Britain. Added to these were more than six hundred mounted sergeants armed very much like their knightly comrades, and nearly a thousand footmen, some free men serving their required time, others mercenaries.

The mounted soldiers were well-armoured and carried both lances and swords. The footmen were protected by leather jerkins and shields, and armed with a variety of horrid weapons including pikes, flails, swords, forks, and halberds, the last being a lance-like instrument with a long, double-edged blade and axe-like appendages. The English army also included large numbers of Welsh archers—bearing long-bows made of yew—as well as several elite companies of Flemish cross-bowmen (the Church's ban on the weapon notwithstanding).

All soldiers owing military service were required by their lords to maintain a wardrobe of armour, which varied according to their station. When service was demanded they were expected to report for duty appropriately accoutred. The *Assize of Arms* declared in 1188 had specified what was required by way of arms and armour for all free men. It was a statute affirming the importance of maintaining an armed society to ensure its defence. Shoulderlock and Sir Baldwin had made sure the rules were followed to the letter among the men of Sir William's *mesnie*.

Generally speaking, knights and wealthy freemen were required to possess at minimum—and at their own expense—a mail coat (armour made of tiny steel links), which hung to the knees, helmet, shield, and lance. Free men of middling means (over ten marks of annual income) were required to own a mail shirt (which hung to the waist), iron cap, and a lance. All other free men were required to own a padded coat, iron cap, and a lance. These demands were not inconsequential, for a mail shirt cost about one pound—nearly two months wages for a skilled tradesman.

The morning of battle, Lord William donned a padded shirt atop his under-shirt, wrapped a set of mail leggings around his woollen hose, which he tied at the back before hanging his thirty-pound mail coat over his shoulders. A young page assisted him, a squire waiting nearby with the knight's weapons. After his armour was properly adjusted, he donned his sleeveless robe, richly embroidered with his heraldic colours, and bound his waist with a wide belt. Lastly, William placed a large, flat-topped helmet under his arm and strode towards his white stallion. The squire handed the knight a long lance and his heavy sword.

Even at fifty-five years of age, the grey-eyed, grey-haired warrior struck a chord of fearful respect as he walked his war-horse through the camp. At six foot two inches, he stood taller than any other in Richard's army. His shoulders, made all the more broad by his armour, were not stooped in the slightest. "Sir Baldwin," he cried to the marshal of his mesnie.

"*Oui*, sire." Baldwin, no youngster himself, was itching for combat.

"Our men are at the ready?"

"*Oui*."

William mounted his horse. "Good. You are to command them. I am ordered to the King's side. Go and fight well, dear friend; go with God." William spurred his charger forward and loped through the assembled camp until he was alongside his King beneath the flutter of the royal colours.

Richard was flushed with excitement. His stallion pawed the earth and tossed his head. "Sir William, look there." He pointed to the castle and grinned, widely. "By nightfall it shall be ours."

William wasn't nearly as confident. He knew that Philip had filled the fortress with a host of his best soldiers: cross-bowmen, archers, well-trained footmen, and a bailey full of knights ready to engage on the ground—a commitment to combat, once made, resulted in either death or victory.

The wise lord surveyed the castle carefully. The curtain wall (the forward wall) was topped by the alternating gaps and merlons of the ramparts. In the gaps William could see many numbers of cross-bowmen crowding forward for a look at their prey. Lord William knew this castle and knew it had an inner wall, also well-fortified. If his men succeeded in breaching the curtain, they'd likely have to breach the second wall as well. He shook his head and wondered why the King had not opted for a siege. But Richard was not only impetuous; he was also at times impatient. Since most castles kept a year's supply of food and had adequate numbers of wells inside, the King had calculated that it would be a very long and expensive wait before his victory could be secured.

William had earlier proposed they undermine the walls, a clever tactic that succeeded from time to time but would require months of heavy labour with no guarantee of success. He turned to the King. "My lord, have we considered a night escalade? I could feign an evening frontal at the east barbican—its gate seems in need of repair—while I send our footmen on ladders there, at the south, under cover of darkness."

Richard stared at the castle and the colours of King Philip waving atop its towers. The pennants snapped and fluttered as if they were taunting him in the morning breeze. He considered his marshal's proposal, then shook his head. "*Non, mon ami*. We charge straight at them in full light. The castle will fall; I feel it in my bones."

Lord William was more concerned with good sense than a King's hunch, but he was a loyal vassal and had little choice other than to obey. "Aye, m'lord."

"Good. Now, general. To the wood." The King turned his horse and the two sprinted to the rear of the waiting army and into a heavily shaded hardwood forest. Here were hidden the mechanised force of the English army, just arrived from repairs in the west. "Look at them, William. Eight bears and five engines. They ought make something of a difference!"

"*Oui*, sire." William was still uneasy.

Richard's "bears" were tall assault towers upon which archers or cross-bowmen could climb and fire into the castle with deadly accuracy. Sometimes also called 'cats' or 'wolves,' they provided excellent cover for ground troops and a bridge to the top of the castle walls if they could be successfully wheeled close enough. His 'engines' were catapults capable of hurling fire into the centre of the castle complex or fifty-pound rocks against its stone walls. Made of heavy timbers, they were designed with long firing beams that were put under tension by cranking them backwards against leather loops wound around wooden cylinders. When released, the firing beams would leap forward until they crashed against a padded crossbar, heaving their ammunition far into the air.

"Lord William, my tactics are simple. We are to wheel the bears within range of our cross-bowmen. We need to kill their archers there, on the east wall. By concentrating fire on those towers, we can send the hired Scots into the moat under some cover.

With proper support they can fill the moat with debris and their corpses. Soon, my friend, we shall have a fine bridge to the gate, which we shall then burn.

"In the meantime, the engines need to keep a constant bombardment of rock against the battlements—I want to see the castle's teeth shattered! And have your Welshmen keep a steady rain of flaming arrows dropping from the sky—we must see to it that the constable is kept busy putting out fires while his soldiers choke on smoke."

"*Oui*, sire."

The King surveyed the land. "Send a company of your quickest knights round about on either flank. I'd be displeased to have Philip's reinforcements surprise us by land. Our scouts say he's with them at some distance, but riding hard. I know if we take his castle quick, he'll turn and ride just as hard away." Richard laughed loudly.

"Of course." William was still uncertain. A castle like this often took many days or even weeks to take. "God be with us."

CHAPTER XI

TO ARMS!

LORD William turned his charger and galloped to a company of lieutenants to whom he barked his orders. In moments the battle began.

First the archers raced forward with their longbows and formed ranks within danger of the French cross-bowmen's greater range. They hurriedly dipped the heads of their arrows in pots of pitch and ignited them on the firepots at their sides. Behind them waited row upon row of dead-eyed footmen. They shuffled nervously, weapons in hand. They were glad to hear the creaking cranks of the engines, but they knew, despite the coming cannonade, it would be they who would ultimately be hurled against the castle walls.

In the rear, armoured cavalrymen stood at the bridles of their chargers. Attended by their squires, groomsmen, and armourers, they rocked on anxious feet. They expected to either storm through the smoke of a well-charred gate or to receive an attack of the castle's own knights.

As the King's archers lofted fiery shafts over the castle walls, the catapults were being dragged forward. Able to release their missiles from two hundred yards, they were positioned without incident. One by one they began to hurl their boulders hard against the stubborn stone of the castle walls. As each giant sling was released, a short rush of wind sounded, followed by a hard thump of the crossbar. Then the rocks flew away silently in a high arc, seeming to shrink in the distance until thudding hard against the castle stone. At impact, some of the merlons held, others burst apart as if exploded into a thousand little stones.

At the trumpets' blast, long lines of groaning men began hauling the towering bears from the wood with thick ropes. The army cheered and hurrahed as the mighty wheels rumbled over the hard earth, but as they rolled past the heaving arms of the catapults, the hiss of crossbow bolts suddenly sang through the air. Those at the lead end of the ropes fell first, screaming and clutching belly or limbs. Lord William galloped forward, commanding those remaining to hurry on. "Just a few more yards, lads!" he cried. On top of the bears, King Richard's own cross-bowmen crowded under their wooden canopies, urging those below to drag them "closer, just a bit closer."

The wretches on the ropes now dropped in waves as each yard gained moved another group within the killing range. On it went, the towers creaking forward, inch by inch, men dying with nearly every step. At last the bears were close enough and the duel of bows began.

For a half an hour the cross-bowmen of the bears traded death with their counterparts atop the castle wall. Men from both sides dropped to the ground in heaps and the moat began to fill with their bodies. But to the chagrin of King Richard and his general, another weapon was suddenly introduced to the combat. Hidden within the belly of the castle was a series of catapults loaded with a fearsome weapon. Huge balls of fire now roared towards the English army and a loud cry went up: "Greek fire!"

Richard, suddenly nervous, barked orders to his lieutenants. "A bucket company to the river at once…form a line, form a line."

The King was right to be fearful. Greek fire was a sulphurous pitch concoction designed to be flung at or dumped upon would-be invaders. When striking its target, it splashed a sticky gum that burned with the "heat of Hades." The castle's constable had wisely aimed his engines at the legs of the bears. It took only a few shots for him to find his range, and when he did, he poured his fire on rapidly.

"Pull them back. Pull them back!" cried Lord William. He knew the bears would easily burn for he had seen they were made of fallen timbers and not with green wood, as they ought to have been. "Hurry, hurry," he shouted.

Companies of footmen raced forward with ropes and hastily

tied the legs of the tall towers. But as they struggled to pull against the great wheels, the fires fell upon them as well. Screaming and rolling, the men died in utter agony, while above, the cross-bow-men stared helplessly at the burning timbers below.

"More men," roared William. "More men." Sir Alan and Sir John d'Erley galloped forward, no longer able to wait for their time. "No," shouted William. "*Sacre bleu*, return to your line."

The two hesitated, their eyes filling with tears as one by one the great bears collapsed, dropping all to their deaths. Stinging smoke now filled the air, along with cries and desperate shouts. King Richard charged to the commander of his engines. "Keep firing your blasted rocks!" He pointed to William. "And keep the archers firing. I want to see smoke *inside* the castle."

The French defenders now cheered wildly at the chaos spreading across the enemy's field below them. They laughed and goaded the English army with every foul blasphemy under the sun.

John d'Erley grumbled to Sir Alan. "Hear them? They are laughing at us."

"Aye, but 'tis not over yet." He pointed to swarm of ladders suddenly rushing from the forest. Ranks of waiting footmen now shuffled nervously as the ladder companies ran past them towards the wall. They knew it was their time.

With a nod from King Richard, the trumpets sounded and a large wave of men were ordered forward. Scottish mercenaries formed the forward line, and with a loud shout they ran hard towards the ladders. Many carried brush and logs or whatever kind of debris they imagined might clog the moat. In moments, however, an unyielding rain of arrows, bolts, and burning pitch began to fill the moat with their corpses.

The Welsh archers were ordered to follow in support and they quickly placed themselves in positions from which they could maintain a withering stream of arrows directed at the battlements above. And, all the while, the King ordered the catapults to keep hurling their great stones, even at the peril of his own men now clambering up their ladders.

Richard's knights were aghast at the slaughter before them, and they edged forward on their horses, impatiently waiting until the wall was breached and the gates somehow opened. Fortuitously, the defenders had fumbled an iron pot of Greek fire just above the eastern gate. It had spilled to the ground and splashed on to the wooden doors, which now were ablaze. Once the fireball hit the ground, Lord William made sure it was quickly fed with logs run forward by brave soldiers daring the defenders' arrows. It soon became a contest between both sides as to whether the water dropped from above would extinguish the blaze, or whether Richard's men could continue to feed it.

William was worried. His war-horse trotted just beyond reach of the French archers. He ordered the battering rams to be made ready and bit his lip as the oak gate blackened. His eyes flew from the contest at the gate to the horror on the walls and he groaned. His thoughts left the battlefield only once and it was to think of his wife for a brief moment. He reached within his collar to feel her relic and it gave him comfort.

"Lord William," cried a voice. "The wall is holding; our men are dropping like leaves." Indeed, King Richard's army was being butchered. The defenders were pushing off the ladders with long poles while archers fired point blank into the desperate faces of those climbing upward. Pikes, forks, hammers, and swords were waiting for those who neared the top.

Unable to watch any longer, young John d'Erley spurred his horse forward. He ignored the commands of William and the shouts of his comrades. Urging on the footmen below him, he reached the moat, dismounted midst a shower of shafts and, under the cover of his shield, stumbled over the pile of bodies that had filled the shallow moat. He leaned his shoulder against the castle stone and looked upward. With clenched teeth he then drew his sword, cast his shield aside, and started up a ladder, crying for others to follow his lead.

Lord William gasped and galloped forward, ignoring the commands of King Richard. His heart pounded as he watched his beloved knight lift one leg above the other, higher and higher. Bodies dropped past the brave lad; arrows and bolts glanced off his armour. "Dear God," cried William. "Stand by him."

John was one man away from the top; the man fell backward, his head split by a defender's axe. John's legs burned, his heart pounded, and his eyes were blurred by smoke. He reached back with his longsword and prepared to swing, but the French defender lunged downward with a long fork. The two prongs missed their mark but ran along each side of the knight's neck. The heel of the weapon jammed into John's throat and the knight gagged, tilted to one side, and lost his grip. He tumbled backward as one leg fell through the ladder's rung. With a loud cry of pain, the knight's knee snagged him and he fell helplessly upside down, dangling precariously.

"Ahh!" cried Lord William. He charged forward, followed by a roaring knot of his knights. At the sight of William Marshal's herald colours rushing towards the wall, the whole of Richard's army lifted a mighty cheer and, suddenly filled with new courage, it pressed the assault savagely.

The old warrior reached the ladder first. He set his jaw hard and grabbed hold of the rails. Ignoring the host of arrows flying all around him, he began his climb, pushing those above to hurry on. Men fell over him, beside him, and atop him, but Sir William climbed ever upward until he fixed his huge hands on John's flailing arms. "Easy lad, I'm with you."

Just behind came the marshal's knights, led by Sir Alan and followed by a panting Baldwin, Sir Ralph Bloet, and a smoky blur of others. Alan stretched his arm past his lord and duelled deftly with two from above as William released John's leg. The lord kept a firm hold on his vassal as he finally wrestled him upright. In another moment John was standing on the ladder with both legs.

"Lad, can y'fight on?" cried William.

D'Erley was flushed red. His eyes flashed and he answered boldly. "Aye, m'lord." Ignoring the pain in his badly sprained knee, the faithful knight set his jaw and turned his head upward.

William pushed through Sir Alan's reach and stared at the flashing steel waiting for him just a few yards above. Peering through the smoke, William recognised the man who had rushed to meet him. It was the constable of the castle, a ruthless brute whom the marshal knew. William snarled and readied his sword. With a cry that rallied all those around him, the ageing man sprinted up the final rungs until he reached the rampart gap. There, with a feigned thrust and one vicious swipe, he crashed his sword into the constable's helmet, cleaving both it and the skull within. With a shout, Lord William then leapt through the gap and onto the castle's wooden wall-walk, striking this way and that as his fellows rushed into the breech.

William's knights and the cheering footmen that followed quickly spread across the walk, freeing gap after gap for their rallied comrades until the whole of the eastern wall was taken. King Richard's men pounced upon their foes now fleeing along the walk with a ferocity and fury seldom seen; they fell like wheat at harvest, thumping the ground below like so many sacks of grain.

Lord William paused to catch his breath and study the smoky, bloodied scene with the trained eyes of a seasoned general. Then, certain the tide had turned, he took a moment and sat atop the constable's corpse to wipe his brow. With a silent prayer of thanksgiving, he lifted the Countess' relic from within his armour and kissed it. "Good Isabel," he muttered. "Good wife." He took a deep breath and closed his eyes. He pictured Isabel reading in a bed-chamber softened by candlelight and he chuckled. "Me always with m'sword, she with her parchments." The man turned to face the slaughter within the walls where he watched with both pride and sorrow.

Within the hour an exited voice cried, "Sire!" It was Sir John. William stood. "Aye, lad."

"The castle has surrendered, the portcullis is raised, and the King is leading his knights into the central bailey."

Lord William smiled. "I see it. God be praised. The day is over. Tell me, John, have we losses to our family?"

"Not a one sire, save an arrow graze to Eustace, and a squire's broken leg."

The lord took a deep breath, relieved at the news. "The cost is light."

D'Erley paused, then, unable to contain himself, he clasped his lord's hand and fell to his knees. "My thanks, sire. You saved my life this day."

"Thanks be to God, good lad."

"*Oui*, sire, but thanks to thee as well." Tears welled in the young man's soot-smudged face. "My lord, I would storm the highest ramparts of Lucifer's most hardened castle keep for you. I would—"

William laid a hand on the knight's shoulder. While he rarely revealed his heart to any but Isabel, he loved this unusual warrior. "I am proud to be thy liege-lord, John. 'Tis my sworn duty under God to defend thee, but is also my joy to do so. You are steadfast and sure, blessed with the heart of a lion *and* a lamb. My Isabel says if Christendom was served by men such as you, the whole of the earth would be a happy place, 'soothed by charity and secured by courage.'"

John d'Erley blushed and humbly hung his head. "She is too kind, sire, as are you."

William Marshal studied the young knight for a quiet moment and raised him to his feet. He then spoke firmly. "You fought well and bravely. You shall receive the praise of many. But I must warn you of this: as thy sword sharpens and thy wealth grows, let neither steal thy soul. Of all your enemies, 'tis the ones that lie within that are the most dangerous. Beware of avarice, sloth, excess, and vanity, and know that the captain of all these foes is pride."

John stared into his lord's grey eyes and nodded. Even in his twenty-three years he had lived long enough to witness pride corrupt the hearts of lords, clerics, kings, and kingdoms.

The pair remained quiet for a moment. The din of trotting horses and groaning carts, a cacophony of men's voices, and the crackle of burning thatch did not distract the younger man from his elder's counsel. But at last Sir John was startled by a loud trumpet and nervously entreated his lord: "I fear the King waits, sire."

William laughed. He was the only man in England who might make a King wait without the slightest sense of dread. "*Oui*, lad. Well then, we dare not tarry. Let us welcome the Lionheart to the castle we've won for him!"

❋

Hearing the news of the defeat at Beauvais, King Philip turned his reinforcements quickly around. Fleeing to safety, he rushed his French army through the streets of Gisors, taking no note whatsoever of the site where he and Richard had stood barely ten years prior as oathtakers for the Third Crusade.

For the next two years both weary armies chose to avoid serious combat and the lull proved to be good for the Marshals as they continued residence in Normandy. In this, the final year of the twelfth century, Lady Isabel gave birth to her seventh child. After a bit of playful coaxing from Lord William and the earnest pleas of the older children, the Countess consented to have the child baptised Isabel.

William and the King's other courtiers were also delighted to be regularly reminded how well Richard's absentee reign was being managed in England. The King's extended absence had left many wondering what mischief Prince John might cause; however, England's peculiar system of common law and decentralised governance proved to be difficult obstacles for the power-seeking prince. King Henry II had refined the ancient Saxon administrations of county and shire government in order to secure his hold over the barons. Now this same structure had gradually grown in such a way as to effect a web of local authority resistant to despots of any sort, whether barons or kings. Though far from being immune to tyranny, England was slowly turning to the rule of law, and not to rulers, for its statecraft.

But all did not bode well for Merry England. King Richard, desperate for money to manage his war debts, heard of a treasure being unearthed on the lands of one of his barons near the castle of Chaluz. The treasure was rumoured to be a golden set of figurines— an emperor and his family seated around a golden table. As overlord of the land, the King demanded that his vassal surrender the discovery immediately. The baron, in turn, denied him. Richard scoffed the lord's defiance and, without benefit of William Marshal's leadership, immediately lay siege to the baron's small castle. Confident from his victory of just two years prior, the proud King rode close to the wall, only to receive an arrow in his left shoulder near his neck.

Severely wounded, the Lionheart was taken from the field of battle and to the tent of a surgeon, where the arrowhead was removed. Unfortunately, even as the castle fell to the King's troops, gangrene appeared and began to spread. Quite aware of his fate, the dying King Richard quickly arranged his affairs. First, he declared his brother John to be his successor and all present were required to swear allegiance. He then declared that William Marshal, presently attending royal duties in Rouen, should be made the Custodian of the Royal Treasury.

The hapless archer who had shot the King had been taken prisoner and was dragged before the fevered monarch. Richard lifted himself to one elbow and eyed the trembling man for a long moment; then granted him full pardon and a generous gift of money.

Satisfied that amends had been made on earth, he demanded his steward do two more things. First, he was to swear that large portions of his wealth would be distributed amongst the poor at his funeral. While the giving of alms at a lord's death was not uncommon, the sums King Richard whispered were to assure him a place in the hearts of the poor for a generation. Secondly, he had the steward summon his chancellor, to whom he offered his final confession. Then, on April 6, 1199, with all things both temporal and eternal in proper order, the forty-two-year-old crusader King, Richard the Lionhearted, Richard *Coeur de-Lion*, released his final breath.

※

Alone in Rouen, Lord William heard the news as he was undressing for bed. "It cannot be!" he cried to the messenger. "It cannot be. I was told it was a small wound to the shoulder."

No words could comfort him. His King was dead, and with him all hopes of justice in the realm. The messenger added news that the archer who had shot the King had been re-captured within an hour of Richard's death and skinned alive by anguished mourners. The news provided no consolation to William.

The lord hastily dressed and sought out Hubert Walter, the Archbishop of Canterbury who was fortuitously also in Rouen. "*Père*," he shouted. "*Père*. A word."

The archbishop bade him enter and soon was weeping with William. "Now we've truly a problem," murmured Hubert. "The kingdom is in grave peril."

"Indeed," answered William. "Philip shall pounce! I know it. He has always a good eye for the chink. We must be about the heir and quickly."

The archbishop nodded. "I've given hours of thought to the matter in these past years. Richard was such the adventurer! He gave no heed to either his welfare or ours, and he spent precious little time in England!" Hubert shook his head. "What say you about Arthur, Richard's nephew? He is, after all, the grandson of Henry, and the law could claim him a rightful heir. The lords here in Normandy prefer him, as do those in Aquitaine."

William shook his head sombrely. "No. Arthur is not fit, and he loves France more than England. More than that, conscience does not allow it. Prince John is Henry's son—the direct heir, and Richard has declared for him."

The archbishop grumbled and poured wine into two goblets. "Was Richard's declaration properly witnessed?"

"*Oui*, by both the court and the Church."

Hubert swallowed a long draught. "John is not fit to rule. He is intelligent and resolute, but he uses these virtues as weapons against all that is just. He is a vile man, given to rage and unspeakably cruel. He is violent, lustful, greedy, and morally deformed. I do wonder if he may not be mad."

William Marshal knew the kingdom was devoid of *any* fit ruler. He knew that John's ambitions were self-serving and wicked, yet he would rule with efficiency and would oppose the French, whereas Arthur would doubtless expose England to the ambitions of King Philip. "John is the better of two poor choices," was William's reply. "Perhaps a hard bit can keep him in check."

"A bit?" cried the archbishop. "What sort of bit could hold a frothing stallion like he?"

William did not like the man's chiding tone. "None of this matters. I care little for what is the most expedient, for it is my conscience that rules me, and it is my conscience, sir, that requires me to swear fealty to John."

The archbishop furrowed his brow and closed his eyes. "Oh, William, I fear thy words shall someday fester in thy mouth. John is evil and not easily bridled. Arthur is yet a boy, still able to be moulded."

"I repeat, *Père*, my conscience turns me to John. As Richard's vassal, I was sworn to obey and he bade all his vassals to swear to the Prince. My duty is clear and my honour demands I follow duty."

"My son, perhaps thy honour ought to beckon thee towards wisdom instead."

William Marshal turned away and strode towards the door.

The archbishop had one more thing to say. He called after the departing knight. "William, art thou so very certain of thy duty, or do thy lands in Ireland and thy hopes for Wales tilt thy honour some?"

✻

"I've hated him since he spat in yer face," whispered Aethel, with a scowl.

Isabel thought she ought to reprimand her servant for such blatant disrespect. It would have been the most appropriate Christian response, for kings were considered God's appointed and, as such, entitled to appropriate respect. But Isabel could not bring herself to do more than remain silent. She knew her own heart on the matter.

Aethel grumbled and escorted her pregnant lady out of the gate of the Abbey of St. Clare in London where Lord William's household had taken quarters in preparation for King John's coronation. Sybil soon joined the pair with the flock of seven children, who had not been seen by their mother for several days. The Countess stepped towards her children and let them engulf her in a circle of hugs. She paused to greet them one by one. "Dear William, before you return to school, you must recite more of *Lancelot* to me." She smiled at her oldest son, and he, at her. William, like his mother, had become something of a free spirit, less bound to the order of things than his father.

Isabel turned to Richard, now nearly eight. He bowed, dutifully. Blond, blue-eyed, handsome like his father, and given to neatness and solemnity, he was fast becoming William's favourite. The Countess mussed the lad's hair and laughed at his predictable outcry. "Good son, let the wind blow it. Learn to roll in the grass, soil thy knees sometimes. Dear boy, I fear you make Shoulderlock happy and *that* makes me anxious." She laughed and hugged the lad.

Her eyes then fell on the others one by one, lingering for a brief moment on each pair of happy eyes. Matilda, now six, was fair and delicate, Gilbert, at five, was dark-eyed and brooding. He had just begun the song-school. Eva, four, was plump and eager; Walter, two, was cheerful and mischievous. She took baby Isabel in her arms and nuzzled her soft cheeks. "I am a woman most happy," said she as she closed her eyes. "I pray God's shield upon thee all and for all time."

A rider dressed in a fine embroidered coat and knee-length boots approached. He removed a gaudy hat made all the more fancy by a long white plume, and bowed. "*Madame*, thy husband awaits at St. Peter's."

Isabel curtsied. It was time for the lord's entourage to make its way through London and on to St. Peter's Church at Westminster in order to witness King John's second of three coronations. "Thank you, good sir. Tell him we come." Two pages took the Countess by the hand and eased her into a decorated carriage along with Sybil and the children.

Behind, Aethel struggled to climb aboard her sway-backed

mare. The woman was nearly forty years old and her girth had continued to spread through all the many years she had served her lady. "I still hate him," she grumbled to herself.

A group of knights dressed in their finest robes and with their polished buckles shimmering under the summer's sun led the Countess' column towards London proper. The entourage crossed over a short bridge spanning the city ditch that rimmed the eighteen-foot high city wall. They then entered London through the heavy oak double-swinging doors of Aldersgate.

The free city was alive on that June day, as bustling amidst its crooked streets as it had been for centuries. From various causes, its population had shrunk over time from nearly fifty thousand souls under Roman rule to around eighteen thousand in the prior century at one point, but as a result of the prosperity of the Norman kings, it had grown again and was now home to nearly thirty thousand persons.

Once the travellers lifted their eyes from the chaos in the streets, they realised that they were in a city shadowed by steeples. William fitz Stephen had recently chronicled the number of monastic churches at thirteen, and that of parish churches at one hundred. The priests of the city served a population of freemen, mostly tradesmen and merchants who lived in wooden houses painted in spectacular colours of pitch. Their neighbourhoods were lined with wooden signs decorated splendidly with the images of the many guilds that served the city so well. The streets were dirt, often muddy, and teemed with carts and wagons, horses, fowl, swine, and oxen.

The air reeked, like it did in all cities of the time. The heat of summer had made the manure, urine, garbage, and human waste all the more pungent. Lady Isabel covered her nose. She had never liked London as a child, and she liked it even less as a woman. She had been happy to spend most of her days outside the city wall and within the quiet of the adjacent Tower Castle.

The entourage mingled with peddlers, legates, and soldiers from the farthest reaches of Christendom as it passed down ten-foot-wide Newgate Street. It meandered alongside the newly built

St. Paul's—its beautiful stone imported from Caen like that of the Templar's Temple Church. The column then passed beneath the two mighty strongholds built at the city's western gate near the Thames—the keep of MontFichet and Castle Baynard. Here the Marshal household found itself funnelled into a heavy press of persons, carts, and horses. It seemed like the whole of London was now moving towards Westminster. The Countess looked nervously across a sea of unkempt heads and rough-spun woollens as the city's poor made their way between the retinues of the wealthy towards the coronation and the likely gifts of alms.

Once beyond the western wall the throngs spread across the narrow roadway and spilled over its green shoulders. Isabel cast a look over her left shoulder to catch a fleeting view of the city wharves piled high with wine casks and barrels, carts of fish, and sheds filled with sailcloth, nets, rope, and iron works. The riverbank was home to long rows of rocking wooden ships, their oars at rest and their tall masts standing bare. It was a peaceful sight that she remembered as always pleasing.

"Did you hear about his first coronation?" asked Sybil, as the carriage rolled past the Temple Church.

The Countess was suddenly lost in memories of her wedding. "M'lady?"

"Eh?"

"I said, did you hear about King John's first coronation—in Rouen?"

"*Oui*," answered Isabel, with a hint of annoyance. "I am glad we were not present."

Aethel urged her horse forward. "I have, Sybil. He refused the Mass!"

Sybil nodded. "And I heard he was complaining at Easter that the sermon was too long—that he was hungry and the bishop ought hurry. 'Tis said he walked out for food."

Isabel remained quiet, still lost in the pleasant memories of former times. Aethel leaned forward and continued in lower tones. "And what about the lance?"

"Eh?" answered Sybil.

"Aye, when John was handed the Lance of Normandy, he made a joke and laughed heartily—alone I should add—only to drop it."

Isabel turned a quick eye to her servant. "He dropped it?" she said, incredulously.

"Yes, *Madame*."

"But that is a terrible omen for Normandy."

"Yes, m'lady."

The three fell silent.

CHAPTER XII

THE GIANT AND A NEW KING

AS the entourage made its way past Charing Cross the crowd had grown all the larger and William's knights were making every effort to tighten their ranks around their lady's carriage. In spite of angry commands from the soldiers, a growing throng of the city's poor began to shuffle dangerously close to Isabel's carriage. They pressed near on crippled legs and crutches; some were carried on litters or in each others' arms. As they approached, they turned their faces towards the Countess in hopes of alms.

Isabel stared at the gaunt faces gazing hopefully towards her. She sighed. Many of these pitiful folk were deformed; others were covered in scabs, filth, and ragged cloths. Some had escaped the manors of distant lords and now claimed their liberty for having remained in free London for the required year and a day. *What price is freedom worth?* wondered the Countess.

A huddle of dirty-faced children clamoured at the wheels of her carriage and begged loudly for alms. The Countess stared blankly at them for a moment before her mounted guard chased them away. She thought their little hands seemed so very small as they stretched towards her. Their helpless faces were drawn and white, coloured only by the soot of the city. Bodies disfigured by poorly mended broken bones slumped and limped this way and that; the lady shuddered for their misery.

Isabel laid a hand on her belly and wondered why the child she carried would soon be so blessed with wealth and advantage while these waifs chased pigeons for a crumb. She turned about on her seat and pointed to a squat chest that rested in the rear of her canopied carriage. "Sybil, William—please drag it forward."

"Why, Mummy?"

Seeing her son in his fine tunic embroidered in Paris and

belted with Spanish leather made her suddenly cringe. "Do as I say," she said curtly.

William's face dropped, as did those of all of her children circled around the inside of the carriage. Sybil hesitated, then dragged the chest forward. Without a word, Isabel flung open the iron-strapped chest and plunged two hands into the heap of silver pennies within. Then, to the dismay of all, she began tossing great handfuls of coins into the mob now clambering alongside her carriage. The silver had barely flashed in the June sunlight when a throng of humankind roared from all directions.

The sudden shouts and rush of grasping hands startled the carriage's team of four. Isabel's young teamster leaned backward on his long reins, bellowing at the horses to hold fast. But they reared and spun, lurched about wide-eyed and frightened, until they bolted directly into the crowd ahead.

The lady fell backward atop Sybil and little Matilda while Aethel's horse reared alongside them, dumping the poor matron headlong into the brawling folk. Isabel's carriage dashed away, its wheels rolling up over the bodies of screaming people desperately trying to scatter. The carriage careened headlong down the street until one wheel ran high up a steep shoulder and dumped it on its side, spilling its occupants out onto the ground.

Desperate to defend their lady, William's surprised knights scrambled to gain control of their chargers and, once in command, galloped through the crowd now running hard for the silver spilled from the upset carriage. Without mercy the knights trampled whomever they might and drew their swords against any they thought threatened their lord's family.

John d'Erley, Sir Alan, Sir Ralph, and more than a dozen other mounted men formed a ring of defence. A group of squires righted the carriage and a passing cart was impounded for use. Blood dripped from Sir John's sword and he looked across the stunned roadway with a heavy heart. Before him lay a dozen or so dead peasants, a few of them mere children. Some had been crushed by carriage wheels or horses' hooves; others had been slain by his own sword. Great cries of anguish began to lift towards Heaven as mourners lay across their dead.

Sir John looked carefully at the crowd and his eye caught more trouble about fifty yards away. He leaned forward in his saddle, peering through the tangle of brown tunics and dusty leggings. In the middle of a scuffle he thought he saw a flash of colour. He whirled about and cried towards the carriage. "Are all here?"

Isabel was in tears and being consoled by Sybil. The two looked up and at nearly the same moment cried out, "Aethel!"

Their words had barely found his ear when Sir John and Sir Alan galloped towards the *mêlée* with swords in hand. Indeed, in the middle of an angry crowd was poor Aethel, bloodied and bent over as she struggled against a circle of raging townsfolk determined to have their revenge. But at her side was a giant of a man spinning on his heels and striking his huge fists at any whom would add further injury.

John and Alan crashed into the ring with a shout, both swords singing through the air atop ducking heads. Their horses knocked folk this way and that until they positioned their steeds rump to rump with Aethel and the stranger in a nook of safety.

"Norman dogs!" cried the crowd. "Devils!"

John calculated his move as Alan grumbled, "As long as we've lands across the Channel, it will always be so."

D'Erley nodded as he kept a steely eye on the murmuring mob held at bay by the edge of his steel. "Aethel, where's your mount?"

Aethel's face was bloodied and her elbow swollen from the fall. Her gown was ripped and one braid had fallen loose from the side of her head and hung to her waist. "I don't know," she cried.

"No matter, can you climb on mine?"

The massive stranger suddenly placed his hands around Aethel's waist and lifted her as if she were a small child. She was set gently atop John's horse as Sir Alan watched in awe. The giant stood taller than any man Alan had ever seen. He was young, black-bearded, and fair of skin. He wore his black hair shaggy and long; his eyes were hypnotic, nearly clear, like two crystals tinted by the faintest hue of blue. "Uh—stranger. Many thanks for our Aethel. Follow us?"

The giant said nothing, but a rock thrown from the crowd landed hard against his back. He barely flinched. Alan lifted his face and scanned the crowd with a scowl. "You, stranger, I beg thee follow us."

The man understood and retreated with the two knights to the safety of the entourage. While a doctor quickly attended the family with wet sponges and wraps, the stranger was welcomed with a mixture of gratitude and suspicion. Henry Hose, a new member of the *mesnie* dismounted and shook the fellow's hand. "You look Welsh to me. Are y' a Welshman?"

The man said nothing.

Henry shrugged. "Fine, as you wish."

The man nodded.

The knights drew closer. The Welsh were renowned for their fighting skill as well as their singing. Many of William's knights had suffered at their hands. "Give us a song, then," scoffed one. "*Oui*, a pretty song and a peck of coal." The knights laughed until Aethel climbed out of a wagon and stormed forward.

"He saved m'life, y'fools," she shouted. "Now leave him be, else I'll send him at you!"

Lady Isabel now came forward. Her clothing was rumpled and her face still flushed from fright. She stared about the corpse-strewn roadway, weeping for her shame. "Look, look about. 'Tis all my fault. I wanted so to help them, and I brought them death instead."

Sybil put an arm around her. "The children are all safe, Madame. Give thanks for that."

Isabel was not to be consoled. "I am a fool of fools. And look, poor Aethel. You could have been killed." She embraced her handmatron, sobbing loudly. "Forgive me, my friend. Please, forgive me."

Aethel hushed her beloved lady and wiped her tears. "You meant well enough. And I am fine, save a few bruises and a head full of manure," She laughed. "And see, a stranger came to save me—a Welshman. He shouted something about his mother at the fools."

Isabel wiped her nose and looked at the gargantuan man. "Aethel, you must have reminded him of his mother." She curtsied politely and gathered her composure. "Good sir, you have the thanks of my lord husband and myself for protecting our friend."

The Welshman stared blankly but made an awkward bow. His sincere attempt at courtesy moved Isabel, who cast a hard eye at the snickers of her knights. She thought for a moment. "*Buidheachas do Dhia*—thanks be to God."

The man brightened. "*Buidheachas do Dhia.*"

The two looked at each other for another moment. Isabel strained to think, then asked, "*Deagh ainm?*"

"*Tha.* Twigadarn, *Poch ab-Rhys.*"

Isabel turned to her household. "All of you, greet our new friend, Twigadarn, son of Rhys."

The obedient soldiers extended their hands to the man one by one. He was then introduced to the Marshal children, who could do little more than stare upward in astonishment. Sybil curtsied politely, but it was Aethel who gave her hero a hug.

❋

Given the excitement of the day, the Countess and her children did not join William, who was already at St. Peter's. He was informed of the day's tragedy and assured that all were well and had been safely returned to the abbey. William commanded Twigadarn be given a generous gift of money, a plain linen robe, and a satchel filled with salted pork and honey cakes. He ordered gifts of robes for his knights and a silver goblet for the doctor.

King John's coronation was splendid, as all were, though the new King seemed more interested in his new wife. The day was filled with ceremony and rites, the King himself being led to the altar of St. Peter's, where he lay prostrate while prayers were offered. He then swore to preserve the peace of the Church and of

Christian people, to prohibit crime, and to maintain justice and mercy in his judgements. The clergy and barons who were called as witnesses were then asked if they wished to have such a ruler, to which all replied, "We so wish thus and grant it to be."

It fell upon Hubert Walter, the Archbishop of Canterbury who had secretly opposed the selection of John, to consecrate the new King with a sacramental liturgy designed to remind all of the sacred nature of the King's office. He had already angered John by wresting the prince's pledge to honour the first King Henry's *Charter of Liberties*, but in his sermon the archbishop angered the man all the more. He reminded everyone present that England had committed itself over time to the laws and customs of its early Saxon rulers. These rulers, such as St. Edward the Confessor and King Alfred, had held that the monarchy was in essence an elective rather than an hereditary position. Rule by consent of the governed was the island's heritage, and King John needed to know it was by such consent that he was privileged to serve.

Hubert blessed oil and poured it upon John's hands, breast, shoulders, and head. He was then girded with a sword—the symbol of his duty to defend the Church and protect the weak—then given a golden ring, a sceptre, and a rod. Lastly, he was crowned with the jewelled, golden crown of King Alfred. This he would wear for the remainder of the day and on those future occasions deemed suitable for crown-wearings.

King John was led into the courtyard by a procession of clergy and lords. The clergy were first and they walked bearing candles and containers of incense. A long column of barons followed. These were the lords of the realm who had consented to John's ascension and they were led by the powerful lord, William Marshal. The newly crowned King came next, walking under the same silk canopy his brother Richard had used. Behind him followed more priests, lesser lords, and great numbers of other laymen.

John, now ruler of England, Ireland, Wales, Normandy, and much of France, stood quietly as Archbishop Hubert raised his hands to the sky and proclaimed, "Almighty God of nations, drive his enemies before him, grant him the blessings of Thy mercies as he serves Thy holy ways amongst us. We have chosen him as our King according to Thy just law and the laws Thou hast consecrated. Grant us all, therefore, Thy holy wisdom as Thou hast bestowed most generously upon Solomon, that we might be the holy keep of Thy justice and mercy. Amen."

Archbishop Hubert then presented King John to the assembled. "Behold the Lord's anointed, given power on earth to defend the good and to punish the evil. We entreat the power of our royal saints, St. Edmund, Hermengild, and Oswald, we yearn for the help of St. Edward and commit this kingdom to the succour and the faithful attendance of all the saints of God."

King John was presented to his people with all that which he had ever wanted—power, glory, wealth, and the approval of the Holy Church. For him it was a good day, a good day indeed. A choir of monks began singing a chant for the King: "Christ conquers, Christ reigns, Christ commands—"

❊

Within months of King John's coronation, the Marshals were faced with good news and bad. King John had recognised the value of keeping Lord William Marshal tied closely to him. The King held the vast estates of Pembrokeshire, a holding once belonging to Isabel's family. Located near the western tip of Wales between two tidal inlets, it was renowned for its strategic castles and productive land. The estates were nearly twice the acreage of William's Chepstow estates. King John, being a man of shifting loyalty, imagined all others to be as he. Had he understood the character of a man like William Marshal, he would have understood how unnecessary it was to buy his loyalty with something as trite as wealth. But King John did not understand the honour of William Marshal and proceeded to invest him as the Earl of Pembroke.

William's fealty was neither enhanced nor diminished by the grant of Pembroke, but he was delighted nonetheless. Pembroke not only made him a man of even greater wealth and prestige, but also provided a convenient port for his necessary trips to his lands in Ireland. He immediately appointed a sheriff to administer royal justice throughout his shire courts and then set upon the business he preferred—the business of war.

Pembroke's castle had been strategically located over one hundred years prior and had never been taken by Welsh rebels. Now, armed with the knowledge of the very latest in castle design, William eagerly set plans in motion for its reconstruction. Of course, he attended quickly to the comforts of his family and to the immediate improvement of the chapel, but his heart thrilled with excitement as he poured over his sketches with architects and engineers summoned from France.

He began by immediately hiring workmen to replace the earth and timber keep—the central stronghold—with a magnificent stone one. It would be nearly seventy feet tall and twenty feet thick, divided by four floors, and topped by battlements and a dome.

The plans for his battlements were ingenious. At the top of the walls he would leave large holes, into which he could place beams to create a platform. The platform would extend out over the heads of attackers and keep ladders from assailing the ramparts. He also planned a curtain wall with round towers and a mounted catapult.

To one side of the castle sat a small town secured by a thin stockade wall. Its residents were a mixture of English transplants and local Welshmen, the latter bearing a stubborn grudge against their Norman conquerors. Theirs was a seething hostility that took form more by night than by day, and William was ever conscious of his peril. Welsh chieftains like Maelgwyn and Gruffudd were known to be raiding the countryside and William was anxious to complete his improvements quickly.

The grant of Pembroke had barely captured the imagination of the Marshals before Isabel delivered her eighth child. The little girl was born on a cool October morning after a long labour and a painful delivery. Sybil and Aethel proved to be champions at encouraging the suffering mother until the child took her first breath.

A weary Isabel smiled at her screaming infant as the bells of matins rang from her chapel. She turned a weary voice to Aethel. "I have spoken with my lord husband and he approved the name, if a girl."

"Aye, m'lady? Shall I fetch a priest?"

"Soon. But hear me," begged Isabel with a weak voice. "We have chosen to name her Aethel, after you."

The ageing Saxon servant stared blankly in the candlelight. She could find no words, no words at all, but reached her thick arms clumsily towards her lady with tears rolling down her round cheeks. Sybil smiled warmly at her friend. No amount of silver or gold could have provided a more wondrous gift than this.

"Ah, dear Aethel. I cannot breathe," laughed the lady, as she struggled in Aethel's embrace.

"Oh, my lady, my dear, dear lady." Aethel was giddy and spent the whole of that night by the child's side. And, in the morning when the priest came and when Lord William came, and Sir John, Sir Alan, Sir Henry, Sir Eustace, and the whole of the household came to witness the child's baptism, it was *her* name that was proclaimed. To hear her name repeated loudly and proudly for the daughter of her beloved lord gave her tears of such joy as she had seldom known.

But, alas, though the love expressed by Isabel to her friend would endure for all time, the little child's breath would not. The day following the baptism, little Aethel began a fever which worsened through the day. A doctor of renown was urgently summoned from Cardiff to consult with William's own physician, but in the two days it took for him to appear, the child worsened. The doctors called the malady "childbed fever," a common condition of infection, resulting in death for many newborns. They agreed on a very mild dilution of barley water, coupled with apple vinegar steeped with raspberry leaves. Isabel, Aethel, and Sybil did not sleep, choosing instead to keep a vigil for the child. While one bathed its head in cool rags, the others prayed with Le Court. Even the busy, eternally pre-occupied Shoulderlock spent many hours on his knees alongside a stream of loyal knights who gladly took their turn before the altar.

But it was not meant to be. The child passed gently on a Sabbath morning and breathed its final breath with the bells of terce. With tears of course, but also with courage and grace, Lady Isabel and her sullen husband prayed with Le Court and his priests as the whole of the household gathered to mourn. There, in the chapel of Pembroke and surrounded by seven children and the world that loved her, the Countess thought her heart might break. She followed her daughter's shrouded body towards the little graveyard in the castle's bailey and watched in horror as her baby disappeared into the black, yawning hole. Isabel groaned and leaned hard against the sturdy frame of her husband. She cast a woeful eye at those gathered and sobbed.

Yet the stricken mother did not grieve for herself alone, nor only for the suffering of her husband and her children. Indeed, she turned a wet eye towards another and walked across the leaf-covered churchyard to hold the hand of broken Aethel.

❈

"Ah, Countess. Here, a tankard of warm cider for thee to chase the chill." Le Court handed his lady a steaming wooden cup filled with hot cider that tasted more of vinegar than apples. "'Tis six months since thy loss."

"*Oui, Père*, almost to the day. And I am with child again." Isabel smiled calmly at the dwarf as she took a seat on a padded wooden stool. She had grown so very fond of him over the winter past. Confined among the terrible draughts of Pembroke Castle she had spent many an hour in the chancellor's chamber reading from his library of parchments and from the few books he had managed to acquire. The grief she suffered for her baby's death had found its place, and her heart, though scarred, had healed—as all must.

"God be praised. Another Marshal for the world."

Isabel smiled, but lowered her eyes.

"Eh? What is wrong, dear sister?"

Isabel hesitated as her eyes swelled. "I–I have spent these months wondering if the curse is now satisfied. To my shame I

176

felt relief in the thought of it. It was as if the loss of little Aethel had served me well, and I hate myself for such horrid feelings."

Le Court walked to the lady and laid a tiny hand of comfort on her shoulder. At his touch Isabel began to sob. The priest continued tenderly, "Thou dids't love that child well. Do not doubt thy love nor the earnestness of your prayers in those dark hours."

Isabel drew a deep breath and nodded. Then, with a trembling voice she recited the curse that had so darkened her days;

> A sword from heaven's gate shall fly
> with wings that none can stay.
> Its edge shall split thee from thy love
> and tear thy heart away.
> Thy tears shall never dry nor cease,
> thy grief shall never fade,
> Lest angels err and brace thee so that
> thou cans't join the blade.

Obsessed with her fears, she pressed timidly. "Oh, *Père*, do you think her death might satisfy these words? My heart *has* been torn away. Yet the curse may not be fully satisfied, for my tears for her *have* ceased." She wrung her hands and stood. Her face was pale and drawn, suddenly showing the weight of her secret agony.

Le Court did not know how to answer. To suggest the curse had been satisfied was to give it credence; to suggest it had not been was to continue its hold on the suffering Countess. The little priest fumbled for words and turned away. "I–I do not know, m'lady." His voice betrayed his own confusion. He was beginning to believe the curse had power after all.

Isabel fixed her red eyes to the floor as if bewitched. "'Twas no 'sword from Heaven's gate'," she mumbled to herself, "unless all death is a sword. Could it be so, *Père?*"

Le Court was troubled. He had to say *something*. He took a breath and with grave reluctance offered the best his shepherd's heart could offer. "Dear Countess, I bear thee witness that thy grief *has* faded. Hence, this empty curse is of no effect."

Isabel paused and pondered his words. "So you think it is of no relation to Aethel's death?" she asked slowly, warily. She felt shame once more, suddenly aware of her self-interest in the question.

"I think not, but more than that, it is of no effect whatsoever." Le Court wanted to drive away his own creeping doubts and punched a fist into his open hand. "If I could find the priest who has so wounded thee, I should gladly hazard my soul to send him to his grave."

Anxious to change the subject, Le Court refilled the lady's tankard and changed his tone. "Now, enough of this. I beg thy leave to speak of other things."

Isabel composed herself with a timid smile, embarrassed by her fears. "Indeed, I do beg thy pardon, *Père*, and I do thank you for your kindness."

Satisfied the crisis had ended, Le Court climbed a small ladder that gave him access to his window. His apartment overlooked the bailey and he had spent many an hour enjoying the activity of the lord's builders. "All the world does change. Our friend, Sir Ralph has died in England, his son Ralph shall soon join the *mesnie*. Aethel's helper Carly is lost to fever. Ah, so very sad. And Ida is injured in Chepstow, I'm told."

"*Oui, Père*. Such news has saddened us all."

The little man nodded, then changed his tone. "Thy family grows as does this castle. I see stone rising all about, stone and mortar, scaffold, heavy timbers, rope—my, 'tis to be a monument to genius."

Isabel laughed. She would enjoy sharing that comment with her husband at pillow time. "Indeed, Father. I have found genius in this room as well. I love thy wisdom as well as what I discover in here." She lifted two scrolls from Le Court's wooden chest.

The chancellor nodded with a grin, happy the woman's mood had changed. He pointed to the scroll in her left hand.

"So, my lady, by the old wine stain I see you hold my copy of the first King Henry's *Charter of Liberties*."

"Of course, *Père*, you know thy library well."

"I was given this parchment as a gift from the nephew of Bishop Maurice of London. I believe it is one of the original copies the King issued at his coronation exactly one hundred years ago. King John took no pleasure in affirming it. Did you find it of some interest?"

"*Oui*, indeed. I have studied each of his fourteen points and I surely found the spirit of piety and justice that I had oft' heard of in his regard."

Le Court agreed. "By granting this charter, the King acknowledged what God requires of rulers—that they are to rule with justice and under the law. His first point was to 'make the holy Church of God free' and after that he pledged to take away 'all the bad customs by which the kingdom of England was unjustly oppressed'. Notice God's place is in the first, then the cause of justice. It is an order of things that never fails; when kings place God first, justice *always* follows."

Isabel's eyes flew over the Latin script—scanning over numbers of tedious injustices that the King had intended to redress—until they fell upon the tenth point. "Here, *Père*, notice he yields to the '*common consent* of my barons on issues of his forests. And here he places *all* England under the King's peace—a way to spread common law over the whole of the realm. But here, Father Le Court, here is what takes my eye. 'I restore to ye the law of King Edward—with the advice of my barons.' The blessed laws of King Edward."

"*Oui*." Le Court smiled. "Edward the Confessor, the patron saint of England! He was a kindly King, chubby, it is said, and an albino. As all know, he was the last Saxon king, yet had been exiled to Normandy where he became learned in many matters of religion and philosophy. Once given the crown, he did his best to keep the peace between the Anglo-Danes in the north, the Anglo-Saxons of the south, and Normans whom he had invited across the Channel to serve in his court.

"Some say he was weak—I say he was a man of peace. Under St. Edward the kingdom flourished. Fine sculpture, illuminations, amazing metalwork, and wondrous architecture bloomed. These are fruits of an eye fixed on the beauty of God. His reign gave blessing to religious life and it secured the folk by honest law and fair administration. It was a fine time.

"Ah, but I am wandering again! Let me say this one last thing: Henry's *Charter of Liberties* says more in whole than it does in part, for I believe it suggests that *law* is supreme—may that never be forgotten. But, now, what hast thou in thy right hand?"

"You ought to guess," Isabel said with a laugh.

The dwarf wrinkled his nose and stared at the yellowed scroll. "Well, methinks perhaps portions of John of Salisbury's *Policraticus?* But thou didst once say he was a bore."

"Ah, quite so, on both counts. He *is* a bore, but now I understand your insistence that I read him." Isabel took a sip of her cider and proceeded enthusiastically. "His writings are quite astounding and I find them of particular interest now that we suffer the excesses of King John."

Le Court smiled. Like himself, John of Salisbury had argued the importance of history as a basis for all learning. "Didst thou know that John of Salisbury had been a witness to the murder of Archbishop Thomas Becket?"

"*Non, Père.*"

"'Tis true, and because of it I believe he maintained a particular interest in the abuse of authority."

Isabel continued. "He first writes that God ordains rulers—even tyrants—and that their laws need to be obeyed—even evil laws—so long as they do not violate God's Law."

Le Court settled himself within the arms of his miniature chair and folded his hands. "*Oui, continuez, s'il vous plaît.*"

Isabel's furrowed her brow and thoughtfully proceeded. "He also reasons that tyranny itself, however, is a violation of God's Law, for it offends the stewardship of authority given to kings. He argues persuasively that, while God may ordain a tyrant for the purposes of chastising His people, the tyrant is not justified for such a role.

"God's Law requires rulers to rule justly, that they wield the sword in His name according to virtue. Thus, when a ruler ceases to rule justly Christian men have both the right and the duty to dispose of the tyrant. If I remember his words—'To kill a tyrant is not merely lawful, but just.'"

Le Court nodded, approvingly. "Interesting words for our times!" he said, with a smile. "And cans't thou see the power of history in forming his understanding. The man draws on the ancient Scriptures, the experiences of the Greeks, and that of the Romans. He sees the effect of sound doctrine and the lessons of prior generations on our times. History's gift is wisdom. Ideas do not simply appear in time, but grow over the centuries.

"But back to his point: I ought to temper thy summary just a little. John of Salisbury was a moderate man and he suggested tyrants be dealt with patiently. If I recall his words, 'it is not well to overthrow the tyrant utterly at once, but rather to rebuke injustice with gentle reproof until his wickedness is proven by his stiff-necked rebellion.'"

Isabel nodded. "*Oui*, prudent words and words respectful of God's anointing." She wrapped her cloak tightly over her shoulders and leaned towards Le Court's hearth as she pondered what effect words like these could have on the England of her time. She was anxious to share these thoughts with Lord William in their bed-chamber. *He needs know his duty towards tyrants,* she thought. *Yet his honour—his pledge of fealty—is always present in his mind. I fear the day when honour and duty may stand opposed.*

CHAPTER XIII

A FEAST TO REMEMBER

THE Countess turned her face to the dwarf and she smiled affectionately. *Soft-hearted, learned, humble, void of bitterness*, she thought, *I do love him so.* The two relaxed quietly, both having had enough of heady thoughts and political conversation. They enjoyed their cider without further comment until Le Court finally spoke.

"My lady, hast thou heard who slept in the stable last night?"

Curious, Isabel shook her head.

"Twigadarn, son of Poch ab-Rhys."

"Who?"

"Ha! Forgotten so soon? The Welshman who saved Aethel on thy adventure in London."

"By the saints! I had forgotten. He's that giant of a fellow—black hair, crystal eyes—yes, I do remember. Why is he here?"

Le Court shook his head. "'Tis an amazing story! It seems the fellow had been in search of me for some years." Le Court threw a large log into his hearth and settled into his chair. "In the first years of service to thy lord husband, I was sent about his many holdings, including the Netherwent of Wales. While passing through the valley of the Wye I had learned of a certain Norman lord, Raimond fitz Gilbert, who was persecuting his peasants harshly. It seems they were showing hospitality to the Welsh rebels who followed a druid priestess named Gwaeddan. The woman was believed to be inhabited by demons. Her body was painted in many colours, her hair unkempt and pinned with human bones.

"The villagers feared her and her pagan followers, so they were apt to yield to her demands for food or shelter. In response, Lord Raimond had responded to his peasants' timidity with fines, beatings, and unspeakable tortures, finally even threatening the bishop with death unless he pronounced an interdict against these hapless Christian folk. The cowardly bishop succumbed to the lord. The churches were closed, priests could no longer offer Mass, children were born without benefit of baptism, marriages were not consecrated, burials occurred without sacred rites, and so forth.

"The poor folk trembled in fear for both body and soul, helpless to defend themselves from the brutality of either side. So when I passed through the valley they begged me to quickly baptise their children and to pray for their dead. I had arrived in Twigadarn's village within the hour of a pagan attack. I remember well choking on the sour smoke that snaked between charred hovels and I remember the bodies and their parts strewn about the place like so much refuse.

"A row of stakes had been set in a circle and atop each sat the head of a peasant. My priests and I stared in disbelief, ashamed of the bishop's interdict and angry with the cruel lord who should have protected his people. I scattered my small company in all directions to offer what pitiful help we could."

Le Court shuddered and reached for his cider. "I was running from ruin to ruin, corpse to corpse, when the voice of a boy turned my head. He was a large lad and his eyes enchanted me as if they were the eyes of an archangel. I ran to his side and he pointed me towards the grey ashes of his hovel. He led me quickly to a tangle of bodies which were the remains of his family.

"The lad took my arm and pointed to the lifeless bodies of a toddler and an infant. He cried, '*Baptismo! Baptismo!*' and I understood. The children had been born during the interdict and their souls were in grave peril. I quickly knelt before them and poured water from my flask over their little heads."

Isabel asked, "And the boy was Twigadarn?"

"*Oui.* It was. It seems he believes he had failed to properly thank me and so he vowed that night to find me and serve me. He claims he has spent all these many years in search of a dwarf priest—an inquiry that must have earned him a few hearty laughs! But, he soon learned I was in the service of William Marshal and has been searching for our lord's entourage ever since.

"I fear I received his thanks yesterday with more astonishment than humility. He embraced me, lifting me higher from the earth than any has ever done! He told his story, then admitted to having killed nearly the whole of the pagan rebels in the years that followed. He wrung the neck of Gwaeddan like a hen for the pot. I assured him it was no sin."

"So the man is devout?" asked Isabel.

"He has no good reason to be, but yes, I believe so."

The Countess thought for a moment. "Shall he serve you?"

"I think not, at least not directly."

"Eh?"

"Shoulderlock tells me that thy husband wishes to provide his family with constant bodyguard. His knights have all volunteered, of course—d'Erley being the loudest—but Lord William is reluctant to remove any from other services. Furthermore, he is awarding each of his knights holdings in his growing lands and they would need to travel from time to time. So, I have asked Twigadarn if he would serve thee instead of serving me—that it would be my desire he do so."

Isabel was not sure. "Lord William hates the Welsh."

"*Oui*, and I intend to rebuke him for it. Scripture instructs us to be 'no respecter of persons.' Not all the Welsh are worthy of hatred and this one is surely not. With thy permission and with Twigadarn's, I should like to propose it."

The Countess remembered Twigadarn's valour in the defence of her beloved Aethel and reconsidered. "Perhaps it would be a good thing, a very good thing. *Oui*, please propose it. I believe it is a particularly good time, especially as we soon shall be among the Irish."

Le Court brightened. "Ireland? God be praised. 'Tis the land of sheela-na-gigs and saints--the repository of the *Book of Kells*, and the bones of St. Patrick and St. Brigid. Ah, wondrous news."

❋

William Marshal growled at the prospect of a Welshman protecting his family. He did trust his chancellor and his wife, however, and reluctantly agreed to the appointment of Twigardan as his family's bodyguard on the condition that his fighting skill be tested by the knights of his *mesnie*. So, after several hours of bruising competitions, a circle of bloodied, limping, and humbled Norman knights advised their lord that the Welsh giant was quite capable of defending the Countess and her children—and, for that matter, anyone else he chose to champion.

✳

The summer of 1200 was stormy and the trip to Ireland was delayed. The delays frustrated the lord but nearly drove Shoulderlock mad. No sooner had he organised the provisions, forwarded appropriate correspondence, and prepared the boarding, then his precious schedule was changed. Furthermore, Steward Roger had died and no new steward had yet been appointed. This left Shoulderlock with countless added details to supervise, including settling quarrels between bickering sheriffs and their judges, suspicious tax collections, angry tenants, a peasant uprising on William's lands in far-off Normandy, and sundry contentions with other lords and their courtiers. The pressures of his duties had taken their toll on the exhausted chamberlain.

By the feast of Lammas—the first of August—poor Shoulderlock thought he might finally lose his mind. He was seated at the far end of the long trestle table and chewing on some pre-dinner cheese when one of his ushers whispered of an argument between the pantler and the butler. "I can bear this no longer," Shoulderlock cried. The hall fell silent.

Le Court, Edward Shoulderlock's persistent foil, smiled wryly from across the table. The two were in Pembroke's hall preparing to enjoy a moderate feast day with their lord, a dozen knights, two ambassadors from London, and an Irish-Norman baron. The little chaplain pointed to the kitchen. "Is it the fresh-baked wheat rolls turned in honey, or the roasting boar that you can no longer bear?"

Shoulderlock would not be mocked. Seeing the dwarf's grinning face drew a whining, "Le Court! Thou art unkind and unkempt! I need not be thy entertainment!"

Lord William and his knights roared. They were already well-oiled from several hours of drinking red wine, English ale, and sundry fermented liquors—by-products of nearly any boiled food. Loud and boisterous Sir Henry was seated next to Le Court and he cried across the table, "Shoulderlock, walk over here; I've a question for thine ears only." The diners tittered.

The chamberlain pursed his lips. He was seated next to Sir Eustace, the troublesome knight who had his ever-present monkey on his shoulder. It was the monkey that made Shoulderlock nervous, and he rose slowly. She was prone to bite and had snatched grievous bits of his forearm at the Easter feast. Relieved to be clear of the monkey's menacing eyes, he took a few loping steps towards Sir Henry. With each step the hall echoed with guffaws. Lord William closed his eyes, wishing for all the world the man would swing his arms. "*Oui*, sir knight?"

The drunken soldier whispered in his ear, "D'Erley needs thy counsel."

Shoulderlock raised his nose and turned his face to the opposite end of the table towards which he quickly walked. The diners' faces broadened with grins. "Begging thy pardon, Sir John, how can I serve thee?"

John d'Erley shifted in his seat. He pitied the man and took no great pleasure in the sport being made of him. "Uh—*non, Père.* They are having their fun." The hall filled with good-natured hisses.

"It is I who needs thee!" cried Alan de St. Georges from the middle of the table. He stood with a big smile and tossed his long blond curls to one side. "*S'il vous plaît.*"

Shoulderlock turned, submissively, and took several long, awkward strides. It was the earl who could bear no more. "Good Chamberlain! I beg thee, could you not fold thy hands in prayer as you walk!"

The hall rollicked. Shoulderlock sighed and obediently held his hands at his chest as he continued towards Sir Alan. "*Oui*, sir knight?"

Alan smiled. He would be merciful. "*Père*, I want to offer my many thanks for thy fine service to us all." He raised his goblet and loudly proclaimed, "To Father Edward, the best chamberlain in the realm."

The knights stood to teetering feet and hurrahed Edward Shoulderlock. The priest blushed, faced the floor, and turned one eye towards his nemesis. But Le Court was cheering as well. He was standing atop the table and crying his hurrahs with all the bravado he could muster.

The game over, the men turned their attention to the cupbearer now bringing a silver tray and two large silver goblets towards Lord William. Following behind was the Countess, and all remained on their feet and bowed their heads. Lady Isabel was dressed in a flowing red silk outergown that was draped lightly over an undergown of green. Her long, redberry-wheat braids were wound in bright yellow ribbons, and atop her head she wore a pale blue wimple. With a smile lightly cracking the small wrinkles at her eyes, she took her husband's hand and the two were seated.

Lord William nodded and his guests took their seats. Their wooden trenchers were presented along with a pile of thick slabs of stale bread which would soak excess fat and water from the meal to come. Drooling dogs began to prowl beneath the table and nose their masters in anticipation of a bountiful morning.

The cofferer was the servant charged with maintaining the lord's table, and he quickly put a silver spoon and long knife at each place. Wooden, pre-meal tankards were replaced with silver ones, and the butler—the man in charge of the lord's beverages—followed his colleague with pitchers of red wine and ale, perry, cider, and even mead—a honey liquor more popular with commoners but occasionally enjoyed by the ruling class as well.

Lady Isabel loved to cook and had often spent many hours with her kitchen staff reviewing their recipes, their supplies, and their techniques. A stickler for good health, she insisted that her staff follow the etiquette prescribed by physicians regarding the proper preparation and presentation of foods. Hence, she demanded strict adherence to the required considerations of the four humours.

The learned men of the times believed the body to be governed by four prevailing fluids, or humours, each affected dramatically by the four associated seasons. Each person was born with a disposition towards the characteristics of one of the four, but it was important for everyone to avoid the extremes of each. If the body's fluids were not kept in a reasonable balance, one's health and disposition would be susceptible to various maladies. The object of treatment, therefore, was to restore balance among the humours.

The first humour was sanguinity, or blood—a hot and moist fluid that was enhanced during springtime. The diffusing qualities of blood allowed for much physical activity and a wide variety of foods in its season. The second was choler, or yellow bile, a fluid adversely affected by summer's hot and dry conditions. During summer, therefore, it was prudent to avoid activities that heated the body and as well as excessively hot foods or beverages. Cool, moist foods—the opposite qualities to the season—such as barley pottages, sour veal, and pomegranates were preferred.

The third was melancholy, or black bile. This fluid was affected by the depressing changes of autumn, and was considered cold and dry; hence hot, moist foods, such as hearty stews and old wines were recommended. Activity might be increased and hot baths were encouraged. The fourth humour was that of the phlegmatic, or winter's phlegm. It was the fluid considered to be cold and moist, requiring hot foods such as roasted meats, hot potions, and activities that would aid digestion by stimulating the body's heat.

Isabel had spent the morning hours in the cramped kitchen to be certain her new cook, her baker, fruiterer, and poulterer were all well aware of her unyielding standards. She had been pleased with their apparent understanding and she eagerly awaited their fare as the ushers delivered silver trays bearing the first course.

"Good wife!" cried William happily. "Capon and pheasant dressed in cherries—and *blancmange*." He lowered his nose close to the *blancmange*. "I smell mutton boiled in almond milk and sweetened with Welsh honey!"

Isabel clapped. "*Oui*. The fruiterer is a clever man from York. He has a peach sauce as well, and puddings of dried fruits and spices!"

The servers brought more platters, these filled with light meats and easy-to-digest broths, a platter of lettuce, and borage seasoned with the clove-like flavour of avens. Plates of cheese were brought, and would remain throughout the meal, as well as boiled turnips seasoned in salt and ginger, and a young crane boiled, then cooled, and soaked in ale.

Between the courses a minstrel with a lute sang numbers of pleasant ballads and a juggler toyed with four daggers and a hammer. His demonstration was cut short, as it were, for a monkey's cry turned his eye and his hand grabbed hold of a blade!

"Good," grumbled William. "I'd enough foolery. I'm ready for my second course." Shoulderlock watched nervously as his kitchen staff hurried forward with wooden trays of heavier meats. At first glance he feared his lady would object to the roasted boar.

Isabel stiffened and turned a hard eye on the cook peering sheepishly from behind a column. The boar had been rubbed red with sandalwood and was presented in bulk surrounded by a circle of partridges coloured green from the parsley and mint in which they had been boiled. But the meat was still sizzling and oozing grease onto the tray in such quantities as to form rivulets of fat that dripped generously over the tray's curled sides. Isabel tossed her head lightly and the usher quickly removed it.

As pots of vegetables and a magnificent bowl of rose-glazed carrots filled the vacancy left by the boar, the earl's eyes raised. "And see, *mortrewes*!" No one knew whether the name of the dish predated or followed the word, 'mortar.' It was a heavy concoction of boiled hens and pork hewed into small bits and ground finely. Grated bread, egg yolks, and handfuls of ginger, saffron, and salt were then added to make a challenging fare reserved for the most hearty of knights.

Two plates of baked eggs in a peculiar sauce arrived, then one of more green salad. Finally, the boar was returned, now devoid of excess fat—it having been soaked away by spongy loaves of bread. Now dressed in clary leaves to cut the grease yet further, it was presented with the reluctant approval of Isabel. Well-trained squires busily carved chunks of pork from the beast and delivered platters of it to the waiting diners. Fingers grasped greedily at the piles of steaming meat, then flew into deep dipping bowls of heavily spiced fruit sauces and deposited succulent morsels into gaping mouths.

To this course was then added boiled cabbage, a plate of dull looking beans, and a scant egret staked awkwardly upon a wooden plank.

"I confess I am relieved to see no fish," chuckled William. He submitted to the Church's fish days but oft' dreaded eel stew, salty cod, roaches, rayfish, tench, or salmon. Isabel was convinced it was the Church's demand that took his pleasure, not the taste. William plunged his hand into the boar's carcass and yanked out a few bones which he tossed to the horde of dogs drooling by the table. He enjoyed watching them dig through the straw and run away gleefully with their prizes. Eustace's monkey screeched and began to fight with Shoulderlock, prompting the lord's hard look. "If you can't quiet that she-devil, I'll have her on a plate."

Isabel had slipped away only to reappear at the kitchen's door as a trumpet sounded. She smiled as the knights and guests rose to their feet with a cheer. The soldiers, dressed in their finest robes, drew their swords and formed a tunnel of steel under which the lady walked as escort to a large gold and silver platter bearing the centrepiece of the day's feast. A huge boiled swan wrapped in a blanket of its own feathers and looking very much like it was floating comfortably on a shimmering pond was delivered to a very pleased Lord William. He rose and clapped as musicians played pipes and lutes. And, as it was positioned on the table, each knight took a turn laying the flat of his sword atop the great bird to pledge oaths of chivalry.

Sir Baldwin bellowed, "Under God, my lord, I do swear to defend and protect thy lady and thyself from all harm for all time."

Sir John quickly elbowed to the fore. "By thy leave, my lord,

I do swear to defend the virtue of the maidens of all Christendom against all foes. I do further pledge my blade, my heart, and my very soul to the wise, the courteous, and the beautiful Countess Isabel."

Isabel smiled. She loved this knight, as did her husband. She could not imagine why he had taken no wife.

Hurrahs followed each vow until Lord William took his turn at the last. He stood slowly, solemnly, then drew his sword and touched the bird. With both eyes fixed on the wife he loved he said, "By all that God has given, by all this sword hath won, by all that warms my heart, I do pledge thee my honour, my every breath, and my eternal love."

Isabel could not hold her tears. The room was silent, save for a few knightly sniffles, and the woman blushed shyly as she dabbed her eyes.

William, suddenly uncomfortable, turned towards his men and raised his sword. "God save King John."

The hall filled with an awkward, half-hearted murmur. William darkened and stared at his reluctant men until a gentle, though unseen tug on his leggings turned his head. Isabel smiled and bade him to sit. "I am thirsty, lord husband, and cannot reach the perry."

The earl hesitated, then grunted as he sat hard atop his chair and filled his wife's silver tankard. Wisely, Shoulderlock quickly ordered the carver to his task. The man was specially trained to carve the delicate meats, and with skill he sliced perfect portions of the swan and laid them gently on a silver tray. Le Court, though stuffed beyond the limits of his conscience, found himself fixated on the tender bird and impatiently waited for his serving. It was a delight of delights.

After the second course was over, an hour of loud, coarse jokes followed, as well as yawn-tempting performances by a tumbler, an Italian troubadour, and a poet. Finally, the third course arrived—a smaller course of lighter fare. The lord and his lady looked across the long table now decorated with tasty treats including plover, sour veal, and snails. Accompanying were bowls of purple seaweed called laver, as well as applesauce, cherry preserves, honey cakes, a large plate of his wife's marzipan, and best of all a tray of her tarts.

Eustace was groaning and drowsy. He had eaten far too much and needed to wash his throat one more time. He tossed his monkey to the centre of the table and cried in a drunken slur, "Pass mee li–qu–or."

"Eh," answered a new arrival to William's *mesnie*. His name was Sir Jordan de Sauqueville.

"What eh? I says pass me *li–cour*."

Confused but accommodating, Sir Jordan shrugged and set his hands upon the unsuspecting shoulders of little Le Court. Then, to the surprise and sudden delight of all, the howling dwarf was jerked from his seat and passed along the table from one roaring knight to the next until he was delivered to the plate of one very bewildered Eustace.

"Eh? Whaat's this thing 'ere?" he mumbled with a wrinkled nose.

"You said you wanted Le Court!" shouted Jordan.

"Le Court? Le Court? Nay, y'fool. I wanted l-i-q-u-o-r."

The hall echoed with laughter as men wiped tears from their eyes. Even Lord William chortled and giggled uncontrollably—a sight none had *ever* seen! As might be imagined, the memory of the tiny chamberlain being handed down the bench would bring many a smile in the dark years ahead.

More time passed with music, ballads, and rowdy sword-play. The room was filled with countless belches, guffaws, titters, and roars. The story of "*li-cour*" was told and retold. The dinner had begun in the late morning, as all should, but it was nearly nones when Lord William faced his stuffed-bellied knights and stood with arms widespread. Forgiving them the disappointment of the King's well-wish, he bellowed, "Are ye glad-hearted, my brothers?"

The room resounded with a loud "*Oui.*"

"Are ye ready for the Irish?"

"*Oui, Oui,*" roared the knights.

"Ha! But are they ready for us?"

"Nay!"

"*Sacre bleu*! They are not. The barbarous bunch need order and honour! It is we who shall bring it to them! They shall see Norman stone rise about their green hills and they shall surely know we mean to stay and hold what is ours."

The hall was loud and noisy. The knights hammered the heels of their boots hard against the floor.

"Our estates lie throughout all the southeast of the island, from the shores where our Viking cousins once lived, through the haunted mountains to Kildare, to Kilkenny, and the ancient lands of Macfaelain, Ua Tuathail, and Mac Murchada. This is the ground once held by my wife's grandfather, King Dermot. King John now honours its rightful rule and 'tis you who must hold it."

The knights stood and cheered, their swords waving wildly. They continued to shout until they joined together in a loud chant roaring, "For God and William Marshal, for God and William Marshal!"

Lord William was pleased and he sat down with a smile. His men were good and true, they would serve him well, and he would defend them to his own death. He took Isabel's hand in his and squeezed it lightly. He was a happy man.

※

It was Christmas in the first year of the new century when Lord William presented his family with two very special gifts. The pair came tumbling out of a large sack as the great lord laughed. There, to the astonishment and great joy of his children, stood two puppies on teetering legs, wide-eyed and panting.

"Oh, husband, what a wonderful gift," clapped Isabel, as a flurry of grasping hands seized the pair. She wished her two oldest boys were not away at school.

The children squealed with delight. The one puppy was an Irish Hound with grey, wiry hair and a long square face. The other was a Boar Hound, a breed popular with the Danes for their savage fighting spirit. Smooth-haired and wheat-coloured, the pup's face was long and bulky, his brown eyes eager and keen.

"Children, what shall we name them?" William laughed.

Walter cried, "Shoulderlock and Le Court!"

The children giggled.

Lord William raised his brows. "So, y'little imp! Do we really need two more of them?"

The children laughed.

Plump Eva chimed, "Sir John and Sir Alan, my two favourites." Her five-year old voice still squeaked a little and her father playfully tumbled her atop the rushes strewn about the floor.

"Nay, daughter! They'd be my best two knights—methinks they'd feel the sting of insult in namesaking a dog."

Matilda was the oldest daughter. She had become ladylike, even at her tender age of seven. The earl had already received numerous requests for her betrothal. "I think, father, good names are Peter and Paul, for the apostles."

The room was quiet. For a few moments only the snap of firewood in the bed-chamber hearth was all that could be heard. Lord William found himself in a predicament, for he wasn't sure if it would be proper to name his dogs after the apostles, but he did not want to offend his daughter's piety. Unable to manoeuvre, he cast pleading eyes towards his wife.

Isabel paused. She re-tied the braids in her hair. "I suppose," she began, "that if we name them after Saints Peter and Paul, then St. John, St. Thomas, St. Matthew, and the others might feel rather slighted."

Like both her parents, Matilda could be stubborn. "Are they slighted at cathedrals named for one or the other?"

Isabel sighed. The girl had a point.

William suddenly blurted. "The apostles were men of peace—our dogs are for the hunt." He smiled, proud of his quick wit.

Matilda countered: "It was Peter who drew the sword to defend the Christ."

The ever-brooding Gilbert, now six, added bluntly, "It seems a wicked thing."

The family turned their faces towards him in surprise.

"I won't have it so," Gilbert continued. He turned his dark eyes hard at his sister. "A dog should not be named like that."

Isabel awkwardly lowered herself into a cushioned chair. Heavy with child, she was due to deliver within the month. Baby Isabel cried and William called for Sybil. "Children, might I offer names?" said the Countess.

The circle consented.

"I have been spending these many months reading with *Père* Le Court. I have learned that good England stands on sturdy pillars. The piety of St. Edward, the wisdom of John of Salisbury, the justice of Henry the First, the order of Henry the Second, and many more. But two ancient pillars hold it all steady, the Kings Alfred and Canute—one Saxon, one Danish.

"Alfred taught his people that rightful law is founded on God's Law. Canute showed his folk that rightful rule is that which submits to the King of kings. Together these two set-stones of England's past are the foundations of free men's liberty. Perhaps these are fitting namesakes for our pups?"

The family paused and whispered amongst themselves for a time; then Gilbert stepped forward as the eldest male child present. "*Oui, Mère*, we agree."

CHAPTER XIV

HOME TO IRELAND

LORD William stood at the dock below Pembroke Castle and stared impatiently at the foreboding April sky. He filled his nostrils with salt air and looked longingly westward across the waters of the inlet. With a good wind and smooth water he could be in Ireland in four days.

The lord's new steward, Richard fitz Hugh of Oxford, stood before him in his black robes. A clerk, the priest was fluent in Latin, adept at finance, and shrewd in political matters and the law. A tonsured, squat, hawk-faced man, Steward Richard had little patience for Shoulderlock and less for Le Court. "Father Edward says it is so and I find the man generally precise, despite his shrill and annoying manner."

William nodded. "If the barons in Normandy continue their complaints they shall bring another war against us—Philip would be their ally and the realm shall surely divide. They must swear to King John. This Arthur business is folly."

Richard agreed. "It seems, sire, that the barons in France think John to be a dangerous man and they argue that Arthur has proper legal grounds."

The two stood quietly, turning their eyes to the crying gulls. "We sail in three days, the devil with the wind. I must secure Ireland before I am called to war in France."

Within hours the steward ordered Shoulderlock to organise the household in preparation for the journey. When the lord's household sailed, however, he was to go to Chepstow in order to review matters of domestic staff and expenditures while Steward Richard travelled to Sussex for other duties.

Before attending to any of the preparations at Pembroke, Shoulderlock sent instructions to his deputies in Ireland via a fishing vessel sailing that very day. It would be important for the earl to be properly received at his various residences and they needed fore-warning. The castle at Kilkenny would be the Marshals' primary residence and it was well-staffed with servants, including cooks, a butler, a pantler, and an adequate host of ushers, cupbearers, fullers, chambermaids, and tradesmen.

Shoulderlock was efficient and decisive, so in three short days four high-prowed ships set sail from Pembroke. Three of the ships carried the lord's *mesnie*, including their horses, armour, weaponry, and wardrobes. On board the fourth sailed the lord's family and those personal servants most needed. Each ship was manned by a crew of six, including a master and assorted seamen hailing from unnamed ports of Britain, Frisia, Denmark, and Spain. They made for a colourful assortment of various hues, tongues, and tempera-ments, all sharing a common knowledge of the sea.

Lady Isabel and her eight children, including the newborn Sybilla, rocked uneasily through the inlet as they cast a final glance towards their limestone castle disappearing quickly against the grey sky. As the ships rounded the most westward tip of Wales, all eyes turned wistfully towards the headlands of St. David's, named for the virtuous founder of a monastery founded there nearly six centuries earlier and the patron saint of the Welsh-Norman lords.

Heavy clouds shadowed the tender green of the rocky coast and sank towards the oncoming ships rapidly. The concerned mas-ters pointed their crafts due north, tacking hard against an increas-ing wind blowing cold and damp from north-northwest. The ships heaved hard into rising swells, tilting first to port, then to starboard. The ruddermen struggled with the crew to tack the ships forward. Below deck, the Marshal children became sick and frightened. Sybil tended her namesake while Aethel and Isabel comforted the others. The lady wondered why she had agreed to bring the chil-dren and now was beginning to believe she had made a terrible mis-take. The day was long and cold for them all. Sheets of rain pelted the ships' decks for hours while salty spray hissed hard against the rails.

The day passed into night and the Marshals fell into a restless sleep atop uncomfortable wooden cots stacked above one another. Aethel had been sick from the first hour of the journey and now lay terribly weak in her bunk, unable to do more than groan. Sybil was drawn and hollow-eyed, begging the angels to either carry her to solid ground or whisk her soul to Heaven. Poor Twigadarn had not been seen save for one brief moment where he was spotted bent over the rails and offering the sea whatever his sorrowful belly possessed. It was a journey none would soon forget.

The second day passed more easily with lessening winds and lower seas. Yet the masters kept their sun-squinted eyes fixed on a troubling western horizon. The travellers climbed out of their horrid quarters now reeking with vomit and waste. The crew tossed buckets of cold water atop each and, though the water was icy cold, it refreshed and cleaned them. Aethel retrieved warm blankets for the children and her lady and the group seated themselves before the deck-hearths, which offered a warm fire set atop large flat stones.

The air was fresh, though bracing, and Isabel liked the groan of the ship as it ploughed the blue water. She watched the baker busy himself by warming long loaves of bread that had been baked a few days prior. At the baker's nod, the children pounced upon the bread-basket like starving serfs at a boon day feast. Fish—both fresh-caught and smoked—was added to the meagre menu, as were cheeses and generous quantities of ale.

That night was one of fading stars and by dawn of the third day, William's flotilla was shrouded in fog so thick it was nearly impossible for the ruddermen to see each other's bows. Wisely, the master of Lord William's vessel lowered his sail and called through the shadows to his fellows. From some distance came a hollow, ghostly voice, "Aye? Aye? 'Ave y'torchlight?"

"Aye, 'tis aft. Where be the others?"

"One's far to starboard, another's off m'stern some bowshot or more."

Thin, muffled voices from other directions confirmed their positions. The masters had no idea where their ships were, nor at what rate they were drifting. The knotted ropes they used to 'dead reckon' speed could not be seen and the sun was not to be found. They had all heard rumours of a navigational instrument in which lodestone was set in water to point south. They thought such a thing might be of good use in times like these, but it was assumed that the rumours were either idle talk or the thing was an object of sorcery.

By mid-morning the fog yielded and the sails were hoisted. But by late afternoon the sky blackened. Sheets of stinging rain again pelted the deck, bouncing off its oak boards like great handfuls of pebbles thrown by giants. The sea turned grey and angry; its swells foamed and raced towards the bobbing ships like wild beasts running hard at helpless prey.

"Mother!" cried Eva. "Help me!"

Isabel gathered her six-year-old daughter while Aethel and Sybil held others. Lord William braced himself against the throws of the ship and cried for all to be calm. The ferocious storm had come quickly. Concerned for the water now pouring over the deck, all male passengers were ordered top-side to help the crew bail. So, clinging desperately to taut ropes, William, three of his knights, some half-dozen squires, and two groomsmen did their best to heave pitiful buckets of salt water back to the angry sea from whence it came.

Night fell and it was as if the darkness had encouraged the wind's wrath. Howling spray and black water crashed against the groaning hull. The mast's cross-beam fell, falling atop a hapless seamen and crushing him on the deck. The hold was filling quickly and the ship listed heavily within waters now rising ever higher to the rails.

Below, Lady Isabel clutched her relic and prayed with her household. The woman touched each of her children in the utter darkness and with each touch a young life was comforted. Dispelling her own fears, she recited the *Pater Noster* until she was nearly hoarse. Wet, cold, terrified, and losing hope, the Countess could do little more than wait for some end to come.

It was the same deep into the night until the master finally cried the words none wished to hear. "It is hopeless, sire."

William would have none of it. "*Non. Sacre bleu, non.*" Exhausted from hours of futile bailing, the ageing earl staggered down the short deck ladder and crashed into his family's chamber, now waist deep in cold water. "Isabel!" he cried.

"Here, William." The woman heaved herself against the roll of the ship and fell into her husband's arms. She pulled herself tight against his warm frame and held him with all her might.

"We must make a vow," cried the earl. "If God spares us, I shall endow a monastery where we land."

As if the vow suddenly angered the Prince of the Air, a huge wave crashed over the bow pouring a river of black water into the lightless galley. Isabel was knocked out of her husband's grasp and toppled backward beneath the flood. William plunged forward, desperately grasping for her in the dark water. He found her arm and dragged her coughing and gasping to her feet.

And so it went through the night. The ship heaved, the men bailed, and in the cold, dark galley the women and children held each other in a tangle of trembling arms. But as the dawn approached, hope returned. The winds began to ease, as if exhausted in their vain attempt to drive the fleet away. The sea rolled hard, but it, too, seemed weary of its own fury.

"Lord Marshal," cried the ship's master. "There. Clear skies." He pointed to the eastern horizon where the faint edge of the sun was creeping out of the sea.

"Ah, Sir William, but turn now about."

The earl set his back to the rising sun and laughed heartily as before him lay a dark silhouette of land. "Ireland," he shouted in a clear voice. "God be praised."

❋

True to his word, William Marshal had barely set foot on the docks of Wexford when he ordered a clerk to deliver a letter to the bishop at distant Dublin vowing the founding of a monastery. He would grant nine thousand acres of land to the white-robed Cistercians of a Welsh abbey of which he was a patron, along with an invitation for them to send a colony of monks to Ireland. Since landfall had first been made near a tiny village by the sea, he would build the cloister there and name it Tintern after the abbey in Wales.

The Countess and her household were both relieved and amazed to learn that each of the lord's four ships had arrived safely. All were badly damaged and several seamen had been lost overboard, as well as two squires from Sir Baldwin's ship. Sad as the losses were, all hurried to give thanks for their good fortune and were directed by William to Wexford's Templar church.

The port town of Wexford was no stranger to Norsemen. It had been settled three centuries prior by Viking raiders who were more apt to create towns than the native Celts. Its streets were designed in the fishbone pattern common to most Norse towns, with a main thoroughfare and many narrow side streets fanning off from each side. Its harbour was surrounded by mudflats and supposedly had been formed by an enchantress who drowned a Celt named Garman Garbh by releasing flood waters from the sea.

Lord William's entourage settled in Wexford for three days while he fasted and prayed with Le Court. The earl then travelled briefly to Waterford where he prayed with his beloved Templars at their modest preceptory. There he vowed generous grants to the Order to be used in the various preceptories located on his other lands, including the ones at Wexford, Kildare, and Kilkenny. During the same time, his herberjurs were sent ahead to advise various vassals that their residences would be used as lodgings during the earl's tour.

After the brief respite, the Marshal retinue formed a column of pack-horses, palfreys, hunters, and chargers loaded with provisions, servants, squires, and knights. These, accompanied by carts filled with tents, weaponry, furnishings, wardrobes, utensils, and a whole pantry of foodstuffs and beverages, began their journey through the lord's lands of Leinster—the south-eastern quadrant of Ireland.

For several days the column passed through the gentle Irish countryside, stopping to pray at pilgrims' chapels and pausing to marvel at the ancient stone circle-crosses that stood tall and ominous like silent sentries staring across the green landscape. They passed ominous megaliths—stone circles and ringed mounds—which reminded all that this was a timeless land of mists and ghostly ways.

Le Court was particularly intrigued with the sheela-na-gigs carved in the stone of so many village churches. He thought these frightening figures of grotesque and hideous human forms were a fascinating, though troublesome expression of mankind's condition. "Only the Celts would carve such things," he remarked.

The company crossed over lands once ruled by the chieftains of families with names like Ua Donnchadha, Ua Cearbhaill, O'Kealy, O Riain, Ua Caellaighe, and Ua Bruadair. These same lands were now ruled by men with other names, names such as FitzRobert, de Valle, Bigod, Devereux, de Clare, and de Hereford. These Irish-Norman lords were reluctant vassals to William Marshal and had shown little interest in paying their overlord his due. Most were pure Normans but some were sons or grandsons of Irish women and felt a kinship to the land they ruled. All proudly called themselves Irreis, not so much as to be identified with the Irish natives, but rather to identify themselves as the toughest of all Norman lords—colonists who had conquered and now held the wildest of all realms. Their counterparts across the Irish Sea— the *Engleis*—were considered soft and comfortable.

For this reason, the Earl of Pembroke was seen as a lesser man, his reputation notwithstanding. The barons would concede their duty but intended to do so half-heartedly and with an eye for opportunities to circumvent or even sabotage the lord's authority. It was a tension that suited King John, for he had always considered Ireland his personal garden and had no interest in seeing any of his barons establish dominance. Though he had allowed William Marshal to retain the Irish lands of Isabel, he would keep a sharp eye on the great knight's ambitions.

Hence, the column that wound its way through Leinster did so with martial order. William's knights travelled in full armour, robed in their lord's colours and readied for combat. The earl was well-aware that his vassals were unhappy and likely to be disloyal, and he also knew that the local population remained stubbornly hostile to all the Norman lords. Were it not for the conquerors' stone castles and impressive military presence, it would be nearly impossible to rule them.

While her husband viewed the passing villages with an eye for danger, Isabel viewed them with a heart of compassion. She, after all, was the true governess of these lands—her husband held them by right-of-wife. When he died, they would pass to her. So, though she was concerned for the well-being of the folk in all of her husband's many lands, she had a particular interest in these.

Like all of Christendom, the villages were populated by simple serfs, called villeins, and were little more than haphazard collections of thatched hovels filled with hungry children, gaunt mothers, weary men, and a heart-breaking assortment of undernourished, deformed wretches, many staggering about mad. The villagers spent their days tilling the land or tending sheep according to the tolling of bells and the turn of seasons. The Holy Church ruled their souls; Norman lords ruled their bodies. They raised what grain crops they could—rye, oats, some wheat and spelt. With this they paid more than a third in tax and tithe, kept a third for seed, and lived on what remained. This they boiled into mush, or paid nearby monks to bake into bread. The villeins were the "third estate" of humankind. They were "those who work." Above them were the other two estates in this Chain of Creation: the first estate, which consisted of "those who pray," that is, the Roman Catholic Church as represented in its many layers, and the second estate—"those who fight," or, the lords and their knights.

So, while the clerics prayed and the rulers ruled, the serfs simply laboured. Some were yeomen—free tenants who rented or purchased small portions of the lord's land. They were required to offer military service when called upon and most commonly served as footmen or archers. Most of the folk were not free, but rather bound-men. They were tied to the land of their lords and exchanged their labour for their lords' protection. They were not permitted to leave their lord's lands or even marry without receiving permission and paying a tax. Some were allowed to buy small parcels of heritable land, but its ownership did not change their status. Only by paying a huge fine, called a manumission, could they buy their freedom. Their only other hope was fleeing to a free-city in which they could safely hide for a year and a day. Having lived unclaimed by their lord for the prescribed time, they were considered free.

Isabel sighed as her horse trotted past the dirty-faced folk. She now knew better than to toss them money, yet she pleaded with her husband to send the almoner for their relief. If the peasants of Leinster had only known the heart of their lady, they would have been glad-hearted and would have cheered as she rode by. Instead, they glared at her with hate-filled eyes, daring to dream of the day they might be free from their oppressors.

Much of Leinster was an easy landscape. Covered in green pastures, rolling hills, and pleasant rivers, it was a temperate, fertile land. Near its centre was the town of Kilkenny and the lord's primary residence. His castle there was perched atop an overlook of the River Nore and from its great hall Lord William presented gifts of expensive robes and announced the grant of lands to many of his household knights, including a large holding to his beloved Sir John d'Erley. The grateful knight fell to one knee and reaffirmed his pledge of fealty. Happy, the good knight ran from the hall and immediately summoned two fellows and a half-dozen squires to accompany him to his new lands and the stone keep that would be his official residence.

Isabel was pleased with her husband and enjoyed her time in Ireland. Her newborn, Sibylla, was healthy, as were her other seven children, and all seemed pleased to be in the land of their grandmother. Isabel spent many hours along the ramparts of Kilkenny Castle, which overlooked the river and the carpet of green that spread to the far horizon. She thought of her mother, Eva, and wondered about the woman's final days. The woman had held some lands in dower right and these were now the cause of some dispute. Isabel paid little heed to squabbles over land rights and "grievances of greed," as she called them. Instead, she preferred to keep her attention on things lovely and good, things just and honourable—pure things worthy of praise. It was as the Holy Scripture instructed and it was as she preferred.

❋

In the months that followed, the Countess played with her children, enjoyed what sunshine Ireland grudgingly offered, and accompanied her husband on his missions to various lordships in the region. Le Court typically followed, as it was his duty to pray with the couple daily and offer Mass for them. Often while travelling, Isabel would seek out her little friend and the two would spend hours pouring over the chancellor's parchments and discussing their contents. The Countess had become learned in philosophy, theology, history, literature, and even higher mathematics. She had become so well educated that Lord William now summoned her to his various councils as his personal advisor. Any who might raise an objection found themselves immediately and discourteously dismiss.

The earl's priority continued to be the securing of his Irish barons' loyalty. It was a frustrating task. One particular baron, Meilyr fitz Henry, was a constant thorn. He was the grandson of King Henry I and had fought for Leinster shoulder to shoulder with Isabel's father, the mighty Richard Strongbow. He saw Lord William as an unwelcome intruder, undeserving of the land and a threat to the interests of the barons who had heretofore done well under the distant eye of King John.

Meilyr had been appointed the King's justiciar in Ireland and as such, he had wide-ranging authority on behalf of the Crown. Unhappy with William Marshal's arrival, he had already planted seeds of dissension. He sent a hurried message to King John advising him that the "ambitions of Lord William Marshal are contrary to the best interests of thy rule." It was enough to bring an oath to the King's lips.

Troubles with resistant barons were not the only matters of concern for the earl and his *mesnie* however. News from Britain proved to be a disquieting distraction for all. It was learned that King John had become utterly obsessed with Arthur, his rival. John's barons in Normandy had abandoned John in droves in favour of Arthur and were finding a sympathetic ally in France's King Philip. John's English barons were beginning to falter as well. They had already grown weary of the man's excessive and abusive ways.

Lord William knew what would soon be asked of him and, as expected, a courier arrived at Kilkenny with a message from King John. The earl and his knights were urgently needed to "defend royal interests in France." William groaned.

When the summons arrived, Lady Isabel begged her husband to delay only long enough for her to satisfy a dream. Torn between the King's command and his wife's pleading eyes, Lord William hesitated. Once before he had abandoned his family for the call of a king and he still doubted his decision. He paced the floor of their bedchamber, then turned to his wife and laid his huge hands atop her shoulders. He stared into Isabel's pleading blue eyes and smiled. "*Oui*. I do grant you this, but I demand you return quickly. I must attend to matters here. Sir Baldwin shall escort thee with two score men-at-arms. Leave the children with Sybil; Aethel may ride with you."

Isabel was disappointed not to take her children or to have William join her, but she bowed her head, gratefully. "*Oui*, my lord husband. *Merci*. We shall return within one week."

❋

Le Court nearly wept out loud when Isabel told him the good news. "By the holy saints, can it be so?" The priest's one wish for Isabel had been that she might lay her eyes on the *Book of Kells*. Fearing this might be her last trip to Ireland, the chancellor had urged her to make the journey to the cloister where it resided.

The column escorting the Countess delivered her to the monks at Kildare on a sun-washed September day. The treasured book was housed within a church built on the site of St. Brigid's double-monastery—one housing both monks and nuns. The clerics serving the cloister also guarded the eternal flame of the ancient Irish saint. "Please, my lady, follow me." Le Court led Isabel, Aethel, and their ever-present shadow, Twigadarn, into a smoky pit where one monk and one nun kept a sacred vigil. "This flame has burned since before Christ's name was ever spoke on this island. It was the flame of an ancient community of pagan priestesses and had burned for centuries. St. Brigid was converted by the Briton, St. Patrick and she, in turn, converted the whole of the community, sending them far and wide to serve the poor. She then consecrated the flame to God and it has burned ever since as a reminder of the Holy Ghost and the mysterious presence of God around us."

The four stood quietly before the flames for nearly an hour as Le Court told of St. Brigid's kindness and remarkable miracles. He picked rushes from the ground and formed a crucifix by knotting two small sheaves at the centre. "This is the Cross of St. Brigid. She would make these and leave them on the roofs of the sick whom she prayed for all over Ireland. She would return to each house exactly one year later. Then she removed the crosses and laid them on the stables so that the animals might be blessed as well."

Isabel knew of St. Brigid and thought of her fondly. She removed her relic and held it to the light of the fire. The tiny gold cross reflected its warm light in such a way as to make it seem alive—a living Cross. She began to weep for the joy of her Saviour. The woman was devout, to be sure, and guided by the light of truth. She communed with her God with her mind, body, and spirit. Secretly however, she had begun to wonder about the stories of miracles claimed so regularly in her world.

The obsession with myths, legends, and magical things that the Countess had encountered, particularly among the Celts, had given her pause enough to form the seed of doubt for all things fantastic. She had never witnessed a miracle as such, nor seen a vision of the Virgin, nor stairways of angels, nor the dead revived. She had been told that St. Brigid's fire needed no tending, yet her eyes had fallen upon sawed logs under a canvass near the pit. Always angered by priests who promised unseen "blessings" for coin-in-hand, she was also troubled by those who took silver in exchange for wild tales of floating rocks and flying bishops. Yet deep in her soul she knew—she *knew*—that her world was governed by an unseen Hand, only partly revealed yet fully present. She knew the Almighty could not be contained by the thoughts of men, yet she wondered how far reason could be stretched—when should she embrace mystery and when should she challenge it?

"*Madame?* I see that look in thy face again."

Isabel nodded. She set aside her questions and answered, "*Père*, I feel God's presence, even in my doubts, and it is enough to give me joy." Her tone was humble and laced with a grateful confidence.

Le Court smiled. "Ah, doubts—the evidence of faith."

Isabel laughed, lightly. "And now, *Père*, to the book?"

"Indeed! Follow me!" The chancellor led the lady's company into a squat stone church. He whispered to a priest, who then bade the group to follow him down a narrow stairway and into a torch-lit chamber in the cellar. "*Non, Frère*, this shall not do. We want to see it under the sun."

The young priest objected lightly, but upon being reminded of whose wife the Countess was, he quietly relented. In moments the *Book of Kells* was set upon a wooden table under the full light of the Irish sun. With a prayer and a bowed head, the priest then opened the book and backed away.

Isabel's eyes widened in astonishment as Aethel gasped. The beauty of the book defied all later efforts at description, for its remarkable artistry was incomparable and beyond words. The Countess turned the vellum pages reverently. The book contained the four Gospels and had been written by unknown persons over six hundred years prior. Most learned men, however, were convinced that such exquisite glory could only have come by the touch of Heaven; hence, it was believed likely to be the handiwork of angels.

Written in black, red, purple, yellow, lilac, sienna, pink, and green, the book rivalled the most exotic flower garden of any earthly king. Its colours tinted and shaded the Holy Word in a proportion most pleasing. The artists varied their use of colour between soft, gentle hues, and strong, shimmering enamels which were masterfully made by heavy layers of inks. No silver or gold had been used, yet the colours of the pages radiated under the sun. Miniature pictures of the Evangelists, the Divine Child, the Holy Virgin, and the temptation of Christ drew Isabel to tears. Along the borders were intricate patterns of coils and Celtic knots, swirling trumpets, gargoyles, the animals of creation, and interlacements of symmetrical patterns all woven into an abundant, harmonious design.

"Such a wonder of man's handiwork have I never seen," murmured Isabel quietly. "Never in all my journeys have I been so smitten by beauty. Dear Le Court, you have blessed me with a gift beyond measure. To know such beauty exists in this world of sorrows gives me hope for things to come. I shall keep my memory fixed on these pages."

The group remained silent, moved by the lady's passion and encouraged by her vision. They lingered over the *Book of Kells* for hours, pausing only to eat a modest meal of smoked fish, bread, and Irish ale. Finally, with grave reluctance, the Countess called Baldwin to her side and requested they be returned to Kilkenny Castle.

CHAPTER XV

TROUBLES

THE four years to follow were tumultuous for Lord William's household. King John had ordered the earl to save Normandy for him, as well as his other lands in France. It proved to be a futile command, even for the likes of William Marshal. The brilliance and appeal of the impressive court of King Philip had enticed many a baron's affections. Given the brutish outbursts of the impetuous King John, the polish and the dignity of the French King was enchanting. Furthermore, John's dubious regard for justice and customary law had discouraged many. As a result, Philip's endorsement of Arthur as the rightful King of England drew increasing support.

To add insult, King Philip cleverly summoned King John to appear before him on a matter of charges brought by the barons of Poitou—a region held by the English throne yet subject to the lordship of the French King. It was a proper demand under the law for King John was technically Philip's underlord for these particular lands. Yet the thought of John submitting himself to the King of France under these circumstances was unconscionable and fuelled the man's fury.

War raged again on the gentle lands of Normandy and the other duchies of France, as it had done under the Lionheart and Henry before him. To fund his new war, King John immediately raised taxes on his barons to levels never before tested. Most of his lords' primary holdings were in Britain and they had less and less interest in royal business across the Channel. Paying taxes for the King's adventures abroad had rapidly diminishing appeal. As news of defeat after defeat criss-crossed England, the willingness to support the war effort with either silver or soldiers waned yet further.

In a short time, King John had lost so much land on the continent that his nickname, 'Jack Lackland,' had become the derisive toast of taverns all through Christendom. By 1203 the situation had become desperate, and King John would respond to the pressure in a way that would ultimately confirm the true character of the spirit wearing the Crown. It is always the way, for pressure does not change a man; it exposes him.

Encouraged by the support of the French King and rebellious barons, King John's nephew, the young Arthur, had begun manoeuvring towards the overt seizure of the English Crown. Old Queen Eleanor, the widow of King Henry, was King John's mother but also Arthur's grandmother. She was residing in France, where she bravely championed the cause of her son against her grandson. Arthur resented his grandmother's hostility and unwisely had her captured and imprisoned.

Arthur's move gave John just the help he needed to inspire a groundswell of support. Queen Eleanor of Aquitaine was the beloved inspiration of courtly love and the symbol of feminine elegance. The English barons would fight for her. John rallied his army and prepared to rescue his mother. But before implementing the whole of his plan, he shocked all by reaching into his dwindling treasury and giving one thousand pounds of silver to the hungry. It seemed odd and out of character to many, but perhaps he believed the deed might relieve his soul of enough prior sins that he could add one more heinous deed without dire consequence.

King John's barons fought hard, less for John than for Eleanor perhaps, but in any event they scored a victory both bloody and complete. Queen Eleanor was joyous and grateful, Arthur humiliated and tossed into the prison of Rouen's castle. Yet that was not quite what John had in mind for his nephew. He quickly sent agents to Arthur's prison who claimed to be under instructions to castrate the would-be king. Considering the penalty suitable, the castle's commander gladly released the prisoner to John's men, only to later learn that the knaves stabbed the helpless Arthur to death.

The vengeful, cowardly murder of Arthur sickened Lord William and disgusted all men of chivalry. Unable to look his King in the eyes, William obeyed his further commands nonetheless.

King Philip was now determined to pry Normandy from the grip of the English King forever. Lord William was called upon to rally John's army and fight for the land the Normans had ruled for three centuries. Lord William obeyed, albeit dispassionately, and engaged Philip's armies bravely until nearly all was lost.

Defeat after defeat stripped King John of his territories until, at long last, he abandoned his troops and fled to England, demanding William follow. From there, he claimed, he would raise the money necessary to send reinforcements. But it was too late. Soon after his arrival in London news came of the fall of King Richard's beloved Saucy Castle, his "Fair Child." With its loss, the inevitable, unimaginable end was in sight.

※

In May of 1204, William Marshal was sent to France to seek terms with the happy King Philip. William arrived quite troubled. He held lands in Normandy and had no wish to lose them on account of King John's failures. He realised that such a desire would put him on dangerous ground and he needed to be meticulous in protecting both his honour *and* his land. Years before he had pledged fealty to Philip for his lands in France. This meant he had never been able to draw his sword against Philip *for those lands*— and he never did. His fealty was legal, understood by all parties, and was accepted as the norm for all barons with mixed homage.

King Philip was no fool, however. In his negotiations with the earl he immediately recognised an opportunity to tempt the worthy knight, insult the defeated King John, and perhaps drive a wedge between the two. "Sir William," he began. "You served against us brilliantly. Thy courage and cunning on the field of battle inspires us."

Lord William bowed, unaffected by such flattery.

"You do come to me now as ambassador for thy defeated King. He wishes to sue for peace."

William bowed again.

"As a Christian soldier, I have no desire to prolong bloodshed among my brothers. After all, in Palestine our knights died for one another. So, my secretary has presented my conditions for peace, conditions both merciful and fair. You have read them?"

"My clerks have read them to me, sire."

"*Oui*, of course. And do you agree to our most merciful terms?"

William had little choice. "*Oui*, sire."

The corners of Philip's lips turned upwards, just a little. "*Bon*. You have the King's seal?"

"*Oui*."

"I see. There is one other thing, Lord William. A small matter perhaps, but one most fitting." His eyes narrowed, almost playfully, but with a glint of meanness. "In the presence of this council, I demand thy fealty to be reaffirmed. It would persuade me of thy honour in all these matters."

William chilled; his mind raced. *If I swear, I've done no more than restate what already is. If I fail to, I lose my rightful lands. Yet by swearing loyalty to Philip, John may dis-endow my lands abroad.* The aged earl was a courageous warrior and reasonably skilled at court, yet he lacked wisdom in matters of proportion, yielding instead to the easier formulas of things clearly divided. *What is legal is right; the devil with the rest.* He walked boldly to Philip's throne and knelt.

The King of France rose and received the man's pledge graciously. He then reaffirmed Lord William's rightful claim to his French lands.

The negotiations concluded quickly. King John was stripped of his title as Duke of Normandy and thereby yielded up centuries of the over-lordship of Viking blood. John's other lands in France remained intact, at least according to the letter of the law. For generations to come, however, they would be little more than fields of blood for future English kings fighting desperately to protect their ancient interests on the continent.

✳

"The world is different now, Isabel," moaned William in the summer that followed. He had returned to Chepstow Castle from the King's court in London, where he had met his wife.

"I have heard, lord husband. Perhaps it is a better place."

William's eyebrows arched. "Better?"

"*Oui*. Less land for the Devil to play on."

William did not respond. His opinion of his King was kept fast in deep places. "The contract for our young William's marriage holds."

"The terms are not changed?"

"No. Good Baldwin is still the Count of Aumale, and so our contract holds. He has served me well as my faithful friend. If his daughter survives to proper age—she is eight now—they will wed. He has agreed, however, that if she dies, William is to be given her younger sister. If William dies, the contract serves for Richard."

"I trust your judgement in the matter, husband, though I do hope she will be a good woman. Our William is a tender soul, deep-thinking and wonderfully artful."

William nodded. His eldest son was not his favourite—Richard was—but he loved him dearly. The lad was still in the Canterbury school, now with brothers Richard, Gilbert, and Walter. "He has spunk, as well," added the earl. "I received a letter from Bishop Hubert that he needed a severe rod for William's 'sundry wrongs, including fighting, insolence, and trickery.' I love it. Soon he begins training as a squire."

Isabel shook her head. "It troubles me some. I think Richard must have goaded him. Ah, but he is thy son, so I suppose the acorn has sprouted close enough!" She took her newest baby in her arms. It was her ninth living child, a boy named Anselm, born one year prior. She nuzzled the happy fellow, whose hand seized upon her braid. "And you? What sort of man shall you be? I only wish Sybil were still here to help." Her dear midwife and nanny had left the service of the Countess just months before. Her husband, Sir Alan, had retired from service in the lord's *mesnie* upon receiving a large inheritance of property. Believing all replacements would fall far short of Sybil, Isabel had decided to tend the little ones herself, along with help from various handmaidens and, of course, her Aethel.

A rap on the door startled the pair. It was John d'Erley. "By thy leave, sire, an urgent summons from the King." Knowing his lord could not read, Sir John handed the message to Isabel and turned away.

The Countess read the message quickly. "King John orders you to meet him in York 'at once and with the accompanying William the Younger.' Husband, does this mean—?"

"*Oui*. So I fear." The lord's face tightened.

Isabel paled. "I would have Shoulderlock make thy arrangements, but he is not yet returned from Usk. A messenger brought news yesterday that he is still quite ill; the doctor says he suffers congestive chill."

William was not interested. "Matters not. Summon his assistants; we leave at daybreak."

❋

"King John, I do swear by all things holy I am no traitor to thy Crown!" William was enraged and sat before the King and a council of nervous barons. The summer day was warm and the day's showers had made the manure-covered streets of York reek. Inside the King's residence, the hall was heated with angry words.

"How dare you lie to my face!" roared the King. "You swore thy fealty to our enemy whilst my acting agent for a truce."

"My homage to Philip is within the law and only on my lands already held. It was required as guarantee of my honour as thy agent."

King John was not impressed. "I find it odd, sir, that my spies say you first paid homage to Philip and *then* gave away my Normandy."

William stormed towards the throne. "None here has served thee better on the field than I. None. I yielded only what terms you approved." He turned towards the council facing him. "Do any here accuse me of treason? If so, I do challenge trial by combat."

The King waited impatiently. He wanted someone other than

himself to make the charge. The King tapped his fingers anxiously on the arm of his oak throne and waited a little longer. Trial by combat was a method of proving guilt that was fast fading. The trial was conducted by a duel to the death—the survivor was deemed the innocent party. Few in the King's hall were foolish enough to challenge either the integrity or the sword of William Marshal. The room remained silent. At last, the King stood with a grumble and walked away.

William took long, proud strides through the Great Hall and out its oaken doors. His son, William the Younger, was there to meet him, along with the recently arrived Isabel. The two had listened angrily through the closed doors and received the man with affirmations. Still indignant, Lord William could barely speak.

"No man under God has ever served a King with more honour than you, lord husband. King John would like nothing better than shoulder you with his failures; you were wise to challenge him." Isabel's words were the brave, affirming words of a loyal wife. Yet deep inside she wondered if her husband had acted wisely, or even honourably. After all, it was true he had a *legal* right to do what he did, but the *spirit* of his homage to Philip cast doubt on both his wisdom—and his motive.

Young William nodded. "Aye, father. The man's a pig—a liar and a pig."

The lord turned a hard eye at his fourteen-year-old son. "The man is your King." He turned to Isabel and then said sadly, "The lad is to be taken to Windsor as a hostage for my future loyalty. I fear he shall be there for some time."

Isabel chilled. A quiet fury filled her chest and she squeezed her fists tightly. She nodded, submissively, but thought, *He gave more heed to his lands than to his family! Could he not see these effects?*

The earl spoke to his son sternly. "You. Guard your tongue; guard your back. Do nothing to give any cause to do you harm or put your family in peril."

Isabel bristled. She thought, *'Tis you who has put our family in peril already.*

The young man stood stiffly, willing to accept his fate boldly.

216

Lord William continued. "Marshal de Hardell shall begin your knight's training. He's as good as any in the realm, and I shall keep an eye on things."

Father and son looked at each other for a long moment until young William finally spoke. "Sire, I pledged no fealty to King John. I shall honour you, father, but my duty is to you, not to him."

Lord William nodded. "Then serve me well, my son, to God's glory and to England."

With heavy hearts, father and mother turned their son over to the royal guard, and began their journey back to Chepstow. For days the Countess hid her sadness and her anger until she could finally hold neither. In the dark of night she walked alone and in her solitude wept loudly.

The earl was not unaware of his wife's displeasure nor was he unaware of his own mixed motives in his pledge to Philip. Suddenly shamed by what troubles his poor judgement may have foisted on his innocent family, he became enraged. He led his retinue to within view of Chepstow Castle, then could contain his fury no longer. Saying little, he directed his household towards home with Twigadarn and a handful of knights. Then, with a loud, angry cry, he turned his horse around and led his soldiers in a six-day raid against the rebels of his Wye valley.

For his part, King John had anger to vent as well. He had not been able to successfully confront Earl William, for the lord had skilfully positioned himself behind the barricade of law. But, as tyrants do, King John decided to ride roughshod over what laws he could and began to prick the man. His first act was to seize all the earl's lands in Sussex. It was a costly loss for William, but as with all acts of vengeance, it was not fully satisfying for the King.

The difficult year of 1205 ended with yet more troubling news. Queen Eleanor of Aquitaine, the mother of King John, died, and with her died what influence she wielded on her son's behalf among his reluctant barons scattered in the minor duchies of France. The Archbishop of Canterbury, Hubert Walter, also died, thus leaving his important office to the manipulations of the

scheming King. It was a loss that gave England shudders. The archbishop had served honourably, championing justice and the rights
of Englishmen courageously while defending order and urging
patience. His death deprived the realm a voice of reason at the
King's court, yet it also deprived the King of a respected buffer to
his barons.

But other news was sadder yet. Alas, as with the passing of
seasons, men's lives must also pass. Chamberlain Edward Shoulderlock succumbed on a Sabbath morning in the small castle at Usk
near Chepstow in Wales. The chamberlain died of "congestive
chill," a disorder related to the accumulation of blood in the vessels.
The doctor claimed that his hanging arms had failed to move his
blood properly over the years. Despite his annoying and sometimes
overreaching ways, his death prompted many tears. The lord's children felt the loss especially hard, perhaps due, in part, to their mer-
ciless mocking of the man. However, they had also known him in
ways only children sometimes can. They remembered him as the
gentle, nervous man who glided about their many castle homes
with no other thought than their well-being. When no other had
seen, it was Shoulderlock who crawled about the floor with them
riding on his back. And though others dismissed such revelations as
fool's talk, it was he who sneaked them little gifts and sweet cakes
while Sybil slept.

Aethel wept openly, as did Isabel. For his part, William
received the news with some surprise, but as death was his constant shadow, the man set the matter aside with relative ease. It
was Le Court, however, who grieved more than all. He mourned
the man's death, to be sure, but he also grieved that the loping
chamberlain had never known of his respect and affection. If he
could have only shared one more meal with the man, one more
passing in the hall, a brief time in the chapel; if only—

❋

Pope Innocent III had been the sovereign of the Roman
Church for eight years, during which he had exercised a zealous

commitment to establish the 'throne of Heaven' as the ultimate temporal authority on the kingdoms of Christendom. His papal throne had extended his authority through coercion and dubious statecraft in ways that later centuries would be quick to recall with alarm. Amongst the Germans, his meddling had precipitated a civil war. In France, he had instructed King Philip to take back his divorced wife—a command received coolly, to be sure. In England, he prepared to dominate the government through the appointment of a new Archbishop of Canterbury.

King John did not fully appreciate the vigour of his pope. Instead, he imagined his own influence at the Lateran Palace to be far more than it was. He was quite confident that his candidate, John Grey, Bishop of Norwich—a pliable cleric—would be installed by the pope with little resistance. Fully expecting Innocent to approve Grey, John supported the pope's decision *before* it was announced. It proved to be an unwise act, for the pope did not approve of Grey, but rather an English theologian—a respected cardinal named Stephen Langton, whom he installed as Archbishop of Canterbury in December of 1206.

Outraged, King John began a war against the Church of Rome, seizing its property and interfering with its authority at every possible juncture. In response, the pope laid all England under interdict. The church doors were closed, none could be baptised, no marriages blessed, no ground consecrated for burial; the bells would be silent.

With her world now darkened by tension and fear, Lady Isabel did what she could to be a proper wife, mother, and Countess to her people. She had spent the last year and a half at Chepstow Castle, travelling once to Pembroke and once to Norfolk for the marriage of her thirteen-year-old daughter, Matilda. The pope's interdict had locked the churches, so the ceremony was performed out-of-doors under the supervision of the oft' independent-minded Father Le Court. Matilda had seemed happy enough, Isabel thought, though the young maiden's portly new husband had left Isabel with the distinct impression he cared little for anything other than her daughter's youth. The Countess had urged her husband to consider other options, but in the end it was William's right to seal the negotiations. Though the earl had neither sought nor considered the opinions of Matilda, in truth, he had spent considerable resources investigating the greying groom's reputation, to avoid abandoning his daughter to a cruel life. Happiness he would not guarantee and hearts' affections would need to be cultivated by the couple themselves.

In this time, Isabel's only other journey was to York, where William had been called to the King's court for Christmas. It was there an unsettled peace had seemed to settle between her husband and the Crown—one that wise Isabel did not trust. Some thought it was reconciliation earned by William's faithful protection of England while the King had visited his dwindling royal holdings in France.

John's feigned friendship mattered little to the Countess; she still held the tyrant in secret contempt and found her anger impossible to disguise when she learned—by way of John d'Erley—that William had presented the King a Christmas gift of fine wine and a considerable loan. Lady Isabel paced the floor of her bedchamber and spoke in a manner uncharacteristically forthright. "Lord husband, I find this deed intolerable."

William stiffened and began to protest, when Isabel blurted, "I am speaking." The grey earl submitted as his hounds, Alfred and Canute, ran for cover.

Isabel's face was tight and flushed, her eyes fixed and flashing. "I find thy manoeuvres at court to be nauseating and ill-suited to the man I married. I am disappointed that you have become the very sort of courtier you once despised. King John is a beastly man, sly and cunning, clever and ruthless. He is no honourable liege to men of virtue. Yet you dance about him with gifts and loans to curry his favour."

William bristled. "Curry his favour? 'Tis not what you thought when I pledged to Philip! Then you accused me of riding two horses for my own gain."

"And so you did! But you have yet to face this dragon squarely."

"I challenged him in his very court. I stared him in the eye and dared him to prove me traitor!" William threw a heavy candle against the far wall.

Isabel clenched her jaw and walked briskly to her window, where she stared blankly at the Welsh countryside spread before her. The next moments seemed so very long to her, and to him. Neither spoke, as time passed slowly. Finally, Isabel took a deep breath and turned about, only to find her husband, the mightiest knight in all Christendom, fumbling for words. His mood had changed and he stood limply in the centre of the room.

"I do love you, Isabel," the old earl said sadly. He reached his long arms for her and she rushed to his embrace. "I fear your words ring true. I have become the man I wished not to ever be and I ask thy forgiveness."

Isabel could not speak; she could only hold this man, whose character she would never doubt again. The couple stood together quietly until William said softly, "We shall sail to Ireland, we needs be away from the troubles at court."

The Countess brightened. "Ireland?"

"*Oui.* I think it is time to return. Someday, perhaps soon, these lands shall return to you. I must put order to them before then. I shall request the King's leave for my men and myself at once."

"But the King may resist. I am told he grows ever more jealous of 'his Ireland,' as he calls it. I think your power there may threaten him."

William nodded. "True enough. All the more reason to go whilst some peace exists between us."

※

Within weeks, Lord Marshal's households were prepared to leave. Provisions had been organised by the new chamberlain—a dour, dough-faced French clerk named Robert de Bethune. Nondescript and without either virtue or vice, the man was adept at his tasks and soon filled six ships with a large army of servants and soldiers.

While standing on his docks Lord William heard a voice calling for him. He turned to see his beloved John d'Erley. "A message, sire, a message from the King." John handed William a sealed letter which was opened and returned to the knight for reading. "It says, 'By right-of-King, I, John, do require a surety of fidelity, namely one Richard Marshal, son of William Marshal, Earl of Pembroke. Such surety to be released upon the faithful return of William Marshal to the King's court from sojourns in the King's lands called Ireland.'"

Lord William cursed loudly and grabbed the letter from d'Erley's hand. "An outrage. An insult."

"Another prick, I fear, m'lord," said the knight.

"*Oui*. He feigns his trust, only to wound me all the more."

"What shall we do, sire?"

The earl shook his head and surveyed the vessels. "We are laden and ready for sail. The sky is blue and the sea invites us."

"Aye, sire. February gives us few days as fine as this," d'Erley added.

William thought for another moment. His eldest son was already held by the King and that lad's forced absence was a daily distress for his wife. Yielding a second son would inflict yet more misery on her. "I have little choice. The Irish barons are rebellious and unfaithful; I need to secure my holdings for Isabel's sake. John, I am no young man. At my death all Leinster returns to her, and if it is not held fast, she shall never be able to keep it for my sons. Send for Richard; we sail at once."

CHAPTER XVI

COURAGE IN KILKENNY CASTLE

IT was a week past the dances of May Day when Lord William received news from England while dining on a light breakfast in the hall of his castle in Kilkenny. Sir Alan de St. Georges delivered the message and, though he was supremely joyous to be reunited with Lord William and his old friends, he was reluctant to inform the earl of what he had learned. "Sire," began Alan. He lowered his head so far that his curly golden mane fell forward, covering his anguished face.

"Speak man. And let me see you. I miss you, lad."

"Aye, m'lord, I beg thy pardon. I do so very much miss you as well. Sybil sends her deep love and most tender affections to you, thy wife, and the children. But I come to bring you a warning most troublesome and, I fear, overdue. It seems the King had wrongly calculated. He thought his demand for Richard would keep you from sailing to *his* Ireland. When the boy arrived, the King went into a rage and I fear he now plots against you."

Lord William sat restlessly within the arms of his large oak chair. He was joined at his table by Sir John d'Erley, Sir Baldwin, Sir Henry Hose, Sir Jordan, and a few squires now squirming on stools at the far end. He slammed his fist atop the table. "*Sacre bleu! His* Ireland? "'Tis I who rule in Leinster." It was a rare display and untrue. King John was the ultimate overlord and William was his vassal.

"Indeed, my lord," added d'Erley, "but the man is a tyrant and tyrants hate rivals of every sort. You, sire, opposed him at court. You, sire, are his better on every count and he knows it well. I think Ireland is the decoy; you, sire, are the prey."

"Aye," growled Baldwin. The Marshal's old friend was weathered and hard, his hair now white. "Beware this King. He covets

223

more than thy land or thy wealth. Nay, m'lord, the King hates thee and all manner of honour others see in thee. He would suffocate thy virtue like the sea swallows a ship, and when he fails, he froths and foams like a mad dog denied its bone."

William shook his head. "Perhaps I wronged him in that matter with Philip, but I have truly never betrayed my oath, not once. I have unsheathed my sword in his defence and have stormed countless ramparts at his command. I do not understand this growing hatred."

John d'Erley spoke with the counsel of a man growing in wisdom. Now thirty-three, he had become a seasoned, wealthy knight of uncompromised valour and devotion. "My lord, in you he sees what he is not. In thy courage he sees his cowardice, in thy piety, his hypocrisy, in thy faithfulness, his inconstancy, in the wealth of thy virtue, his depravity, and in thy happy family, his loneliness. It is thy very character that shames him, and, like all men of terrible want, he shall make you suffer for it."

The earl blushed. Sir Alan remained uncomfortably quiet, however, and his shuffling feet caught the attention of the wary lord. "You, sir, have more."

"*Oui.* Uh, sire—King John has stripped thee of the forest of Dean and its castle of St. Briavels. He has taken direct control of the castle and shire of Gloucester, and the castle of Cardigan."

The hall echoed with loud curses and oaths. William silenced his men. "Is there more?"

"Only this, that others have told me of the King's growing affection for his justiciar for Leinster, Meilyr fitz Henry—thy tenant. It seems Meilyr is the one who counselled the King against thy coming and now he urges that you be summoned to England again so that you might not interfere with the King's business."

William darkened. "Meilyr. Fool, ingrate."

Sir Baldwin stood. "Sire, few of these barons in Ireland have any liking for the King. It would be wise to consider turning them against Meilyr as well."

The earl thought carefully. "Well said. You there, squire, summon my clerk. "'Tis time to move the pieces on the board. We shall petition the King in a complaint against Meilyr and have our barons sign it. We shall soon know who we dare trust."

＊

Lord William was a veteran of the political intrigue he despised, and most considered him to be reasonably adept in matters of the court. Unfortunately, his years of experience had not prepared him for the likes of King John. Late in the summer of 1207, William, the barons of the petition, two former knights of William"'s *mesnie* (John Marshal— his nephew, and Philip Prendergast), and Meilyr fitz Henry were summoned to England for a council with the King at Woodstock. It was to be a council on all matters pertaining to Leinster.

In preparation for his departure, the earl gathered all the knights and lords of his Irish lands to his fortress castle at Kilkenny. Before addressing the throng of soldiers now milling about the bailey, the lord called for a brief council of his *mesnie*. Lady Isabel, pregnant again, was invited to the assembly. Her participation in Irish matters was particularly helpful because both the Norman lords and their Irish vassals respected her lineage.

After each member of William's table had spoken, Lady Isabel was invited to the fore. She stood politely and began. "My lord husband, beloved knights, I do thank you for thy patience in my fears. King John is our common King and the liege-lord of all here gathered. He holds two of my sons as hostage for my lord husband's faithfulness and I would not dare urge him tarry against the King's summons.

"But heed my warning: as my hounds scent peril in the forest, my nose lifts to an evil wind blowing from Woodstock. King John shall poison the loyalties of the barons you believe are with you. He shall buy their allegiance against the interests of our Lord William.

"See whom the King summons: William of Barry, Richard Latimer, Adam of Hereford, Gilbert of Angle. He draws our most loyal barons to the snare. Not only shall he woo them to his side, with them and their *mesnies* out of Ireland, we are ripe for the picking by Irish raiders, traitors, and barons from the north."

John d'Erley rose. "I, *Madame*, remain here as thy bailiff in all parts of south Leinster. I shall defend thee with my very life."

Isabel smiled. She remembered the same pledge by her beloved John so many years before. The Countess bowed, respectfully.

"But begging thy leave, m'lady," continued d'Erley. "If this is so, it would be better for you to join thy husband." A murmur of agreement rumbled along the table.

Lord William rose. "My heart is warmed by thy love for my wife. She insists—and I agree—that our cause is better served with her here, sheltered by your steel. Some Norman lords who might rebel would give long pause before raising their arms against Strongbow's daughter. And their Irish footmen still honour King Dermot, her grandfather."

The knights nodded.

"So, my brothers," continued William, "stand with me. It is time for me to address my vassals."

The earl took his wife by the arm and the pair led their most faithful knights through the chambers of the castle and onto the sun-washed bailey. As they emerged, a flurry of trumpets sounded. The courtyard was filled with pennants boasting the herald colours of the Marshals, and scores of Irish nobles dressed in finely embroidered robes and gaily decorated hats crowded close together to listen to the great earl. Lord William led his wife to a small stage of rough-cut planks where Aethel helped her lady step to her place.

A trumpet blast hushed all. The earl raised his arms and drew a deep breath. "Lords of Leinster, I thank you all for honouring my summons. As thy overlord I am proud to defend you.

"Now, hear me. Behold this fair woman who stands before you. She is *la grant amore e de l'onor*—the great love and honour—of my life, the daughter of Strongbow, the mighty warrior who enfeoffed you all with these green lands. See her, growing with child and kindled with a mother's love for all Ireland.

"I leave on the morrow to obey my King's command and

when I sail, I do so without my beloved wife, your gracious lady. See her, filling with the fruit of womanhood, soft and tender like the fragrant bloom of honeysuckle. She is a precious, most delicate treasure, and I leave her to your faithful care. Draw thy steel to defend her from the wicked intentions of evil men. Secure her behind a wall of sharpened edges, hold her safe against all enemies. Swear it as thy sacred pledge."

The bailey filled with the roar of chivalry. With fists and swords raised to Heaven, the lords of Leinster vowed the fair lady's protection. Le Court then climbed awkwardly atop the stage and on to a barrel, from which he raised his little hands over the crowd. He reached into his pocket and retrieved a piece of bone, a relic that was claimed to be from the leg of St. Margaret of Antioch—a saint believed to help women with child. The priest laid the bone on Isabel's belly and prayed loudly for her protection. He then prayed over Lord William, the mesnie, and then over all those now kneeling in the bailey. "*Eripe me de manibus inimicorum meorum, et a persequentibus me. Domine, non confundar, quoniam invocavi te. Fiat misericordia tua, Domine, super nos, sicut speravimus in te. In nomine Patris, et Filii, et Spiritus Sancti*, Amen."

With a final flourish and a cheer, Lord William waved farewell.

❋

Despite his confidence in the chivalry of his lords, the earl left for England reluctantly. His *mesnie* had begged him to take hostages from his barons, but the man refused, convinced that his lords would remain loyal. Unfortunately, once again William Marshal had measured men according to his own character.

Arriving at the King's palace in Woodstock, it took little time for William to learn that his wife's instincts had been correct. King John greeted his guests with a sumptuous feast and glad tidings. Meilyr fitz Henry, the King's centrepiece, was presented with accolades and honours, while Lord William was immediately humiliated by being seated at the far end of the table. Such dishonour did not go unnoticed and, now believing their lord to be out of the King's favour, the barons' loyalties quickly listed.

Through that long evening, clever King John heaped gifts of silver and gold upon William's vassals, adding promises of position and titles with such eloquent flattery that William left the hall in disgust. Upon his eventual return, however, the earl further learned that his former household knights, John Marshal and Philip Prendergast, had joined Meilyr as the King's principals in Ireland. John was given the title "Marshal of Ireland," and Philip was given huge grants of lands in Cork. The authority and influence of William Marshal, Lord of Leinster, had been seriously compromised.

In the meantime, Countess Isabel faced sudden peril in Ireland. It seemed that Meilyr had secretly conspired with disloyal Norman lords and hordes of angry Irish tenants to rebel against the interests of William upon his departure. John d'Erley and the loyal mesnie of William Marshal did their best to defend the villages and towns of the earl against a series of bloody raids. Unfortunately, loss of life and property was mounting, and the rebellion spread.

The rebels did not expect to topple Lord William's legal rights to his holdings, but, as with most warfare of the times, the purpose of their uprising was to seize or destroy property, including silver, furnishings, wardrobe, harvest goods, and armaments. The rebels attacked William's port at New Ross, slaughtering nearly two dozen of the earl's men, burning storehouses of grain, and riding away with wagons weighted with plunder.

Secretly learning of his agents' successes against William, Meilyr urged King John to summon the earl's primary knights to England. It was a ploy to further weaken Marshal's position. The King agreed enthusiastically and sent his message to Ireland by way of Meilyr himself, accompanied by Philip Prendergast and young Thomas Bloet, a son of Ralph, the former knight of William's *mesnie*. Upon his arrival in Ireland, however, the treacherous Meilyr learned that William's men had begun to turn the tide against the rebellion. Suddenly desperate, he immediately summoned William's chief knights, including John d'Erley, to a meeting, where the King's command was presented.

Staring dumfounded and confused at the summons, John d'Erley sought the counsel of his comrade, Sir Jordan de Sauqueville. "The King requires us to remove ourselves at once to Woodstock. If we go, this Devil shall retake the advantage."

Jordan was a dashing young knight with close-set brown eyes and close-cropped hair. He nodded, angrily. "Aye, but if not, the King shall take all thy lands—all thy wealth is to be lost."

John and the others talked in low tones; then it was John who spoke. "Our duty, Lord Meilyr, is to the oath we pledged under God. The King may take our fortunes, but he shall not ever take from us the love we dearly hold for our liege lord. We choose honour, sir; we shall not go."

Meilyr hissed and cursed the knights, warning them of the dire consequences of such deliberate disobedience. He turned away from William's knights and hurried towards Wexford. From here he ordered his followers to press hard and quickly. As for him, he secretly believed his cause was now likely to be lost, and he made hasty arrangements to flee to England.

※

"My lady!" cried Aethel. "We are under siege."

The words struck a sickening chord deep within the Countess' swollen belly. Feigning courage, Isabel climbed awkwardly from her chair and into the bracing air of Kilkenny's castle in January, 1208. She peered through an archer's slit at an army of wild Irish rebels assembling in front of the walls. A footman ran past crying that boats filled with archers were floating in the river.

The day was bitter and grey; a cold wind driving stinging sleet blew from the north. Baldwin Bethune, John d'Erley, Jordan de Sauqueville, young Ralph Bloet, Henry Hose, Eustace de Betremont, and another half dozen of Lord William's *mesnie* were accompanied by Sir Alan de St. Georges, six knights of lesser lords, two dozen footmen, a score of archers, and numbers of squires fit for battle. In total, the castle defenders numbered about seventy men-at-arms. Though they faced an army of several hundred, Lord William's hurried improvements to the gatehouse towers, the western curtain wall, and other outworks would provide the fortress with some advantage.

The terrified townspeople of Kilkenny had begun streaming into the castle the night before, as rumours of an approaching army reached their ears. Their needs would surely tax the well-stocked granary and the pens of swine and cattle. Sir Baldwin, the castle's temporary commander, immediately arranged the town's men into tithings, each under the command of an appointed captain. These tithings—groups of ten—were to perform any number of duties, including bucket lines for fire, the gathering of incoming missiles, and help on the ramparts repelling ladders.

Sir Baldwin knew this would not be a siege of attrition, for it was the wrong season. Instead, he had properly anticipated a frontal assault and was well-prepared. He had hung the hoardings— wooden balconies—over the north wall the night before and now ordered them filled with archers. He took his position on one of the round towers of the gatehouse and began barking orders as the new day's sun struggled to push light through the heavy skies. "Bucketmen at the ready. Soak the thatch and hurry about it. You, captain of the archers: have your men direct their fire in front of the gate. Forget the flanks. Do you understand?"

"Aye, m'lord."

Baldwin surveyed his assembling men, then pointed to the bustling courtyard below. "D'Erley, set a barricade one hundred paces from the gate. If they begin to break through, send a company of archers behind it. You've command of the bailey guard."

"Aye, sire," cried Sir John.

The old warrior turned his seasoned eyes towards his enemy. The army was led by a dozen or so Norman knights dressed for battle in full mail armour and boldly boasting the colours of their treasonous lords. Their footmen were comprised of dishevelled, unkempt, and ferocious Irishmen protected only by leather jerkins, small shields, and steel caps. They brandished a menacing assortment of weapons, including short swords, axes, two-handed hammers, flails, maces, halberds, and pikes. A company of fearsome Scots from the western islands were spotted carrying their double-edged axes over their shoulders. The very sight of these wild, Viking-Celts dried mouths and caused many to tremble.

On the parapets, the nervous defenders waited anxiously, shifting in their boots and awaiting their duty. To a man they wished William would hurry home. A piercing cry rose from the rebels and chilled those inside the walls. The attack had begun.

As Baldwin expected, the enemy focused its primary attention on the gate, sending wave after wave of men forward with large ramming poles. A rain of arrows poured atop them from the suspended balconies above, dropping them in droves. But as quickly as men fell, others filled the void, only to join the horrid pile of corpses and writhing wounded covering the berm.

In the meantime, the archers in the river successfully launched a barrage of flaming arrows over the eastern curtain wall and into the bailey. Though the thatch of the various buildings had been soaked, the penetration of the arrowheads drove the flames into dry tinder. Within the hour the castle had begun to fill with smoke, while tithings of firefighting townsfolk ran hither and fro futilely tossing sloshing buckets of water onto the rising flames.

A large body of rebels had hidden themselves in the forest some three bowshots from the western wall. They suddenly charged from their cover, catching Sir Baldwin by surprise. The commander ran along the parapets, barking orders for archers to adjust their positions as scores of shrieking Irishmen threw themselves upon their ladders. The defenders quickly reorganised themselves.

A sour, choking smoke filled the air within Kilkenny Castle, and the cries of men brought tears to Lady Isabel, who was tucked safely deep within the dark bowels of the fortress. She huddled quietly with Aethel, Twigardan, Le Court, her son Anselm, now five, and daughters Isabel, Sibylla, and Eva. She stroked nine-year-old Isabel's hair, and squeezed Eva's plump cheeks affectionately. "All shall be well, dear children."

Aethel was frightened but also angry. "Cursed Irish devils. I tell you, *Père*, cast a curse upon them!"

Le Court was pacing back and forth within the chamber, mumbling indiscernible words. Aethel's voice caught his attention. "*Oui*! Here is my curse on them." The dwarf snatched a dagger from his belt. "Should they breach the wall they'll taste my steel on their way to Hell."

The door flew open and Sir Alan stumbled inside. An arrow was stuck in his neck. He had unwisely lowered his coif to hear a command and at that very moment an arrow had arced into the exposed area. The brave knight staggered forward, blood running freely around his collar. "M'lady, have a care. Twigadarn, bar the door. Traitors pulled the portcullis up whilst others knocked the lock-beam away. The gate's been breached by the Scots." He fell to one knee. "M'lady, tell my dear Sybil of my love—" The man collapsed.

Isabel ran to Sir Alan's side and held his head upon her lap. "No!" she cried. "Oh, please God, not good Alan." The man's eyes closed and he lay still—perhaps worse. Aethel groaned loudly with her lady, but the sounds of battle gave neither woman time to grieve.

The Countess laid Alan's head lightly on the straw-heavy floor. She then stood slowly with her jaw set hard. To the amazement of her attendants, she ordered an immediate change in wardrobe and within moments was dressed in her husband's herald colours. "Aethel, fetch me guards for my children." Saying nothing more, she smoothed her clothing atop her swollen belly and took the sword of Sir Alan from his limp hand. Then, over the loud objections of all, Isabel stormed out of her chamber and towards the smoke of battle. Followed by the giant, Twigadarn, and the dwarf, Le Court, the woman hurried through the passages of the castle until she emerged on the bailey at the stone stairs leading to the ramparts of the southern wall.

Twigadarn was armed with a sword in one hand and a hammer in the other. "Please, my lady," he pleaded.

Isabel shook her head stubbornly and began to climb the stairs.

Le Court cried from behind. "*Non, Madame!*" Unable to dissuade her, Le Court pulled the dagger from his belt and began praying loudly.

The giant's crystal eyes now glowed like two red embers readied to consume all things evil. He followed close to Isabel's heels to the top of the stairs, then past fighting men along the wooden wall-walk of the ramparts. They rounded the corner of the south wall and turned northward along the treacherous eastern wall, ducking below a steady flight of arrows from the riverboats. Below them in the bailey a vicious combat was spreading like the flames now eagerly consuming storehouses and sheds.

As the trio neared the high towers of the north wall, the walkway became more and more crowded with friend and foe fighting for control. Irish footmen were breaching the gaps and Twigadarn stepped to the fore. With a wild, unearthly cry he began clearing his lady's path like a harvester in a grain of ripened wheat. Bodies fell before the giant Welshman in such numbers that eyes began to turn upward, and when they did they saw the Lady Isabel. Cheers began to rise above the din of battle and they grew louder as the Countess neared the tower steps.

Twigadarn continued to fight savagely, like the Archangel Michael engaged against the hordes of Hades. Behind Isabel was little Le Court, and he, like her, suddenly turned to face the shrieks of a shaggy-haired, soot-faced Scot rushing towards them. The man wielded a bloodstained axe and he swung hard at Isabel, tearing her cloak and barely missing the top of Le Court's head. Before Twigadarn could whirl about, the angry little priest lunged forward with his dagger. With the force of ten men he plunged it beneath the hem of the Scotsman's leather vest. The man cried out and staggered forward, dropping his axe in disbelief. Still enraged, Le Court thrust his weapon into the man again, then again, until Twigadarn wheeled about with his hammer, knocking the wretch off the wall and into the bailey below.

The Countess was pale and trembling, yet her courage was of such bounty that it overwhelmed all her fears. She hurried up the steps of the gate-tower and when she, great with child, emerged at the top, a rousing hurrah echoed within the stone walls. Then, like the Saxon Emma of Norwich, Isabel Marshal, daughter of the mighty Richard Strongbow, fixed her hands around the handle of Sir Alan's sword and raised its point to Heaven.

Blood-splattered and staggering, John d'Erley looked up, and upon seeing his beloved Isabel standing tall and brave above the battle, his weary heart lifted, his aching arms suddenly surged with new strength, and his stinging eyes filled with tears of love. "Press on, my brothers!" he cried. "Press on."

Inspired and freshened with new-found resolve, Lord William's men fought on bravely. Though badly outnumbered, they regained their order and now formed a tight block of resistance in the centre of the bailey. At each corner stood an armoured knight, the sides lined with large shields guarding footmen bearing lances and small arms. Against this human fortress flew the savage Irish and Scots in frantic, desperate waves. Again and again they charged in their vain attempt to break the block of steel. Finally, as the corpses of their soldiers mounded high in front of Lord William's stubborn defence, the rebellious lords lost all heart and began to falter.

Seeing the day could be won, Sir Baldwin ordered his men to rush forward and drive their beaten enemy through the gate. With a spirited cry, Kilkenny's defenders obeyed and charged. The slaughter that ensued was one not soon forgotten. Sir Baldwin refused all quarter and at the hour of vespers, the battle ended, leaving Kilkenny Castle awash in blood.

CHAPTER XVII

TWO TYRANTS

AETHEL held her lady close. "Oh, dear, dear Countess. God be praised! God be praised. I lay prostrate on the floor and begged His mercy on you whilst yer children wept around me. You saved the castle, m'lady, God be praised."

Isabel kissed Aethel upon the cheek. "I do love you so, old friend. And by mercy Sir Alan does yet live."

Aethel smiled. The chamber was heavily shadowed by a small fire now flickering in the hearth. The battle had ended just hours before and the Countess now rested in her chamber, far away from the justice being administered outside. The townsfolk were now prisoners of the castle until Baldwin could find the traitors among them whom had opened the gates. Carpenters were building the gallows.

Isabel's children clung to their mother and begged her to not leave their sight, and she was happy to oblige. In the morning a circle of cheerful faces enjoyed a breakfast of bread and cheese chased to their bellies with a little red wine.

The days to follow passed slowly for Isabel. She yearned for news of her husband, though Sir Alan had earlier told her he was likely to be kept at court for some time. The knight had also told her it was his opinion that the treachery of Meilyr was grounded in a conspiracy with the King himself. Isabel wondered if the King's anger was still kindled by her husband's dubious judgement in the matter with Philip, but Alan had assured her that the King was consumed by a much larger issue regarding William—that being envy.

Isabel now pined for those sons not under her wing. William and Richard were still hostages and she knew little about the welfare of either. Brooding Gilbert was completing his grammar school and had informed his instructors of his desire to become a priest.

It was a choice that did not surprise Isabel, and she hoped it might finally give him reason for joy. Cheerful, mischievous Walter had just begun his grammar school and had been left behind in Chepstow. She missed his happy ways and twinkling eyes. She turned her attention to little Anselm and the three daughters still at home.

Within two weeks of the Kilkenny battle, Isabel entered another struggle. For nearly eleven hours she suffered terrible labour in the delivery of her eleventh child. Aethel maintained a stubborn vigil and acted as midwife—she refused to trust the Irish women in the castle. Le Court prayed faithfully while Sir John d'Erley paced the hallway just beyond the lady's chamber. The knight cried words of encouragement from time to time and denied himself both food and drink until he knew his beloved Isabel was safe. Finally, sometime deep in the night, the Countess gave birth.

"Aethel, cover me and warm the child. Then call Sir John to my side," whispered Isabel weakly. The woman was now thirty-six and her face, still beautiful, surely belied the passing of the years. She took a sip of wine and secretly prayed this child might be her last. She had now born eleven and had been blessed with ten who had survived. Knowing that God had been kind, she also offered her thanksgiving.

"*Oui, Madame*? You summoned me?"

Isabel looked into Sir John's kindly eyes. He, too, was beginning to show the signs of time. Now thirty-four and well-seasoned, he embodied all that was good in a Christian warrior. "*Merci, bon* John. I am well; the child is well." She took his hand. "Hear me, sir. My lord husband loves thee like no other—save his children and myself."

John smiled and blushed.

Isabel hesitated. She looked at him closely, and then added quietly, "And I love you, too—like no other save my husband." She squeezed his hand, knowingly.

The knight's eyes filled and his heart soared. They were the words he had longed to hear for these many years.

Seeing the sudden contentment in the man's face warmed

Isabel's heart. She was relieved to say that which she had always felt. She smiled tenderly. "You are to be a godfather again and Aethel a godmother. The child is to be named in thy honour; she shall be baptized Johanna."

Bursting with joy, Sir John wiped his eyes and kissed Isabel's hand. His lips did not linger. "No better wonders could you have granted me this day, m'lady. I am humbled and have no words."

※

Within a fortnight the first news of Meilyr's defeat reached the King's eyes. Scanning a hastily written message, he learned how his agents had been crushed at Kilkenny. He cursed the name of Countess Isabel when he read how she had ordered the rebels to be dragged from "every corner of Leinster." She had succeeded in even seizing Meilyr—his own royal justiciar. The man now languished in prison and his sons were taken as hostages. The King was furious. He crumpled the message and tossed it into his hearth. His eyes darted round the ring of councillors shuffling to safe shadows. "How? By the saints, how can it be?" he roared. "He shall be all the stronger, all the wiser—all the more wary now."

King John paced and cursed, at one point drawing his sword and crashing it against chairs and cupboards standing about. When his tantrum was over he bellowed, "Get me Marshal."

Within the hour, Lord William was on one knee before his liege-lord, ignorant of the news from Ireland. "*Oui*, sire?"

"Rise, William Marshal." The King laid a finger on one side of his long nose and stared at the old earl silently. He sniffled, then feigned sympathy. "Good man, I've sad news."

"*Oui*, my lord?"

The King's lips moistened as if they were about to form themselves around a delicious morsel. "It seems the lands in Leinster you hold for me have been the subject of a treasonous rebellion."

William stiffened.

"Forgive me, sir. No harm has come to either thy good wife

or children. But, alas, thy brave knight, Sir John d'Erley to whom you so recently granted generous holdings of our lands, has been slain." King John stopped, letting the words pierce the man.

William's heart broke, but he would not reveal his pain to this king. "Pity for thee, sire," he stated flatly. "For he was thy man as well."

Frustrated by the man's calm and chastened by his words, King John stared incredulously at his better. "Indeed!" he shouted. With that, he stood from his throne and hurried away, pausing only to whisper to his clerk, "See that d'Erley is stripped of everything. See to it at once."

The grey earl walked out of the King's hall alone and into the penetrating air of mid-March. He stood erect and contained as he peered through a cold drizzle at the lifeless landscape before him. He drew a deep breath and walked until he found himself deep in a dripping wood. There poor William's shoulders sank and he slid downwards along the wet bark of a thick-trunked tree until his body rested on wet leaves. He stared aimlessly until tears blurred his vision, and, no longer able to deny his utter grief, the great knight wept like a heart-broken child for the loss of dear John.

❈

Safe and faraway in his chapel in France, the English Archbishop of Canterbury prayed for peace. A godly man by all standards of virtue, Stephen Langton opposed tyranny in all its forms and was committed to the principle that no man had the right to dominate another.

King John knew little of Langton's convictions, but opposed his appointment on reasons of jurisdiction. He was still fighting with the ambitious Pope Innocent III on matters of control and insisted that he, as King, had the customary right to elect and install the archbishop in England. After all, John argued, the position was both ecclesiastical *and* lay. The archbishop was the superior authority over matters of the soul *and* the overlord of astonishing temporal wealth. The pope was not impressed with

John's arguments. He had no interest in the English customs that John had so suddenly and conveniently embraced. He intended to keep England under his suffocating interdict as long as it took King John to yield. And, for added measure, he excommunicated John as well.

John's excommunication provided a particular disadvantage to the agitated King. It absolved everyone of their foresworn allegiance and granted all of his enemies the sacred status of Crusader. To oppose King John was now to embrace the Holy Church. In response, John looted England's monasteries, cathedrals, and manors, filling his royal coffers with a bounty of spoils. Silver, gold, precious jewels, the finest art, illuminated manuscripts, and even relics poured into the royal treasury. Furthermore, he began conspiring with his cousin Otto, the emperor of the Germans, to join him and an assortment of disaffected French counts in a conspiracy against King Philip of France.

※

Meanwhile, in Ireland, Countess Isabel Marshal was giving little heed to the news of these events. She had been overjoyed to welcome home her beloved William, who had been greatly relieved to learn of King John's cruel ruse in the matter of d'Erley's supposed death. As he disembarked his vessel, it seemed he was as anxious to embrace his favoured knight as he was his wife!

The lady prepared a feast fit for the saints and cried for joy as Lord William gathered his *mesnie* close. The great lord honoured his household knights for their courage, chivalry, sacrifice, and honour with gifts of magnificent robes. With a rare display of emotion, he assured all whose lands had been confiscated by the King that he would work tirelessly to restore their losses and indemnify their honour.

Concerned to fix his grip more securely on his Irish lands, the earl spent the next four years directing a fierce campaign against all rivals. His soldiers imposed harsh order on the villages and helped themselves to many numbers of hostages from Norman lords whose loyalty was suspect. Though William made sorties into the countryside from time to time, he primarily supervised his campaign from Kilkenny Castle so that he might remain close to his family.

On sunny days, when his chambers were reasonably quiet, it was his pleasure to escort Isabel on pleasant jaunts by horse across his green, rolling countryside. From time to time he dabbled in boar hunting with his hounds or ventured with Isabel into an empty landscape with their falcons.

During these years the Countess and her children enjoyed the relative comforts of the castle. Her daughters enjoyed fishing in the river and picking bouquets of fresh wildflowers. Their few sojourns into the countryside made life all the more interesting and everyone delighted in picnics spent in the company of Aethel, Twigadarn—now unofficially called *Messire*, or *Sir* Twigadarn by Isabel for his bravery at Kilkenny—and the dogs Alfred and Canute. On two occasions, Le Court had managed to escort the family to Kildare and the *Book of Kells*, and once spent a day in search of sheela-na-gigs carved in parish churches throughout the legendary mountains of Wicklow. On other days, Isabel fed her appetite for reading by spending hours in Le Court's chamber or at the scriptorium of the monks in Ossory. So, as the Year of Grace 1212 unfolded, the happy world of the Countess was well-rested and refreshed.

Ah, but while Lady Isabel had been occupied in matters of respite and inquiry, another had been secretly engaged in matters of the heart! Aethel—dependable, staunch, and ever-reliable Aethel—had served her lady nobly and selflessly. She had remained the joy of her lord's household and everyone's favourite companion. Yet, despite her love and devotion to the Countess' family, she had spent years in secret sadness, lonely for a companion that might touch her heart in ways her beloved friends could not.

During the feasts of the Christmas just passed, Aethel's heart-strings had been tuned by the shy attentions of an ageing English yeoman named Harold Cutter. Harold was a good-natured, kindly fellow who had been a free tenant on Lord William's former lands in Sussex. Stout, balding and a few years beyond fifty, he was still fit and hale. His face was round and ruddy—like Aethel's— but most of his teeth had disappeared, leaving him with a smile that could lift the sagging spirits of any.

As a free man who owned heritable property, Harold had dutifully provided his military obligations under William's banner. While serving the lord's army as a simple footman, he had learned from afar to respect the earl's character. When King John stripped Lord William of his lands in Sussex, however, the great earl was no longer Harold's overlord. Unhappy and tired of years behind the rumps of oxen, the man sold his land for a gold Venetian ducat and a bag of silver pennies freshly minted according to the new standards that King John had imposed for the whole of the realm.

A few years prior, the yeoman had travelled to Pembroke, where he had been hired by Shoulderlock as a fuller. Harold was grateful for employment, but had little interest in washing clothes and bedding. He had begged to be transferred to the *mesnie* where he might work as a groomsman and armour-keeper, and Shoulderlock had graciously complied. So Harold followed the *mesnie* to Kilkenny and had fought savagely in defence of the castle during the rebellion.

Though a bold and tenacious soldier, it had taken Harold years to find the courage to address the Countess' fetching servant, Aethel. And when he finally fumbled through a speech he had rehearsed so very often, the confused woman had no choice other than to politely ask him to say it again. But when Aethel finally understood the man's intentions, she nearly flew to Heaven's gate.

For months the two kept their growing affections to themselves, and when the giddy handmatron finally asked Lord William's permission to marry, Isabel nearly swooned. Happy to grant it and happy to waive all fees, the earl had given them his unqualified blessing.

Harold and Aethel wanted to marry on a sunny day under a blue sky. They waited anxiously for several weeks until one May dawn finally broke pink and glorious. The pair impatiently watched Le Court finish his vespers prayers, then nearly dragged from his chapel. "Today, *Père*," they cried.

Isabel hurried about the castle, chasing her servants in all directions to prepare the long-delayed wedding feast and crying for the trumpeters to assemble the whole of the lord's court. Within the hour the bailey was filled with a colourful assortment of delighted guests, and when the bells of nones pealed over the ramparts, all was ready.

"Look above you, Aethel," cried Isabel. "The sun shines upon you; the angels sing for you."

"Aye, m'lady." Aethel was grinning ear to ear. "I am so very happy. Tell me again, do you think Harold a good man?"

Isabel smiled. "I hardly know him, but Lord William is told there is no finer man in all his working company."

Aethel tittered and adjusted the over-gown sewn by Isabel herself some weeks prior. It was blue, like Aethel's shining eyes. Her grey hair was rolled at her ears, as it was always. Isabel had gently urged her to let her braids fall, if only this once, but Aethel had politely refused. She reminded her lady that the modern trend was to roll them like she had for all her life!

Isabel wrapped a silk chin band round Aethel's jaw and over her head, then set her gauze wimple in place. The Countess walked round about her friend, directing others to stitch this or loosen that until she was satisfied. Then she took Aethel's two hands in hers. "You are a bride most beautiful."

Aethel turned nearly purple. She attempted a rather stiff-jointed curtsy. "Thanks, m'lady. Praise be to God above for you."

Isabel embraced her friend. "I thank Him each day for you. Now, 'tis time for a wedding."

Le Court presided over the simple ceremony in front of the door to the castle chapel. The priest assured all that the pope's interdict could not possibly have found its way to the wild shores of Ireland, and if it had, he cared little. He offered fine prayers and large smiles, a few winks, and the mercy of a short homily. Attending as witnesses were the whole of Lord William's household, including his officers and clerks. D'Erley and what other knights that could be spared from duties elsewhere were arranged in handsome ranks, and behind them stood numbers of glad-hearted household servants. Aethel was beloved by soldier, servant, and churchmen alike, and Lord William's great household was soon delighted to share a hearty, happy feast in celebration of the joy of Harold Cutter and his bride.

✳

News from England was always received with mixed feelings. Rumours of increasing tensions had been arriving on Ireland's docks for months. The common folk were growing ever more restless over the strangulation of their souls by the pope's interdict, and fears of the coming Judgement and the perils of hellfire had taken a terrible toll. In addition, a conspiracy to assassinate the King was uncovered amongst the barons of the troublesome northern counties. In response, the anxious monarch felt compelled to secure as many friends among other lords that his wealth would allow.

King John suddenly appreciated the fealty of Lord William and he made every effort to guarantee it. Despite the King's prior conspiracies, insults, deceptions, and penalties, Lord William had, indeed, remained true. But the earl's fidelity had been rooted in neither affection nor self-interest. Like all true virtue, it held fast to things eternal.

Regardless of the King's sudden flattery, Lord William served him in his time of danger by rallying his own Irish-Norman barons in support of the Crown. More than that, he had even offered his coming to London in order to provide advice, counsel, and personal defence. Delighted by the earl's unshakeable loyalty, King John politely declined the offer, but rewarded him by summoning d'Erley to England to accept the release of the royal hostages, William the Younger and Richard.

The lord's eldest sons were now knights in need of armour, robes, war-horses, and weapons. Whether the King truly intended to please the earl or whether he wanted to avoid the costs of keeping the men any longer was of no matter to Lady Isabel. She wept and danced for joy at the news, though later cursed the King's name.

It was true, he had released them from their status as the King's hostages, but he would not give them permission to leave England.

Another bit of news had circulated along the Irish wharves, odd news from the Continent that was quickly the centre of discussion in the taverns and the halls throughout all Ireland. Aethel had informed Isabel who, in turn, summoned her daughters to her side.

"Children, I've grave news from Wexford." She looked about the curious faces gathering in a close circle. As they settled, she suddenly felt a tug for those no longer present. Matilda had been long since married and she knew little more than that she was with child. William and Richard remained trapped in England. Dour Gilbert was studying theology in Canterbury, cheerful Walter was in school in Chepstow, young Anselm was in a grammar school in York.

She turned her thoughts to those still present. She looked at gentle Eva, still plump and rosy-cheeked. Aged seventeen, she had been betrothed to Lord William de Briouze, but the man seemed reluctant to have her. Daughter Isabel, thirteen, was betrothed to Gilbert de Clare, but it was the Countess who had delayed the marriage for fear of her child's unhappiness. Sybilla was now eleven and betrothed to one William de Ferrers. The young maiden was willowy and tender like her namesake; her husband-to-be was a young squire with a bright future. Johanna, the youngest of the Countess' ten children, was now only four and the apple of her father's eye. White-haired and feisty, the little girl scooted and scampered about the castle like a glad-hearted fairy.

"I love you all so very much," began Isabel. "I wish you could be my prisoners for always."

The circle giggled.

"I am told by *Père* Le Court that your tutoring continues well for all, save Eva and Isabel. It seems embroidery suits you both better, but I should remind you that a beautiful mind is as worthy a thing as nimble fingers.

"Now, I have learned of something that shall be of interest to you. It seems our Christian knights are faltering in Palestine. The infidels have pressed them near to the sea and have long-since seized the holy places. We continue to pray for the safety of our brothers serving God in that horrid place. Your father speaks often of the courageous, selfless sacrifice the knights of Christ have suffered.

"Never forget why our Holy Crusades were ventured. Many years ago the heathen followers of Islam swept through our Lord's holy lands and seized them. They slaughtered Christian pilgrims and degraded our sacred sites. Then they sent their hordes into Spain and into Byzantine. They lusted for the kingdoms of our Christian kings and had pressed far into France before the mighty Charles Martel defeated them with his army of Franks."

"*Oui*, mother, we know these things."

Isabel nodded. "Yes, of course, I beg pardon; but the crusaders' hopes have dwindled and now other news has come."

The girls were quiet.

"Thousands of German and French children are forming columns to march to Palestine in crusade. They follow the visions of two and believe the sea shall open for them like the Red Sea did for Moses! They plan to march to Jerusalem where God shall honour their faith by driving away the infidel."

The Countess' daughters were as astonished as she. "Have they done so?" asked one.

Isabel shrugged. "The last news was simply that they had begun to march, thousands of them, it is said."

"Who goes with them?" asked Eve.

"They are sent alone, though the priests insist God goes with them. Some say they are being escorted by butterflies and birds."

Young Isabel's brows furrowed. "But how shall they eat? How shall they know where to go? Who shall protect them?"

"*Oui!*" cried Johanna. "What about wild boars and wolves?"

The Countess nodded. "I am told they make their pilgrimage without food or defence. Some say it is their faith that shall protect them; they say a great miracle is upon us."

The girls were quiet until Eve asked, "And what do you say, mother? Is it possible?"

Isabel drew a long breath and released it slowly. "With faith all things are possible. I do believe this with all my heart. Yet I also read in the Holy Scriptures that, though we are to live by faith, we are also to pray for wisdom. I confess I see little wisdom in this crusade, and I fear God is not pleased when we cast prudence aside in favour of visions."

"But what of miracles, mother?"

Isabel thought for a long moment, unconsciously fingering her relic. She answered slowly and deliberately. "I have seen much in my time. I have learned to neither deny miracles nor demand them."

The room was quiet until the silence was broken by the sudden sobs of Sibylla. "I fear for the children, mother. It is as if I can see them in their graves. I fear they are already perished."

The room fell silent again.

❋

It was May 1213 and the Marshal family was enjoying the springtime gardens of Wexford when a messenger arrived from the court of King John.

"I am summoned to England," said William sombrely.

Isabel nodded, submissively.

"Disaster looms. King Philip has taken Crusader vows and is allied with the pope against King John. He is preparing an invasion."

Isabel groaned.

Lord William took a deep breath. "I confess, Isabel, I find this pope to be heavy-handed and ambitious and my King is difficult to serve. The world is weighing upon me."

Isabel would normally have responded with a gentle touch and kindly words; her husband was old and growing very weary. Instead, frustrated by both her King and her Church, and most certainly no longer patient with William's stubborn ways, she answered in a scolding tone. "John is an evil man and the pope is grasping and shrewd. We have a duty to oppose tyranny in all its forms."

William stared at Wexford's harbour. "I am a simple man. I can do only what I know."

246

"Then you must know more." Isabel would not yield.

"Perhaps," grumbled William. He lifted his face angrily and scowled. He would accept no more reprimands from his wife. "Enough. I want things set to order so I may sail to England within three days. The King is at Windsor and I shall expect you to follow within the fortnight." With that, the earl spun on his heels and walked quickly away.

As he demanded, the lord's vessels were ready within three days and he sailed away to England on a breezy Thursday dawn. The Countess stood by Wexford's muddy harbour shore and waved a sad good-bye, hoping to be restored eventually to her husband's favour.

By the Wednesday next, Isabel, Aethel, the children, a host of household servants, and an armed escort climbed aboard two large cogs and began a quiet voyage across the Irish Sea to Pembroke. There they rested for two days while the chamberlain prepared for the final leg of their journey, and within another week they arrived safely at Windsor Castle, near London.

CHAPTER XVIII

THE BARONS PRESS

LORD WILLIAM met his wife as her carriage halted by Windsor's gate. His mood had brightened and he helped her to the ground with a cheerful word and a gentle kiss. "Ah, good Isabel, I am pleased you have come so quickly. We've good news: the King has restored all the lands he had taken from me."

Isabel was not impressed. She had hoped to talk of other things.

"But I've more." His eyes twinkled, and he suddenly looked like a playful boy. He clapped his hands loudly, and from behind a heavy curtain stepped Isabel's two eldest sons.

The Countess gasped, then raced to embrace each, kissing them on their cheeks and weeping for joy. "Ah, look how you've grown."

Indeed, the boys were now men. William the Younger was twenty-two and handsome. His shoulders were broad and he was tall like his father. Isabel took his face in her hands and studied his eyes. Her brow furrowed. She remembered him as a tender lad, soft-hearted and gentle. Now he had the look of a man deeply wounded. "My son, I fear you've suffered some at the hands of King John."

The very words, "King John," caused the young man to stiffen. He pulled his face from his mother's hands. "I am so very pleased to see you, mother," he said. "I am called to service in the north, near Richmond. I am very sorry, but my men are waiting for me, even now. Please, give my love to my sisters."

Isabel nodded, sadly, then took him by the shoulders and kissed his cheek. Young William's eyes reddened and he lingered in his mother's touch. "I love you, my son," said Isabel softly.

The young man nodded and turned, hesitated, then faced his

248

mother again. He looked at her for a long moment, then bent towards her ear. "Have a care, mother. And give thy love to father; no greater man has ever walked the earth." It was all he said, and he walked quickly away.

Poor Isabel was heartbroken. She took a half-stride towards her departing son, then stopped and wiped her eyes. "Oh, my poor son. What did your King take from you?"

The woman turned to Richard. "My Richard." She sighed and wrapped her arms around him as if to bind him to her. Richard had grown into a hardy lad of middling height. His blond hair was long and his eyes twinkled. He was mischievous and daring, still his father's favourite son.

"Mother," he cried. "I have missed you badly. Give no heed to brooding William. With time away from the King, he'll be set to right. Now you. You look a wonder."

Isabel laughed. "I have aged some."

Richard smiled, broadly. The young man was twenty-one and had become a skilled soldier. Unlike young William, who had been long betrothed to a maiden of some wealth, Richard was an errant knight in need of employment. He could not be betrothed himself, since his life was surety for William's bride-to-be. If William died, it was he that must fill the obligation.

"So, please tell me you shall join thy father's *mesnie*."

Richard shook his head. "Not just yet, mother. I've some business in Lancaster."

"Lancaster," boomed Lord William. "A garden of treason. The whole of the north is naught but trouble. Two sons in those troubled places is not good for any of us."

Richard turned an angry eye towards his father and the two began shouting at one another. Finally, Lord William would have no more and he shoved his son to the ground with a loud oath. He stood over him like a looming colossus and bellowed, "Tell me you'll not go to Lancaster."

Richard climbed to his feet and spat. He fixed his eyes hard on his father. "I go to Lancaster, father. Fare thee well." The young man adjusted his garments and walked towards his grieving mother. He held her for a moment and whispered in her ear. "I do love thee, mother." With that, Richard Marshal walked quickly away.

✳

Excommunicated King John had apparently been less troubled with the destiny of his soul than he was with the future of his kingdom. He had found it uncomfortable to consider the torments of Hell, but imagining the likely loss of his kingdom to the combined forces of the papacy and the French was more than he could bear. Somewhere between Hocktide and Midsummer's Day, King John had calculated his repentance. He submitted himself to the Holy Church and granted his entire kingdom as a fief to the pope.

Casting all plans with the French aside, the pontiff pounced upon his new realm. He immediately declared to all his absolute authority over all matters in England, both earthly and spiritual. In exchange, as both shrewd men had no doubt agreed beforehand, the pope then returned the over-lordship of England to John as his sworn vassal. In addition, mistakenly assuming Stephen Langton would quietly support his manoeuvres, the pontiff immediately loaded the cleric on a fast-sailing ship and set him upon the seat of Canterbury as Archbishop.

All sides reeled from the reversal. John's enemies were suddenly the enemies of the Holy Church. King Philip of France was outraged. He had spent vast sums of money preparing an invasion under the auspices of the Church's blessing, only to have this ambitious pope turn all events to his own advantage.

In England, the barons were outraged as well, for their grievances would surely go unheeded, despite Innocent's ceremonial demand that John right all wrongs. The barons feared what mischief this tyrant might now make behind the shield of the pope's ghostly powers. Even the English clerics were troubled and they immediately resisted such a dramatic, unparalleled interpretation of papal authority within their dioceses. Influenced by the persuasive arguments of John of Salisbury and others, they gathered to affirm the principle that no one office and no one man had ever been intended to wield such absolute authority.

"Lord husband," asked Isabel, soon after hearing news from Canterbury. "What do you think of this Stephen Langton?" Her question was sincere, her mood inquisitive.

William shrugged. He was glad peace had been restored between his wife and himself. "I had thought him to be another lap dog for the pope, but his words gave me pause. When he met the King in Winchester Cathedral, he embraced him, but he had the boldness to remind John that a condition of his vassalage to the pope was that he redress injustice. King John nearly fell off his throne! Now he has summoned a council of bishops and barons to St. Alban's in order to reaffirm ancient English liberties."

Isabel brightened. "Ah, Le Court shall be pleased."

"Where is the little fellow?"

"Serving Mass to a leper colony near Dover."

William shook his head. He remembered the horror of leprosy in Palestine and he shuddered. The terrible disease had followed the Crusaders home. "*Oui*; well, other news. The French fleet is defeated."

Isabel clapped. "God be praised. My prayers have been that neither tyrants nor Frenchmen rule in England."

William laughed and poured them each a tankard of warm red wine. "So then, to Isabel. May she breathe free air in a free England."

❋

"My lady, I have heard talk of yer sons." Aethel squirmed a little as the two snooped about the pantry in Chepstow Castle.

Isabel turned a curious eye towards her. "*Oui*? How so?"

"The barons are growing weary of the King's abuses. He taxes them beyond all reason, to pay for his adventures in France; he gives no heed to their complaints. He imprisons them without jury trial, dispossesses their lands, and uses the Holy Church as a weapon."

"And?"

"Well, in the market the Welshmen are saying they've heard that young William and Richard are joining with barons in a rebellion."

Isabel was quiet. "I know nothing of my sons. I've sent messages, but have received none."

Aethel regretted bringing the matter up. She laid a hand on Isabel's shoulder and showed her a basket of green beans and watercress. "I am glad to be back at Chepstow again, away from London and talk of our fool King. The dunce dances about the whole of his realm like a nervous rabbit."

"More like a sneaking fox." The Countess shook her head, troubled for her sons but hardly surprised. She had known that the Anglo-Norman barons were very dissatisfied and approaching the point of civil war. The King's support was primarily in the south of England and was provided by those who had either been browbeaten or bribed. She also had learned that the pope had recently allowed King John to take the vows of a Crusader and hence, John now had the authority to invoke excommunication on any who would oppose him!

Other news had added to her fears. The King's cousin and ally, Emperor Otto of the Germans, had been defeated by the French at Bouvines. It was a crushing defeat that had utterly ruined John's fresh designs on France. With the English King so discredited, the barons would find increasing support for their rebellion.

A familiar voice turned the women's attention. "My lady, and Aethel."

"Ah, Sir John."

D'Erley bowed. "Aethel, you are looking more beautiful than my last memory."

Aethel blushed.

"You are happy with thy Harold?"

"Aye. Never so happy as now, sir."

"Good. Now, m'lady, seems we are off to another council. Thy husband sends his regrets that he has rushed off ahead and I am to escort you to London."

The Countess sighed. "Another council, dear John?"

"*Oui*. Archbishop Langton is struggling to maintain a peace. He loudly opposed the King for his stubborn and foolish adventure in Normandy and now the King and the pope are angry with him. Their fury does not wilt him in the least, however, and now he demands to hear the barons' grievances so that he can put order to them and present them to the King. In truth, m'lady, I doubt civil war can be avoided. The King has abused all manner of law, raided the barons' treasuries, and now he has excommunicated all who oppose him."

"And where do you stand in these matters, Sir John?"

John d'Erley was a man of uncommon character. No mere King could buy his loyalty or badger him for fealty, yet the knight proclaimed himself a royalist. "I serve thy husband, my lady, and he has sworn to remain faithful to the King. It is a matter of honour."

"Honour, dear John? Honour or stubbornness?" Isabel thought. "I see no honour in serving tyrants. There is a higher duty."

"With pardon, we serve no tyrant, we serve our honour."

The Countess' face tightened and she wrung her hands. "It is justice that ought be served and it is *this* that ought be served honourably."

Though always present, Twigadarn rarely spoke and was rarely seen. He suddenly stepped from a dark corner and drew his sword. Startled and not a little frightened, Sir John paled and reached towards the handle of his own blade. The giant rushed towards him and d'Erley jerked his sword from his belt only to watch the Welshman fly past him towards a dark passage at the rear of the pantry.

Aethel and Isabel cried out as Twigadarn fell upon two hooded men. One lunged at the Welshman with a long sword, only to be instantly felled. The other nimbly dodged both Twigadarn and Sir John's swords as he sprinted for another doorway. Dashing away, he cried over his shoulder, "A curse on all the Marshals!"

❋

The surviving hooded man was never caught, but the one whom Twigadarn had slain was believed to be a priest or monk, given his tonsure. Some thought he had the look of an Irishman, but who could really know? He was broad-headed, like many of the Celts, and his hair was red. Another thought he smelled of Irish ale. It seemed like a logical conclusion, for Lord William had aggravated numbers of the Irish clergy in his efforts to subdue the irascible population. The earl never did understand their hostility. His almoner had faithfully and generously supported their poor and he had endowed many monasteries.

Shaken and glad to be leaving Wales, Isabel and her entourage packed quickly and departed for southern England with Sir John and his escort. Upon their arrival in London they were met with frantic activity. King John had commissioned troops from the few territories he still held in France and he had dispatched these to attempt the collection of overdue taxes from the infuriated barons. In the meantime, he ordered royal castles to be quickly filled with provisions and readied for siege.

The Marshals took residence in a pleasant and most familiar manor house in Surrey. The home brought a smile to the Countess, for it was the very house in which she had honeymooned so many years before. The owner was the son of the prior owner and was a courteous, generous host.

Isabel and Aethel walked about happily, reminiscing about the many things they had endured between their stays at this home. "Ah, m'lady, 'twas here that Sir Alan defended my honour," laughed the servant.

"Ha, ha! I wish I had seen that. Oh, Aethel, so much has happened in our lives." She paused in her melancholy and ached for her children. Suddenly, another memory seized her.

"Forget the curse, m'lady. 'Twas cast by an old, miserable Scot who had no power."

Isabel nodded wearily. "Indeed. So it was. Now, Aethel, I've news of young William. He sides with the barons against the royals."

Aethel grimaced. "I thought as much, but I would as well and, methinks, you, too."

Isabel's eyebrows lifted in surprise. It was a bold, treasonous statement. "Aethel, mind your tongue," she scolded. "You'll find yourself tossed in prison or hanged and thy husband with you. Such talk puts all of us in danger."

The handmatron hung her head. "Aye, was unwise—but true enough."

❋

Christmas came and went with little notice. Isabel had so wished to spend the holy days far away from the troubles. But it was not to be. Lord William had spent most of December shuttling between Surrey and London, hoping to negotiate a solution to the rebellion now spreading rapidly from north to south.

The Epiphany of 1215 followed with a moderate feast and a sad, cold rain. Then news came that, on the advice of Archbishop Langton, the barons had finally presented their grievances to King John's advisors. Theirs was a long list of complaints organised under the counsel of the archbishop, who had insisted that they base their petitions in English law rather than in economic loss. To the barons' grave distress, King John casually dismissed their presentation out of hand, even insisting that further discussions be postponed.

So, while a host of furious barons returned to their homes, Lord William finally was relieved to enjoy a few weeks of winter respite with his family. 'Midst the damp, cold air of late January and early February, the earl and his wife enjoyed heated cider and heavy wines. But, as all men who steward their duties in earnest, William remained preoccupied with the troubles of the realm and found himself spending more and more time in clandestine meetings with the archbishop at Westminster.

William had learned to respect his wife enough to share with her the nature of his discussions. For her part, she was pleased to be included in such disclosures and fascinated with the information. As the weeks passed, however, Isabel had done more than listen. For these many years she had learned so very much from Le

Court and his treasure chest of scrolls. She had been a voracious student of history and law, philosophy, and theology. Now her learning was coming together as if it had finally found its intended end.

Isabel shared her bounty with her husband so that he might attend his secret meetings with Langton more aware of the great principles of law and liberty. It was true, Stephen Langton needed no tutor on these things, but it was William Marshal who was enabled to better understand these principles in play. It was he who was suddenly able to relate the reality of the barons' experience to the abstract concepts presented by the archbishop. Such an amazing match would soon prove to be the fountain of great things to come.

※

"I am to represent the King at Oxford," grumbled Lord William.

"Travelling to Oxford in February? I hope it serves your purposes well," answered Isabel.

"The barons are practically begging for a hearing. We've rumours they've sent delegates to Philip and I fear they may bring the French in on their side."

"Never," snapped Isabel. As sympathetic as she was for the cause of the barons, she hated the French.

"I fear so. Our royal castles are well provisioned and at the ready. The barons know a civil war would be costly on all counts, but the French could ensure their victory."

"Then they'd not be fighting for English law at all."

William smirked, ever so slightly. "*Oui*, well said."

Isabel shook her head. "They *must* understand it is for *law* they rebel, not profit."

"Now you sound like Langton." William lowered his voice. "But, dear wife, guard your tongue. Another might think you are disloyal to the King." He raised his brows.

Isabel sighed. "I am loyal to *you*."

"And I am loyal to King John."

The Countess felt the snare closing. "But I would that you were—"

"No more of this," commanded William. "If honour is to be King, then prudence must be Queen."

Isabel folded her hands neatly on her belly. "God is to be King, and prudence is Queen. Honour would make a pleasant Prince." She smiled, playfully.

"Ha! I do love you so. Now, I'm off to Oxford."

Lord William made the cold journey with Archbishop Langton and a column of men-at-arms. Upon their arrival, however, they learned that King John had cleverly avoided inviting more than a handful of barons, and they now cried foul. They quickly understood that the earl's report would state that a meeting had occurred but with poor attendance. The King, in turn, would claim he offered redress but few had bothered to attend and their disinterest would be used to minimise their grievances. It was a cunning ploy. The conference ended abruptly and bore no fruit.

In the early spring, soon after Hocktide, the barons did gather in force, this time at Brackley, the home of the agitated Earl of Northamptonshire. Here they assembled under arms in an overt display of rebellion. As they prepared to make war on their King, they dispatched agents to a delighted King Philip. Here was the Frenchman's opportunity to avenge King John's endless meddling in France and to wrest a penalty for the pope's double-cross.

The outbreak of open warfare grieved the archbishop. Knowing the barons still trusted him, he begged them to meet with him and the respected Lord William. A gathering took place from which another petition was drawn and delivered to King John. With Langton's support, the barons expressed their demand that the King reaffirm the just laws of Henry I—laws that had re-established the ancient liberties of free Englishmen. Again, the obstinate tyrant dismissed the earnest pleas of his subjects. Civil war was now inevitable.

Lord William found himself suddenly in the unenviable position of defending a king who had betrayed his trust, deceived the realm, abused his power, and disregarded nearly every legal precedent that had kept peaceable, just order in England for centuries. It was an abrogation of royal stewardship that had already earned the King the dubious distinction of infamy.

The old earl did give the wicked King some due for his charity to the poor, and he gave him credit for his admitted skill at manipulating the world around him. Furthermore, though England itself was on the verge of collapse, King John had achieved dramatic victories over the Scots, the Welsh, and the Irish.

The earl was too old to re-evaluate the code of chivalry that had shaped the whole of his long life. Now in his early seventies, he was not about to wrestle with what notions Isabel and Langton had confounded him. He would follow duty as he had always thought it to be and he would defend the Crown without regard for his personal feelings.

With the realm now at war, the royal camp would need to begin immediate manoeuvres. "You are to follow the King to the south-west," cried D'Erley to Isabel. "Lord William demands we leave at once for Salisbury."

The lord's entourage packed quickly, and the domestic household hastily wound its way towards the Salisbury plain under heavy escort as William and his *mesnie* rode far ahead. D'Erley, however, was sent with a company of scouts towards Essex to reconnoitre the counties just north of London. William sent the man there out of due diligence, but had fully expected him to return with a report proving his own conjecture—that the rebels were assembling much farther to the north, probably near the river Trent. It was William's strategy, therefore, to plot a campaign that rallied support from the lords of the Welsh Marches and from England's royalist south-western barons. With a large army properly organised near Salisbury, he could then march against the rebels from south to north.

In late May, however, d'Erley returned with shocking news. He had stumbled upon the barons' army and had barely escaped with his life.

"*Sacre bleu!*" cried Lord William.

"I fear it is so," answered d'Erley. "They have swept south and are already prepared to take London."

"London! Will there be resistance from the city's guard?"

D'Erley was surprised that Lord William was so ill-informed. "No. The officers are believed to be in sympathy with the rebels."

William planted his fist hard into his palm. "We must strike them, but where? Tell me, what do we know of the French army?"

"We are not certain Philip is in the war yet. It seems the rebels are in some division over the matter, though we do know their agents have crossed the Channel. If Philip enters, I fear it would be to crown his son, Louis, as King of England."

Lord William stared blankly, gathering his thoughts. "May it never be," he mumbled.

✵

In the days that followed, London fell to the barons and its fall incited extreme numbers of defectors from the royal camp. Furious, desperate King John took the occasion to berate William for his strategic miscalculation, as well as for other news recently received regarding young William's defiant defection to the barons' side. "An outrage. A grand deception by you, old man, and thy treasonous son." King John threw himself about his chamber like a wounded bear. "William Marshal, pledge thy fealty once more."

William was angry and humiliated. He lifted his jaw. "Sire, I have pledged my fealty to thee before; it is enough. To pledge it again suggests I am being restored to a tryst I have ne'er broken."

John scowled. He hated men of principle. "That, noble sir, did not prevent you from swearing twice to Philip." He tossed a flask of wine at a wall and cursed the man with every foul oath a despot might know. Then, realising no better sword served his Crown than William's, he relented with a laugh. "Ha, Marshal. I jest. Thy word is fixed to thy soul like sheep to Wales."

The courtiers tittered, but Lord William set a hard, unyielding eye on the man he despised. "Sire, London is gone, our own lords and barons creep out of our camp each night and fly to our enemy. Agents are known to be in France negotiating with Philip."

King John roared. "I excommunicate them all! Let their souls burn always. I shall demand the pope pronounce interdict on all of France. 'Tis a terrible fear the French have of such things, you know, and it shall be our defence. You, William Marshal, are said to be the greatest knight in all Christendom. Lead my army against these traitors and crush them where they be."

William's mind was racing. "Sire, if that is thy command, I shall obey. But I am quite certain you jest—as before. You know what loss an ill-timed attack might mean. Their army is now positioned west of London in force. Surely your wish is to sue for peace, to buy time for a better day's fight."

The King sat quietly, then turned to his counsellors and whispered. He rose and approached the earl. Standing close to him, he smiled. "Ah, good William. You know me well: you know my mind." He embraced the stiff-backed earl, then backed away. "Windsor still holds for us, and the meadows by the Thames in that country are so very agreeable in June. Perhaps one may provide a good place to make a peace? Yes, of course. So, you and Langton call the fools to a meeting, and have them write their demands plainly. We shall see if we can make some sense of this pudding."

William left the court sweating and relieved. He had hoped to avert bloodletting and wanted desperately to keep the French out. He huddled with the archbishop, and the day following he led King John's shrinking army towards Windsor and a pleasant, flower-dappled meadow called Runnymede.

CHAPTER XIX

MAGNA CARTA

"AH, my beloved friends," sighed Isabel as she looked deeply into three faces now shadowed by the setting sun. "I have so enjoyed this picnic!" She rose and proceeded to kiss the cheeks of Sir John d'Erley, Aethel, and Twigadarn. "I am so very thankful for the way that our lives have been woven together. We are like a wonderful tapestry of times gone by. I thank you all for thy love and friendship for these many years."

Aethel embraced her lady in a firm, almost suffocating hug and wept on her shoulder.

The four smiled at one another for one last moment before d'Erley said sadly, "My lady, I do fear we needs return to camp. 'Tis getting late; 'tis no longer safe here."

Isabel nodded, obediently. "I wish the day had never ended." She mounted her horse and waited patiently as her entourage assembled. Her mind turned to her husband and she wondered what manner of Sabbath he and Archbishop Langton had endured with the King's councillors. She smiled as she watched Aethel plant her rump in her saddle, and spent a moment thinking of Harold in far away Pembroke. Then, with all in order, she and her entourage trotted away to the royal camp pitched near Windsor Castle.

❋

The morning of June 15, 1212, broke fair and warm. A light breeze ruffled the pennants of the King's camp and sent gentle ripples across the tents' dew-laden canvas. The bells of Prime pealed softly from nearby churches and Lord William entered his tent with a tray of cheese, fresh wheat bread, and red wine. He had not slept all the night, yet he looked bright and hopeful. "Good morn, fair maiden," he said as he pulled the blankets off his wife.

"Oh, William," scolded Isabel playfully. She quickly donned a white chemise and wrapped her shoulders with a light stole. "You have spent the whole night in council?"

"*Oui*. But not in vain." His eyes sparkled like they had so oft' in years prior.

Isabel brightened. She kissed her husband and held his hands. The man was now seventy-three, but on this morning he seemed hardly past his prime. "Tell me."

"I believe you shall be proud. I have listened well to all you have shared with me. I think my pillow ought be called my 'university'." The two laughed. "Langton is a genius. With my help— little as it may have been—he has redrafted the barons' grievances into what they have titled the *Articles of the Barons*."

"Is it a fair and proper charter?"

"*Oui*, most certainly, though Langton says it needs some final reduction and a great deal of better order. But I say you shall be pleased because it is as you have wished. It is a restatement of the ancient liberties of England. It addresses taxation with consent, trial by jury, and freedom to the English Church. Langton had much to do with *that* one. And he wrote the words, 'English' Church, not 'Holy' Church. If I recall his language: 'That the English Church shall be free and enjoy her rights in their integrity and her liberties untouched.' Our good archbishop hates tyranny in all forms, including the tyranny of the pope."

Isabel felt chills tingle through her body. "'Tis all the things Le Court and I have dreamt of for England."

"*Oui*. Of course the barons also have a tangle of sundry particulars—forest boundaries, mercenaries, guardianships, debts to moneylenders, Welsh hostages, bridge building, and so forth. You should be glad to know they demand rights for widows as well."

Isabel did not appreciate her husband's morbid humour. "Go on."

William shrugged. "Langton also tells me I should take special note that the *Articles* speak on behalf of all English freemen, not just the barons. He intends it to address the rights of all—the simple yeoman with one hectare or an earl with a whole county."

Isabel nodded and poured her husband some wine. "What I am hearing, William, is a great principle ringing loudly in the sum of thy words. It is *law* that is to be finally supreme, not king or pope. And that, dear husband, is what I believe God has always intended."

William smiled, and had begun to speak, when a soldier called from outside the tent. "Lord William?"

"*Oui*, lad."

"The King is ready."

The old earl faced his wife. He took her by her hands and stared at her lovingly. "I pray England is about to be served well. I pray my honour does not fail me, nor my King fail this moment."

Isabel embraced him. "Would that all Christendom know of thy matchless manhood. Indeed, lord husband, you shall serve well."

William adjusted his long tunic and belt. He laid a gloved hand on the hilt of his sword and turned on his heels. With a shout and a flurry of commands, the great lord then mounted his charger and followed his King into destiny.

※

The mounted royal cavalcade trotted quietly towards a tent set neatly in the centre of the flower-dotted meadow of Runnymede. Nearby, the Thames flowed full; enlivened by late spring rains. Accompanied by a small, armed escort, the retinue included a variety of notables. These included King John of course, as well as Stephen Langton, the Archbishop of Canterbury and Primate of England; William Marshal, the Earl of Pembroke; Henry, Archbishop of Dublin; Bishop Pandulph, the papal legate; Brother Aymeric, Master of the Knights of the Temple in England, and a sundry assortment of clerks, lesser lords, and men-at-arms.

Waiting on foot at the tent were twenty-five barons acting

as the ambassadors of the rebellion. While an army of others waited nervously at some distance, these twenty-five stood boldly, fully aware that their defiance might very well cost them their property and their lives. They waited nervously, but bravely. Unfortunately there were few among them that truly risked such peril for lofty principles.

Lord William dismounted and followed his King towards the tent within which a small throne had been set. Impressed, King John immediately claimed the throne and surveyed the barons facing him. William scanned their faces as well, but when it fell upon one certain face, his heart nearly failed him. Just yards before him, standing as surety for the barons' cause, was his own eldest son, William Marshal the Younger. King John had noticed the young man as well and he cast a wry smile at the earl.

Archbishop Langton offered a prayer for peace and a quiet negotiation began in which the general principles of concern were reviewed. It was agreed that a truce would protect the parties and be in force for the duration of the negotiations. The barons swore that the King of France had not yet been granted safe landing anywhere in England, Wales, or Ireland, and that none knew of any present conspiracy between Philip and the Scots. For their part, the King's men swore that messengers had been sent to all royal officials demanding they desist from all punitive measures taken against any baron in rebellion.

Believing all matters to be in order, the archbishop designated himself and William Marshal as chief negotiators for the King. The barons presented three of theirs and, with all preliminary formalities addressed, the meeting began.

The affair was tedious, at best, and while Langton and William Marshal conducted themselves with dignity and respect for the barons' grievances, King John languished on his little throne, bored, suddenly hungry, and eager for the matter to end. It was obvious to Lord William that the King was demonstrating no meaningful interest in any of the many articles under discussion, and it gave the wise earl pause. He began to wonder if King John had entered this negotiation devoid of good faith. Could it be that the King was simply stalling for time and pretending capitulation to disarm the rebellion? If that were true, William Marshal would be the instrument of betrayal.

The lord's mind wandered over the King's possible strategy as Langton and the royal lawyers reviewed the barons' *Articles* one by one. The morning wore on until, at eleven o'clock, dinner was served. Each side went separate ways to find their respective tables now set under a glorious blue sky. It was a quiet affair for both the barons and the royalists, each enjoying summer fare of vegetables and game. The ale flowed and moods softened, bringing the negotiators back to the tent refreshed.

King John, however, became all the more agitated as the afternoon began. He felt suddenly humiliated by his predicament and his anger rose. His eyes flashed about the tent and the negotiators felt an immediate sense of urgency to their purposes. However, knowing it was too late to abandon that which he had begun, the King abruptly stood and declared the *Articles of the Barons* approved. With that he stormed away, leaving the details to Langton.

✳

As the King galloped towards Windsor Castle, Lord William and Archbishop Langton stared blankly at the barons. "My lords," began the archbishop at long last. "I shall remove the document to my chamber and, with permission, shall refine it. When all is ready, I shall have it returned with the King's signature, and I shall then witness your signing. Is this agreeable?"

Lord Robert FitzWalter stepped forward. "*Oui, Père,* and on behalf of our Army of God, I offer our deepest and most profound gratitude for thy service."

Stephen Langton bowed, humbly. "I trust all of you shall now serve the King as Christian vassals ought."

The comment drew a few grumbles, then a few nods.

"Good, my sons. The King is God's ordained servant. With our common liberties now reaffirmed, he has acted as a proper steward of his throne. Serve him well and with honour."

The day's business over, William called to his son. "Lad, good lad, a word?"

Young William answered coldly. "Aye, father?"

"Let me look at you! Ah, strong and determined—I see it in your face."

"Yes, father."

"You've won the day; you ought be proud."

The young man nodded, then took his father aside. "Sir, you still serve a wicked King. I know him well. He has no intention of honouring this charter. I can *feel* it. As soon as we disperse he shall betray his own word and you will bear your sword against us once again."

The earl scoffed. "But, my son, the King shall soon sign the charter; it will be law. I doubt even he would dare flaunt the very law he signs."

William the Younger shook his head, sadly. "Father, by now I would have thought you'd understand that few men are as honourable as you. No, sir, he shall flaunt it indeed. This King is sly and wicked, clever, and a master of deception. I swear to you, father, that he shall undo what he has done, and it shall cost England much."

The old knight shook his head, stubbornly. Deep within he did fear the King's ways, yet he could hardly fathom such a betrayal, even by this wicked King. "My son, we have all read the final words of the charter. When he signs it and puts his seal to it, he would never recant." As if to reassure himself, William called for Langton.

"Peace to you, young William," said the archbishop kindly, as he approached the pair.

"And to you, *Père*."

Lord William bade Langton read from the parchment. "There, at the end. Read again the covenant of the King."

"He has not yet signed it," answered the archbishop.

"*Oui, oui,* I know, " answered William impatiently. "But read what he is about to sign."

"With joy, my friend. I shall translate the Latin as I go:

"Wherefore we shall, and do firmly charge, that the *English* Church shall be free, and that *all* men in our kingdom shall have and hold *all* the aforesaid liberties, rights and concessions, well and peaceably, freely, quietly, fully and wholly, *to them and their heirs, of us and our heirs, in all things and places forever*, as is aforesaid. It is moreover sworn, as well on our part as on the part of the barons, that *all these matters shall be kept in good faith and without deceit*. Witness the above named and many others. Given by our hand in the meadow which is called Runnymede, between Windsor and Staines, on the fifteenth day of June in the seventeenth year of our reign.

"Do you wish more of the document, Lord Marshal?"

"No, it is enough."

Young William shook his head. "I hear the words, father, as I heard them before. You, *Père*, many years ago witnessed the King's reaffirming of the *Charter of Liberties* of Henry the First, yet he mocks them. This King is utterly faithless and without virtue."

The young man's doubts were well founded, as King John was infamous for his arts of cunning and clever calculation. Yet the day's events had softened many of young William's comrades, for it seemed incredulous to them, as it had to the earl, that any but the Devil himself might recant these words, once sealed.

※

It took days for Archbishop Langton to complete his refinement of the *Articles of the Barons* into a more formal charter of liberties. During the delay the King's mood had darkened all the more, and by Thursday, the nineteenth of June, it seemed that the cause of peace might be hopeless, after all.

"Never. I shall never stoop to such a disgrace as this."

"But, my King, you have given thy word to the barons. The

word of a king ought to be sacred." Archbishop Langton was desperate.

King John's face twisted like a madman's facing a full moon. "I will be the ridicule of all Christendom! Me, the King of England, *forced* to yield redress." He spat.

Lord William spoke. "Sire, consider this. Our army is but a paltry huddle of weary footmen and a few loyal knights. Thy treasury is nearly spent, you've the crown jewels, but little more—you gave the pope all the wealth you once had. As your general and as your royal marshal, I counsel you to reconsider. If you fail to sign the charter, the barons will simply destroy our army, kill you, and set Philip's son, Louis, on the throne."

King John writhed in his chair. He cursed and threw a dagger across his hall. Leaping to his feet he shouted, "I will not sign it!" He then folded his arms and dropped into his seat like a little boy whose comfit had been suddenly snatched away. The court fell silent and still. William and Langton had argued their cause for four days and were weary of battling their foolish King. They had offered every possible argument and had presented themselves persuasively.

King John abruptly stood. For all his vanity, in the end he was not unintelligent. "I have reached my final decision on this horrid matter. I do not intend to sign my name, nor do I intend to affix my royal seal to this outrage." He paused to enjoy the defeated looks of his slack-jawed counsellors. "No, I shall not endure such humiliation. Instead, Lord William, since you are so keen on our shame, *you* shall affix my seal in my stead. Let this degradation fall upon the memory of you, sir, and not this King of England."

Langton stiffened. *A tyrant and a coward!* he thought. He gave the straight-backed earl a subtle nod and, wanting nothing more than to protect the charter at all costs, he smiled at the King. "By God's grace, my liege, and according to thy wisdom."

The King sneered and left the hall without a word. Langton turned to William and sighed. "I fear all the soap in England would fail to cleanse my mouth from what putrid puffery it just belched." He spat.

Then, without wasting any more time, the archbishop and

William hurried to the King's chancery, where the charter lay atop a large desk. The chancellor bowed and yielded the King's seal, wax, and a candle. A handful of clerks and the King's lawyers were summoned as witnesses and, with little ceremony, Lord William Marshal affixed the Seal of King John to the amazing parchment later to be known as *Magna Carta—the Great Charter*.

❋

An uneasy peace settled over southern England for the rest of June 1215 and into early July. Neither side fully trusted the other, though the rebel armies slowly dissolved into the various shires, earldoms, counties, and towns of their origin. London was once again considered the unofficial capital of King John's England and Langton's churchmen worked feverishly to maintain the peace. But John's lacklustre enforcement of the *Charter* quickly affirmed the reluctant suspicions of the barons and fuelled a growing resistance to the duties of the royal officials.

By August it was clear that King John had never intended to honour the *Charter*. Instead, believing his enemies to be vulnerable once again, King John began a punitive campaign against the former rebels, particularly in the north of England. His armies set fields to the torch, put peasants to the sword, robbed treasuries, and destroyed storehouses and workshops.

The chaos that he spread over England created other troubles for the King, however. The Welsh saw a fresh opportunity to strike their Norman occupiers and a rebellion in the Marches—the wild frontier between England and Wales—created a second front for the royal army. It was here that William Marshal was sent.

❋

"If you must take arms again, lord husband, I am thankful it is against the Welsh, and not yet against our son in England." Lady Isabel was weary and frustrated. The joy and hope of just three months prior had quickly evaporated. The precious *Charter* had been abandoned and her beloved England was being torn asunder. Now, within the cold walls of Pembroke Castle, she stared angrily at the sea and wondered how it could be that her husband and her son might someday face each other on the field of battle. "It was a joyous day when I saw both you and young William affix your names on the *Charter*. I thought all Heaven must be rejoicing. Instead, this evil King has betrayed the trust—and he made you the fool, again."

"Enough, woman. I am so very tired of this old song. My duty stays with the King, whatever I may think of him." His words trailed at the end, sadly. "Young William serves in the north, far away from my army. But know this: I shall never draw my sword against my own."

Isabel turned away. "I will not speak of it again, though I have heard that Richard is with the barons as well."

A heavy rap sounded on the door.

"Enter," boomed William.

John d'Erley came into the room, white as death and trembling. "Sire, we've news."

"Speak, man."

John cast a nervous, almost shameful glance towards Isabel. "I—I—we've a courier that claims the pope has annulled the Charter and demands Langton excommunicate all the barons of the rebellion."

Isabel gasped. It was an outrage. Furthermore, thinking of her son's soul being damned on the verge of war was terrifying for her. She began to weep.

The earl was furious. "Annulled the *Charter*? It is good law, right and true. The King ought to yield to it."

John grumbled. "*Oui*, m'lord. A king of virtue surely would."

William began to pace. "Tell me, John, how is it that this meddling pope is in this matter?"

"King John appealed to him for relief as his vassal. I am told that the pope nearly swooned with rage when he read of a free, *English* Church and was not the least bit pleased that free men might impede his authority. Some say that his lawyers advised him that a contract approved under threat of force is invalid and he acted on that point."

William nodded. "I fear it bears some truth." He rubbed his head and groaned. "I tell you this, Sir John. The pope has just blown air into embers. The barons not yet in revolt shall cry foul and go to arms quickly. They'll join the others and soon we'll be facing the Scots and the French."

D'Erley had more to add. "Sire, I've also learned that the pope is sending large numbers of Italian and Spanish mercenaries to bolster our army. It seems we'll have enough to press hard against the rebels if they rise up."

William was furious. "By the saints. Mercenaries? Seeing dark-eyed little men running about on English soil will turn the folk against us as well. The Saxons won't have it, I tell you, nor the Danes. The barons will fill their ranks with every English yeoman that can shoot a bow or carry a pike."

Isabel spoke with a voice sharpened by fury, but weakened by exhaustion. "Sir John, what of Langton, shall he excommunicate my son?"

"*Non, Madame*; he refuses to obey the pope."

"Ha!" cried William. "Good fellow. He's vinegar in his veins."

"*Oui*, my lord, but now he has been excommunicated himself and ordered into exile. I am told he has marched to Rome to protest."

Isabel shrieked. "What sort of madness is this? Two tyrants in league to avenge their wounded pride. And you two serve them both."

❈

The winter that followed was miserable for the Countess and her household. The Marshal daughters remained with their mother and continued their studies under the masterful eye of Le Court, who had finally returned to Pembroke Castle from far-flung duties at the lord's other estates. The dwarf faithfully performed his religious duties on behalf of the anxious family, and, as the lord's chancellor, was privy to all correspondence from England. The messages he read to the earl gave them both reason for grave concern.

The earl had successfully organised resistance to the Welsh rebels in the Marches, but much of north Wales was under the control of the skilled Welsh warrior, Prince Llewellyn. To Aethel's great horror, her beloved Harold had been sent to the north of Pembrokeshire where he now served Lord Baldwin as a footman in the battles with Llewellyn's troops. She had heard nothing of the man for months, but had learned that the fighting had been terrible and bloody.

By March, Le Court read a message to Lord William which confirmed what all had dreaded: the barons were in armed rebellion and had formally invited King Philip's son, Louis, to come to England with an army. He would be elected King of England.

In the meantime, King John's military position had greatly improved. Though he was now fighting both the barons and their ally, King Alexander of Scotland, his own army had been swollen with foreign mercenaries happily supplied by the pope. As a result, the King had successfully besieged London and defeated its outlying rebel garrisons. In addition, he had scored a decisive victory over the castle of Rochester, a loss that had affirmed the rebels' unqualified need to call on the French for help.

Though he was successfully engaging the Scots and the rebel barons, King John was deeply troubled by the prospect of battling the French. He decided to appeal to Philip directly, so he sent a message to Lord William. "Sire," Le Court began, "it reads that you are to 'come under heavy escort to Pavensey and meet with my delegation. You shall sail to France to secure a lasting truce with our beloved brother and Christian kinsman, Philip.'"

"Why Pevensey?" asked Isabel.

"The other ports are still in rebel hands," answered William. He looked wearily into Isabel's eyes. "I do beg thy leave, good wife. I pray the French stay home and let us settle our matters amongst ourselves."

Isabel nodded angrily. "You once wished for me that I might breathe free air in a free England? My air is no longer free and I fear my England shall soon be under a French heel."

William shook his head. "Pray for me, pray for us all." As the man turned to leave, his wife caught him by the arm.

"Take me with you," Isabel insisted.

The earl hesitated. The voyage would be dangerous in March and they would be at considerable risk on French soil. He could easily imagine Philip seizing him as a hostage.

Sensing his reluctance, Isabel became forceful. "I have been your faithful companion for all these many years. We have travelled together throughout all of England, Normandy, and the duchies of France. We've braved Wales and Ireland side by side and faced perils of many kinds. Now, in our sunset, I see no reason to become timid."

"The daughters do not come."

"*Oui*. They shall remain here with Le Court."

The lord sighed. He looked carefully at his wife and reluctantly agreed.

"Have I thy leave to ask one more thing?"

"How could I stop you?"

Isabel smiled. "I should be very happy if you would recall Aethel's Harold from service to join her on our journey."

"But we've no time."

"If you send for him now, I am quite certain nothing could keep him."

"Travelling alone is perilous."

"Not as perilous as the north of Wales."

William looked away. He hesitated, then said, "I have not yet told you but Harold Cutter lies wounded. He was slashed across the belly in a battle near Machynlleth."

"Oh. Say it is not so!" Isabel exclaimed.

"D'Erley only informed me of it yesterday."

Isabel clutched her hands together. "Aethel must be told at once."

"*Oui*, of course. Our troops have a stronghold near the mountains and Harold lies in under tent there. Perhaps you ought give her leave to attend him."

"Oh, most certainly. I shall send her at once."

"'Tis dangerous."

"Have I leave to send Twigadarn with her?"

William paused. "No. I need him to guard our daughters."

"You've knights enough to spare for a fortnight."

The earl disagreed. "No. Twigadarn must remain behind. He's a Welshman and I'd be a fool to forget that."

Isabel scowled. "He's as loyal as Sir John."

William would not be dissuaded. "Have the commander send her with an escort of sergeants."

The Countess submitted.

"Now, I've more: Isabel, I received a message yesterday which I intended to present to you at supper. The King offered Young William amnesty and safe conduct to Pembroke under protection of the Templar Master, Aimery St. Maur."

Isabel's eyes widened with hope. "Home? To us here? And St. Maur—yes, I've met him. You claimed him to be the most faithful man in all Christ's Kingdom."

"And so he is, but our son declined."

Isabel's heart sagged. "Perhaps he was wise to do so. Your Templars may be the finest men on this earth, but even they cannot keep the King from treachery. I fear it was a trap and so must have he."

William sighed. "But I long to see him."

Isabel took his hand. "We shall see him again, William. I feel it."

CHAPTER XX

SAOIDH NA AIRC

ISABEL hurriedly informed Aethel of her husband's condition. "But he is yet alive and Lord William says he lies in a mountain stronghold."

Aethel fell to her knees, trembling. She groaned a prayer to the Virgin Mary, then stood and clutched Isabel's hands. "That means they are fighting the Welsh in the open. Else he'd be behind good English stone."

Isabel held her tightly.

"M'Lady, might I have leave to go to him?"

The Countess smiled. "Indeed, you may. Lord William says you may have an escort of sergeants, but it is a dangerous journey."

Aethel kissed Isabel's hands. "Oh, m'Lady. God be praised, Lord William be praised. Thanks be to you."

"God go with you, dear friend. But have a care on the highway." With that, Lady Isabel pecked Aethel on the cheek and began her preparations for travel.

✻

With all things in order, Lord William's entourage made way to Pevensey from which the company set sail in five vessels on a windy, rain swept April morning. Travelling with the earl were Isabel, of course, a portion of their domestic entourage and three knights, including D'Erley, Jordan de Sauqueville, and Henry Hose. The earl's assisting agents were the Bishop of Dublin—a man who hated William for past events in Ireland— two loyalist barons, and a small retinue of clerks.

After nearly twenty-four hours bobbing atop turbulent seas,

the ships finally reached the mouth of the Boulogne Harbour where the masters waited impatiently to follow the tide. By the bells of nones they then entered the harbour, passing the smouldering beacon fires of the old Roman lighthouse atop the harbour's hill. The ships' masters then ordered all sails furled and the oarsmen to their posts. In moments, the ships began to lurch gently forward atop smoother water until they rested quietly at their moorings.

Glad to be ashore, the earl's company disembarked hurriedly as William paid the appropriate fees and presented the town's magistrate with the necessary papers. His clerks exchanged English pennies for French *deniers* and his chamberlain's deputies scattered quickly to acquire French wine and cheese for the land journey ahead. Isabel was sick and sallow. She missed the comforting presence of Aethel.

By noon, William's retinue was rushing south through the heavy forests that bordered the margins of Normandy. Over the next few days they sloshed along muddy roadways, sometimes sinking in slurry to their calves. Horses struggled, wagons fell into deep ruts, and all the while Isabel wondered why she had pleaded so vigorously to come.

After passing odd assortments of travelling monks, peddlers, pilgrims, and soldiers, the column finally reached the abbey of St. Dennis where the brothers delivered them to warm fires and hearty stews. The next morning broke bright and warm and Lord William wanted to press his company hard over the seven miles remaining to Paris. He led them quickly around the walls of St. Dennis and to the Roman road that would lead them to the city. The ancient highway was bordered by a delightful landscape of vineyards and fields touched by spring's first hints of green. The travellers enjoyed these delightful harbingers of the summer to come.

Though the earl was anxious to meet with King Philip, he decided to grant his wife a special moment. It was late morning when the column arrived at the three-tiered town of Montmartre. The hill against which the town was nestled was sided with vineyards, and its top was decorated with a clutter of Roman ruins.

Nearby was a newly constructed convent and it was here that Lord William bade his lady bind her eyes with a kerchief.

"Trust me, Isabel," he laughed.

"You've never asked this of me before."

"Well, a new trick for this old hound. Now, all of you, follow me slowly." Despite the weight of the times, Lord William was suddenly and uncharacteristically playful. He remembered Montmartre from his youth and had been praying for this day's sunshine since he sailed from Pevensey. He led his company into the convent, offered a generous sum of alms, and exited at the far side.

Upon hearing the hushed exclamations of the others, Isabel began to complain. "May I remove this now? Please, William, now?"

The earl laughed. "Indeed. Now."

Isabel tore the kerchief off her eyes. She gasped and clapped and stared in wonder at the green-blushed panorama of France spread before her. Then, with a cry of joy she cried, "Oh, 'tis beautiful! Look, husband, there—the turrets and walls of Paris."

"Indeed, and the winding Seine. 'Tis always beautiful to me." He smiled. "So, good wife," he boasted, "I've done well?"

Isabel laughed loudly. "Well indeed, my lord."

William beamed and pointed to Paris. "By the bells of nones we shall take our quarters somewhere in the centre of that place."

The pair stared quietly and basked under the warm French sun until, with reluctance, they abandoned their lookout and descended from Montmartre to begin the final leg of their journey. The column quickly passed the Martyrologium—the place of St. Denis' martyrdom. It then followed the Seine River to the suburbs of the city where an armed escort awaited. Lord William presented his papers and directed his company to follow the King's mounted sergeants over a drawbridge, through the gate of Saint Merri, and into Paris.

❋

In Pembroke, Aethel had spent the days demanding that the castellan release her escort. Wringing her hands, the frustrated woman insisted that the Countess' permission had been granted.

"She only said you had permission," grumbled the castle's commander. "She did not order you to go. My information is that the roads are more dangerous than ever."

"But permission is permission, y'dung-breathed dolt."

"You might have her permission but you needs mine as well. Now, you old cow, go back to minding your business."

Twigadarn had been standing near. He had a soft spot in his heart for Aethel since the day he had saved her from the London mob; she was like the mother he had lost long ago. The giant said little but he noticed everything. He heard her sobbing alone in her chamber; he saw the dullness in her eyes and heard the sluggish step of her feet. He knew that Harold was the love of the woman's life; her heart beat for the bald fellow like it beat for no other. Despite the restraint of his emotion, Twigadarn did feel for others—deeply, and now he had an idea.

"Aethel," Twigadarn said flatly.

"Aye lad?"

"Your husband?"

Aethel nodded and teared. "I've been told he's suffered a belly wound. He probably has fever and may be dead by now. Contemptible, cursed castellan. Who will wash my Harold's body? Who will lay a flower on my Harold's grave?"

Twigadarn turned away and faced the tender green buds of early April that swelled on the forests beyond. He loved his homeland and he longed to see his people free from English domination. But he also loved the family he served, including the red-eyed matron at his side. "I will take you at dawn."

Aethel paused. "You?"

"*Seadh*. Yes."

"Lord William has not granted you permission."

Twigadarn grunted. "Did he deny it?"

Aethel shrugged. "I doubt it ever was discussed. But you need to stay with the children."

The Welshman looked kindly at Aethel. "The children are safe enough. I will take you on the morrow. I've heard that a company of footmen are leaving for Lord Baldwin's position and we will travel with them."

"But are you sure about the children?"

Twigadarn nodded. "I will see that the lord's knights are aware and we shall return home quickly...with your Harold. But do not speak of it to any, not even Le Court."

Aethel was uncertain. It would be a bold move, one she doubted that her master would approve. Her mind went to Harold and she took a firm hold of Twigadarn's forearms. "God bless you, friend. We go on the morrow."

❀

At dawn the pair joined the column of twenty grumbling footmen and for the next six days, they marched quietly under April skies. Spring rains slowed their hurried pace, but the commander demanded his company press forward as quickly as possible. They crossed through the sprawling Teifi Valley, passed beneath the bluffs by Tregaron and, at long last, arrived at the dramatic environs of Machynlleth. Steep, pine-clad slopes rose to either side as the column rounded a sweeping curve in the roadway and they found themselves facing the looming mountain known as Cadair Idris.

"'Tis magnificent," exclaimed an exhausted Aethel.

Twigadarn said nothing. He had been troubled for some time. He looked about the rugged landscape and adjusted the long-sword fastened on his back.

"Lord Baldwin should be just east of here, 'bout an hour's march," grumbled the commander. His men were weary. Carrying an assortment of pikes, hammers, bows, and a few swords, these were yeomen--free farmers--fulfilling their military obligation to Lord William and others. They were not pleased to be slogging through mud to fight Welsh rebels this far from their homes.

"The courier said the camp is just beneath a tall outcrop past a pine gorge with a waterfall. That would be it." The leader pointed. "Now, hurry on. I'm hungry."

The small column jogged forward, now drawn by hopes of steaming stews. They stumbled a bit over the stony path, and they continued to descend until their trail was cramped by cliffs and steep rises on either side. The sky was grey and darkening beneath the setting sun.

Suddenly, the leading soldier screamed and clutched an arrow that had punctured his belly. With his eyes wide with surprise, he tilted and fell to his side. The yeomen began to scramble in all directions as more arrows flew from the rocks above them. Twigadarn grabbed a terrified Aethel and dragged her uphill where he stuffed her roughly in the cleft of a protruding boulder.

The yeomen began to shoot back, wildly. Most missed their targets and as the raiders burst from their cover the majority tried running for their lives. Twigadarn, however, pulled his sword from his back and clenched his jaw as he prepared to greet a rushing company of Welshmen. With Aethel hidden behind him, he suddenly charged towards his enemies with a wild yell.

The giant swung his steel in vicious circles, first this way, then that. With every long sweep he removed a head or split a belly. Striding ever forward—driving the raiders away from Aethel—he cut his way through a toppling column of shrieking Celts. He slowly made his way to the centre of the trail where he held fast.

Englishmen lay dead all about, but those who hadn't run now made their way close to the giant and defended one another bravely. The Welsh fell upon them with short swords and spiked clubs, with maces, and with pikes. Mad with bloodlust, they surged towards Twigadarn and his knot of farmers in screaming waves.

From her cover, poor Aethel trembled. She had kept herself deep within the cleft with ears covered until she finally dared to peak beyond her rock. When she saw brave Twigadarn slaying his countrymen for her, her eyes blurred.

The giant was beginning to falter, however. His sword was

heavier than most men could lift and the endless waves of attack had left his arms burning. With one eye on Aethel's screen and the other on his foes, he fought on.

One by one the Englishmen at Twigadarn's side fell away and soon it was only he and one other to face the horde. It was then that the Welsh raiders paused. Their commander—a bony devil with long, black, braided hair barked a command and his men slowly formed a circle. He looked at the writhing bodies of his fighters piled about, and then at Twigadarn who was panting in the centre of the ring. The terrified young yeoman was leaning on him back to back.

The Welsh commander pointed his sword at Twigadarn and shouted to his fellows. "*Cridhe nach sgithich an trod* (A heart that will not tire in battle)."

Twigadarn lifted his chin. "*Innsidh mi dhut de as coir dhut a dheanamh* (I will tell you what you should do)." He was about to order their surrender when the sounds of approaching heavy horse shook the earth.

Aethel's heart leapt for joy. "Sir Baldwin's knights!"

Indeed, the sounds of the Welshmen's shrieks had found the ears of Lord Baldwin's soldiers. A company of knights were now rushing from their stronghold to rescue the reinforcements they had expected.

The Celts looked at their commander. The man lifted his nose to the air like a wolf, and then scowled. With a few words he ordered his men hastily into the walls of the ravine, but he had not run more than twenty paces when he spotted Aethel from the corner of his eye. With an oath he changed direction and made his way towards her.

Twigadarn saw the man make his move. Trumpeting like a raging bull he rushed towards him, the savage now nearly upon the speechless woman. An arrow sang over the giant's shoulder, however. It was lofted by the lone yeoman still standing on the trail. The shaft flew true and as the raider neared Aethel, it pierced his back and the man dropped dead to the ground.

Twigadarn stopped and spun about. He raised his sword in

thanks to the Englishman, and then turned towards Aethel with a smile. The woman sprung from her cover to embrace her friend, but she had not taken three steps before another arrow—a Welsh arrow—flew through the air. It pierced the base of Twigadarn's neck with a sickening sound. Aethel screamed and the giant stared at her, blankly. Another arrow flew from the rocks and hit him squarely in the chest. The force of it rocked him backwards. Yet another came from farther away and sank into his thigh.

Angry, Twigadarn broke the wooden shaft from his leg and bellowed. His voice echoed through the gorge. He raised his sword helplessly and a shower of arrows then found their marks. The sword fell from Twigadarn's hand and he arched his back, crying loudly, "Aethel...*na biodh doilgheas ort*. Be not grieved for me."

With that, the beloved giant with the crystal eyes fell like a mighty timber atop a forest floor. Aethel screamed and ran to his twitching body with open arms. She collapsed by his side, sobbing and wailing. She rested her head on his chest and prayed for God to raise him up. It was not to be.

Lord Baldwin's knights thundered through the gorge and two charged towards Aethel and the body of Twigadarn. "Woman?"

"I am Aethel, servant of Countess Isabel," she sobbed. "This is my friend."

One of the knights looked at Twigadarn and cursed. "I know him. He shielded Isabel at Kilkenny Castle. A fighter like no other."

Within the hour, Aethel was taken to her husband's side, forlorn and heartbroken. Seeing him alive and smiling lifted her spirits a little. She reached for him and buried her face into his shoulder. "Oh, Harold. I love you so," she sobbed. But the reunion was bittersweet, indeed.

✸

In the meantime, Lord William's entourage was passing through the streets of Paris. It was as if the whole city was clogged with every imaginable variety of man and animal. Jugglers and troubadours, merchantmen, clerics, knights, ladies of various reputations, pilgrims, farmers, men-at-arms, oxen, horses of every colour and description, caged birds of every sort, monkeys on chains, and even a bear passed by the Countess' small carriage. The company was jostled by hay wagons and carts laden with ells of silk or linen, baskets of fish, spices, utensils, tinkers' wares and the like. Like London, however, the air was pungent with foul odours and smoke. Isabel suddenly wished she might fly away to the clean, salt-scented air of Pembroke Castle or the fresh breezes of the hills near Kilkenny.

That night the lord's company was hosted at a string of merchantmen's homes near the King's palace. All were treated to fine French wine and a delicious light supper of fresh bread and fish—the day being Friday. Unfortunately, Henry Hose drank a bit too much Bordeaux and began swaggering about his host's hall demanding English ale. The butler then made a mistake of his own. He suggested that English ale might best be found by holding one's tankard near the latrine. The resulting brawl left both Henry, the butler, and their comrades nursing bruises for days to come.

The next day's discussions were formal and rather severe. Lord William presented King John's position to the French King directly and without apology. "As you know, sire, it is the pope, and not John, who is liege-lord of England. Should you support the rebellion with arms or silver, or by sending thy son Louis to secure the throne of England, you would be making war on the Holy Church."

Philip smiled wryly. "Lord William, the Holy Church will forgive—once it has profitable reasons to do so. I am quite certain that the pope will gladly receive the homage of Louis, once he sits on the English throne."

William was a warrior, not a politician. He had argued that very point to King John in the past and he had no counter. The earl bowed. "Perhaps, sire, but–but I needs remind you that–that the pope will supply King John with arms and men to oppose you. This adventure of yours shall be costly and without surety."

The King stood. "And let me remind you, Sir William, that you are my vassal as well as King John's. Shall you take arms against me?"

William stiffened. He was well acquainted with the subtleties of vassalage; his honour depended on it. "I am thy vassal for my lands in France, sire. In England I am John's man."

"Ah, so it is," mused Philip. His courtiers tittered. "Before you go, Sir William, I should like to introduce you to the man who shall be your next king. Prince Louis, come meet your future vassal."

A sly young man crept forward like a wary spider towards a wasp. The prince was dressed in gay colours and plumes. "*Bonjour, Monsieur*," he quipped. "It is my honour to welcome the great William Marshal to my father's court." He bowed dramatically.

William darkened. He returned the bow stiffly, keeping his eyes fixed hard on the dandy. He hoped he might face this fellow on the field of combat.

"Sir William," continued the prince. "My father tells me you are a man most steadfast and stout-hearted."

The earl remained quiet.

"Ah, and humble: I like that. *Merveilleux*." Louis pranced about the hall with his sword drawn, feigning swordplay with the shadows. "It shall be my great joy to hear thy pledge of fealty in London. It shall happen soon enough, I think." He stopped and smiled.

William had had enough. He suddenly rued the day his Viking ancestors had ever brushed elbows with these French *délicats*. With a scowl he tipped his head to King Philip and stormed away.

❁

"Again, sire, I do humbly beg thy pardon." Lord William presented his bowed head before a furious King John at Windsor.

"Beg my pardon? Beg my pardon?" roared the King. "You kneel before me and dare beg my pardon? You, you dimwit, fool, dolt! Philip only needed a nudge, a clever word, or some reasonable assurance of profit. Instead he sends you away with your tail tucked neatly between your legs and prepares to steal my kingdom!"

The King's eyes bulged and he spoke rapidly. "Tell me, William Marshal, is Philip still your liege-lord in France?"

William reddened. "*Oui*, sire."

John stood and circled the kneeling knight. He kicked at the rushes covering the floor. "Ah, I see." He tapped his fingers rapidly along his bearded chin. "Yes, I see clearly now. And upon hearing of Philip's intentions, did you forfeit your precious lands and vassalage in my favour?"

"No, my lord."

John snatched a sword from a surprised guard. He pointed it at William with a menacing eye and slowed his words into a dramatic, sarcastic tone. "What manner of man are you, William, Earl of Pembroke? I am told England has no finer Christian knight. You are called by troubadours and minstrels the 'Flower of Chivalry.' Yet I find thy ways suspect."

He flared his nostrils and roared, "Swear to me, Lord William, swear on these holy relics that you did not betray my trust in Paris!" The King shoved a small wooden chest, his personal reliquary, towards the earl.

Lord William stood from his knee and faced his King with blazing eyes levelled like the points of drawn arrows. "Nay, sire! I have once sworn you my fealty and no other oath is required."

King John's fury distorted his face into a turning mass of knots and folds. He sputtered and cursed, then flung his sword into the air. He ordered William and all others to leave his hall and cursed each by name as they disappeared from his sight. The tall doors of his chamber closed and, once alone, he fell to the floor and gnawed the rushes like a madman.

Outside the King's hall, Lord William, d'Erley, Henry Hose, and Sir Jordan sighed and shook their heads. "We've trouble for certain," mumbled Henry. He ran his fingers through his mussed hair and groaned. "We know the French have garrisoned many thousands of soldiers near Paris; we all saw them. I fear they're about to sail."

William nodded. "I agree. But where shall they land?"

"The Cinque Ports are still in rebel hands. I think more northward, perhaps Yarmouth?"

The knights shrugged and Jordan added another thought.

"King Alexander and his blasted Scots are massing on the moors in Durham. I fear Philip might reinforce them and sweep away what few royalists remain north of Lincoln."

William sighed. "I was wrong before, but it seems reasonable. It means that we must yield the counties above the Humber for now. Our strength is here in the south, particularly in the southeast, save London, and in the upper midlands. Kent is ours, except for the coast. We've support in Cambridge, Norwich, Nottingham, Lincoln, Oxford, and Winchester. From here in Windsor we can keep London under watch. The barons have it, but can do little with their prize for now. I say if Philip wants the north, let him have it. 'Tis a wasteland of bald mountains and thin sheep."

His fellows laughed. "*Oui*, and bony Scotsmen."

William smiled, and then proceeded to consider the King's predicament. "Wales is in stalemate, though we dare not draw a single bowman away. Llewellyn is penned in the north country for now but would burst through at Shrewsbury at the first sign of weakness. My own soldiers are keeping a strong line in the south. Ireland is quiet for once, may God be praised for it. If we can only hold what we have, the barons may grow weary and retire. I will call a council of war this evening and try to convince the King of our strategy. Let us pray God wills us wisdom."

After sending his knights to tasks, Lord William hurried towards his apartment and Lady Isabel, who had been resting quietly. The May afternoon was warm and sunny, and the wildflowers sprinkled about the bailey of Windsor Castle caught the old earl's eye as he walked. He paused to pick a small bouquet and held them to his nose. The war-worn knight had rarely taken time throughout his life to enjoy the fragrance of such a simple delight and he closed his eyes in wonder. He lifted his leathery face to the sun and felt its warmth penetrate his skin. "Oh, to lie about in green Kilkenny—" His mind carried him to the River Nore and a day of fishing with his sons. He smiled.

"Lord husband," said Isabel. "You are smiling." The Countess had risen from her nap and was enjoying the May sunshine as well. "Did you pick these for me?"

William laughed loudly. "Ah, my dear, indeed I did. Yet I could find no flower more fair than thee."

Isabel blushed and buried her nose deeply in the bouquet. "The perfume of Heaven." She took William's hand in hers and the two walked slowly through the busy courtyard. "What news have you?"

William shrugged. "The King's position is perilous. We are surrounded by enemies with more on the way. He is agitated and confused, and I fear nearly mad. King Philip will attack soon, though I am not certain where. Our mercenaries are faltering and I fear the pope has been surprised as to how costly this war has already become. The King's treasury is dwindling and he must carry what is left in a few wagons that follow him."

Isabel listened, quietly. "He should never have abandoned the *Charter*."

William nodded. "You are right to say the realm ought to be governed by law, not men, and Langton was right to see the virtue in a free English Church."

"Why then—" the Countess hesitated. "Why do you still serve tyrants?"

The old knight shook his grey head. With a hint of exasperation he answered, "Dear wife, I do not serve tyrants, I serve the Crown of England. My sacred pledge is to John, 'tis true, but it is to *King* John. It is the Crown that must be preserved, and if it is worn by a fool for a season, I must defend the fool rather than lose the order of things."

Isabel was not going to argue the point again. It had been a source of frustration for her for years and she knew her husband would never yield. His ways were fixed in a magnificent order of chivalry that was fast fading away. The Countess loved and admired the man's character and only wished the world deserved such a man as he. "Indeed, lord husband. God's blessings on thy virtue." It was all she said, for Isabel, like her husband, was a person of character, and she, perhaps more than he, was a person of wisdom as well.

CHAPTER XXI

INVASION

IN the third week of May, 1216, an expeditionary party of French soldiers landed on the north-east coast of England and joined forces with the barons and their Scottish allies. As Lord William had predicted, it took only weeks for the royalist barons to be driven out of the northern counties. The rebel army seized York with ease, then pressed below the Humber and now besieged Lincoln Castle, a stubborn stronghold for King John.

Lord William remained in Windsor with the anxious King and dismissed the defeats in the north as of little consequence. Rumours of a French fleet approaching the south-eastern seaboard, however, troubled him deeply. For the great earl, losing "the worthless moors and wretched villages" of England's northland was not nearly as threatening as an invasion into the rich south-east.

Rather than face the French army on English soil, King John demanded his little navy be dispatched into the mouth of the Thames where they could confront Philip's convoy on open sea. William was not enthused about the plan, for the English navy was little more than a handful of galleys and squat cogs. With London filled with sedition and intrigue, the royal fleet had not been properly maintained. The guilds that provided sail makers, carpenters, rope makers, and shipwrights had virtually abandoned the docks, and many numbers of seamen had mutinied in favour of the rebellion. Lord William, the supreme commander of all royal forces, had little confidence in his navy's ability to set sail, let alone defeat the French fleet.

"I say we sail," roared King John. "We must keep them standing on deck boards and not English soil!"

"*Oui*, sire, but our navy is in dire condition and—"

"I command it."

Lord William sighed. "As you wish." He walked sombrely out of the King's hall and sent couriers to London. "D'Erley, we'll load the ships with Italian archers. Keep spies spread across the whole of the coast. If the navy fails—and it surely will—I need to know at once where the French land."

"*Oui*, m'lord. And thy wife?"

"Isabel has chosen to stay with me. I fear sending her to Pembroke, for the journey is now too dangerous. I choose you to defend her, and you may choose others. It shall give me some peace."

Sir John fumbled for words. Though he loved Isabel, he wanted to be at his lord's side in the battles sure to come. "*Oui*, my lord. Though when she is safe, I shall beg leave to follow you."

The earl smiled. "Guard her well."

"*Oui*, sire." The knight bowed, then left his beloved lord to find his dear Countess, who was sitting just beyond Windsor's walls with Le Court.

"My lady," Sir John began, as he approached. "I am assigned to your side until ordered otherwise."

The Countess nodded, grimly. She knew her husband would only command this under the most dangerous of circumstances. She looked at the man, now forty-two and ageing. She herself was forty-four, and the passing of time had added wrinkles to her face—as it had to John's. He stood erect and alert, but his hair was grey and his eyes reflected the strain of years under arms. The woman felt sudden sympathy. Good John had never married and few had ever considered what loneliness might accompany him each waking day. A tear formed in Isabel's eye, and she took her old friend by the hand. "I am so very glad to have you by my side."

John blushed and scratched Alfred's old head. "This bony fellow hasn't much time left." He bent and rubbed the dog's face. "I'd wager you miss your old friend, Canute. 'Tis not good to be alone."

Isabel watched the knight as he toyed with the dog and she felt sympathy for him once again. She had always known that it was his love for her that had kept him alone for all these many years. Tears began to form below her eyes. "Will you not take a wife, dear John?"

The man was startled by the question. He released Alfred and faltered for words. "I…I do not think about it."

"Look at me, my friend, and speak truly."

John's eyes met Isabel's. "I love one that I cannot have." He looked away, quickly.

The Countess nodded. "I know your heart, John, and it is true to all those you love." She took his hand and held it, tenderly. "There is no man in all the world with a heart a large and as faithful as yours. I believe that you have enough love within you to love yet another."

The man's eyes moistened. "I do not wish to love another, m'lady, for when my precious one is near, the stars are the brightest; the sun the warmest. She is the light of my life and I should rather love her from afar in my loneliness than turn my heart away." John's chin quivered and he closed his eyes as he placed his hands over Isabel's and thought, *forgive me, my lady, for I cannot rule my heart.*

✳

English fishermen spotted a large French fleet approaching England's south-east coast, and their reports confirmed Lord William's latest suspicions that they would attempt a landing near London. A French army in the south and the rebel army in the north would squash the royalists in a vice. William immediately sent the royal navy into the Channel just beyond the mouth of Thames, where it waited nervously in a strong wind and under a sagging sky.

For two days King John's ships rocked in high water, buffeted by heavy gusts and driving rains. Conditions worsened by the hour until the bobbing vessels were finally recalled into the relatively quieter waters of the river's mouth. The heavy winds and pelting rains that had forced the English navy deeper into the shelter of the Thames was also wreaking havoc on the French fleet. It was fortunate for the English, for what King John and Lord William did not know was that Philip had sent an invasion armada of some six hundred ships—nearly as many as delivered the Normans to Hastings one hundred and fifty years prior!

Conditions being unfavourable for a landing near London, the French admiral sailed past the mouth of the Thames and landed his fleet at Sandwich, farther to the south-east. News of the landing reached the ears of Lord William within a day and he immediately recalled his ships. His army was hastily assembled and sent quickly around London towards Canterbury, only to be immediately repelled by staggering numbers of Frenchmen, who had made an astonishing advance from the port. In the few days that followed, the royalists retreated quickly from all territories south of London and reluctantly yielded the city to some thirty-five thousand French soldiers. A few days later, on June 2, 1216, things more terrible were announced.

Safe in nearby Windsor Castle, the Countess received news of London's occupation. It had come as a terrible blow, for imagining this symbol of Anglo-Norman rule in the hands of King Philip was cause for grief. To make matters worse, she then learned that the rebellious barons, including two of her own sons, had elected Prince Louis as King of England.

The day's woes were not over, however. The Countess was recovering from this news when a white-faced Aethel arrived with Le Court. Isabel rushed to greet her much-missed friend. "Oh, Aethel, where have you been? I've not heard a single word for all this time."

Aethel collapsed at her lady's feet. "Forgive me, m'lady. Please forgive me. We sent couriers but I fear they've been killed along the road."

Isabel suddenly paled. "Have you bad news of my children? Tell me, are they safe?"

"They are safe, m'lady," answered Aethel, trembling.

Le Court stepped forward looking grave. The dwarf was uncharacteristically sombre and he took Isabel's hand. "We've heavy news to bear, m'Lady. Our beloved Twigadarn was slain."

Isabel gasped and tilted to one side. "Oh, dear God above." She sat, trembling. "Tell me of it, I beg you."

Tearfully, Aethel recounted the horrid day. It was a story soon to be told to a stunned Lord William as well as the servants of the household now serving in Windsor. "A black day," moaned Isabel. "The children loved him so. I loved him so."

"It is my fault, m'Lady. It is all my fault." Aethel hung her head in shame.

Isabel looked at her servant with a taut face that quickly softened. She could not bear to see her beloved Aethel suffer so. She was angry with the woman, to be sure, but she understood. "You are forgiven all, dear friend. You are forgiven all."

※

Louis' election was a blow that heralded yet more trouble for Lord William, the infamous King John and their dwindling army. The symbol of John's rule had been violated when the French occupied London. Now he was confronted with a humiliation of grave proportion. Added to that was the failure of the pope to provide more mercenaries and he had not provided more money.

William quickly gathered his counsellors and, together, they estimated Louis' army in England's south-east at about fifty thousand strong. In the north, the opposition army was smaller, though still formidable, considering the numbers of Scots streaming southward. The size of the royal army could not be determined because many deserted every day. There were pockets of royalist support sprinkled about the realm in places like Lincoln Castle, still under siege, but the earl estimated that less than ten thousand men (mostly mercenaries) were under arms in his command and these were near desertion. In addition, the King's treasury was lighter than ever, and, at a cost of eight cents per man per day, it would not last very long.

By July, King John's royal army had retreated from Windsor and was fleeing northward to the midlands. Cambridge was still sympathetic to the Crown and William collected his army there.

Not one to retreat for any purpose other than tactical advantage, the general decided to strike hard at the forward French troops nipping at his heels. As a strategist, Lord William was brilliant. He chose a campaign of quick strikes that were delivered with punishing affect. He conducted this strike-and-run war all through the mid-summer and his successes bolstered his army's morale. Then, feeling ready to swallow a larger fish, the earl targeted a wealthy prize in England's west midlands. "Worcester Castle. We shall take it back and seize its treasury." Lord William was animated, enlivened by the challenge.

His council agreed, but Henry Hose hesitated. William noticed his old friend's sudden change. "What is it, Sir Henry?"

"Sire," the knight began slowly. "We've learned that thy son, young William, is in Worcester and served in its capture just weeks ago."

William darkened.

"Sire," added another voice, "we might move against Brackley instead, or even Banbury." The comment earned a hard-eyed stare and the man's face turned quickly downward.

Towering over his war council, Lord William puffed his chest and stood stiff as old oak. "We take Worcester within the week." With that he left his chamber.

It took less than an hour for news of the lord's decision to find the ears of Aethel. She, in turn, hurried to share the rumour with the Countess. "I fear it is so, m'lady."

Isabel's jaw pulsed and she said nothing more. She bade Aethel remain behind and she hurried through the streets of Cambridge until she found the round-walled Norman chapel where her husband often prayed with Le Court. True to form, the pair were on their knees begging Almighty God for mercy and wisdom. Their piety did not move the Countess. "Husband," she barked.

Le Court scurried away like a little mouse. He knew exactly what Isabel was about to say and he was quite certain that he wanted no part of the battle to come.

Lord William groaned and stood quietly. "*Oui*, my dear?"

"You say 'my dear' as if nothing were out of order. Tell me, sir; no—assure me that the rumour is not true. Tell me you are not sending the army against thine own son in Worcester Castle."

The earl sighed and faced his angry wife squarely. "It is true."

"You *vowed* to me, sir, that you would never take arms against our sons."

Lord William remained silent.

"Did you hear me?" snapped Isabel.

"I did."

"And?"

The knight's voice faltered. "I—I fear I've little choice. Worcester holds a treasury we desperately need. I believe we may take the castle by surprise without need for blood."

"And if it resists?"

William looked down.

"I feared as much!" cried Isabel. "You place your oath to a king higher than your word to your own wife. I pity you. You are blind. Your honour is mulish, devoid of sound judgement. Your character is strong, like a lifeless cliff of stubborn rock. It lacks wisdom, it lacks love." The Countess spun around and stormed away.

Lord William stared blankly at the back of his beloved wife as she abandoned him to the quiet, dark walls of the chapel. He remained there for a time, silent and confused, torn by his dilemma and without means to resolve his predicament.

Le Court slipped back into the chapel and walked slowly towards the man. He reached his side and looked up at the mighty warrior. *Tall as giant timber*, he thought, *fixed like tempered steel, sincere as soft rain, yet in want for depth and a mind neither bendsome nor supple. He is an oak, not a willow.* The priest laid a gentle hand on the small of his lord's back and prayed.

※

"If you do, Marshal, you shall give them time. It will serve as a warning." King John was unhappy.

"One hour under truce, 'tis all I ask." William's tone was

pleading and the King suddenly enjoyed seeing the man beg.

"I am not sure. You say young William is under arms inside the castle?"

"*Oui*, sire, so our spies tell us."

"Hmm. *My* spies tell me that your son was amongst the first to swear homage to Louis."

The earl said nothing.

"Tell me, old soldier, why I should risk defeat and the loss of treasure so that you might coax thy treasonous son to safety?"

William answered quietly. "I have served thee well, sire. I have honoured my fealty beyond all—" he caught himself, then continued. "I have honoured my fealty through all manner of trial. Yet I do not ask to be rewarded. I ask this of your charity."

"My charity?"

"*Oui*, sire. I know of your generous alms—I know your heart can be soft."

King John was suddenly befuddled. It was not the sort of plea he had expected. Indeed, as wicked a man as John had been, his heart had been touched from time to time by the terrible want of the poor. "Well, yes, I am a charitable King, and am not the dragon others say I am."

"And this too, sire," continued William. "Thy young son Henry is now safe in Devizes, but I remember seeing him at your side. I've seen the two of you playing at 'knights' and kicking the ball about the bailey. You do love your son, sire, as I love mine. I beg thee—as a father—to suffer the pleadings of another father."

John shifted uncomfortably on his throne. He thought of his nine-year-old son Henry, the future King of England. His mind wandered over the few happy moments he had spent with the white-haired lad. The King had rarely displayed his paternal affections and his family life had been one marred by scandal and unhappiness. Yet, to the surprise of all, the King suddenly mumbled with a dismissive wave, "You have my leave to enter Worcester under truce. Save thy son, then seize the castle."

William Marshal bowed, truly grateful. Relieved, he hurried to inform his wife, whose reception of him proved to be disappointingly cool. Nevertheless, anxious to resolve his predicament, the earl mustered his army and made haste across England's heartland.

It was almost Lammas when the surprised garrison of Worcester Castle stared over their ramparts dumbfounded and anxious at the sight of the royal army now encircling them. Lord William wasted no time in personally galloping to the gates under a flag of truce, demanding to speak with the castellan—the commander. In the rear of King John's army, just behind the footmen and atop a small, grassy knoll, Lady Isabel watched, breathlessly, under a hot July sun.

"I have prayed with grave earnest these past days, m'lady," assured Le Court. "God's Will be done."

Isabel said nothing for a long moment. Squinting, she pointed. "See, the gate opens."

"Aye, m'lady," answered Aethel. "It gives us hope."

An hour passed, then two. The Countess' company peered nervously across the heads of the infantrymen shifting impatiently in their ranks.

Isabel suddenly cried, "Look, I see two! Yes, two riders in our robes."

It was true. After pleading and begging, threatening, and finally weeping, Lord Marshal had successfully convinced his son to abandon his weapons and retire from the castle with a pledge of neutrality to Worcester's castellan. Now riding alongside his exhausted father, the young man stared blankly forward. The two hurried towards the King's camp, each in full chain mail and dressed in the Marshal colours. The earl addressed the King briefly, his son bent a stiff, forced knee to the ground, and in moments trumpets sounded for battle.

Isabel began to weep and as her son dismounted, she ran to him. "Oh, my son, my dear son."

"Aye, mother," answered the young man wearily. "I do love thee as well." He received her embrace, warmly. "It is the only reason I abandoned my oath to Louis; 'tis why I left my duty at the castle." He turned a wistful eye to the assault now beginning. He gripped the hands of d'Erley and Le Court and happily received a hug from his beloved Aethel. "I am sorry for my cold heart, mother. I have missed you and my brothers and sisters."

Isabel held his hands, tightly. "All are well, my son, save Richard. I've no news of him."

Young William nodded. "Aye, he was last in York. He's joined with us against the King. And I'm told that Walter is with Lord Robert de Rost and the Scots near Lincoln."

Isabel hung her head. "So I've heard. Gilbert is still in Canterbury; Anselm is in knight's training at Warwick. I've heard naught from them."

"And my sisters?"

"Matilda has had her third son. The others are safe in Pembroke waiting for their weddings."

"I've heard sister Isabel is betrothed to Gilbert de Clare?"

"*Oui*."

"He's with the barons, you know. He's in the siege against Lincoln."

"*Oui*, and your father is displeased."

"And Twigadarn?" asked the young man. He looked about. "Is Twigadarn in Pembroke?"

Aethel choked. She had never forgiven herself, nor had Lord William forgiven her—though he had taken out his rage on the castellan at Pembroke.

"No, son. We've lost him as well." Isabel laid a gentle hand on Aethel.

William stared in disbelief. "How?"

"Taken by Welsh archers."

The young knight looked into the distance wistfully. "I loved that fellow." Young William sighed. "How life changes." He turned to the dwarf and smiled. "I'm happy to see Le Court still with us."

"And so am I," chimed the little priest.

Isabel held her son's hand yet more tightly, so very happy that he was once again the son she had remembered. "Tell us you shall not leave."

"I cannot say it, mother; my agreement was to return to Pembroke and serve in its defence. I pledged to raise no arms against John, nor remain in England."

Isabel nodded. "I wish the same for all your brothers."

The group quieted and turned their eyes to the battle before them. Worcester's castle was well-built but undermanned. Its commander had thought he might be supported by reinforcements long ago, but with no news of any, he finally decided to negotiate an immediate surrender. Worcester Castle and its treasury were presented to a gleeful King John and a very much relieved William Marshal.

※

The ambitious and suddenly confident King John immediately decided to send his army against other rebel garrisons spread across the midlands. For the next two months his troops crisscrossed the realm between Hereford in the west and Norwich in the east. From time to time they ventured north and south, moving quickly and striking hard at unsuspecting pockets of Louis' men. For his part, Louis was frustrated with the nimble movements of William Marshal's army. The Frenchman suffered a considerable number of casualties, and the successes of Marshal were costing him the respect of the rebel barons.

By early October the royalist forces were becoming weary, however. They had, indeed, inflicted harm on their enemy and had inspired respect, but it had come at a heavy price. The men were foot-sore, the horses lame. King John was now growing desperate to deliver a blow that might finally turn the tide and inspire more help from the pope, who had become conspicuously removed from the costly conflict. With his army in England's extreme east, near Norwich, John decided to order a surprise rush northward against the Scots partisans.

"I want to cross the Wash," the King said flatly.

William shook his head. "Is perilous, at best. Filled with bogs and deep channels. Our army could be caught in the muck, trapped by Louis' army on either side."

"It is more direct and if we venture out far enough, we might pass unnoticed."

William shook his head slowly. The Wash was a shallow bay on the coast of eastern England. It was an estuary some twenty-two miles wide that was filled with salt-marshes, sand banks, and gravel pits. A race through its shallow waters would certainly catch the enemy off guard; it might create the illusion that the royalists had simply disappeared. Unfortunately, it could easily prove to be a disastrous, costly error.

William yielded. The King had made up his mind and nothing would change it. So, on a cool October morning, a column of mounted warriors, footmen, archers, pack-horses, wagons, tradesmen, armourers, cooks, fullers, seamstresses, and sundry servants splashed tentatively into the shallow tidal waters of the Wash.

Lady Isabel and her small entourage climbed into a wagon, much to the howling protests of John d'Erley. For a knight to ride in a cart like a common peasant was considered a high insult. Of course, the Countess asked the whining man if he thought she should be protesting as well. "Well, perhaps, my lady," he answered.

"But I'm not, Sir John. I'm not. Lord William believes the wagon is best for our safety in this place and that, good sir, should be the end of it."

The wide waters of the Wash proved to be a fascinating interlude for the travellers. Isabel marvelled at the numbers of geese, ducks, and waders. A few terns were spotted here and there, and other water birds such as Oystercrackers could be seen probing the shallows. Occasionally the wagons tipped precariously on the soft, sand edge of an unseen channel and at mid-morning such a tip tossed Aethel headlong into the water.

The column struggled forward until noon, when King John raised his gloved hand. He huddled with Lord William, then reared his horse and spun about. Seeing black clouds forming ominously in the west had convinced the King that he had best abandon his plan and quickly. With a loud oath and his fist shaking at Heaven, John splashed southward past the astonished faces of his army. "Turn about. Turn about y'fools," he cried.

The tide was rising and the return journey through soft sand and knee deep water proved disastrous. Rain had begun to fall in the late afternoon and high winds quickly battered the waters of the Wash. White-caps rolled along the thighs of the struggling army and horses began to collapse into underwater ditches and hidden channels. Dusk fell and the southern shore was in plain view when shouts could be heard from the front of the column. "Can you hear? Can anyone hear?" asked Isabel. Each of the travellers cocked their ears and the wagonner reined in his team. "Something about the King—something about, well, I can't make it out," shouted Le Court over the wind.

A rough word from behind urged a slap of the wagonner's reins and Isabel's wagon lurched forward. They travelled for another hour and finally arrived on the rain-soaked shore, wet to the skin and shivering. Within another two hours, the whole of the King's army had returned to the Wash's south shore and was working hard to start fires under the heavy rain.

Lord William found his wife and climbed into her wagon. "The tent master shall set our camp shortly. Until then, all of you, follow me to the fires." The earl led his wife and her company to a smoking bonfire that had been miraculously lit along the shoreline, and they all held their palms out to the heat of the flames. William was sullen, grumbling something about "King's folly." The fire cast hard shadows into the crags and wrinkles of his face and when he turned to Isabel she thought him to look suddenly very, very old. "Have you heard?" he asked in a whisper.

CHAPTER XXII

PEACHES, CIDER, AND THE REGENT

ISABEL shook her head.

"I told the King this was foolish beyond words. Our men and horses are exhausted from slogging all these hours through soft sand and water. By the saints, if they had to fight now they couldn't."

"But worse." William spat. "The King's lost his crown and the royal jewels."

The circle gasped.

"*Oui*, 'tis true. They were packed with bags of silver on a sturdy wagon. But a wheel slipped off a sand ridge of some sort and the wagon slid away into a bottomless channel. The horses drowned, the wagonner disappeared—we sent men to the bottom but when they surfaced they reported that the strongboxes had spilled from the wagon and were lost beneath the sand."

"Fool!" barked d'Erley. "Fool. What manner of King loses the most precious things of the realm?"

William threw up his hands. "There's a brawl among his councillors even as we speak. Some say a few things were packed in other places. I hope it is so."

"An omen, to be sure," mumbled Le Court.

The fiasco in the Wash had left the King exasperated, weary, angry, and hungry. In the morning he emerged from his tent cursing and throwing tin plates and wooden tankards. "Marshal, hold the column. I am exhausted and famished, and if I face another salted fish, I shall surely die."

"But, sire, we needs hasten north and relieve Lincoln Castle. This flat, open ground exposes us to danger."

King John cursed. "I've pockets of friends all through this region, and Louis is still far behind. I need a few hours more rest and some food."

"*Oui*, but the northern barons and the Scots are just ahead. We would not want to get caught here."

"Oh the Scots, 'tis always the cursed Scots. I wish those savages would scurry back to their rocky dens and leave us be. Do you know what they eat?"

"*Oui*, sire; I've heard."

"No wonder they've such a horrid disposition. Well, no matter. They'll soon regret they've come."

The army had camped in the vicinity of several small villages set along the shores of the Wash and purveyors were immediately sent to forage provisions. They returned before noon with a bounty of harvest goods taken by force.

"Well done, Marshal. Such peaches I have never seen. Join me!"

The earl helped himself to two plump peaches and a swig of fresh cider. "*Oui*, my lord. Very tasty."

"Eat, eat more!"

Lord William was growing anxious. His eyes were fixed on the horizon. "My lord, we must hurry forward. I've news the French are on to us and are making their way north. They skirted Cambridge two days ago. We've a royal garrison at Gloucester under the Earl of Chester. I think we must commission their aid at once."

King John quickly agreed to his commander's advice. "*Oui*. But the earl will never release troops to me unless he hears the command from you. Go; ride hard and return quickly. We shall move north, towards Lincoln."

"But, sire, I—"

"Enough, Marshal. Do as I say. The army is safe enough for now. Now go, hurry on."

Surprised at the sudden turn of events, William soon found himself thundering towards Gloucester, with his wife left far behind in the King's care. It was a situation that did not please him, though he hoped the Earl of Chester would have a garrison of fresh soldiers at his disposal.

Meanwhile the King delayed his army's departure so that he

might rest a little longer and continue to enjoy great quantities of peaches and fresh cider. A few jugglers entertained him and he played with his hounds, until he suddenly clutched his belly and collapsed.

"What is wrong, sire?" asked his aide.

"*Sacre bleu*, call my doctors."

In moments the King was surrounded by his physicians and their aides. "Bad cider, I say," cried the King.

"Sire, I fear poison," answered a stern man.

"Nay, it cannot be. A bad peach, perhaps?" The King vomited again.

"I have never seen a peach do this to a man."

The King retched loudly and groaned. His doctors huddled. "His colour fails before our eyes and he has vomited everything but his entrails. His bowels run loose and horrid."

One turned to the King. "Sire, with respect, I suggest we hurry to the bishop's palace at Newark. It is just a half-day's ride from here. It is fortified and the bishop is loyal. There we shall find remedies; here we've none—our wagon tipped in the Wash and we lost all."

"Cursed Wash," whined the King. "*Oui, oui*, to Newark then."

A confused cacophony of trumpets sounded and the army quickly assembled. Rumours of a poisoning flew up and down the long column as it began a hurried march towards Newark. John d'Erley climbed aboard the Countess' wagon with a grave look on his face. "The King is ill."

"*Very* ill?"

"*Oui.*"

"Poisoned?"

"I do not know. The purveyors are being harshly tested now. Each is being forced to drink the King's cider and eat his peaches. One just died, but I am told he choked on a pit. "

Isabel nodded. "God's Will be done."

❋

303

King John arrived at the Bishop of Lincoln's palace near Newark late in the evening. Advance couriers had advised of his coming and the bishop had already summoned the abbot of Croxton—a famed doctor—to come. All that night the King suffered loudly, his body bent forward in a painful nausea and his skin turning sallow. At first light he groaned, "Send for the Marshal."

"Sire, he is coming from Gloucester as we speak."

"And why is the fool in Gloucester?" His words faded to a whisper. All that day and into the early evening the King suffered terribly. By mid-evening, a few hours before midnight, he knew his end was near. "The Marshal, where is the Marshal?" he whimpered.

"Riding hard, sire, riding hard."

King John nodded, weakly. "He shall be too late, far too late. For the sake of heaven, can you not deliver him quickly?" He closed his eyes, then rolled to his side to retch. "The bishop," groaned the King. "Send for the bishop and my court."

Within a quarter hour the King was surrounded by the Bishop of Lincoln, several lesser clerks, his secretary, and two royal lawyers. Behind them, numbers of courtiers stood on tip-toes to witness the King's final scene. King John drew long, halting breaths, gagged and retched weakly, then sunk deeply into his bed. His eyes fluttered, then opened. "I wish to make my confession," he began slowly. The bishop, dressed in his finest vestments, bent to his knees and murmured his prayers. He then laid his hands on the King's head and listened as the dying man proceeded to review the vices of his life, his terrible deeds of deceit and betrayal, his bitterness, his hatred, his sloth, avarice, and pride. The dying man rambled over a litany of sins, some public, some private, most of which would soon become eager fodder for the gossip of his petty courtiers.

Then, as he became even weaker, John scanned the faces staring down on him and begged for William Marshal. "Say he is here, here with me."

His audience shook their heads.

The King's eyes filled with tears. "Then tell the earl I have wronged him—tell him of my great sorrow in this hour for all my wicked deeds against him. He is a man most faithful and—I beg his forgiveness."

The chamber was quiet. The King slipped away, only to jerk awake with a start. He looked about blankly, as if he was not certain whose faces were staring back or why they were there. Then, as his mind cleared, he drew another breath. With a sudden surge of vigour he raised himself on one elbow and stated loudly, "Hear me, hear me all. It is to William Marshal, Earl of Pembroke, that I entrust both my kingdom and my good son, Henry, thy future King."

The room gasped.

The King trembled, fell to his back, and gagged faintly, all life now draining away. He breathed a few shallow breaths before his eyes rolled and he wheezed. Then, amidst prayers for his fleeing soul, John, King of England and Lord of Ireland died.

❄

William Marshal heard the news by way of a courier who intercepted him on his way to Lincoln. Shocked, he listened numbly as he was further informed of the King's wishes to be buried in the cathedral at Worcester and of his wish that William be Regent of England. With hardly a word, William turned his men towards Worcester.

The abbot of Croxton had embalmed the King's body and dressed it for burial in a Benedictine habit. The Benedictine monks ruled the cathedral at Worcester, and it was hoped that the King might benefit after death by the wearing of their black cowl to his grave. William quickly bought bolts of silk and brocade to cover the tomb and prepared bags of his own coins to be distributed to the poor in the King's name.

The funeral was conducted with solemn pomp and the King's remains were yielded to the earth with proper ceremony. But few gave their full attention to the funeral. Instead, all knew that the war for England had just been turned upside-down, and the implications of this astonishing reversal were staggering. Lady Isabel attended the services with her thoughts fixed on the hope suddenly shining over England. She believed that John's death could be the death of tyranny and she had nearly wept for joy upon learning of William's nomination as Regent. As such, he would be entrusted with the kingdom until the soon-to-be-coronated Henry attained adulthood.

News of John's death spread across Britain like flames racing over a dry field. It created a stir in the taverns and the halls of every county and shire, for now many of those barons and freemen who had rallied behind Louis were no longer so enthused to owe fealty to a Frenchman. In a matter of weeks, the rebels began to divide, many abandoning their cause and returning happily to the royalist side, now defending the regency of William Marshal.

Louis of France was taken aback. He cried foul and cried it loudly. Just days before, he had been eagerly anticipating the utter destruction of King John and his pathetic little army. Now he was suddenly faced with the prospect of a long, bitter, expensive war on foreign soil against growing numbers of defectors.

William found himself abruptly cast into a whirlwind of decisions, not the least of which was whether he wanted to accept the position of Regent of England. He would need to be elected by the barons—a jealously guarded custom rooted deeply in English tradition. But before he could decide, he wanted to face the young Prince Henry, his would-be ward. He had seen the boy from time to time, but had never really spoken with him or looked him in the eye.

The old earl met the young Henry on a roadway where the two dismounted in the midst of a large contingent of knights. They walked warily towards one another until the boy spoke first. "I, sir William, am Henry, son of King John, grandson of King Henry."

William bent to one knee. "I am here to serve thee."

The nine-year old was regal in his countenance, bright-eyed and eager. He immediately impressed the old earl. "Sir, shall you be my protector?"

Perhaps it was because the lad reminded him of his own boys, perhaps for other reasons, but Lord William looked deeply into the blue eyes of the straight-shouldered lad and a lump filled his throat. "Upon my soul, there is nothing I shall not do to defend you and thy kingdom, young sir. On that I pledge my honour." Midst loud hurrahs the two embraced.

Guardian and ward shared a pleasant picnic but were quickly reminded that before the prince could become king, he needed to become a knight. Time was of the essence and plans were quickly made. On October 28, 1216, Lord William dubbed the boy as Sir Henry amidst a circle of cheering men.

The urgency of the day demanded the young, knighted prince now be made King. So, within hours of his dubbing, young Henry was elected by the barons and blessed by the papal legate. The bishop then laid a small, hastily fashioned gold circlet atop the boy's head and, midst prayers to Heaven and loud hurrahs, the lad was introduced to all the world as King Henry III.

※

Young Henry might now be King, but since he was under-age it would be the Regent who would need to save England. Isabel knew that no man on all the earth could better serve the realm in that position than her husband. So, during the coronation banquet, she exercised great skill in influencing the barons towards the formal selection of William over the others who had begun to whisper of their own ambitions. Hers was an effective voice, but her efforts were stunted when a messenger barged into the hall and rushed to the earl's side. "Sir, thy castle in Goodrich is under siege."

William rose, immediately. "I beg thy leave, King Henry, but the Welsh are engaging a fortress of mine."

The barons rose, suddenly fearful that the man might abandon them to fight Louis on their own. A voice cried out, "I vote William Marshal as Regent of England."

All rivals abandoned their cause. A great shout of approval was raised.

William was confused. He had not intended to leave the

young King's side, but had simply wanted to excuse himself in order to organise a detachment to be sent to Goodrich. He stared about the hall blank-faced. He was not used to matters moving so quickly, and he bowed respectfully. "Good sirs, faithful sirs. I must dispatch arms to my relief at Goodrich. I will not leave the King's side."

Another voice cried, "William as Regent!" The hall resounded and the young King cheered.

William looked helplessly at his nodding wife. He turned to the barons. "I am humbled by thy kind approval and I shall answer you by morning."

Lord William strode out of the hall quickly and sent a flurry of orders and a column of his own men to relieve Goodrich. Duty done, he then took a bottle of red wine and some glasses to a small chamber where he met with John d'Erley and his beloved wife. The old soldier collapsed on to a wooden chair and sighed. "What should I do?"

Isabel remained quiet. She yielded to John, who looked carefully at his ageing lord. "I love you, sire. I see weariness in your eyes and a stumble in your step from time to time. Would you not rather hunt in Ireland or fish in Wales? Might you not want to sleep under the sun with fair Isabel at your side?"

William nodded. "The sound of it is very good to me, John." He turned to Isabel. "And you, dear wife?"

Isabel wanted England to be saved, yet, she, like Sir John, loved the man. "Good husband, I want nothing more than your joy. None has served their honour like you, none is more deserving of a Sabbath rest in the twilight of life. I yield to your wishes, for I love you with all my heart."

William's eyes reddened and Sir John left the chamber. The earl took his wife into his arms and said nothing more.

※

In the morning William Marshal walked slowly into the barons' council, and as he entered a cheer rose up. The grey earl humbly bowed and took his seat. He had barely settled into it when he was asked the simple question.

"So, do I want to serve England, you ask?" answered William slowly. "I am nearly eighty years old; what say you?"

To a man they stood, save John d'Erley. He wanted no part of pushing his old friend into that which he did not want. With another resounding hurrah the others reaffirmed their choice.

William rose, slowly, and turned to John. He nodded to his friend, signalling his decision to accept. The little nod was all Sir John needed. He immediately stood and strode towards his lord with a smile, shouting, "Together then, my lord, we shall turn the tide. The devil has had his due and shall drool no longer over this good land. My lords, my brothers, stand firm with us. We shall never falter, never stop, never yield our England!"

The room echoed loudly with wild cheers. Inspired by his friend's words, Lord William filled his lungs with air and puffed his chest. He stretched his arms over his fellows and begged all for silence. With a confident smile he began. "Thy words, good John, ring true. I say this to every man standing here: If all be lost save the boy King and myself, I pledge that I shall carry him on my back and hop from island to island, from country to country, begging for bread if I must, and all the while I shall bear my sword until the very day the lad sits upon his rightful throne."

✵

William Marshal, Earl of Pembroke, was now Regent of England, the lord protector of the realm and the guardian of its future King. A papal legate named Gualo served by his side, at least in name, but his greatest assistance would come from King John's former justiciar of England, Hubert de Burgh. Both a soldier and an ambitious politician, Hubert had been a zealous defender of the Crown, though he had acknowledged some sympathies for the cause of English liberty.

The leadership of the royalists met in Bristol during the first days of November, and a complicated military strategy was devised to defeat the rebels and their French King. During the many hours of heated discussions, William and Hubert worked well together, each respecting the other and both loving England. They, along with every other member of the royal council understood that the destiny of generations to come was now resting upon their shoulders.

❀

Lady Isabel had more on her mind than the manoeuvres of men-at-arms. While she surely understood the need to destroy the resistance to her husband's regency, she was aware of something of equal, if not greater, importance. On the Sabbath night before St. Martin's Day, she welcomed her husband to their bed-chamber with some fine French wine stolen from Louis' army by Sir Jordan and his men. William was delighted with the treat and quieted by the warmth of the drink as it rolled over his tongue and into his belly. "Ah, good wife, no better balm for a weary old man."

Isabel smiled and refilled his goblet. "I trust that you and Hubert have made plans for the winter?"

William sighed. "My dear, indeed we have. I fear we shall spend each day hunting rebels, Frenchmen and Scots. I do believe with all my heart, however, that many of our English barons will desert their rebellion. They were driven to it with great reluctance in the first place and our offers of amnesty should be a great temptation. Hubert calls them—the *reversi*—the returners."

"*Oui*, but some are stubborn and their pride will never let them come back," Isabel answered.

"Indeed, and those that are shall suffer for it. I also doubt the French will simply sail away, so we must grow our army and do it quickly. I have given Hubert the task of raising the money we need."

The Countess laid a gentle hand on her husband's shoulder. "Dear William, as the *rector noster et regni nostri*—our keeper and the keeper of our kingdom—is it not you who is issuing grants, letters, and royal decrees in the name of King Henry under your seal?"

"*Oui*, the young King has no seal yet."

"Of course, but it is you who wields the power of law in the kingdom."

"*Oui.*"

Isabel fell lightly to her knees and took her husband's large hand in hers. She looked at him softly with pleading blue eyes. "Dear William, God has given you a moment unlike any other in all your long life. We have crossed this kingdom together from Kilkenny to Dover and we have seen the folk of this good land suffer the cruelties of their masters. They, like we, have endured the tyranny of their King and their pope, and the greed of the barons.

"Dear husband, you now have the power to reclaim the ancient liberties of England. You, my lord, have the authority to reissue the great *Charter*. With thy seal you can save that which King John and Pope Innocent have stolen from this realm—the supremacy of just law. With one word from your mouth you can affirm the rightful claims of *all* English freemen. If *you* reissue the *Charter*, none could annul it; none could claim it was issued under force. It would be legal and binding. It would be the rebirth of liberty!"

William Marshal stared thoughtfully at his wife, then rose to his feet and walked to his hearth, where he faced the flames silently. He drained his goblet, and then slipped away.

✳

On Saturday, November 12, 1216, William Marshal, Regent of England, boldly reissued the *Charter* later to be known as *Magna Carta*—the *Great Charter*. It would be the first of three reissued versions, each varying slightly from the others on matters of fine detail. *Magna Carta* would be reaffirmed thirty-eight times in the decades to come and would eventually be considered England's fundamental, guiding law of laws. As such, all future law would be tested against the spirit of *Magna Carta* and any statute failing its standard would be declared null and void. Hence, Lord William's rescue of the *Great Charter* secured the very life of the English Constitution and the liberties it guarded.

Lady Isabel and Father Le Court wept in the church at Bristol. They cried for joy, believing with all their hearts that a seed had just sprouted in England, a seed that might grow into something far greater than what their most fanciful dreams could dare envision. Le Court read from the *Book of Galatians*:

"Stand fast therefore in the liberty wherewith Christ hath made us free, and be not entangled again with the yoke of bondage."

He then closed his eyes and raised his arms to Heaven, praying loudly from the prayer of St. Anselm, *Hail, Holy Cross, Our Strength*:

>*Ave, crux sancta, virtus nostra*
>Hail, Holy Cross, our strength.
>*Ave, crux adoranda, gloria nostra.*
>Hail, Adorable Cross, our glory.
>*Salve, crux, victoria et spes nostra;*
>Hail, O Cross, our victory and hope.
>*Salve, crux libertatio nostra.*
>Hail, O Cross, our liberation!

Together, the Countess and her beloved Le Court then sang psalms and prayed prayers of thanksgiving to the "Creator of all Things Free" until late into the night.

❄

At the bells of Matins, a peaceful Lady Isabel joined her husband in their bed and at prime they walked together to the hall of their Bristol residence to enjoy a breakfast of cheese and bread, red wine, and a few strips of salted fish. The Countess sat contentedly with her husband before a warm fire on the damp November morning and she repeated the pride she felt for William's act. "The *Charter*, sir, is your crowning glory."

"*Non, Pucelle*. It is *thy* child. It is *you* who taught me the virtue in its spirit while I laboured with Archbishop Langton over its words. It is *you* who kept it alive within my thoughts. Had you not urged me to reawaken it, I doubt my mind would have ever gone beyond the enemy in the field."

"Yet it is you, lord husband, who has held England as England. I see now that had you not stayed stubbornly fixed on serving thy oath, the English Crown would have gone to the French. No Frenchman would have ever issued the *Charter*, for no Frenchman has put roots into the ways of this grand island."

The earl was silent for a moment; then he said, "I have oft' wondered why I was unable to break my homage to King John. He was a tyrant, indeed, and a wicked, foolhardy man in many ways. I always knew that he never deserved the Crown, yet I always believed it was more than a man that I had been pledged to. My oath was to the order of things."

"*Oui*, lord husband. And that order of things must hold fast against things foreign. You, sir, have preserved the kingdom, and the *Charter* has given it the life of liberty."

Now William blushed. He had rarely engaged in such introspection and was bashful for praise. He took his wife tenderly in his arms. "*Non*, my fair damsel, *non*. I pray that those who follow us might know the good and worthy name of the Countess Isabel de Clare Marshal, for it has been you who have been my guide and my certain ground in all these things."

CHAPTER XXIII

SWORDS AT LINCOLN

GOOD news of victories in Wales was of some comfort to Lord William as he spent the next months in a dreary campaign across all of England. The weather was damp, and the skies seemed heavy and eternally grey. Inspired by the reissued *Charter* and the magnetic effect of William Marshal's integrity, many *reversi* had joined the ranks of the King's army, gladly donning the new royal robes which bore white Crosses as a sign of the Regent's righteous cause. For the earl, however, no 'returners' were more joyfully received than his two sons, William—just arrived from Wales—and Richard—recently arrived from the moors of north Yorkshire. It was a happy reunion.

"By the saints in Heaven, I have not the words for this moment!" cried the earl.

His sons strode towards him with broad smiles and opened arms. The man clasped their hands roughly and embraced. "Father, you still look hard as iron," exclaimed Richard. "I always feared facing your lance on the field."

Lord William stiffened and his jaw set. "I would have impaled my own heart before crossing steel with either of you."

Richard nodded. "Indeed, and we as well."

Young William, now relaxed and relieved laughed loudly. "My fellows would sweat in their beds at the thought of facing 'Old William.' It was the sort of thought that brought night terrors to many."

William laughed. "Old, indeed. You've seen your mother?"

"Aye," answered Young William. "And I was happy to set things a'right with her." The young man hung his head. "I had been so bitter about so many things."

"It is easy to become bitter in a world as this. You lads are the love of her life, you and the others…and me…and England. The woman has love enough to warm the hearts of the whole Creation."

The men laughed, then wrapped their arms about each others' shoulders and walked happily towards the hall, singing. Courtiers and comrades applauded as they crossed under the lintel into the firelight of the great hearth.

The feast that was waiting would be one to remember through the difficult times that lay in wait for, despite improvement in England's prospects, Prince Louis remained a formidable enemy. His army of stubborn rebel barons, Scottish adventurers, and well-trained French troops continued to wage a costly war against the royalists. Castles were taken and retaken, whole counties put to the torch, and the hapless English folk slaughtered without mercy.

By February, however, Louis had not only failed to defeat Lord William, but had found his position growing more tentative each day. Concerned, he sailed home to Paris to solicit the aid of his father. King Philip, however, had become increasingly frustrated with his son's failures and was under increasing pressure from the pope. He virtually abandoned Louis' cause and left the prince to fend for himself.

In April, 1217, Louis returned to his battered army with little more than the empty bravado of a scorned dandy. Swearing to turn the tide, he gathered his generals to determine where a great victory might be won, one that would catch the eye of his father and regain his much needed support. To a man it was agreed that the victory they needed could be had by overcoming the deadlocked siege of Lincoln Castle.

In the meantime, Lord William's royalists were suffering. The winter had been hard and costly. Men had died from all manner of disease, such as congestive chill, chin cough, camp fever, *la grippe*, and king's evil. The Marshal's doctors could do little, for medicinal herbs had become nearly impossible to find anywhere. The herbalists of the towns had been long since the victims of plunder, and the monasteries had been so stripped by raiding parties that their herbariums were bare.

In battle William's knights had suffered few deaths though, for their armour had continued to prove its worth. The royal footmen, however, had taken huge casualties and their ranks were badly depleted. Fortunately, the English folk had rallied to the regent's cause, and for every ten footman that fell, at least five brave lads appeared from distant villages and shires to fill the void.

William pressed his army hard through the rest of that winter. He directed most of its movements along the eastern coast in order to hamper all communication with France. He took several small, but valuable castles, and continued to welcome a steady stream of "returners." Despite minor successes, he soon realized that his tiring army needed to strike a stunning, fatal blow against Louis before it collapsed from exhaustion. He turned his attention to Lincoln Castle.

The stubborn defence of the fortress had become something of a symbol and, therefore, it—like all symbols—had acquired more importance than it might have otherwise enjoyed. The royal castle sat perched above the city of Lincoln and its high walls had withstood every assault of the rebel forces since the first days of the rebellion. The city had fallen victim to Louis' army, but to the Frenchman's great frustration, the stronghold would not yield and his soldiers bore the daily insult of having to stare at England's royal pennants flapping arrogantly above their heads. The Prince was further aggravated to learn that the castle's stubborn commander was a woman, one Dame Nicola de la Haye, the widow of Lincoln's sheriff. Described as a 'vigorous old hag,' the incredible female castellan proved to be both mulish and clever.

Louis' army had constructed huge siege engines and catapults. For months his men had launched torrents of arrows and hurled countless numbers of small boulders at the castle. It had all been for naught. He had broken and battered the fortress' walls but had not breached them. Instead, the old woman and her castle held fast, perched smug and defiant above the occupied city.

✸

It was May 1217, when Lord William's royal army began its

twenty-five mile march from Newark. Urged forward by the earl's impassioned pleas, his men rushed along the banks of the Witham River and raced northward in the full knowledge that they were headed to *the* battle for England.

Prince Louis, too, had ordered the whole of his army to Lincoln. He had managed to swell it with surprising numbers of Scots and men from the northern counties, and hoped to overwhelm the castle before the Marshal arrived. To his great vexation, however, no sooner had his army crowded into the city then his scouts reported the royal army's approach. His generals decided they would turn their backs on "the hag" and greet the Marshal's men in the streets of Lincoln.

With the stalwart castle in view, William Marshal and Hubert de Burgh assembled their men outside the city's gates. The earl knew his army was considerably smaller than Louis', but he also knew his men could fight and fight well. He mounted his huge war-horse and trotted to the head of his troops. Sitting tall in his saddle and dressed in full battle armour, he faced his men. "Men of England!" he cried. "This day is the day of reckoning for those who would steal thy lands and corrupt the Holy Church. I ask you to fight for God, for honour, for thy families, thy land, and thy liberties under *English* law."

A great roar resounded.

"Who among you is faint of heart?" Lord William listened to the wind. "Who among you is wont to lay courage aside and fall away from this place?"

None answered.

"Then, men of England, point thy lances, aim thy arrows, thrust thy gleaming swords at those who stand by Satan's side. Follow me, my brothers, follow me in battle for the glory of God and for our Mother England!"

The army shouted and hurrahed, shaking the earth with stamping feet. The grey earl whirled about and spurred his charger into a quick trot. He called to officers riding by his side and directed them to their appointed positions.

Old Dame de la Haye had sent a secret message to William informing him of a weakened gate in the city wall and it was there that the earl would focus his assault. Within the hour, the whole fury of the English army was thrown against that one point and soon William's troops crashed through the city gate with a deafening cheer. The battle for Lincoln had begun.

❅

On a low rise a safe distance away, Lady Isabel strained her eyes to find the herald colours of her husband. Her escorts, Aethel and John d'Erley were by her side, as well as a contingent of other body-guards. The woman wrung her hands as she watched her husband's army funnel into city's gate. "There, John, I fear he leads them."

John d'Erley was pacing. He could hardly bear standing in a safe place while his comrades stormed into the horrors of battle. "*Oui*, m'lady. It would seem so."

Isabel suddenly turned white as snow and nearly swooned against the shoulder of Aethel. She clutched her necklace desperately.

"What is it, m'lady?" Aethel steadied the Countess as others rushed to her aid. She was helped to a blanket upon which she collapsed, weeping.

John knelt to her side, alarmed. "*Madame?*"

Isabel wiped her eyes and groaned. "'A sword from heaven's gate shall fly with wings that none can stay. Its edge shall split thee from thy love and tear thy heart away—'"

"Enough," scolded Aethel. "No more of that curse. No more."

Isabel hung her head. "I have born its weight so very many years, I–I hear the words each time my William has faced danger. Now, see, he leads his men—he *leads* them. He is near to eighty years old and he leads his army against men a mere third of his age. How can he survive such a thing?" She began to sob. "And he refused to take my relic."

John d'Erley stood up and set his jaw. He could bear this no longer. "Forgive me, Lady Isabel. I must take thy leave and fly to my lord's side." He did not tarry for an answer. He leapt upon his charger and dashed quickly away towards the streets of Lincoln.

❋

Lord William's sons rode shoulder to shoulder with the great warrior as the King's army crashed into the waiting lances of their foes. Heavily armoured in chain mail coats and large helms, the Marshals quickly cut a bloody swath through the French footmen. Behind them poured a roaring column of English manhood falling furiously on their enemy. Louis' army was slowly pressed deeper and deeper into the city. Retreating street by street they were pressed closer and closer towards the shadow of the castle until, at the shrill command of Nicola, they received volleys of cross-bow bolts directed with terrible accuracy into their ranks.

William continued to push his mount forward with the instincts of an old veteran. He knew his enemy was faltering and he knew *now* was the time to strike the deathblow. With his sons still by his side, he smote a company of Scots, and then paused to catch his breath and survey his situation. "There," he cried. "Turn them downhill, towards the south gate."

His troops obeyed and followed the earl's sons as the lord stood in his saddle. Seeing the colours of a traitorous baron he hated, William suddenly raised his sword. With a growl, he charged forward and engaged a spirited young knight, one Robert of Roppesley. The two duelled furiously on horseback as the din of battle rose about them.

John d'Erley now arrived, desperate to fight at his lord's shoulder. He crashed forward against a rising tide of enemy footmen, slaughtering them without mercy. Then, just as the faithful knight reached Lord William, the old warrior thrust his sword deftly under Robert's helm, killing him instantly.

Panting, Lord William turned in his saddle to see d'Erley. He raised his hand to lift his face guard when a sword from behind crashed atop his head. Stunned, the earl tipped forward, almost falling. Sir John leapt from his horse and on to William's with a cry and held the man upright. Sitting behind his lord, d'Erley then began a desperate defence of both their lives.

The French knight struck again and again as good John bravely deflected each blow. Another joined the attack from the front, smashing a withering blow to the drooping Marshal's helm. Now fighting two men and terribly disadvantaged, Sir John knew he and William were in grave peril. He fought well and ferociously, blocking first one's blow then the other's.

The Frenchmen nudged ever closer and they were soon landing hard edges against John's mail coat and atop the shoulders of the stunned earl. Lord William's helm was badly creased and his vision blurred, but he was conscious and he drew upon the resolve that yet remained. With a loud oath the old man came alive. He threw his body forward into the saddle of one of his foes and the two fell to the ground with a crash. No sooner had the armoured soldiers landed then a host of footmen pounced on the pair.

Now reduced to one opponent and alone on his lord's horse, d'Erley felt free. He dispatched his remaining enemy with a deftly placed thrust beneath the man's armpit that burst through his shoulder. As the French knight tumbled off his horse, d'Erley leapt off his mount and waded into the savage butchery surrounding his lord. For a few deadly moments the air was filled with the horrid sounds of breaking bones and torn flesh as Sir John lopped limbs and battered heads.

At last the ferocious knight had cut his way to the centre of the combat where he stood over his fallen lord. Sir John was then joined by a blood-splattered Henry Hose and wild-eyed Jordan de Sauqueville. Back to back these three valiant knights stood like an impenetrable wall around the stunned earl.

Steel clanged loudly as here, around the knights of the prostrate Marshal, both armies strained to take the day. The battle raged furiously as the war for England's destiny hung in a blood-splattered balance. Finally, a mighty cry resounded from the throats of the Marshal's sons. Richard and young William rallied the royalists into a final, frantic surge forward. It was enough. The French troops faltered, then recoiled, and finally turned to flee for their lives.

Midst a rousing cheer Lord William climbed slowly to his feet. His helm was split and badly bent, his head aching and welted. He tipped weakly into the arms of his sons and thanked them each. Then, with a determined breath and a set jaw, the resolute commander of the King's forces climbed back upon his horse and drew his sword once more.

＊

William Marshal's victory at Lincoln resulted in a rapid collapse of Louis' dreams. The English rural folk had expressed their thoughts on French rule by summoning the warlike spirit of their ancestors. These Saxon and Danish peasants slaughtered Louis' retreating army on its flight to London. There the Frenchman learned that the Scots were abandoning his cause in the northern counties. Despondent, the pouting prince abruptly called for a council of peace in order to provide for a face-saving withdrawal of his aspirations.

In June 1217, Lord William, Hubert de Burgh, numbers of bishops and magnates of both sides met along the Thames River near Staines remarkably close to the meadow of Runnymede. Unfortunately, they had nearly settled upon a treaty when a messenger informed Louis of his wife's fresh efforts to coax King Philip into sending reinforcements. Hoping for the best, Louis ended the discussions as abruptly as he had begun them.

Angered, William Marshal had had quite enough. He ordered his navy to prepare to sail from Sandwich and intercept the arrival of the new French fleet while his troops were positioned to greet any possible survivors. True to form, the obstinate French did arrive with a small fleet of ships, against which the earl promptly sent his navy. Under the command of Hubert de Burgh, the English navy destroyed the French fleet and with it all hopes of Prince Louis. Watching from high cliffs by the sea, Lord William and young King Henry III cheered the happy day.

The months that followed were filled with tugs and whispers of barons and courtiers plotting their political fortunes. The English government was slowly regaining its footing and supporting itself with the reputation, if not the political savvy, of William Marshal. For his part, Lord William had grown weary. He had never been fond of the court and had neither patience with, nor interest in the quarrels of petty men squabbling over position and title.

In October he took some qualified joy in marrying his eighteen-year-old daughter, Isabel, to a very grateful Lord Gilbert de Clare. While the Countess approved of the marriage, the earl had not quite forgiven the thirty-seven-year-old groom for fighting against him at Lincoln. It was there that the man had been captured but, in the interests of national healing, Lord William had chosen to lay the unfortunate matter aside.

Through that autumn and in the months that followed, Lady Isabel was often seen at her husband's side. She was happy and her husband seemed to be at some peace, though he had begun to speak almost obsessively of his old friends, the Knights Templar. It was a distracting interest that she found odd and troubling. She prayed that age was not beginning to affect his mind.

Isabel also had begun to fear for Aethel. The kindly matron had begun to stoop with age and her husband Harold had recently been beset with quinsy. Aethel was now approaching fifty-seven and suffered stiff joints and some shortness of breath. Isabel knew that the woman had never really ever forgiven herself for the death of Twigadarn. She had seen her spending many an hour whimpering in the chapel. Isabel ached for her; she had been her faithful servant and friend for over forty years.

※

The Year of Grace, 1218, delivered an agreeable Advent season to the Marshals at Pembroke Castle. It proved to be a cheerful time of warm fires and feasting, and the Countess delighted in sharing her table with much of her family. Three of her sons were present in this year, these being young William, yet unmarried, Richard, also unmarried, and Gilbert. Gilbert had become a priest in Canterbury and his superiors had been pleased to report of his likely advancement through the layers of ecclesiastical authority. "Perhaps bishop or better," they had said.

Elsewhere, son Walter, now twenty-one, was engaged in royal

business in France. He was serving his father's ambassadors in efforts to guarantee control of lands in France still claimed by the English Crown. These had been contested for years, of course, but the recent treaty had supposedly acknowledged English rule. Anselm, fifteen, was approaching his knighthood but had taken ill in Dover on St. Nicholas' Day.

Matilda and young Isabel were celebrating the season in their own homes, those being Norfolk and Hertford, respectively. Sibylla, Eva, and Johanna were seated at the Marshal's Christmas table. Sibylla, seventeen, was married to Lord William de Ferrers, the wealthy young Earl of Derby, who was presently abroad in France.

Plump Eva was still round-faced, cheerful, and a bit loud. Aethel loved her. The twenty-three-year-old had married a man of middling means named William de Briouze of Bramber. He was a jolly fellow and happy to plunder the Marshal feast. Johanna, now ten, was not yet betrothed, though her eldest brother had recommended a respected lord named Warin de Munchensi of Swanscombe.

Surveying her Christmas hall, Isabel smiled. The faces lining both sides of the trestle tables were now the faces of the future. She paused to look at each one and quickly recalled their special moments: bumps and bruises, their laughter and their sobs, their recitations of the Psalms—and their occasional outbursts. She thought each to be intelligent, wise, and charitable. Her young men were chivalrous; her daughters, gracious.

As the cooks delivered trays of roasted boar and venison, Isabel called for Le Court and Aethel to join her family. Together, the Marshal household enjoyed the bounty of their lives midst the siblings' stories of days past and dreams for days yet to come. By mid-afternoon, all were sleepy and well-stuffed with every manner of saffron-coloured fowl, water bird, and hare. They washed their plenty away with fine wine and English ale as they sang tavern songs and recited the best poetry of the French court. Then, to the added pleasure of all, Sir John d'Erley arrived from duties in the north of Wales, weary and hungry, but smiling.

Lord William rose and greeted his faithful friend with an expensive robe made of fine wool and fox fur. "A gift, good Sir John. A gift of the season."

The knight bowed. "The years together, sire, are thy greatest gift. I accept this in honour of all that we have shared. And I've this for you." He handed William a finely crafted silver goblet depicting the twelve apostles and a Templar Cross. "From the preceptory in the Vale of Glamorgan."

Isabel smiled at the sight of the earl's grey eyes shining with affection for the man.

John then turned to Isabel and handed her a magnificent Celtic cross of gold and emerald studs. "In memory of your great affection for the lands of your good mother. 'Tis from Tara, the home of the High Kings." The two looked into one another's eyes for an instant—a look that did not go unnoticed by William.

Isabel quickly turned her face to the cross in her hand. She was astonished by its beauty. Depicting the great doctrines of the Faith, it was a masterpiece. She kissed the man upon both his blushing cheeks and clutched the gift to her heart. "I love it, good friend, as I love you."

Smiling broadly, William filled his goblet with red wine and lifted it high as he spoke. "My beloved. I am a man most blessed. I sit by a warm fire and eat from a table of bounty surrounded by hearts of deep affection. I live life with a woman of virtue, honoured by children most pleasing, and served by men of chivalry who call me friend. 'Tis more than any man ought ever have, and I do heartily thank you all. May this Christmas cheer follow us all of our remaining days."

CHAPTER XXIV

THE WISE, THE GRACIOUS, AND THE BEAUTIFUL, ISABEL

THE twelve days of Christmas passed far too quickly for the Countess. By the Feast of the Epiphany on January 6, 1219, her sons had all departed for various places and sundry tasks, and in the middle of that cold month she accompanied her husband to London, lodging at Westminster where he conducted the affairs of the kingdom.

It was late in January when William fell terribly ill and was found writhing in pain by his horrified wife. By Candlemas it was apparent that his condition was worsening and whispers began to grow in the corners of the court. By March 7, however, the man had regained some strength and climbed atop his war-horse to ride to the Tower where he and his wife remained for nine days.

Days in the Tower proved to be a time of melancholy reflection for the Countess. How very many memories it restored. While her weakened husband slept, she wandered quietly about and quite alone, remembering times past, such as her beloved King Henry and his magical dream. She closed her eyes and imagined Prince John playing with his wooden sword and she thought she heard the gentle voice of old Father Adderig. Her mind carried her to the painful memory of King Henry's harsh declaration of her first betrothal. She now knew why the man had been so terribly abrupt—he had loved her so and their parting had torn his heart. She then thought of her wedding day and she wept.

Lord William's health continued to fail and on the fourteenth day of March he summoned his wife to his side. His skin was pallid and his eyes were fading. He feared his end was fast approaching— and so did she. "Beloved Isabel, my darling wife. My time is short and it must be so."

The Countess knelt to his side and bravely fought her tears. She stroked the man's sweated brow and nodded.

William smiled, relieved that she would release his soul without anger. He could pass to his next life without feeling the shame of failure. "I should like to die in Caversham, the home of my birth."

Isabel nodded.

"Please, summon my men, all that can come. And send word to our sons. I should not like to die without them in my presence. Also, send for my daughters. I have given them too little of myself, yet I have loved them with all my heart."

Isabel nodded, again. She would have Le Court send messengers throughout all the kingdom.

William took her hand. "From here to the end I shall be surrounded by many. It is the way of the world. So allow me to say things that are only for your ear."

Isabel held her breath and squeezed his hand, lightly.

The earl grimaced in pain and rested for a few moments. The bells of Nones rang loudly from the churches of London. "My dear wife, when I die I would not want you to suffer loneliness."

Isabel began an immediate protest.

William laid a finger gently on her lips. "Nay, my dear, just hear me. You are a tender flower in want of holding. So it should be." He lowered his voice. "It would give me joy to enter my grave knowing you will be yet loved upon this earth." He looked at her carefully. "I have seen the way my beloved John serves you. He is a good man, dear Isabel, the only man I know who is deserving of you."

"But…"

"Hear me. This I do not command, but I do permit. Should it be your wish, receive him as your husband with my blessings." The man coughed, weakly, then smiled. "But perhaps you could first grieve for me a little?"

Isabel was not amused. Her eyes were swollen and tears dripped from them freely. "I love *thee*, good husband. I have always loved only thee."

William nodded. "You are a woman of rare virtue. This I know. But I have noticed your affections for d'Erley."

Isabel was uncomfortable. She answered, insistently. "I have loved him as a brother and respected him as a man. But I have loved you in all ways and more than any other."

William nodded, and smiled, tenderly. "We shall speak of it no more." He closed his eyes and rested for a few moments, his hand resting on hers.

Isabel laid her head on her husband's breast. She knew he had more to say.

The earl lay still, but not peacefully. His chest began to heave and he opened his eyes. "I now must ask something of you that no man has a right to ask."

His wife raised her face and waited, suddenly anxious.

The earl hesitated, and then spoke. "I once served with the Templars in Holy Crusade. I witnessed their power, their skill, and their utter virtue. They touch no women, they possess no wealth, and they deny themselves all selfish comfort. No better warriors live in all Christendom then these brave monks. They bind righteousness to order in a holy cause."

The Countess nodded and stroked her husband's hair. *The Templars, again*, she thought.

"Over thirty years ago I vowed to give myself to their brotherhood and now comes the time I must honour my vow." The earl drew a deep breath and stared sadly at his wife. His look was suddenly haunting.

The Countess' eyes widened as she attempted to comprehend the shocking implications of the secret her husband had just revealed. "I do not understand. You've never shared this with me before and–and what does this mean?" A twinge of anger suddenly pricked her. She pulled away.

William answered ashamedly, "I could not bring this upon you before this very last moment. I beg thy forgiveness, but my love for you has kept me from this duty all these many years." His chin trembled.

Isabel was so confused and shaken that she simply stared at him, blankly.

William took a deep breath and continued. "Beloved wife, as a Templar I must take certain vows; among them, of course, is chastity. The brethren are forbidden marriage and even the touch of a woman."

Isabel's mind whirled and her breath quickened.

"Dear wife, before I am received as their brother, I must…" he struggled to form the next words. "I must end our marriage." His voice fell away.

No words of any language could have captured the sudden agony that Isabel felt from such a stinging announcement. She struggled desperately to gather the pieces of her broken heart in the futile hope of offering some dutiful display of selfless honour to the man she so deeply loved. Instead, a fountain of tears poured from her eyes and she stared helplessly at William's face. Shocked and dismayed, she was unable to do more than say nothing. Trembling with a confusion of emotions, the poor woman rose stiffly, and hurried away.

❋

William decided he would be delivered by boat to the manor house of Caversham which he had inherited many years prior from his deceased brother. The modest estate was located along the Thames upstream from London and had remained an affectionate reminder of a family long-since gone. So, on March 16, the regent, members of his *mesnie* (including a weepy John d'Erley), the numbed Countess, three of Marshal's daughters, Le Court, Aethel, and various attendants were loaded into a small flotilla of wide-bottomed boats.

London's spires quickly disappeared and the view became one of a grey, flat landscape. Within an hour or so the travellers passed by Richmond, followed the bending river to Chertsey, and finally came to the banks of Runnymede. Here Lord William bade his oarsmen to hold for a moment as all eyes fastened on the quiet meadow of rumpled, brown grass.

Isabel stared at the field and her mind filled with memories of those five days in June-- memories of *Magna Carta*. Still wounded by William's revelation, she turned to him, nonetheless.

"You saved what was begun in this place." Her tone was matter-of-fact, obligatory--devoid of the emotion the memory had otherwise evoked in her.

William lifted her hand to his lips. "It was you, Isabel. The world must know that it was on account of you." His eyes searched hers for a hint of softening. Denied, the earl ordered his oarsmen to row on.

The company travelled under a heavy sky and soon followed the meandering Thames past Windsor, Eton, and Hurley, until they finally arrived at the docks of Caversham. Servants scurried to assist the flotilla as William paused to relish the memories now reawakened. The very sight of his boyhood home had immediately invigorated him. He laughed, though weakly, and happily disembarked to stand atop the lawns that he had loved to dash about so very long ago.

During the weeks to follow, the enlivened earl ignored the pleas of his doctors and quickly re-assumed direct control of his duties. Sitting up in his bed, he spent long hours surprising all by producing a constant stream of official documents and proclamations. The old warrior was fading, but he would not yield his soul just yet.

In the meantime, King Henry III and his tutor were delivered to the town of Reading, which lay just across the river from William's house. From there the young King could be kept abreast of the affairs of state and be close at hand for the regent's death. Despite the rally in William's health, news of his condition had also drawn many numbers of barons, legates, ambassadors, and well-wishers. A growing encampment now spread along Reading's riverbank, forming something of a morbid death-watch.

William Marshal saw death as did others of his time. Unless it came suddenly and without warning, it was seen as one's final opportunity to sustain the moral order by passing forward the virtues and worthy traditions of one's life through ceremony and deliberate sequence. By early April, the earl recognized that his recent recovery had been only a merciful interlude and that his passing was imminent. He was often racked with pain and his mind was fast failing him. It would be good, he reasoned, to relinquish all political authority now. Therefore, during the week following Easter, he summoned a council in which he yielded his regency to Hubert de Burgh.

Next, it was William's duty to confer the guardianship of the King to another. Young Henry stared at his aged friend tearfully as William apologized profusely for his inability to defend the lad any longer, and, like a good father, he proceeded to instruct the boy on his duty towards God and his fellow man. "Live a life worthy of thy sacred title. Know this, too. I have prayed that God would strike you dead if you dishonour your Crown as others of thy lineage have done."

William took the lad's hand and placed it within the papal legate's. With that gesture he legally passed the young King's care to the Holy Church.

Having nobly and wisely surrendered his public duties, the suffering earl needed to turn to his private ones. Believing death to be now fast approaching, he summoned his auditors, his lawyers, his wife, what children had arrived, and sundry courtiers. He was disappointed to learn that Young William had not yet come, and he was also told that Richard had not yet been reached in France. His other sons were either *en route* or unable to be found. All of his daughters except Matilda were present, however, and he was glad-hearted to see them. Nonetheless, this day required a complete accounting for his temporal blessings before the sun would set all matters would need to be settled.

Greed, for the Marshal, was a vice he despised. He placed it third amongst the sins he hated most-- below pride and envy, and one ahead of sloth. It had been his great joy to have spent a lifetime granting huge sums of wealth to any number of abbeys, cathedrals, and works of the Church. It had given him solace to serve the poor and the sick and he had done so with astonishing generosity. So, after the mid-day meal, when a huddle of eager clerks pushed past Le Court to coerce the dying man for more, he scolded them loudly. "You churchmen shave us too close. I can do nothing more for God now than give myself up in repentance for all my many sins. If more is demanded, no man can be saved."

Much of William's wealth had been by right-of-wife. Therefore, upon his death, most of his vast holdings would be returned to Isabel, and upon her death his sons would be granted it all, according to their birth order. What the earl held by his own right was rather modest and he disposed of it with relative ease. To his eldest son, William, the earl bequeathed a reasonable, though not lofty, sum of money, lands, and titles. The younger sons received inheritances of descending value.

To William's relief, four of his daughters were already married and well cared for. He was worried about young Johanna, however, and he had shared his concerns with Isabel. "I would go to my grave in great sorrow were I to believe I left my dear Johanna without merit for a good man. Hence, I grant her a sum of thirty pounds income per year and a trousseau of two hundred marks." Isabel hoped it would be enough to attract a worthy groom.

William then ordered his immense collection of robes and fine clothing to be distributed amongst his beloved *mesnie*. These were garments of silk and squirrel, otter, sable, and embroidered velvet. Such a bequest was more than one of comfort, for in William's world a man would be feared and properly served according to his wardrobe. Then, with his temporal affairs put to proper order, the dying earl fell to sleep peacefully, delaying the more agonizing matters of heart and soul for the day to follow.

✻

The Countess went to bed that very same night, aware that in the day to follow she would be stripped of the name, 'wife.' She had spent many of the days past walking alone. During these times she had wrestled with her feelings, working hard to reconcile her anger at William's betrayal. *But is it truly a betrayal?* She asked herself. *He does not leave me for another woman. He leaves me for an ideal—and it has been ideals that he has truly loved for all his life... But he could have told me! Could not he have loved me more? A curse on the Templars!*

In the darkness of deep night, the woman struggled with her heart. She had wanted to kiss him in his final hour and hold his hand—as a wife should-- while he released his soul to the Will of God. Instead, she would be abandoned; she would be set aside to watch from afar as his 'brothers' knelt by his side. "Oh, God above, hear my cry," she wept. "I do not understand."

Alas, Isabel finally lay still atop her empty bed. Exhausted, she rested a hand on the pillow where the great knight had once slept and simply stared into the shadows of her room. No longer able to war with either herself or with heaven, she quieted her mind and her heart and finally allowed the mysterious wisdom of the silence to fill her.

As the hours past, slowly, like the swirling mist of an angel's balm, true love began to heal her wounds. Isabel began to breathe evenly, then deeply, and she fell to sleep, at peace with her world.

Then, like the golden edge of the springtime sun now rising beyond her window, Isabel awakened and rose calmly from her bed. She knew that her heart was about to be torn from her chest-- yet she would surrender it, willingly. She knew that she was about to face a force far greater than herself-- yet she would not fear. This was the appointed time to simply yield her love to her husband's desire-- and in so doing, love him all the more.

※

The wise, the gracious, and the beautiful Lady Isabel stood quietly as sobbing Aethel draped a yellow silk under-gown over a pure white chemise. Unable to contain herself, the servant stopped and wrapped her loving arms around her lady. "Oh, dear one. I...I cannot bear this day for you."

Isabel could not answer. She patted Aethel's heaving back gently until the woman resumed. Aethel pulled slowly away and reached for a rich, green over-gown sewn by the Countess' own hand in faraway Kilkenny. Isabel finished winding red ribbons in the plaits of her long, hanging braids and stood numbly as Aethel set a red silk wimple neatly on her head. Now dressed very much like the day of her wedding, Isabel drew a deep breath and turned to her friend. "Dear Aethel, pray for me that I shall bring glory to God as I yield my husband to the arms of others."

John d'Erley silently escorted Isabel from her chamber through the musty corridors of Caversham manor and to the door of Lord Marshal's room. Overcome by feeling, he fell to one knee and took Isabel's hand. "I do swear, my dear Isabel, that I have not seen such love in all my years. To willingly release that thing most precious to you is a gift of grace, given by the angels."

Oddly, John's touch was suddenly discomforting to Isabel. Looking at the man her husband had offered, she wanted to turn away. *Oh, William, do not leave me*, she thought. She took a breath and then smiled courteously at poor John. *But it is not his fault.*

Now thinking only of William, Isabel envisioned his face as it had been the first moment she had seen him in the Temple Church. She then pictured him romping with her sons, sleeping peacefully by a Christmas hearth, and making ready for battle. She sighed and knew she must stand against all these memories now. She needed to be brave and selfless.

Isabel entered her husband's chamber and gazed upon the frail frame of the dying warrior now lying atop his bed draped with the white robe and red Cross of the Knights Templar. Aimery de Sainte-Maure, the master of the Temple in London, was standing at a respectful distance holding William's new sword and waiting to administer the vows of the Order. Others, including Sir John, lined the damp walls solemnly.

William raised, himself weakly. "Oh, my beloved darling wife. Come close." He stared at Isabel for a long moment. "I have not known love except from you, and I do beg forgiveness for this moment." Another difficult pause followed. "Sweet one, embrace me, for you shall never do so again." The earl began to cry.

Isabel collapsed to his side and held him closely. "I shall always love thee, dear husband."

Midst a chamber filled with muffled sobs, the two lay close, each crying softly until Lord William groaned in the grip of pain. He then drew a deep breath and set his eyes upon his wife. "Dear Isabel…it is time."

The Countess could not speak. She nodded obediently and waited.

Lord William laid his hands tenderly by Isabel's throbbing temples and drew her face near his. He lingered a long, precious moment and stared at her in wonder through grey eyes blurred by tears. Then, preparing to yield to that which he had vowed, he touched his lips slowly to hers for the last time.

The moment tarried; the springtime birds of Caversham sang lightly out-of-doors. But, alas, the man finally released his lips from his beloved and pushed her head softly away. He paused, still holding Isabel's face in his hands. He knew when he released his hold his hands would never feel her skin again.

Isabel remained fixed within her husband's hands. She, too, understood this would be his last touch. Suddenly, nearly panicked, she slipped one hand forward to rest it securely on the man's breast. At the touch William closed his eyes and released his hands from her face. Isabel stared blankly, her eyes now blinded with tears. She felt the beat of her husband's heart and wanted for all the world to embrace him once again.

William now lay behind closed eyes, savouring every loitering moment of this final touch. He yearned to carry the warmth of his wife's hand into the cold grave that awaited him, but, alas, that he could not do.

Isabel slowly, so very slowly, slid her hand off of William's heaving chest and turned away. She raised the hand to her lips, then dammed the flood of feeling erupting from within, and, without a word, hurried through the door.

Isabel stumbled through the crowded corridor now filled with tear-stained faces. She ran quickly, far, far away from William's chamber and beyond the manor's gates. Weeping loudly, she sprinted towards a green meadow by the Thames River. There, surrounded by the dapple colours of buttercups and feverfew, purple willow herb and white clover, the Countess fell on her face where she lay sobbing.

After a time, a light breeze rustled through the woman's green gown and its gentle touch nudged her upright. She wiped her eyes and gazed sadly about the beauty spread before her. "My William," she whispered, "how I love thee."

❋

In the death chamber, the Marshal marriage was dissolved and Aimery de Sainte-Maure administered the prayers and oaths of William's sacred induction as a warrior-monk of the Knights Templar. A Templar long-sword was laid atop his breast and, now at peace for having finally honoured his vow, Lord William fell into a deep sleep.

For several more days the dying man drifted in and out of consciousness. Three knights were assigned to stay with him at all times, though the fearsome night shift—when Satan prowled—was reserved for the recently arrived William the Younger, Sir John, and one Sir Thomas Basset. Father Le Court, displaced by the Templars as the lord's chaplain, prayed all the night to comfort the three as they stared fearfully into the heavy shadows of the eerie chamber.

All the while Isabel had kept a vigil from afar until she and her daughters were summoned to the lord's side. John d'Erley whispered to them, "My lord wishes to hear a song."

"A song?" Isabel's lip quivered.

"*Oui.*"

"Then a song he shall have." Isabel entered the man's room once more. It was a painful entry and the hard eyes of a knot of Templars kept her at bay from her husband's bed. Biting her lips, she proceeded to lead her daughters in a gentle tune. No more difficult a song had any of the Marshal women ever sung.

The day following, a desperate William called for Isabel, his children, and his faithful John d'Erley. The night before he claimed to have seen two heavenly figures dressed in fine white garments standing on either side of him. He now knew that this day, this

Tuesday the fourteenth of May in the year 1219, would be his last. As they gathered near, he fell silent and listened to the soft bells of sext. It was noontime and the sun was high above Caversham Manor.

"John," William murmured. "Hurry. Open the doors and the windows. Is my beloved Isabel here?"

"*Oui*, sire, I am." Isabel leaned over him with tears now dropping freely.

"Oh, John, have you washed my face with rose water?"

"*Non*, my lord, but I shall do so." The weeping man plunged a cloth into a nearby basin and gently wiped the man's brow and cheeks.

Refreshed, the grey earl drew a deep, trembling breath and opened his eyes wide. "I commend you all to God," he said weakly, "for I cannot remain with you any longer." He turned sad eyes to his beloved Isabel. "I cannot defend myself from death—" His words trailed away and his breathing stopped. William Marshal, Earl of Pembroke, was dead.

❋

Isabel stared lovingly at the still face of her William. No longer restrained by the man's vows, she slowly spread herself across his breast for a time, and then knelt by him to kiss his face, tenderly. She took his lifeless hands in hers and raised them to her cheeks where she held them until all warmth finally drained away. Then, sobbing lightly, she crossed his hands over his heart and walked slowly from his chamber and into the outstretched arms of Aethel.

In the cool of that springtime evening, the Countess strolled alone along the banks of the quiet Thames. She picked a bouquet of wildflowers and held them to her nose. She wiped her eyes and turned them heavenward. She drew a deep breath and exhaled slowly, whispering, "Thank you," to her love.

Isabel walked for some time, lost in her thoughts and pausing to cry from time to time. Finally the sun set, and cool, blue twilight settled over her. A fresh breeze wafted through her gown and Lady

Isabel smiled faintly. She shook loose her hair and let it blow freely in the wind. "William, my darling, you've blessed me with thy love, with dear children and a most wondrous life." She paused and sighed, then smiled as if she were suddenly standing face to face with her beloved. "And this, as well: you've granted me my heart's desire—for our children *do* breathe free air, dear William, free air in a free England."

THE END

EPILOGUE

All of England mourned the death of William Marshal, though none more so than his family and the circle of knights who had served him so very well. The essence of the Christian knight, Lord William embodied the virtues of chivalry, courage, and charity so regrettably absent in our modern times.

The last days of his dear Isabel are noted below, though historical data is scant. It is the author's contention that it was she who provided William with the wisdom and direction that ultimately influenced his role at Runnymede and initiated the rescue of *Magna Carta* during the first days of his regency. Consequently, it is she who ought to be celebrated at the very least as Liberty's handmaiden. Sadly, her time on this earth has been unfairly swept into oblivion by the historical account of others, many of whom were little more than coarse figures whose vanities survive by the chronicling of their lives.

Following William's death, Hubert de Burgh, King John's ambitious justiciar and William's high counsellor, assumed the regency and ruled the kingdom for twelve years during the minority of Henry III. With a passion for England's welfare (and perhaps his own), Hubert abandoned all adventures for French territory, though others would later revive them. He expelled foreign interests that threatened English institutions and allowed his bishops to resist the reach of the Roman Church. During Hubert's regency, the river of time completed its melding of Saxon, Dane, and Norman into a single identity, complete with a merged language, a common law, and a united destiny. As Winston Churchill said, he "restored England to England."

Like William Marshal, Hubert de Burgh was determined to keep order and enforce the King's Peace without compromise. In

1224 he crushed a group of self-serving barons who had attempted to undo lawful governance and disrupt the quiet of the realm. After hanging two dozen rebellious knights outside the walls of Bedford Castle, Hubert wisely sought a way to steady a kingdom suddenly nervous about the balance of power. He turned to that which he had learned from William Marshal to be the symbol of the supreme declaration of rightful order. Hubert reissued *Magna Carta* in its third and nearly final form, and he reissued it as a statute, forever to be part of English law and tradition.

Until that moment, it could be argued that the spirit of *Magna Carta* had not yet been fully appreciated, for many had given more heed to its particulars than to its true meaning. Hubert's timely affirmation, however, gave the document its enduring stature. From this point forward, *Magna Carta* would be part of the corpus of English law and as such, all future law would be tested against its precepts. For Englishmen and all the generations that would be touched by the hands of Mother England, the claims of arbitrary power had been forever displaced by the principle that it is law that rules, not men.

❊

The Countess is based on characters both actual and fictional. In the preceding story, the author has taken necessary licence with the remarkable lives of formerly living persons. Therefore, it may be of interest to review the information about them that has survived.

The Marshal Household:

Sir William Marshal, Earl of Pembroke (1142? - 5/14/1219) Middle son of John Marshal, trained for knighthood in Normandy, where he earned his living in tournaments. His skill caught the attention of England's King Henry II, who recruited him into the royal court as the Marshal of England—effectively the commander of the royal army. As such, he sponsored the King's eldest son for knighthood. Upon the prince's untimely death, William bore the young man's robe and heart (according to legend) to Palestine, where he buried them before serving in the crusading cause alongside the Knights Templar, whom he revered.

Later, William served King Henry against the ambitions of Prince Richard. Upon Henry's death he defended King Richard against the ambitions of his brother, Prince John. After Richard died from wounds in a petty conflict, William served King John against the rebellion of the barons.

It is believed that William, in close communication with Archbishop Stephen Langton, helped in the drafting of *Magna Carta*. Upon King John's death, William was elected Regent of England. As such he used his authority to rescue *Magna Carta* for posterity while he saved England from the French. Known as the "Flower of Chivalry," he is considered England's most famous knight. His remains lie in London's Temple Church.

Isabel (de Clare) Marshal, Countess of Pembroke (1172 - 1220): Our beloved Lady was described by her contemporaries as "the wise, the courteous, and the beautiful" Isabel. She brought grace and intelligence to her marriage. Raised by Henry II, she, unlike her husband, was literate and probably very well educated. She attended knights' councils and is known to have been consulted on matters of policy.

Isabel must have loved her William very much, as it is known that she and her children accompanied him on nearly every journey. Sadly, after receiving his final kiss, she learned of a curse cast against her husband at his death by an angry Irish priest. The curse was that their sons would bear no children; the dread of it ruined Isabel's final days.

Isabel died in Pembroke Castle within a year of William's passing, perhaps of a broken heart? Her remains lie at Tintern Abbey in Monmouthshire, Wales. Little more is known. It is a pity that history has been denied the full fragrance of this woman's amazing life.

The Marshal Children:

The dates of death appearing below are as accurate as can be determined. Birth years of all are speculated and birth order is uncertain. Furthermore, given the times, it is assumed that Lady Isabel may have given birth to one or more others that would have died in infancy and left no mark.

William the Younger (1190? - 4/1231): Upon his father's death, this eldest son of William and Isabel was given the office of Marshal of England, which he held until his own death. He married Alice, the daughter of Sir Baldwin, but Alice soon died. In 1224 he married King Henry III's nine-year-old sister, Eleanor. William retained the King's favour and spent years defending royal interests in Ireland. While serving there he also directed a war with the Welsh rebels who were harassing Pembrokeshire. He died suddenly in 1231, just days after the second wedding of his sister, Isabel. Though never proven, Hubert de Burgh, old William's former ally, was accused of poisoning him. It is this son who hired the author of *The History of William the Marshal*.
William died with no children.

Richard (1192? - 4/16/1234): After his brother's death, Richard was given the office of Marshal of England. He became the immediate beneficiary of William's estates, though some chroniclers state that Hubert de Burgh attempted to coax King Henry III into denying the man his rightful due. Richard married a woman named Gervase and received many lands in France from the marriage. His holdings now stretched from Ireland to France and envy soon spawned many enemies.
King Henry eventually conspired with the Bishop of Winchester against Richard. Richard's brave sister, Isabel, warned him of a trap and his escape earned him the label of traitor. He was stripped of title and lands and was betrayed by many.
Outraged at the violation of *Magna Carta* rights, Richard did rebel. Finally, on the bailey of Kilkenny Castle, he stood with fif-

teen loyal men (probably including his brothers Gilbert, Walter, and Anselm) and fought the King's troops—some one hundred and forty men-at-arms. Rather than yield to tyranny, Richard is quoted as crying, "'Tis better for me to die with honour than incur the disgrace of cowardice!" Trained well by his father, Richard could not be unhorsed in the battle that ensued. His enemies promptly cut off the legs of his war-horse, then stabbed the toppled Marshal in the back. Yet the man would not die easily. He was dragged to the bowels of Kilkenny Castle, where a surgeon finished the deed. Richard's body was hastily buried and King Henry denied all complicity in the matter.

Richard died with no children.

Matilda (1193? - 3/23/1248): Also called Maud, she married Hugh Bigod, Earl of Norwich and so became a Countess. Matilda bore seven children, including a son named William and a daughter named Isabel. She is interred in Tintern Abbey, England.

Gilbert (1194? - 6/27/1242): The third son of William and Isabel, Gilbert abandoned his clerical robes and supported Richard's rebellion against the King's tyranny. Upon Richard's death, he returned to England where King Henry granted him (and his brothers) pardon. He was knighted and given Richard's lands and offices, including that of Marshal of England. On November 12, 1239, Gilbert took Crusader's vows but delayed his departure. On June 27, 1241, he participated in a tournament where he fell from his horse and was dragged to his death. He is buried near his father in London's Temple Church.

Gilbert married twice, once to a Margaret de Lanvallei, and then to Margaret, sister of the King of Scotland.

Gilbert died with no children.

Eva (1195? - 1246): Married William de Briouze, a lesser noble of Bramber, England. She had four daughters, including one named Isabel. In 1230 her husband was hanged by an angry

Welshman. Later, Eva's daughter Isabel married the son of the hangman.

Walter (1197? - 3/24/1245): In October 1241 Walter inherited the lands and titles of the deceased Gilbert. On January 2, 1242 he married Margaret de Quincey, widow of the Earl of Lincoln. Little more is known other than that he died in Goodrich Castle for reasons unknown and that he is buried near his mother's side.

Walter died with no children.

Isabel (1199? - 1/17/1239): Young Isabel married an older man, Gilbert de Clare, in 1217. The pair had seven children, including those named William, Isabel, Richard, and Gilbert. Through her daughter Isabel's marriage, she became the great-grandmother of Scotland's hero, Robert the Bruce.

In 1230 her husband died and in April 1231 her oldest brother, William, married her to Richard, the Earl of Cornwall and brother to King Henry. It was at this wedding that some believed William was poisoned.

Sibylla (1201? - 4/27/1245): Married William de Ferrers, Earl of Derby, and bore seven daughters, including one named Isabel.

Anselm (1203? - 12/23/1245): This youngest son of William and Isabel married Maud, daughter of the Earl of Hereford. Little more is known, for, since his brother Walter had died so shortly before him, he never had the opportunity to inherit the family wealth. After his death the family fortune was distributed among his sisters' children. He is buried near Walter and his mother in Tintern Abbey, Wales.

Anselm died with no children.

Johanna (1208? - 1247) Also known as Joan, she married Warin de Munchensi of Swanscombe. She had three children—a daughter named after herself, and two sons, one named William and one named John.

The Knights of William Marshal:

The knights named in our story were drawn from the actual men of Lord William's circle. Few facts are known about them but it is hoped that what little we have is of some interest.

Sir Eustace Beautremont (dates uncertain): While William's other knights were Anglo-Normans (except Henry Hose), Eustace was the only true Frenchman in the mesnie—a landless knight who served Lord William his entire career.

Sir Baldwin de Bethune (dates uncertain): A childhood friend of William Marshal, Baldwin was not officially a member of the *mesnie*. This lord owned many estates in his own right, but his close association with William over a long lifetime of shared experience prompted the author's use of him as the lord's de facto marshal.

Sir Ralph Bloet III (? - 1199): The Bloets were a wealthy family with vast holdings in England and Wales. Their influence at court was particularly enhanced by Ralph's marriage to the adventurous Nest, a former mistress of King Henry II. Their marriage produced Ralph IV and William, both of whom also served in the Marshal *mesnie*. The Bloets, though vassals of William Marshal, were extremely important to the great lord's financial and political interests.

Sir John d'Erley (1173? - 1229): Young John came into William Marshal's care at about age fourteen. He was William's most beloved knight and served his lord with honour and distinction. Contemporaries described him as a courageous Christian warrior devoid of vice and filled with a heart of charity. He was the founder of Buckland priory and ultimately held lands throughout Britain and Ireland. He was the co-executor of William's will.

While most historians believe it was John the Troubadour who wrote the poem of William's life (the *Histoire*), others contend that the "John" whose name appears is none other than John d'Erley.

John married a woman named Sybil on a date unknown, but probably after Lord William's death. He left three children—two sons named John III and Henry, and a daughter. His cause of death is unknown.

Sir Alan de St. Georges (? - 1230?): Sir Alan served Lord William between 1189-1204. Alan held lands as the Earl of Arundel and served as Constable of Knaresborough Castle. He was elected to Sussex juries four times. He was married twice, his second wife being Sybil. He had no surviving children.

Sir Henry Hose (? - 1233?): By his name it would seem that Henry was most likely to have come from old English (Anglo-Saxon) stock. He was the son of a landholder in Sussex and was the patron of Durford priory. He had two sons, Henry and Matthew.

Sir Jordan de Sauqueville (? - 1230?): Jordan was an opportunist whom, some believe, had won his way into William's *mesnie* through his charm and eloquence. For whatever reasons, William welcomed the man into his household where he served as steward, soldier, and lawyer. He was granted lands in Ireland and had a son named Bartholomew.

The Monarchs:

King Henry II of England (1133 - 1189): As the son of England's would-be queen of England, Matilda, and Geoffrey, Count of Anjou, Henry became the first of England's Angevin (a derivative of Anjou) kings in 1154 and served until his death. As King of England he also became Duke of Normandy upon his father's death. When he married Eleanor of Aquitaine his French holdings exceeded that of the French King. Four of his sons survived to adulthood, but his eldest and his third-born died before their opportunity to receive the crown.

An intelligent, ambitious, bow-legged man, Henry reorganised the English monarchy and extended royal jurisdiction effectively over Britain. In so doing, he established the basis for common law. In addition, he strengthened local governments, secured large regions of France, regained England's northern counties from the Scots, and established rule over much of Ireland.

The murder of Archbishop Thomas à Becket darkened what was otherwise considered a supremely successful reign. While Henry did not wield the blade against the cleric, his agents did, and the crime drove him to his knees in repentance.

King Richard the Lionhearted of England (1157 - 1199): Richard, second son of Henry II, loved the romance of the Christian Crusade more than any earthly duty. Consequently, his vision of England was as a source of revenue to finance his adventures. A brave, intelligent, and devout man, King Richard reigned between 1189 and 1199, but spent precious little time in England—six months, to be precise. Most of his life was spent in France where he defended his interests against the French King. He served nobly in the Third Crusade but was captured on his return and held in an Austrian prison. Eventually he was ransomed by the barons of England who wanted desperately to avoid the ascendancy of Prince John. John, it should be noted, had offered huge sums of money to the Germans to keep his brother in prison! While Richard's reputation conjures pleasing notions of chivalry and courage, he did not rule his Kingdom well. It was the administrative efficiencies that his father had imposed that maintained the realm in Richard's absence. Curiously, this King's inattention helped strengthen the movement towards the decentralisation of authority.

King John of England (1167 - 1216): The tall, handsome, youngest son of Henry II, John became King of England upon his brother Richard's death in 1199, and served until his own death in

1216. He was twice married, first to Isabel of Gloucester, whom he divorced on grounds of consanguinity (blood relationship) while at the same time scheming to keep her wealth. His second wife was Isabella of Angoulême, who bore him five children.

John's reign was marked by strife and ambition. At one time or another his enemies included his father, his brother Richard, the pope, most of the barons, and the greater part of England's good folk. He lost most of England's French possessions, broke his father's heart, deprived his people of the comforts of the Church, lost the Crown jewels, and committed acts of renowned stupidity. Occasional alms to the poor seem to be the single redeeming quality of the man's life of infamy.

John's crowning achievement is that he so abused royal prerogative that his subjects were finally pressed to rebel. As a result of their rebellion, *Magna Carta* was issued and the foundation stone of English liberty was set.

King Louis VII of France (1120 - 1180): A contemporary of King Henry II, Louis reigned from 1137 until 1180. He was a pious man, sometimes thought to be doting and melancholy. He served in the Second Crusade, which was a dismal failure. He lost many French holdings to English interests, and lost his wife, Eleanor of Aquitaine, to the younger and more virile Henry II of England. He supported the revolts of Richard and John against their father, but to no avail. His son, Philip, succeeded him upon his death.

King Philip II of France (1165 - 1223): A contemporary of the English Kings Henry II, Richard, and John, Philip Augustus was the shrewd son of King Louis VII who had once joined Richard the Lionhearted on Crusade. Philip more than doubled the royal domains of France during his reign (1180 - 1223), primarily at the expense of King John of England. He warred with King Henry, conspired with Prince John against King Richard, then supported the barons' cause against King John. At home he created an administrative class, systematised the collection of tolls, taxes, and the like, continued the construction of Notre Dame, built the first Louvre, and paved the main streets of Paris.

Prince Louis of France (1187 - 1226): The son of King Philip II, young Louis participated in the pope's slaughter of the Albigensian heretics. Later he invaded England in support of the barons' war against King John. He became King Louis VIII in 1223 but only served three years. During his brief reign he successfully fought against the English for control of Poitou.

The Churchmen:

Pope Innocent III (Lotario de Conti) (1160 - 6/16/1216) Pope Innocent III was a zealous protector of the Roman Church and an opponent of heresy. He claimed supremacy over every Kingdom of Christendom and managed to exert his dominance aggressively. He meddled in fine details, including the excommunication of Alfonso of Leon for an improper marriage, annulling the marriage of the crown-prince of Portugal, crowning Kings of his own choosing, excommunicating others who had fallen from his favour. He mediated disputes in Hungary's royal family, renounced the tyrannical Sverri of Norway, arbitrated the Crown of Sweden, rotated his support for claimants to the throne of the Holy Roman Empire, and attempted to void *Magna Carta*.

He watched silently over the tragedy of the Children's Crusade, launched the disastrous Fourth Crusade, and encouraged the Albigensian Crusade, which resulted in the wholesale slaughter of legions.

Ironically, he died in the same year as his sometime-vassal, sometime-foil, King John.

Archbishop Stephen Langton (1156 - 7/9/1228): A great theologian and scholar, Stephen Langton was English born and educated in Paris. Pope Innocent III made Langton a cardinal in 1206 and nominated him as Archbishop of Canterbury under John's reign.

Langton was no friend to tyranny of any sort. When he was finally received by King John as Archbishop, he insisted the King redress the grievances of the barons. Out of the storm that followed came *Magna Carta*—much of which is believed to have been written under Langton's guidance.

Stephen Langton was considered to be wise, prudent, courageous, and without personal ambition. When the pope insisted that Langton denounce both *Magna Carta* and the barons who signed it, the Archbishop flatly refused. In retaliation, the pope excommunicated him. As fortune would have it, however, the pope soon died and Langton's soul was presumably pardoned.

In the years that followed, Langton devoted his time to maintaining peace and an orderly liberty in England. He was committed to maintaining an independent English Church and his writings, called the *Constitutions of Langton*, provided a foundation for the Church of England's final break with Rome three hundred years later.

A final word:

While we are pleased to acknowledge these living souls now departed, we would be remiss should we not fondly salute those who exist only in our imagination. With some sadness, therefore, we say, "Fare thee well, good Aethel and brave Twigadarn, Father Adderig, Father Shoulderlock, and our beloved Le Court. May you all live long and bide well in our most pleasant nights' dreams."

"Here, Ruthven, you take a spell now," he said.

Although the rowers had from time to time glanced over their shoulders, they could not, through the mist, form any idea of their position. When Ruthven took the helm he exclaimed,—

"Good gracious, Frank! the shore is hardly visible. We are being blown out to sea."

"I am afraid we are," Frank said; "but there is nothing to do but to keep on rowing. The wind may lull or it may shift and give us a chance of making for Ramsgate. The boat is a good sea-boat, and may keep afloat even if we are driven out to sea. Or if we are missed from shore they may send the life-boat out after us. That is our best chance."

In another quarter of an hour Ruthven was ready to take another spell at the oar.

"I fear," Frank shouted to him as he climbed over the seat, "there is no chance whatever of making shore. All we've got to do is to row steadily and keep her head to wind. Two of us will do for that. You and I will row now, and let Handcock and Jones steer and rest by turns. Then when we are done up they can take our places."

In another hour it was quite dark, save for the gray light from the foaming water around. The wind was blowing stronger than ever, and it required the greatest care on the part of the steersman to keep her dead in the eye of the wind. Handcock was steering now, and Jones lying at the bottom of the boat, where he was sheltered, at least from the wind. All the lads were plucky fellows and kept up a semblance of good spirits, but all in their hearts knew that their position was a desperate one.